Here's what readers are saying about *All Her Own*

'Diane Deeming is a gifted writer. Her story will appeal to many readers, particularly those women who identify with raising children whilst tolerating a difficult husband.'

'Mary Bray is an exemplary woman. Her courage, strength, and drive to find a better life for her children is admirable. I loved reading her story.'

'A sprawling family saga that I could not put down.'

'Mary, Alice, Kathy, Archie ... such vivid characters. I really enjoyed reading about them. It felt like we were right there in the Glasgow slums.'

All Her Own

All Her Own

If only she could take back
that moment of weakness...

Diane Deeming

Published by Misty Publishing

All Her Own
© Diane Deeming 2024, All rights reserved

First (eBook/paperback) edition: March 2024

A catalogue record for this book is available from the National Library of Australia

www.trove.nla.gov.au

ISBN: 978-0-6459175-3-6 (print)
ISBN: 978-0-9756631-0-3 (epub)

Author's note

The Glaswegian dialect featured in the pages ahead showcases the breadth in which the English language can be used. Words such as:

wean — child
hen — an endearment
burn — stream
baw — ball
greet — cry

These are not regularly used in such a fashion in standard English, but they are outright common in Glaswegian English. The salt of the earth Glaswegian accent is also tonal on occasions, with the mood of the speaker adding meaning to a word in their pronunciation. For instance, the word *you* in regular conversation with a Glaswegian might sound like *ye*, but if the speaker is trying to make a point, is angry, frustrated or trying very hard to enunciate for whatever reason, it will sound like *you*.

In other words, accents can grow broader or narrower depending on the situation. People can also lose their accents over time. All of this is to say, just enjoy the story as you read this book. Let the characters of *All Her Own* into your heart as they tell their story, their way.

Diane Deeming

For My Girls

Remembering my mother, Mary Patricia:
11.10.25 – 02.06.86

For my beautiful daughter Maryanne
and
My precious granddaughter Mayah

Strong women aren't simply born,
they are made by the storms they walk through.

Scotland: 1950

Chapter 1

Mary, on bended knee, threw up. Her retch mingled with a streak of recent spit dripping from the stone stair of the tenement building. Hands numb with cold, she reached down to the edge of her apron to wipe saliva from her chin. Her frail body shook as she coughed into the grey waters of the tin pail.

On the floor above, a door rattled and banged loudly as it slammed into its shaky frame. A familiar shuffle could be heard on its way down the winding stairs. Bella was a small, overweight woman wrapped in dark woollen shawls coiled loosely around her body and head, almost completely covering her round, weathered face. Bright, defiant eyes glowed under a heavily creased brow. Her breath came in short bursts, her jaw working hard, every now and then grinding down on loose dentures as she grunted loudly. Thick men's socks and old worn slippers a size too big made her shuffle even more.

'Och, Mary, ye poor wee thing, have ye no seen the doctor yet for that cough? I hear ye in the middle of the night coughing and spluttering and I get that worried about ye. Are ye alright?'

Mary nodded, then she tilted her head back and rubbed the nape of her neck. Her bright eyes had long lost their glow, her soft English accent almost a whisper. 'I'm fine, Bella, honestly, I am. It's the weather. It really does sound a lot worse than it is. Please don't worry about me, I'll be alright.'

Bella grunted, shaking her head while leaning heavily on the stone wall, passing Mary on the stair. 'That's awfie good of ye, Mary, to dae ma turn on the stairs this week. My legs are that weak ah can hardly walk. Well then, can ah get ye anything at the shop? Maybe some Vicks to rub on yer chest?'

Mary shook her head. 'No thanks, Bella. I'll soon be finished, then I'll have a break. Maybe if I have a strong cup of tea and an aspirin and put my feet up for half an hour I'll find some energy.'

'Okay then, darlin, but you tell that man of yours to get aff his arse and get ye to the doctor. It's a bloody disgrace so it is, coughing and spitting at aw hours. It's no right, so it is. It's just no right.'

'I will, I will,' Mary said wearily, knowing only too well that she wouldn't.

She brushed a strand of dark blonde hair from her eyes and breathed deeply. If only it was that easy! If only a trip to the doctor could find a cure for regret, a remedy for heartache, or therapy for constant torment. Tears welled as memories of the past loomed before her. Visions of what she had lost were almost unbearable. She covered her face with her apron, sat down and wept.

The last stone step outside the communal toilet door was caked in human faeces. Mary retched again, closing her eyes before turning her scrubber to the job ahead. She burrowed into the human waste, then she upturned the tin pail into the cracked toilet bowl.

For tenement dwellers, 'The Close' was their vital connection to life. Entrance to the condemned stone building was through a long passageway with a narrow staircase reaching from the ground to the third floor. It was a meeting place, somewhere to chat and gossip with the neighbours, have a bet with the bookie or feel the warmth and comfort of a lover and a goodnight kiss.

Most of the stairs had eroded and cracked over time from decades of weary footsteps. The curve of the old walls had worn to a dull shine, a testament to the failing elderly bodies and the many inebriated souls hugging it for comfort and support over the years. Gas mantles flickering at night struggled to light the way for families living there; families trying desperately to scratch out a meaningful existence in wretched and hopeless conditions.

Climbing the last stairs to the door of her Rooken Road home, Mary cringed. That wonderful feeling of euphoria of having her own place had long since faded. Now she found the reality of her surroundings at times unbearable. The building was destined for demolition. Only the needy and desperate had grasped at offers of the run-down shells masquerading as rooms. Only they would ignore what the local government would silently call 'uninhabitable'.

Many of the outhouses at the rear of the building had been bombed during the war and were unsafe. Rats roamed unchecked, homeless tramps bedded down in any unlocked toilet they could find, and drunks from the nearby pub relieved themselves wherever they fell in the confines of the narrow close. No one complained.

Number twenty-three had a peeling painted wooden door that opened to a small passageway leading to a single room. Slipping quietly into the room, Mary glanced at the floral curtain with a feeling of dread as she sat down.

There were two recesses. A double bed concealed by a faded floral-patterned curtain in one; an old mirrored wooden wardrobe, a threadbare rug and an armchair with exposed bare springs filled the other.

The dark wooden dresser standing flat against the wall had four large drawers. The bottom drawer was permanently open, a bed for her baby son Scot. Two vinyl wooden armchairs pulled together at night was a bed for her five-year-old daughter Alice. A small wooden Formica-topped table with two aluminium chairs was in the centre of the room. One of the table legs was short, propped up with wads of newspaper.

Looking around at her surroundings with the necessities of their meagre life, she sighed. The room was dark, the only natural light coming from four small windowpanes overlooking the street. Placing the pail under the sink, she held her breath. No matter how hard she tried, she could never get rid of the smell of mould and dampness. She started to cough and wheeze, desperately holding the corner of her apron to her mouth to dull the noise, but to no avail.

There was a rustle then a swish of curtain from the recess. With a racing heart, she turned around.

'What the fuck are ye doin, woman?'

Mary froze. She looked to the recess dreading that tone, that anger, that person … her husband. She peered wearily into the low light, searching for his face. A heavy dark stubble emerged. She shuddered, speaking slowly, choosing her words carefully. 'Oh Archie, I'm sorry if I woke you with my coughing. I must have picked up an infection again. There was a lot of coughing in the steamy when I was washing the clothes. I'll get some more medicine from the doctor, I'll—'

'Shut the fuck up, that's right, aye, gas-bagging wi aw they women at the steamy, eh? Telling them how hard done to ye, ye are, married to me, eh?' His voice escalated. 'And while I'm at it, what have ye been doing aw day anyway? Look at the state of this place. Nay fire, nay tea ready, I'm supposed to be on the night shift the night and they weans will be back any minute. I'll get nay peace. For Christ's sake, get aff yer arse and get me ma tea!' He pulled at the curtain and stumbled out of bed, grabbed Mary by the collar and pushed her head down into the stone sink, smashing her brow against the brass tap in the process. The neck of her blouse tightened around her throat. She blacked out briefly then cried in pain, begging him to let her go. The warm blood had started to drip over her eyes. Trying to fight back was useless, his strength was intensified by his temper, his fist coming down on her back like hot embers. She could feel her body failing until the pain from his blows brought a high pitch scream for mercy.

Letting out a grunt he threw her aside. Weak and losing her balance, she fell to the floor. He staggered back to the recess, crawled under the coats and glared back at her while shaking a clenched fist. 'You just watch it. Dae ye hear me, Mary? Are ye listening to me? Next time, I'll break yer fuckin arm!'

Wiping the blood from her cheeks, she looked over pleading with him. 'Oh, please, Archie, I had to help Bella with the stairs today, she hasn't been well. I'll get everything done, really, I will.'

Archie didn't reply. He pulled the old coat over his head, dragged the curtain closed and turned to face the wall.

Loathing for her husband intensified as Mary looked at his protruding curled-up bulk. Tears mingled with blood as she slowly pulled herself up from the sink and turned on the tap. The icy cold water shocked then comforted her as she attempted to stop the blood flow with her hands. How she hated that sink! It was the cornerstone of the cramped, miserable room. They bathed there, washed dishes, prepared food, laundered clothes, concealed bruises, and combed heads rampant with lice right there ... now it was splattered with her own life's blood.

As the crimson flow slowed to a trickle, Mary grabbed a cloth, found disinfectant under the sink and dabbed at the wound, wincing as the antiseptic took hold. Still holding the torn cloth to her head, she looked into Archie's shaving mirror above the sink. It was only a surface gash, but a large lump turning blue had started to encircle it. She covered it with her turbaned headscarf, taking comfort in not having to explain away yet another bruise.

Mary's head throbbed. She felt powerless, weak, alone, humiliated, but she was not defeated. Strange as it seemed, and as bad as it was, this moment gave her another injection of strength, another stride toward her goal of escaping this miserable existence. Her determination had intensified. She would never settle for this life for her children, never concede to the poverty. She would find a way ... but she would have to be patient.

It was getting colder, and the children would be home soon, so she went to light the fire. Archie was sleeping soundly; his snores thankfully muffled beneath the blankets.

Mary had trouble starting the fire. On hands and knees, with her face in the grate, she blew on the coals. Soot from the chimney blackened her cheeks and caught in her throat, racking her thin body with a rasping cough. Her head ached. The cinders responded with a dull spark. She coaxed them repeatedly, adding more paper balls and cardboard until they finally caught and the flames slowly snuck up the chimney.

She sat back on her heels exhausted. The outside door letterbox rattled.

'Are ye there, Mary?'

Chapter 2

Mary stood up quickly, wiped her hands on her apron, patted her turban headscarf and called out, 'Yes, yes, Kathy, the door's open, come in, come in.'

Kathy King bounced into the room like a harlequin ball. Her rich red hair fell in giant curls over a corded jacket. Light green woollen pants clung to her slim legs, with black rubber wellington boots ending at her knees. Her face was glowing fresh and pink from the cold air.

Kathy smiled at her friend. 'Jesus, Mary, look at ye. Ye should see yersel wi yer elbows poking oot of that bloody cardigan and your curlers hanging aff your turban.'

Mary laughed while coughing into her handkerchief. Kathy pointed to a chair piled high with clean washing. 'Can I move that pile and sit doon?'

Mary nodded. 'Of course.'

Kathy lifted the folded washing, placing it on the table and then throwing herself onto the chair. A loud screech came from beneath. The cat, hiding under the warmth of the laundry, had connected with the seat of Kathy's pants. She screamed, then jumped up, as it wailed, racing off to its hidey-hole behind the door.

'Fur fuck's sake,' Kathy muttered. 'Why the hell do ye keep a cat? Ye can hardly feed yer family, never mind that thing.'

Mary smiled and shook her head. 'I know, I know, Kathy, but Alice found it when it was a kitten behind the bins outside. The poor little thing was crying inside a potato sack. She brought it upstairs to me. It was so little I just couldn't say no.'

Kathy looked kindly at her friend. 'Yer just a fuckin softie, Mary, so ye are.'

Mary nodded. She could never understand why Glaswegians had to swear so much. Looking sideways at her friend, she said, 'Well, at least it keeps the mice on their toes!'

The women looked at each other and let out a roar of laughter, the noise resonating in the confines of the small room. Abruptly the snoring stopped.

'What the hell's going on here? Who's that? I'm trying to get a bit of kip before I start work. Have ye nay consideration for a worker? Mary, where the fuck is ma tea?'

Archie Bray reared his bleary face from behind the curtain while scratching his head. Looking around the room, he caught sight of Kathy and glared. 'Oh aye, I might have known it was you. What the fuck are you dayin here?'

Mary put her hand to her mouth and held her breath. She never understood why Archie disliked Kathy so much, and she was never sure of his reaction whenever she was mentioned.

Kathy squared her shoulders, stood up and stared directly into his unshaven, haggard face. 'Stick a sock in it, Archie, eh?'

Mary opened her mouth to intervene, but Archie quickly cut her off. With bloodshot eyes and expanding nostrils, he answered, 'You shut yer face and mind yer ain business, ya slut.'

Rising up onto his elbows, exposing green striped pyjamas and a brown cardigan, he pointed at Kathy. 'This is ma hoos and ye are no welcome here, shoutin yer mouth aff. What you need is a man to keep ye in yer place.'

There was a split second of silence as Kathy moved toward him, eyes wide and shining with a defiant half smirk. 'Oh aye, and I should be setting my sights on sumdy like you, is that right? That *will* be the day. Yer a fuckin head case, Archie Bray, ye'll never change.'

Mary began to wheeze and cough loudly, spitting into her handkerchief. She was nervous and tense, trying to keep the peace, but it continued.

Archie glared at Kathy. 'See what ye've done, ya stupid bitch? It's your fault she's sick, your fault she's getting big ideas, making her cough and splutter. Get out of my hoos! Go on ... fuck off!'

Mary rubbed her forehead, shocked at this ferocious outburst. She spoke slowly. 'Archie, you need to leave for work in a couple of hours, so why not get up and sit here by the fire? Marilyn will be back from the park any minute with the children. You could maybe play snakes and ladders with Alice for a while before you leave, she would—'

Archie had already dismissed what she was about to say and instead snapped back, 'Are ye kidding me, Mary? I'm away back to bed.'

Archie mumbled as he climbed back under the coats in the recess. 'Anyhow, I'll no have time to play snakes and ladders. I need a kip before I go and find Tam to get a couple of fags aff him. The wee shite owes me ye know.'

Mary went to Kathy putting her thin arms around her shoulders.

'Come on now, Kathy. Tell me what happened last night with that fella from the cafe, did he ask you out again? Was he nice? I've been dying to know, come on, tell me!'

Kathy raised her voice, winked, shaking her head in Archie's direction. 'Och, Mary, I'm sorry I need to go hame. I have tay wash my hair.'

Both women held their mouths tightly, terrified one giggle would escape and alert the now comatose Archie. Kathy raised her eyes to the ceiling, clenched her sheepskin mittens into fists punching above her head mouthing silently, 'yes!'. Her smile said it all. Buttoning her jacket she winked, heading for the door.

'Well, I better be going noo, anyhow. I only called in tay tell ye that Tony wants ye at the café in the morning at half ten.'

Mary nodded. 'Okay then, thanks for letting me know. Can you wait a minute and I'll walk you down the close?'

Mary grabbed her coat, then the two friends clambered down the stairs and huddled in a sheltered corner of the close.

Kathy pulled off her mitten before fishing for a half-smoked cigarette from the farthermost corner of her jacket pocket. The flimsy matchbook held only three comb-like thin matches. Striking the side, she cupped her hand. The flame quickly flickered and died. 'Shite,' she said and moved further into the corner to try again. Mary held her coat up to Kathy's face. 'Yes!' Kathy whispered loudly as the flame embraced the tipless Woodbine. She looked back at Mary with a gurgling laugh. 'Do you remember that big lorry driver that comes in on a Tuesday, the cheeky one with the black curly hair?'

Mary nodded.

'Well, we went to the pictures last night and then ...'

'And then what, then what?' Mary persisted, laughing loudly, as she grabbed Kathy's arm, shaking it gently.

'Well ... we did it. We did it, Mary! Staunin up at the back of oor close behind the bins. It was great, so it was, I canny tell ye how much ah—' Kathy stopped suddenly, looking at Mary. 'Day ye think I'm terrible, Mary, eh?'

Mary drew in a deep breath, coughing and laughing at the same time, she stared wide-eyed at her friend. 'You did not. I don't believe you.'

Kathy's face lit up and she squealed, 'God strike me dead if I'm lying! Don't you tell a soul, Mary. Ye promise me, okay?'

'Of course, I promise I will never tell, but Kathy, listen, I don't think you're terrible. I think you're very brave and that you are following your heart.' Mary shook Kathy's arm again. 'C'mon. C'mon then, tell me more. Was he a good kisser?'

'Oh aye, he was a great kisser, we just got carried away. He smelt great, ye know whit I mean? He wis wearing a real strong spicy aftershave and his hands, they were just ...'

Mary stopped laughing. She grabbed Kathy's arm, shaking it. 'Kathy, wait a minute. Did you take any precautions? I mean did he come out or did he, you know, wear anything?'

Kathy froze. She was quiet for a moment; rubbing her forehead, she frowned. 'Shite, I canny remember. I had too many brandies, ma heed was spinning so it was. He was well on as well. My God, Mary! I never even thought aboot that. What if I'm up the duff?' Kathy's brow rippled slightly while inhaling the last of the nicotine. She then extinguished the cigarette with the toe of her boot and regained her humour. 'Och no! Whit am I sayin? Me wi a wean? That'll be the day. It's no gonna happen.' Her face was expressionless, her eyes cold and wild, gazing up at the flickering gas mantle she turned to Mary. 'Oh aye, and wouldn't your Archie just have a right laugh at that, eh?'

Their eyes met ... it made Mary shiver.

A loud clatter and banging came from the entrance to the close, followed by excited voices and laughter. Mary's children were home. Marilyn, the twelve-year-old who lived in the next close was pushing baby Scot in his 'go-chair' pram. Five-year-old Alice was running ahead and calling for her mother. Catching sight of her she ran to her outstretched arms. Her little cheeks expanded, blowing hard on gloved fingers. Her blonde hair shone and bounced. It was the colour of simmering sunshine and had never faded from the day she was born. The curls were a legacy from her father.

Her biological father.

Mary's first husband, her only love, Charlie. Much to her mother's disappointment, Alice had quickly picked up the Glasgow slang.

'Mammy, we had a great time. Marilyn took us to the swings and I went on the iron shovel by myself and I wisni scared wan bit, wis ah, Marilyn?'

'She was really good, Mrs Bray, honest, and the wean slept the whole time, but I think he's done a shite in his nappy, it's stinking.'

Mary smiled. She liked Marilyn, who enjoyed taking Scot out for a walk in his pram, and Alice adored her.

Kathy came over to the pram, looked at Scot and smiled, bending down to kiss the sleeping baby gently on the cheek. She then leaned forward so Alice could throw her arms around her.

'Cheerio, you gorgeous weans, Auntie Kathy has to go noo. Be a good wee lassie for yer, Mammy, Alice, do ye hear me?'

Alice looked up and beamed, showing two rows of perfectly white baby teeth.

'Aye, Auntie Kathy, I will, but did ye bring me any sweeties?'

'Next time, hen, I promise.' She winked at Mary and headed for the front of the close before turning back. 'See you in the mornin, okay?'

'Right,' said Mary, their eyes locked knowingly. 'And stop smiling. You're like a contented cow.'

Kathy waved and whooped loudly before running out into the street.

Mary bumped the pram up the stairs then pushed it into the small hallway at number twenty-three. She lifted the sleeping Scot. Marilyn was right, he stunk to high heaven, but he did look so lovely, those eyebrows were perfect, not a stray hair and shaped to perfection. He didn't stir as she quickly changed his nappy before wrapping him in a flannelette blanket.

Archie was shaving at the sink, he had his back to her. Mary glanced at him and shuddered, wondering what his mood would be. She could barely recognise the handsome fresh-faced soldier who was besotted with her when she worked in the mess hall of the army barracks just after the war. It was hard to believe it was only a few short years ago. His hair was now receding and lank, he was always picking his nose or cleaning his ears with a matchstick, he never changed his socks and his feet stunk. Turning around, he gave her a sideways glance while deftly running the blade through the lather on his jaw, dropping bits of foam dotted with black stubble onto his vest. 'And whit were yous two whisperin about then, eh?'

'Nothing really.' Mary sighed, looking down. 'Kathy was telling me about someone she met at the café weeks ago. They went to the pictures last night, that's all.'

'Whit do ye mean "that's aw"? It's never "that's aw" with that trollop. She's bad for ye, Mary. Keep away fray her, she's nothing but trouble.'

Mary stood up straight talking to his back. 'Why don't you like her, Archie? She is a good person. She's been so good to me and the children, she makes me laugh, and her heart is always in the right place. What has she ever done to you?'

'Don't try to be smart wi me, Mary. I'm tellin ye again, she's fuckin trouble.'

Archie chose not to see things the way Mary did. His contempt for Kathy was like a throbbing abscess that would never heal. He knew her.

Mary knelt down again at the fireplace. It was smouldering now, showing glimpses of red-hot cinders and oozing hopes of warmth and comfort. She blew as hard as she could, coaxing it with scraps of cardboard until eventually giving life to the chilled room.

Archie ate the stovies that Mary had prepared. It was their staple diet; potato, carrot, and onion boiled to a pulp and smothered in salt. Alice had asked for more, so Mary scooped half her plate into her daughter's bowl. She was not so hungry anyway.

Archie called out a hurried cheerio as the outside door banged loudly. The dogs were racing that night. She had watched him earlier scribbling on a folded newspaper with a pencil stub. Mary knew that he had found the money hidden in a candlestick for Christmas decorations. She wanted so badly to brighten the room at Christmas, especially for Alice. She would have to find another hiding place.

Scot was awake. It was getting colder; she lay him on two cushions on the floor, the gas mantle was flickering low, and the heat from the hearth was slowly fading. She put on her overcoat, then found another cardigan for Alice, who had climbed into her chairs to sleep. Mary sighed. Her daughter had never slept in a bed.

Later that night, Mary sat by the fire gently rocking Scot to sleep. She lay him down on his pillow in the drawer, then she bent down to kiss his warm brow. He never stirred. The glow from dying embers shone on her daughter's hair, glowing like a halo. Feelings of dread mingled with feelings of love overcame her. What life was this for her children? How would they survive a life of poverty, cold and hunger? Mary knew she was trapped with a violent man, a gambler, and an ill provider, but she had nowhere else to go.

How different life would have been with Charlie. What would baby Jonathon have looked like now, had she not buried him at barely six weeks old? Memories overcame her. How easily she could visualise his face. The very thought of him made her stomach ache; the heartbreak would live with her forever. A lonely tear escaped her tired eyes. He was Charlie's son, he was her son, he was Alice's brother … and he was gone.

Pulling on a clean, thick pair of Archie's socks, she stood on a chair, turning off the low gaslight. By the last dull glow of the fire, she climbed into bed, encapsulating herself into the thin blanket and heavy coat. In the worn flannelette sheets, Archie's odour was still trapped. It filled her with nausea. She coughed; it was always worse at night. Mary held her head under the blankets, trying desperately to muffle the racking sounds, but her mouth filled with phlegm, and she knew she had an infection again.

A drunken man was abusing himself outside in the street that was otherwise silent. He was swearing and crying. Mary heard him fall as a bottle smashed inside the close. She shuddered, knowing there would be another pool of urine and beer to stain and smell the stairs that she had cleaned earlier.

Closing her eyes, she was comforted by the soft, steady breathing of her son and daughter. Right then, Mary Bray made a pact with her heart. She would find a way to escape this life. She had no idea when or how she would do it; all she had was hope, vision, and a goal. She owed it to her children … she owed it to herself.

Chapter 3

Kathy ran up the last few steps of her close, thoughts of Mary troubling her all the way home. She was concerned about her friend's everyday struggles with a young family in that cramped room, and her choice of a brutal, selfish irresponsible man with no ambition or means to provide for his family. She agonised over whether or not to tell Mary what had happened all those years ago, how those carefree reckless days had eventually morphed into a life of loathing ... but it was too risky. Mary would never understand.

At the door on the first floor, Kathy pulled off a sheepskin mitten with her teeth and blew on her numb fingers before turning the key. The room was small and cosy, but lonely. Kathy missed her mother and pined for her father Stan, who was now languishing in prison, found guilty of the manslaughter of Pat Murphy, a hostile and violent criminal. An unpaid gambling debt, a burst of anger and a switchblade knife all led to the violent death of someone's husband, someone's father, someone's son. Her mother's health deteriorated as she struggled to cope with the scandal and notoriety. She had died in the arms of her eldest daughter.

The bedroom door burst open.

'Kathy, where have ye been? Ye've been away fur ages!'

Helen, Kathy's fourteen-year-old sister stood in the doorway, shaking.

'Yvonne's had a turn. I didne know what to dae. I've given her two

Aspro. Is that okay?' Clasping and unclasping her shaking hands, she looked at her sister. 'She still keeps spewing up, she's shivering, and coughing. What'll we do? Should we take her to the hospital?'

Kathy put her arm around her sister. 'Don't worry, hen. I'll go in and see her, then I'll get Dr Nelson to come round after his surgery. He should be finished soon.'

Kathy slipped quietly into the next room. Yvonne was asleep. The pillowcase was damp and the sheets covering her were bunched and entangled. She stirred as Kathy quickly changed the pillowslip and straightened the sheets loosely over her thin body. She picked up a wet facecloth from the dresser placing it gently on Yvonne's burning brow. Her bronchial rasping breath made Kathy cringe.

She left the room calling out to her sister, 'Cheerio, Helen. Yvonne's asleep, I promise I'll no be long.'

Closing the door quietly on her worried sister, she ran out into the street. The cold air quickly found her throat as she tightened her woollen scarf. She ran most of the way to the surgery, stopping occasionally to catch her breath. Thoughts of her sister lying pale and still beneath the sheets haunted her, spurring her on. Turning into the street, she saw Dr Nelson locking the surgery door. He looked around, catching sight of Kathy.

'My goodness, Kathy, what are you doing here? Surgery is closed now for the night and I am on my way to see a patient.'

Kathy quickly gave Yvonne's symptoms to the doctor; she begged him to come and see her. The elderly doctor nodded. 'I'll be there as soon as I can, Kathy. Just keep her warm until then.'

Kathy smiled weakly. 'Thanks, Dr Nelson.'

When Kathy arrived home, Helen was at the door clasping and unclasping her hands. 'Did ye see him, Kathy? Is he coming soon? Is she gonna be alright?'

Kathy wrapped her arms around her sister.

'Aye, hen. Don't you worry, she will be fine. Dr Nelson is on his way shortly. He's making a call on a patient, not far from here, before coming to us.' She looked straight ahead, afraid to blink.

The thirty minutes until he arrived were dragging. Kathy found keeping her cool in front of Helen was stressful. Dr Nelson went directly to Yvonne's bedside where he methodically checked her temperature, chest, and pulse, then he took her blood pressure. He prodded around her ears then her throat with a flat wooden spatula. He disengaged his stethoscope, folded it and placed it carefully back into its black box, then he took out his prescription pad and scribbled quickly. Closing his bag with a resounding snap, he stood up and whispered quietly to Kathy, handing over the prescription.

'Nothing serious, Kathy, but she does need plenty of bed rest and make sure she keeps warm. This prescription is for cough medicine. Just follow the instructions, it will help break up the phlegm and ease the rasping. When she wakes up she will be very thirsty. Give her plenty of water and flat lemonade. Goodnight to you, lass. I'll see myself out.'

Kathy put on her coat. It was late. Outside, it was getting dark and the streetlights were on. She had to go out to get lemonade for Yvonne, the only place open to buy it was the pub. If she left now, she would be back in half an hour. Helen came into the room as she was knotting the scarf tightly around her neck. Grabbing her basket and mitts, she turned to her sister and said, 'I'll no be long, hen, just runnin doon to the pub for some lemonade for

Yvonne. Lock the door behind me and don't open it to anybody, okay? And don't look so worried. I'll be that quick, ye'll think I've just gone for a pee.'

After hugging her sister, Kathy pulled the door closed behind her and ran down the stairs into the street. A cold wintry blast enveloped her as she buried her mouth and nose into the knot of her scarf. Not many people were out and about. She half walked, half ran through the streets, only slowing down when the neon lights of the pub appeared in the distance. Getting closer, she heard muffled voices and laughter. A door burst open to the sound of breaking glass followed by jeers, taunts and swearing.

The off-license at the pub faced out into the street. She could buy lemonade without going near the bar. Pushing open the swing doors, she walked confidently to the counter.

The stocky barman, his thick arms covered in tattoos, came towards her, grinning. He spread his arms widely on the counter, his smile exposing yellow teeth and shrinking gums.

'What can I get ye then, bonnie lassie, eh?'

Kathy smiled confidently, ignoring his leer. 'Two bottles of lemonade, that's aw. Thanks a lot!'

Bending down, he brought up two bottles from beneath the bar. With a smirk, he pushed them slowly toward her with nicotine-stained index fingers. Leaning forward, he flashed her a sickly grin whilst wiping his hands on a grubby apron. 'Righto, then! Here ye are, lassie. Big party the night then is it, eh?'

Kathy glared at him. 'Aye right, very funny, and your no invited!'

Placing the bottles into her basket on the floor, she pulled up the collar of her coat and turned to leave. The shutters to the public bar were wide open. Glancing into the packed room—she held her breath, amid the smoke, the haze, and the escalating noise—she saw him. A solitary dishevelled figure with a heavy black stubble and thin, lank greying hair trying unsuccessfully to cover an expanding bald patch. Hunched over sodden beer mats and empty glasses, Archie Bray was oblivious of his surroundings.

He couldn't see her. With a pounding heart and trembling hands, she watched him as he leant over a frothed-up pint and two empty whisky glasses. A half-smoked cigarette had metamorphosed into a long cylinder of ash that was aimlessly drifting onto the bar. He frowned and scratched his head whilst jotting with a pencil stub on a folded piece of newspaper. Through the smog and the stench of stale beer, tears of anger and frustration were building within Kathy. The torment was never-ending. She wiped her eyes, picked up her basket and moved silently away.

The heartbreaking sobs of Kathy King went unheard in the deserted streets, as her tears flowed freely in the chill of the night.

Archie had been at the pub for over an hour. Leaning back, he scratched his head and dragged the old army coat closer to his body. Two buttons were missing near the top. The football scarf tied twice around his neck prevented the wind outside from getting to his chest. He wore only one glove, inside the other were two one-pound notes he found stuffed in the brass candlestick at home. With an hour to kill before clocking on at the power station for his night shift, he decided that a quick trip to the pub and a few pints was well in order. The dogs were running at Sheffield Park and he had a tip for a sure thing in the third.

Downing another Scotch, he pulled a half-smoked cigarette from behind his ear. Tapping it on the bar, he turned to the drunk on the end barstool. 'Any chance of a light, pal?'

A heavily lined hand with black fingernails pushed a box of Vesta's toward him.

'Thanks pal!'

Archie struck the match, lit up and inhaled deeply. Shaking his head, he muttered to no one in particular, 'Oh aye, that's the ticket.' He went back to studying the form. Disrupting his train of thought came a strong, high-pitched voice, heard clearly over the hum of jovial patrons. A few close bystanders looked up, staring in anticipation.

'Archie, ma man, where have ye been? Have no seen ye for ages.'

Archie turned around slowly and blinked, narrowing his eyes as he looked to the back of the room. All he saw was smoke.

'Over here, son, it's me ... it's me, Dave. Look. Here, over here. How's it goin?'

Archie peering through the haze, raised his hand in the general direction. 'Oh, aye, hello there. Aw the best, eh! Aw the best!'

The voice came again, this time louder and stronger, the intent was clear. 'Any chance of getting that fiver ye owe me, eh? It's been six weeks, pal!'

Dave Taylor was feared in the crime scene of Glasgow. He was a man who had defied the law numerous times. He had served prison time for assault and battery, attempted murder, and rape. Dave Taylor was feared even in his own circle. His voice was insistent as he sat comfortably with a group of men behind the door, keeping a watch on Archie. Dave's bloated face with its blackhead-infested nose wore a stiff grin; his eyes were cold and fearsome. The meaning was unmistakable. Pay up or else!

Archie was nervous, he was scared, he was trapped. He felt a lead weight in his chest—there was nowhere to run and nowhere to hide.

The noise eased to a lull. Many turned away, embarrassed. Some blatantly stared at them both, waiting for a showdown. Archie turned quickly back to the bar, lifted the pint to his lips, took a great gulp, and faced his fears.

'Aye, Dave, nay problem,' he uttered weakly. 'I`ve got a pound here and I'll get paid the morra so I'll square up then, is that okay?'

Subdued sighs of relief wafted from the surrounding drinkers. Dave's eyes narrowed. He nodded, walked toward Archie and pulled the pound note from his clenched fist, then heading back to his table, he turned and glared at Archie.

'Aye, right-o then, wee man, see ye then. Don't forget, okay? Or you'll be sorry.'

The air grew thicker, the noise louder. Somewhere in the near distance, a lone drunken male voice was belting out the lamenting *Nobody's Child*.

Archie pulled the loose change from his pocket and tossed it on the bar.

'Gie us another pint, eh, pal?'

He picked up the crumpled piece of paper with the night's races circled in pencil, nodded to himself, and muttered, 'Aye, just enough time to bet on the sixth afore my shift.'

Chapter 4

Peggy Bray was a spoiled child. Her middle-aged parents adored her. Many thought she was aloof, some even described her as a 'bloody snob'. She lived a contented life with her family in an old established council house in Leighton Avenue. It was a conservative part of the district. The neighbours were quiet, the gardens and pathways were trimmed and tidy, and they all went to church. Her mother, Sadie, was small and well rounded, a kind woman who saw her sole purpose in life as keeping house for her family: husband Bob, daughter Peggy, son Archie, widowed brother Frank, and her elderly, incapacitated father. This was a very conservative household with no tolerance for smoking, drinking, or coarse language.

Although not a striking beauty, Peggy was an attractive girl. Her hair was set in waves that sat just above her collar, with hazel eyes that seemed to dart around the room whenever she spoke. She wore sensible shoes and plaid skirts with fine woollen twin sets and a double string of pearls. Voluptuous lips that had never seen lipstick enveloped her straight teeth. Many thought she resembled a young Princess Margaret.

Archie, being the youngest, was protected growing up in these surroundings. He was very bright at school but lazy and disrespectful, often in trouble with teachers and students alike. He grew into a tall, fine-looking young man.

Not long after his seventeenth birthday the visions that Sadie and

Bob had for their son were to be crushed underfoot.

It was a day in late autumn. They were sitting in the living room. Bob was reading the paper and Sadie had just poured a cup of tea. The front door closed with a bang.

'Are ye there, Ma?'

Sadie turned around. 'Aye, we're here, son. I've just made a pot of tea.'

Archie came into the room and flopped down heavily on the settee. His face flushed with excitement. He was talking quickly and waving papers above his head.

'Here, look at this. I was doon the main street and there was this man sittin at a wee table outside the town hall. He was wearing a kind of khaki uniform and a hat and he said that he was recruiting for the army. I talked wi him fur ages; he thinks I'll make a great sojur. He said the money was good and if I left after a couple of years, I would get a good job. I just need to fill in these forms. I don't know half of whit they need to know, stuff about yous two and when I was born and aw that.' He laughed. 'Can ye sort it oot for me, eh?'

No one spoke.

'Did yous no hear me?' Archie laughed and shook the papers again. Bob didn't look up from his newspaper, he only held out his hand for the forms.

He nodded, speaking slowly. 'That sounds good, son. Just leave them here wi us and we'll have a wee look at them later on, awright?'

'Okay, Da, that's great. Can ye no just see me in a uniform? Whit a laugh, eh?'

Archie got up and left whistling loudly, banging the door behind him.

Sadie hadn't said a word, or moved from the chair. She covered her face with both hands while mumbling between her fingers. 'My God,

Bobby, whit do we do, eh? Oh! What do we do noo?'

Bobby put down his paper. He took her hand in his, squeezing it gently. 'We'll do nothing, Sadie. No a thing. It's likely to be another one of his flash in the pan ideas. We'll no say a word, he'll probably forget all aboot it. Stop yer worrying and drink yer tea hen.'

Archie didn't mention the army at all that week, nor the next. Bob and Sadie relaxed. However, the following week when Archie was upstairs in the bathroom with a face full of shaving foam, he called out to his father downstairs.

'Da, ye know that army thing I telt you aboot the other week? Did ye remember to fill in the form? Ye know, the bits that I couldnie answer? It's just that I met that man at the recruiting place again yesterday and he asked me fur them.'

Bob closed his eyes, held his fist to his mouth and blew softly before answering. 'Aye, son. Sorry, I've been that busy. I'll talk to yer ma and we'll get them done, don't worry.'

Sadie, sitting opposite him, put her knitting needles down and mouthed, 'Oh no.'

Bob stood up and walked into the kitchen, then turned back, looking at his wife. 'We need to tell him, hen. We need to.'

Later that afternoon, Bob and Sadie sat outside in the back garden watching Archie digging a hole to plant a rhododendron bush. They called him over. He looked up, waved, then thrust his shovel into the hole and rolled down his sleeves.

'What's up, Ma?' he asked, wiping the sweat from his brow. 'Is the hole no big enough?'

Sadie laughed nervously, quickly glancing at Bob, who was coughing and tapping his fingers on his knee, which he did when unsure or nervous. Reaching out, she stilled his hand.

Bob looked at Archie with a half-smile and a breaking heart.

'Archie, there's something we need to talk to ye about. It's something that happened a long time ago. We should have telt ye before this, but somehow we kept puttin it aff, we just ignored it.'

Sadie's voice started to waver as she looked into the eyes of her son. 'This is awfie hard for us, son.'

'What is it, Ma? Ye look like a ghost, you as well, Da. What have I done this time?' Archie tried to make light of the moment.

Bob started to speak. 'It's like this, son—'

Sadie cut him off. 'No, Bobby. No, I'll tell him. It's better comin frae me.' Swallowing deeply, and pushing her shoulders back, she looked straight into Archie's eyes. 'The day ye were born, son, brought us aw that much joy and happiness. Ye were such a bonnie wee baby; everybody wanted a cuddle. Ye had a great head of black hair and the most perfect wee man's face.'

She smiled at the memory then paused, took a deep breath, pulled a handkerchief from her apron pocket, blew her nose then dabbed at her eyes. Her heart was aching as she looked at Archie's confused face. 'It was just the happiest day for all of us, son, but it was the saddest day as well, especially for me. It was so tragic, so unexpected I don't think I've ever gotten over it.'

Archie frowned. Raising his voice, he sat up straight and leaned forward. 'Get over whit, Ma. Whit do ye mean tragic? Whit are ye talkin aboot?'

Sadie braced herself. 'It was the day my sister died.'

'Your sister, Ma? I didnae know ye had a sister. I've never heard ye talk aboot her.' He looked at Bob waiting for an explanation, but Bob shook his head and looked away.

'Whit was her name, Ma?'

Sadie answered in a whisper, 'Her name was Jean. She was such a bonnie lassie, no just wi her lovely face, she was lovely inside as well, everybody liked her. She was clever too, she could add up sums in her head and never needed to write anything doon, and she made people laugh. She was … och, well, she was just that funny. We were best pals. We went everywhere the gether. I still miss her. I miss her every day, son.'

'So, I had an Auntie Jean then. How come you never spoke about her? Whit happened to her?'

Sadie didn't answer.

Archie tensed. 'Ma … whit happened to ma auntie?'

'Well, son, ye see she was no really yer auntie. This is awfie hard … it's difficult.'

Bob put his arm around Sadie. He was shaking.

'No ma auntie? Whit do ye mean?' Archie looked at Bob. 'If it was Ma's sister, she must have been ma auntie, eh?'

Bob looked away; Sadie stood up.

'No, son, she wasn't yer auntie.'

'Well, if she wisnae my auntie, who was she then?'

She braced herself putting shaking hands into her apron pockets then taking a deep breath. 'She was your ma, Archie. Oor Jeannie was your ma.' Sadie trembled, making fists in her apron pockets as she looked down.

'I'm your auntie, Archie. I'm your Auntie Sadie.'

There was silence.

Sadie sat down, weeping quietly, as Bob wrapped his arms around her. Archie stood up and looked at them both. Frowning, he shook his head.

'Whit are yous talking about?' he leaned forward, a half-smile now on his face. 'Are yous kidding me on? Yer no my ma? Fuckin rubbish! Where did aw this come fray? Are yous aff yer heid or somethin, eh? Anyhow, how come yer comin oot wi this noo then, eh? Whit's brought aw this on?'

Sadie stayed silent while Bob, who was shaking, took over and looked at the man he had always treated as a son.

'The forms that you asked us to look at for the army, son, well ... ye see, they wanted to know all the details of where ye were born and the names of yer ma and da. When ye asked us for them, we just didn't know what to tell ye, but here it is, this is yours noo, all the information ye need. We're sorry, son.'

Bob reached into his inside jacket pocket and handed a worn folded paper to Archie—it was his birth certificate.

Archie, shaking his head in disbelief, opened the paper, taking time to read it slowly. Without looking at Sadie and Bob and with tears welling, he held out the certificate and pointed to the heading of the father's name.

It read 'father unknown'.

Sadie stood up, she was wringing her hands and holding back the tears. 'Archie, yer mother was a lovely woman. She was very kind and caring, never a bad word to say aboot anybody. None of us had any idea that she was seeing somebody. She never talked aboot him or said where she was goin whenever she went oot. She was five months pregnant when she told us. She was crying, distressed and that scared. We didnae know what to do, we were shocked, honestly, but we never let on to her how we felt. She asked us to help her, and, of course, we said we would, there was nobody else. We arranged it in secret, nobody knew. We took her to a minister that Bob has known for years, he lived just outside of Edinburgh. She stayed with him and his wife till she went into labour. It was a very difficult birth, she had postnatal bleeding. Yer ma was very weak son, and couldnie fight back. Even wi all the hard work and efforts from the doctors, her body just gave up. She lived for twenty-four hours after ye were born, she was able to hold ye for a wee while and touch yer cheek. We were with her when she died, son. She knew what was happnin and made me promise to look after ye. I said of course we would, and that we would raise ye wi our Peggy. Her voice was weak, she wanted to say something to me, so I bent doon closer. She reached oot for ma hand and with the smallest wee smile whispered, "Sadie, he must be called Archie, ma boy's name is Archie." Then her hand fell away frae me, she closed her eyes and was gone.'

Sadie paused to wipe her tears before continuing. 'We told the neighbours and our wee group of friends that we had been planning to adopt for a long time. We told them that we got news of yer arrival very quickly and had to leave in a hurry to collect ye. Naebody ever questioned us, and everyone was happy. Jean's death was a terrible blow, but having you helped us heal, knowing that in you our Jeannie was still here. I hope you can forgive yer da and me for no telling you sooner, son. We know we should have, but this makes nay difference to us. Ye'll always be our wee boy.'

Archie sat motionless with his head bowed whilst listening to Sadie. He didn't say a word, he just stood up then went inside, closing the door quietly behind him.

Sadie and Bob clung together in silence. What had weighed so heavily on them for all these years was now out in the open. The veil of sadness and guilt that had enveloped them had been lifted.

From that day on Archie Bray was very restrained. He didn't ask any more questions. He seemed to accept that the only family he had always known were still his family, only not on paper.

Much later, Sadie would say that discovering the facts of his birth marked the beginning of the decline of Archie Bray.

Chapter 5

Whilst in England with the army, Archie met Mary, a shy English girl with a tinkling laugh and great legs. He would come into the camp canteen where she worked, chat to her, and flatter her, he made her laugh with his broad Scottish accent and humour. He wanted to see more of her outside of the army barracks, but Mary always refused, telling him she was very happily married with a child, and that her heart belonged to Charlie.

'Och, Mary, why don't ye come to the pictures wi me? I know yer married, but it'll no dae any harm while yer man's no here. It's just a wee talk. It'll give ye a break.'

He was insistent and charming, reassuring her that nothing would happen, they were just friends going to the pictures. Mary was lonely and missing Charlie, who was often away with work for weeks on end. Archie was wearing her down with his persistence, and she finally said that yes, she would go with him, but only this once. Charlie's sister often looked after Alice while she spent time with friends from the barracks. Mary still felt guilty at not being completely honest, but she convinced herself an innocent little break with a man from work would be nice.

On the afternoon they met, Archie said that a wee drink would be better, they could relax a bit more and have a chat and a laugh. Mary told him she wasn't fond of alcohol but reluctantly agreed to go for one drink. They sat in the corner of a quiet pub on the edge of town. He was very attentive and made her laugh. He bought her two Pimm's with lemonade: she giggled at his jokes and basked in his flattery while walking her home.

Passing a closed shop in the deserted street, he gently pushed her to the side, guiding her into the farthest corner of the doorway. He pulled her toward him as she tried to resist, but the Pimm's had made her head spin, and she relaxed as his lips, soft and gentle, found hers and lingered. She pulled away, looking at him in horror.

'Oh no! What have I done? I'm sorry, so sorry, that was wrong of me I have to go home. Please, Archie, let me go.'

He stood back grinning broadly. 'Och, lovely Mary, I think ye enjoyed that just a wee bit, eh, did ye no, eh? Don't worry, darlin, naebody will know. Come back anytime and we'll finish what we started, eh?'

He reached out for her again, but she drew away quickly, turned around and ran down the street, his mocking words and laughter ringing in her ears.

'See ye again soon, wee Mary.'

Mary struggled every day with her conscience. She was terrified that someone would find out, and even more terrified of his further pursuit of her. She tried hard to avoid him, but he was relentless, looking for her every day at work. She rejected all his advances, but rejections never fazed Archie, he continued his pursuit. With his magnetism and persuasiveness, he had won the heart of a young female clerk in the office who gladly disclosed to him that Charlie was on a three-day assignment and Mary was on a day off. He knew where she lived so he decided to walk the mile or so to her home. Arriving at the back gate, he climbed the stairs to the top floor flat, rattled the letterbox, waited, then rattled again. The door opened wide. Mary began to smile then stopped and covered her cheek with one hand when she saw Archie.

'My God, Archie! What are you doing here?'

He propped one shoulder against the wall and crossed his legs at the ankles, hands deep in his pockets. Raising one eyebrow and grinned. 'Well, hello there, lovely Mary. Here I am, on ma way tae the pub when right away I said to masel Mary lives here, maybe I'll chap the door and see if she's in. Any chance of a wee cup of tea, lassie?'

Mary, in disbelief, tried to close the door, but he put his boot down firmly.

'Don't just stand there, ma bonnie wee lassie, let me in.'

She started to shake biting her bottom lip. 'No Archie, please go away, the neighbours might see you. Alice is playing outside; she might come up the stairs and see you. Please leave, Archie, please go now!'

He pushed the door open, walked past her, then slowly ambled into the room.

'Oh, it's a nice wee place ye've got here, Mary.'

Ignoring him, she rushed to the window and checked on Alice, who was playing with the next-door neighbour's children.

Archie sat down on the sofa, stretching his legs. Mary, in a state of panic, put the kettle on. Her hands shook as she brought out the cups and saucers; since their last encounter she found herself thinking of him, and although she was anxious, deep down, she was also a little thrilled.

He called out to her, 'Come on, Mary, come and sit wi me for a wee while.'

She couldn't look at him. 'Archie, it will only take a minute. I'll just get the cups.'

He laughed. 'Come on now, Mary, I'm no gonna eat ye.'

Grabbing her arm, he pulled her down beside him. She protested, calling out and breathing heavily, trying to resist, but all he did was pull her closer. His breath reeked of cigarettes, laced with mint chewing gum.

It was somehow strangely exhilarating.

She didn't mind the cigarettes, the heavy breathing, or the tender caresses she was intoxicated by the moment. He covered her mouth with kisses that were long and lingering. She knew it was wrong, but she was helpless to stop him. He lightly stroked her breasts, whispering husky words of love in her ear as she melted into his pulsating body. Lost in a world of warmth and protection, Mary Bray released her conscience and surrendered to her guilty heart.

The shrill whistle of the kettle died as Archie turned it off on the way to the bedroom. Together they crawled under the soft, inviting eiderdown.

When it was over, Mary felt bad, empty, vacant, unfulfilled, and let down. It had happened so quickly. The warmth and pleasure so brief, the words of love somehow lost. After his heavy breathing and commitments of love, Archie turned his back to her, lay on his side and quickly fell into a dead sleep, snoring loudly.

Gazing up at the ceiling in a haze, Mary tried in vain to absorb exactly what had just happened. How could she ever have betrayed Charlie like this? He must never find out; she would tell Archie that. Charlie was her whole world, her daughter's father, and she loved him so much. If he ever found out she would deny it ... all of it.

Getting out of bed quickly, she looked out the window to the street below. Alice had thrown her ball to the older children and it had landed in a water trough. There were howls of happiness in their laughter. Satisfied that her daughter was in safe hands and suddenly feeling very weary, remorseful, disappointed and sad, she lay back down on the edge of the bed to rest her eyes just for a moment.

The banging woke her. It didn't register at first. It sounded like a loud tapping rather than a bang, but the voice was unmistakeably Alice.

'Mammy, Mammy, open the door.'

Mary was scared hearing her daughter's voice, afraid that she may have hurt herself. Without a thought to the snoring mass beside her, she flew out of bed in her underwear, covering herself with a towel, but before she could get to the door it was pushed inwards toward her. She recoiled in shock.

'Charlie!'

Standing there in disbelief, she was momentarily frozen. No words came, just a pounding of her heart and trembling knees.

Charlie stood there smiling with a key in his hand. Dropping his bag, he reached out and lifted her off the floor and then did a full turn, hugging her tight before putting her down. Alice was laughing, singing, and holding onto Charlie's leg; he held his wife at arm's length, his voice breaking.

'Oh Mary, I have missed you so. I managed to get away a day earlier, I just couldn't wait to see you. Now, let me look at you.'

Mary struggled to hold onto the towel that barely covered her decency, but Charlie didn't seem to notice. Tears rested heavily in her eyes.

The bedroom door behind her suddenly burst wide open.

'What's all the fuckin noise and carryin on aboot?'

Archie stood at the bedroom door in his underpants. With his dishevelled hair, and the start of a heavy stubble, he looked directly at Charlie. 'Oh, it's you. Mary? Whit the fuck's going on here? Ye told me he widnie be back till the morra. Yer making me look like a right fuckin ejit!'

Charlie stood back, looking from one to the other. He began to speak and then fell silent. Mary was sobbing, still struggling to cover herself with the towel.

'Oh Charlie, I'm so sorry, it doesn't mean anything, honestly, please forgive me, it was the only time. I missed you so, and—'

Charlie's eyes were static, his face ashen, expressionless. He turned away, bending down to lift Alice into his arms, holding her tightly. His voice was strong but hoarse. 'Daddy has to go now, Alice, but I'll see you again soon, pet, okay? Always remember that Daddy loves you very much, and I will say a prayer for you every night. Come on now and give me your biggest hug before I go.'

Alice stared wide-eyed at her father then threw her arms around his neck and started to cry. She watched as he picked up his bag and ran down the stairs. Sobbing uncontrollably and reaching out with both arms, she cried, 'Come back, Daddy, come back! Where are you going?'

Mary picked up her writhing daughter and dashed to the top of the stairs crying out, 'Please, Charlie! Please let me talk to you! Please don't leave me!'

It was too late. Charlie heaved his bag over his shoulder and walked quickly down the street. He never looked back ... He never came back.

Two years later, Mary and Charlie were divorced, and she was carrying Archie's child. They were married quickly in the registry office. Archie had left the army and returned home to Leighton Avenue, a small close-knit community in a district of Glasgow, bringing with him his new bride, her daughter, and their unborn child.

His family were not happy. This was not what they had envisaged for the young Archie Bray. They were polite to Mary but disappointed in Archie. The only option was to make the best of the situation. To house another three people in their home was going to be difficult for them, but manageable.

Mary hated it all.

The cramped room, the crowded house, the night noises: snoring, coughing, farting, and whispering. The old man sat in his chair all day, grumbling, complaining, and puffing on a clay pipe.

The family were very restrained, appearing only to tolerate both her and Alice. They silently blamed her for putting this burden on the young Archie. Mary desperately wanted them to like her. She wanted family. She lived with regret; regret that Charlie had discovered her betrayal, regret that she had married a man whom she now realised was lazy, uncouth and a poor provider, but her biggest regret was that her daughter was no longer with a father who adored her.

The weeks dragged on. Mary was growing bigger and more uncomfortable. She spent much of the time lying on their lumpy bed in the cramped room trying to entertain Alice. Archie often left her for hours on end without saying where he was going, and then he would slip into bed late at night smelling of beer, smoke and sweat.

Six weeks before the baby was due, Mary went to hospital for complete rest. Her blood pressure was very low and she was exhausted. Sadie looked after Alice whilst Archie found casual work.

After a long and difficult birth, baby Scot came into their lives. Mary was overwhelmed; Scot was a beautiful baby. Although he was healthy and a good weight, she was fearful of losing him like she had Jonathon. She tried not to compare the two, but it was inevitable. Recalling that time in her life was agonising. Jonathon had been born with an exceptionally low birth weight; he had advanced heart disease. The doctors had said his survival was slim but she prayed, maintaining faith for six long weeks. Sadly, her baby son would never grow up. He slipped away one cold, wet winter's night. Charlie was overseas on special duty with the army, so there was no one to take her home from the hospital with her lifeless son. He lay in a small wooden box beside her in a taxi. Mary was inconsolable; Jonathan's short life weighed on her like a tombstone.

Things were bearable for a brief time when she returned to Leighton Avenue, even pleasant. Scot's birth brought boundless joy to the family. This was Archie's son; the family name would carry on. Even Peggy would smile when she held the baby. The old man gazed through watery eyes at a new generation and just nodded his head. Sadie, as always, kept everything running smoothly; she cooked, cleaned, and helped with the children. It was a happier time for Mary, but the euphoria was short lived. Trying to juggle two adults and two small children in the cramped back room became almost unbearable.

Archie had found work as a window cleaner to support his young family. The money he brought home was a pittance. Most of his pay went to the pub, bookie, or cigarettes before he got home on payday. Sadie was feeding them all. Mary was at breaking point, the tension was only growing with the children unsettled, the cold, the silences, the forever-beholding feeling that she felt to the whole family. But mostly it was the loneliness, the need for support. The yearning for a friend.

Scot was six weeks old when she finally realised that her marriage was never going to get any better. Archie would never change. He would forever be irresponsible, abusive and a poor provider—all she felt for him now was contempt. She was determined to rise above this wretched life. She would succeed, and ensure that her children were raised as well-mannered and educated citizens.

Slipping silently out of bed one morning, she crept downstairs and stood motionless at the open kitchen door.

Sadie was standing at the sink with her back to her, humming a tune whilst washing the dishes. Mary hesitated, for a moment she almost silently crept back upstairs, but instead stood straight, and spoke clearly.

'Sadie, I have to speak to you.'

Sadie turned around quickly. 'Oh, Mary, hello! I didnae hear ye come down. Aye, pet, sure, c'mon and sit here. I'll put the kettle on.'

'No, Sadie. Please, no tea thanks, I have something to say. I mean, I have to say it now before I lose my nerve, so please, please, listen to me, it won't take long.'

Sadie frowned, putting the kettle down then drying her hands. Mary stood there, clasping her hands, and twisting her wedding ring. The words flowed from a weak, hoarse voice, the tears running unchecked.

'Sadie, I'm sorry, but I am so unhappy here. Everything is so cramped, I am exhausted trying to keep the children from upsetting anyone, I'm scared, I don't feel comfortable, and Archie is no help at all, he just tells me to get on with it. I know you don't want to hear this, but I have to leave, really, I do. I've found out there is a women's refuge in Edinburgh where I can go temporarily until I sort things out. There's a train leaving Central Station in three days. I told Archie, but he doesn't believe I will go, but I will, Sadie, I have no option. I just can't live like this anymore.'

Sadie was silent. She leaned heavily on the door, not interrupting, just listening to the outburst. She desperately wanted to keep them all here in Glasgow. She needed to see Scot grow up, he brought such joy to the family. She reached out, grabbing Mary's arm, pleading with her. 'Oh, Mary, I had no idea ye were so unhappy. Please don't do anythin yet, please don't catch that train. I promise I'll try to get ye a place of yer own. Would that help? Would ye be happier then? Would ye stay here if ye had yer own place with Archie and the children? Mary, please, Mary, I'm begging ye, please don't do anything yet, will ye?'

Mary's shoulders slumped as she rubbed her bent forehead. 'Oh, Sadie, I'm sorry, but that sounds almost impossible. I don't know how you can find anything for us at all with housing being so scarce, but I will hold off for three days, I promise.'

With that, Mary climbed the stairs slowly to her room and closed the door. The floor creaked as Mary fell onto the bed, her muffled sobs shredded Sadie's soul.

Glasgow was having a major housing crisis. There was a desperate shortage of accommodation. Buildings that had been bombed during the war were leaving slums in its wake, but they were occupied and lived in by desperate families. High-rise 'skyscrapers' were being built to accommodate the long waiting lists of needy and desperate families, rehousing them from congested and slum areas, but all this was taking time. Mary and Archie were not classed as urgent, so they were low on the waiting list.

The next morning, undeterred by the housing shortage, Sadie set out early, heading for the local Housing Corporation, a government office that sourced homes for the population. There was always a constant queue of families. Most would leave disappointed; many would be distraught and crying. Today, Sadie had no time for queues. She was on a mission.

At the reception desk, a middle-aged woman dressed in black

frowned whilst looking down her nose over tortoiseshell glasses. She attempted a distorted smile. 'Yes?'

Sadie spoke quickly. 'I need to speak to someone urgently about getting a house.'

The woman pushed her glasses back up her nose and leaned heavily on her elbows. She pointed one bony finger across the room. 'Well then, Mrs, see that line over there? Ye'll need to wait in it, everybody needs to speak to somebody urgently nowadays ye know. Ye need to take yer turn hen ... okay?'

Sadie looked at the woman blankly then walked away. Not sure exactly in which direction she was going, she aimed for the back of the room. Behind an array of indoor plants, there was a side door with a laminated sign that read: Staff Only. Holding her bag close and looking back around the room, she noticed everyone seemed to be engrossed in conversations, sharing their miseries and complaints. No one was looking her way. She quickly opened the door and climbed the stairs to the first floor. All was quiet, not a soul to be seen. There was a long corridor of closed-door offices, so she tiptoed along silently until she came to the last door on the right. It was slightly ajar. The wooden sign said: District Manager.

Sadie knocked gently, then pushed it open gingerly. An older grey-haired man looked up, put his pen down, and smiled. 'Yes, can I help you? Are you lost?'

Sadie swallowed adjusted her scarf and spoke quickly. 'Oh, I'm no very sure, I should say I don't think so, I mean, I really just need to talk to somebody ... about something.'

Ted Buist sat back in his chair and smiled warmly. 'Well then, why don't you come in, sit down, and talk to me about your something!'

He listened intently as she breathlessly told her story, whilst jotting down notes on a yellow lined pad. Ted Buist shook his head. 'Sadie,

I do understand your dilemma and I can see you are worried, but the housing in Glasgow right now, or should I say lack of housing, is quite dismal. I am sure you're aware of this. We are currently working on high-rise developments and searching for solutions to supply more homes for the people of Glasgow. I can't offer you all that your family needs right now, I understand your problem, but as you can imagine we have a very long waiting list … I'm sorry.'

Sadie, nodded, listening to Ted, while gripping her bag and watching his face, she moved the chair back getting up to leave. 'I understand, Mr Buist. Thank you for listening to me.'

Ted shuffled through some papers in his desk drawer. 'Wait a minute, Sadie. I don't want to get your hopes up, but I could have a temporary solution that may be of some help. It might only be for one year or could be for ten, I can't say, it depends on the new constructions and the waiting list. What I can say is that this place needs a lot of attention and work, and it's extremely basic and small. Do you think they would they be interested?'

Sadie, sat down quickly, laughing, and nodding vigorously. 'Oh, aye, Mr Buist, anything at all, that sounds great, thanks so very much. I'm sure they'll be so happy. They just need to be on their own. They will take it; I know they will.'

Ted sighed and opened the folder. 'Well, hold on there a minute, Sadie. I'll just tell you a wee bit about it. It's only one room in a tenement building on Rooken Road. It's small but still bigger than where they are now in your house. It's a condemned tenement building that's due for demolition in the future. There are about 50 families living there at the moment. It does have running water, and there is a shared toilet situation with other families. As I said before it's very basic, not great really, but it's all I can offer right now.'

Sadie flinched slightly as she listened to him. 'I do understand,

Mr Buist, thanks for yer honesty. It's just that this family are really desperate, I am sure they will make something of it … aye, aye, we'll still take it. I need to go and tell them right now.'

Ted Buist stood up and opened the door, as she went to leave, he put his hand on her shoulder and smiled. 'Good luck to you, Sadie, and God bless you.'

She smiled broadly. 'Thanks for seein me Mr Buist.'

Walking slowly to the bus stop she stood patiently at the end of the queue until the bus arrived. It was crowded and she was exhausted. Clutching her bag tightly, she stood in the aisle and hung on to the strap on the rail above her. A young boy stood up and tapped her on the shoulder.

'Here, Mrs, take ma seat.'

Sinking down gratefully onto the torn viny seat she closed her eyes. It had been a long day.

At Leighton Avenue, Sadie leaned against the back door, gripping the doorknob for support. Her brown woollen coat was half-unbuttoned, the headscarf resting loosely on her shoulders. Breathing deeply, she closed her eyes and came into the kitchen. Mary was sitting at the table shelling peas. Sadie slipped off her coat and sat down at the table.

'Mary, can ye stop for a minute? I've just been to the Housing Corporation and spoke to a manager there …. I've got ye a place, Mary, a place for you and Archie.'

Mary looked at her in disbelief, frowned, then started to wipe her hands on a tea towel whilst laughing nervously. 'A place? What sort of a place exactly, do you mean a house?'

Sadie nodded.

'What? I don't believe it, what's it like? How did you get it?' Mary was talking fast and laughing. 'When can we see it?'

'Well, hold on a minute, hen. I don't think that it's that great. I havnie really seen it maself yet, but ye can move in straight away, and it's a place where ye can be on yer own with Archie and the children. It's a start, Mary. It's small and needs a lot of work, *and* a lot of love, but please give it a try.'

'A home for us, on our own, really? Oh Sadie, I don't care what it's like I'll take it, I'll make it nice. Oh! I don't know what to say. Thank you, thank you so much.'

With that, she threw her arms around Sadie's stooped shoulders, hugging her tightly.

Sadie held her breath.

Chapter 6

Kathy worked in a transport café at the start of the M8 Motorway. She had been working there for two years and was well liked and respected by both staff and customers. Her boss, Tony, expected dedication and hard work from his staff; friendly chat and banter was mandatory. He liked his waitresses to be attractive and flirt with the punters.

Kathy was his best worker, but when she came in one day asking if he could give Mary a job, he was adamant. 'Married wi kids? Yer kidding me on, Kathy, right? Naw, cannot do. Sorry, too unreliable.'

'Aw, c'mon, Tony. She's a hard worker, very trustworthy, I widnie ask if I thought she would let you down.' Kathy lowered her voice and winked. 'Nice looking and wi a great wee figure. What about it, eh?'

Tony half smiled. He trusted her, and he *was* short staffed and in desperate need of another waitress. He nodded his head grudgingly and sighed. 'Okay then, I'll gie her a month's trial, awright, Kath? That's only cos *you* asked me.'

Kathy laughed and ruffled his hair. 'Ye'll no be sorry; I'm telling ye that noo.'

Tony ducked down and turned his back.

'Away ye go!' he mumbled. 'Keep that nonsense for the drivers.'

Kathy met Mary the next day in the main street café; she could hardly wait to tell her the news. They sat down at a corner table and ordered tea and biscuits. Shaking Mary's arm, she grinned widely. 'Guess what, Mary? I got you a job in the café wi me. How aboot that, eh?'

Mary looked at Kathy and laughed. 'What?'

'Honest to God! Tony is gonna give you a try out for four weeks. We'll be working the gether. That's great, is it no?'

Mary's eyes filled as she bit her lip and nodded. 'Oh! Kathy, that's wonderful. I don't know what to say.'

'Don't say a word, hen. Just drink yer tea and pass me they biscuits.'

Mary looked down trying to hide the fear in her eyes. She was terrified.

Archie was lying on the bed reading the previous night's paper when she got home. He looked up scowling while shaking the paper in his hands. 'Whit time do ye call this then, eh? Ye said ye would be away an hour, it's been nearly two. I need tay leave for the afternoon shift in ten minutes. Where the fuck have ye been?'

Mary put her bag on the table and sat down. She looked into her husband's bloated face, trying hard to smile. 'I had a cup of tea at the Bakeries with Kathy.'

Archie sat up slowly. He raised his arm and pointed into her face. 'Whit did ye say, eh? Whit was that again? I don't believe whit I'm hearin. I've telt ye afore tay stay away frae that slut.'

'Oh, but Archie, she's got me a job at the café. It will help us out and Sadie will mind the children, and—'

Mary didn't see his fist. It came at her stomach fast and hard. She rolled off the chair as his boot dug into her thigh. Screaming in pain, she tried to get up, but he pushed her down again, dragging her along the floor by her hair. Scot woke up screaming. Mary tried to reach him, but Archie lunged at her, pushing her into a corner and spitting in her face.

'Yer no goin tay that café wi aw those fuckin truck drivers. Ye'll be the same as her, just asking for it. Ye'll stay here and mind these weans. Do ye hear me, Mary? Do ye hear me?'

Mary tried to stand, but her stomach was throbbing and there was a burning in her thigh. Archie pushed her back down on the floor as he continued to rant, then he grabbed his jacket and left, slamming the door behind him. Mary tried to lift Scot, to soothe his cries, but the pain was too much. She managed to heat his bottle, then fed him where he lay until he fell asleep.

Archie didn't mention the café until late the next night. He was undoing his boots after a late shift and didn't look at her. He just mumbled, 'I'm gettin nae mare overtime at the power station. They said it was a cost cuttin thing, but ah know the Gaffer disnae like me, he's trying to get rid o me, but I'm no goin anywhere.' Then his voice, barely audible, muttered ...

'Ye'd better take that café job. I'll need fag money.'

Mary started at the café, working closely with Kathy for the first week. She was a quick learner and after two days she was managing on her own. The work was tiring, but she enjoyed the challenge, the banter of the drivers, and the extra money. After four weeks Tony pulled her aside.

'Got a minute, Mary?'

She was carrying a fully laden tray into the kitchen.

'Yes, of course. Is everything alright?'

'Aye, oh aye, everything's just great. Just wanted to ask ye how ye are gettin on? Have ye settled in awright? Ye seemed to be managing okay.'

Mary looked at him with a sigh of relief. 'Oh yes, I think I'm getting the hang of it. They're a good crowd here, always joking.'

Tony smiled. 'Well, Mary, yer doing a good job, I've nae problems wi you, so I'll be keeping ye on. Just keep up wi the smiles, okay?'

Mary dropped her shoulders and sighed with relief. She lifted her tray walking purposely into the kitchen, she called out to Tony, 'Okay, boss.'

The café was busy with a constant stream of truck drivers, bringing with them big appetites and cheeky one-liners. Mary was always friendly, and her shapely figure bound tightly in a faded floral pinafore didn't go unnoticed. Her infectious smile and soft English lilt gave great fodder for the drivers, especially the Glaswegians. They loved to tease her.

'Hey, darlin, how about it, eh? Fancy a wee bit of scotch sausage?'

Mary, always embarrassed, was unable to come back with anything quick witted. Not like Kathy, she was the expert.

'Fuck off, Jimmy. Leave her alane, yer aw talk so ye are. Yer wife telt me hersel the other day that yer scotch sausage shrivelled up years ago.'

This drew howls of laughter from the customers. Mary blushed and Kathy let out a roar, laughing loudest at her own bawdy comments.

It was the sixth day in a row that Mary had worked. The café seemed busier than usual, or maybe she was a little more tired than usual. After placing an order for the two young drivers seated by the door, and in her newfound Glasgow dialect, she called out to the kitchen, 'Lavvy break.'

Passing Tony in the passageway, she heard him grumble to no one in particular. 'They should pee in their ain time, no mine.'

The toilet was outside behind the rubbish bins. Mary always cringed when she had to go. There was no lock on the door and no toilet seat; it was mostly used by men. She closed over the door, wiped the rim with newspaper, and slumped down wearily, leaning her head against the back brick wall. It was quiet. She didn't really need to go to the toilet, she just needed to rest, hoping that five minutes off her feet would generate some desperately needed energy, she closed her eyes. It was peaceful ...

Silence was the only sound in the front parlour of Aunt Maud's house. A skinny woman with small eyes and grey skin, she had thin hair caught up in a bun that dragged tightly back from her forehead. Having contracted polio as a child, she was now confined to a wheelchair.

In the whole ten years of her short life, Mary had never been in her father's sister's house. She would have remembered the smell, like dying violets mixed with musk. It seeped in from places unknown, swirled through the air then burrowed into the curtains and the heavy upholstery.

Her brother Jack was a year younger. He sat on the hard sofa beside her, his hair flattened by his father's Brylcreem, wearing his best short trousers that made his legs itch. Their sister Ellen was only four years old. She sat on a stool and pulled at threads from her skirt. They had waited and fidgeted in this room for a long time. They could hear their father in the kitchen next door talking very quietly to Aunt Maud. She moaned and sighed, sometimes she ranted loudly. Mary and her brother Jack were troubled. Their mother had recently died after a lengthy illness and they had not told Ellen yet. Their father was taking it very hard; he had not been himself these last two weeks.

He cried a lot and drank beer, shouted at them, and banged doors, then he would go out, leaving them alone at night. Mary had told her siblings that their father was asking if Aunt Maud could mind them while he worked, just until got things sorted out. Ellen looked up frowning, at her sister.

'Hey Mary, when's our Mam coming home from the ospital?'

Mary coughed into her cardigan sleeve. She couldn't answer straight away, she looked over at Jack, pleading for support but finding none. 'Not for a while, Ellen, love. Mam is still very sick, so not for a while, but don't you fret; she will want you to keep busy. Now go find Golly, I think he's in the hallway.'

Ellen jumped up quickly and ran out of the room, Jack faced up to his sister, tears but a blink away.

'Why don't you tell her the truth, our Mary? Why not tell her that the angels have taken our Mam right up to heaven, and she's never coming back? They've taken her forever and she's watching over us. You have to tell her.'

Jack was muttering behind closed hands clamped over his mouth, he was trying very hard to be strong, but a sob escaped, followed by a tear. Mary leaned over to her brother and spoke gently. 'No Jack, not yet. Maybe next week. She can't understand right now, she's not ready.'

Next door, she could hear raised voices. Her father was the loudest asking, 'Why not, why not?'

Aunt Maud was wailing, 'It's not my problem, it's yours!'

Ellen had found her golliwog. She pulled it along, holding it by one arm, trailing it along the floor. Kneeling down and putting her ear to a crack in the parlour wall, her little brow coiled into a frown. Getting up slowly, she then ran over to her brother and sat quietly on the floor at his feet. Mary and Jack looked at each other, both aching to protect their mother's baby.

Ellen pulled Golly up from the floor and held it close to her chest, her innocent little face, framing dark eyes, was troubled. Holding her head to one side she looked at her brother. 'Jack? What's a orfnige?'

'Mary, Mary, are you okay?'

Kathy pushed the door open. Mary fell off the toilet in fright. Kathy helped her friend stand up, trying hard not to laugh. Mary was frantically trying to straighten her skirt.

'Oh dear, I must have dozed off! I'll be okay in a minute. Is my hair alright?'

'Ye look fine, Mary, but hurry up. Tony's having kittens out there, and the place is packed.'

She stood up, flustered and dazed. She regained her balance, grabbed Kathy by the hand and raced back inside.

Mary avoided Tony's glare as she followed Kathy to the servery. The two young drivers she had ordered for were long gone. She looked tearfully at her friend.

'Oh Kathy, I'm really sorry, I fell asleep. Was I away for long? Is Tony really angry with me? I'll try and get to bed early tonight. Tell him I'll work at my tea break, will you?'

Kathy put her arm around her and laughed. 'Don't worry, hen. He'll get over it.'

Chapter 7

Kathy ran her fingers through tousled hair, shook her head and smiled into the mirror. She liked what she saw. The henna hair rinse she had used the previous night had worked its magic.

'No bad, no bad at aw,' she said aloud. 'God, I'm that like Hedy Lamarr so I am. Just wait till Mary gets a load of this. It'll cheer her up, so it will.'

The house was quiet. Both of Kathy's sisters were out, so she fluffed up the chair cushions, dried the dishes, then sat down and painted her fingernails red. It was Mary's birthday and they were going to the pub. It was the perfect time to talk to her about Archie, about the past, her sorrow, her regret, but more importantly about their friendship. A back booth in the pub away from the crowd and a gin and orange would ease her road to confession.

She pulled on a pair of tight denim jeans, then added a canary yellow woollen jumper with a very low neckline, exposing her ample breasts. Reluctantly, she draped a black chiffon scarf loosely around her neck; it was her contribution to modesty.

Kathy released the four little hairpins on her forehead; they sprang out into fine little ringlets, coiling back and softening her brow. A touch of shadow in the corner of her sparkling green eyes, then a slash of bright mandarin orange lipstick ... she was ready.

Mary was excited; she had been looking forward to this night for so long. Kathy had not visited for weeks, and the last time she and Archie had almost come to blows here in her home. Everything was prepared so that he would have little to do, and even less to complain about. The children were already in bed. Scot, all snug and warm in his blue blanket, was sound asleep in the drawer. Alice, with her long flannelette nightdress and thick socks, was dozing on the chairs.

Mary had no special clothes for going out, so she borrowed a blouse from Kathy. It was a dark, rich coffee colour with a hint of silver thread. The tight sleeves had turned back white cuffs, with small cream pearl buttons from the waist up to the neck, joining a dainty white Peter Pan collar. Her short, straight black skirt was very old and shiny, thanks to many years of wear. The zip would often stick, so she was very careful not to break it. The old skirt still felt good on her hips. Never having had nylon stockings, she rubbed cheap fake brown tan on her legs, then with a stub of eyebrow pencil she drew a straight line from heel to thigh. At a glance, anyone would think she was wearing the best of silken hose. Her old down-at-the-heel suede shoes came up a treat after a steam over the kettle, adding height to her tiny frame and making her ankles look even slimmer.

Archie was sitting in the chair by the fireside, unshaven and still wearing his greasy grey overalls. He was poking his ears with a matchstick while studying form for the meeting at the Ayr racecourse the next day. Strands of greasy hair had fanned over his receding patch, his stockinged feet exposed to the hearth flames stunk to high heaven. He never mentioned that it was her birthday, he never did. Earlier in the morning, Alice had run excitedly down the stairs to pick some dandelions from the side of the pavement. She had rushed back with a wide smile and handed the wilted weeds to her mother. There was a little note hiding in the stems that looked suspiciously like a Kathy imitation child scrawl.

'To my Mammy. Happy birthday, from your wee lassie, Alice xx.'

Mary smiled and swallowed as she put them in a glass jam jar in the centre of the table, their golden heads bowing to the faded Formica tabletop. Even in their dying hours, the dandelions gave a glow to the dark, miserable room.

The letterbox rattled. Kathy called out, 'Are ye ready there, Mary?'

Mary quickly looked in the wardrobe mirror, patted her hair and pinched her cheeks. She grabbed her coat from the hook behind the door and called out, 'I'll be off then, Archie, okay?'

Archie did not look up, he only mumbled loud enough for her to get the message. 'Aye, right-o then, ye'll need to be back to feed and change the wean at half past ten, so don't let that trollop keep ye out late, awright?'

Mary's heart sank as she turned round and pleaded with him. 'Half past ten? Oh, Archie, that's way too early! By the time we walk all the way there and back it will hardly give us any time for a drink. You only need to heat up the bottle in the pan and change his nappy, he'll go straight back to sleep. Please, Archie, I've been looking forward to this for weeks.' Mary was wringing her hands. 'I never go out. It's a special occasion. It won't hurt you, only this once, please!'

Archie didn't answer straight away, nor did he raise his head from the paper, he only looked sideways at her and snapped, 'Half ten is late enough, when ye are oot wi her, she is up to nae good, Mary, I've told ye before. You listen to me, ye'll come to a bad end with that yin. Take heed of what I say and get yersel back here at half ten. That's final.'

Mary didn't answer, she just glared at the top of his head. Slipping on her coat, she closed the inside door quietly and stood in the hallway.

Taking a broken lipstick tube from her coat pocket, she smoothed the pink tint gently over her lips.

Kathy was waiting outside the door she threw her arms around her friend. 'Oh, happy birthday, darlin, ye look fabulous. Day ye like ma hair?'

Mary immediately brightened up, she laughed 'Oh Kathy, it's lovely.'

They ran down the stairs, out of the close and into the street, linking arms and laughing loudly. It was a rare night for the two women at that moment, shedding a lifetime of sadness, on their own for only a few hours ... they were free spirits.

It didn't take long for them to get to the pub. Kathy chatted the whole way.

'Och Mary, this is great so it is. We'll have the night to wirsels and have a good gab and a laugh, and who knows what else?'

Mary whooped and laughed.

The Workman's Rest was well lit and in full swing when they arrived. Kathy pushed open the glass-panelled swing door with one arm, and deftly slipped off her coat with the other. A long, low whistle greeted them, followed by a sluggish male voice.

'Hey gorgeous, where have ye been aw ma life?'

Kathy had no idea where it came from, but without missing a beat, she flashed a dazzling smile and said, 'Running the other way, darlin.'

Everyone laughed, Kathy loudest of all.

The pub was packed. The piano player sat in the corner of the room; he was hunched over a stool and swaying to the music. Encouraged by three heavily tattooed men in dark blue overalls, they were belting out some unmelodic lyrics of *Danny Boy*.

Cigarette smoke hung heavily in the air. Feelings of anticipation, laughter and excitement filled the room. Heartaches were hidden.

This was post-war Glasgow, battle-scarred and suffering. Freezing winters, unemployment, hunger, lack of housing, lack of money, lack of food, all contributed to a life of struggle and desperation. But not tonight, for Kathy King and Mary Bray this was solace, this was escapism, this was exhilaration.

Kathy pulled her friend closer to her. 'Come on, pal, let's sit in this booth. I'll get ye a drink. Whit's yer pleasure?'

Mary's face was flushed with expectation. She was scared, yet excited. The feeling of elation at being dressed up, of not having to worry about constantly cutting corners to feed and support her family, and a break from responsibility and worry was exciting. For the first time in many years Mary was alive.

'Whatever you are having, Kathy, I'll have.'

Kathy quickly dropped her coat in the booth and strode confidently up to the bar, throwing back her mane of thick hair. A middle-aged blonde barmaid with dark roots, black pencilled brows and circled eyes called out to the group that had gathered.

'For fuck's sake boys, gie the lassie a break, eh, have yous never seen tits afore?'

Kathy winked and flashed them a smile before placing her order, then she headed back to the table with a laden tray. She had left Mary in a quiet corner booth where they could talk. She was feeling relaxed and comfortable, the timing was right. At last, she could unburden herself after all these years. She would tell of the torment and guilt that plagued her every day. She desperately wanted Mary's support and understanding.

However, the long-awaited unburdening would not be tonight. Two men had joined Mary and bought her a drink. Her face was glowing and animated, her legs were crossed at the knees and she was listening intently, laughing along with them.

Kathy sighed and walked up to the table shaking her head. She looked fondly at her friend. 'My God, woman, I canny leave ye by yersel for five minutes withoot been chatted up. Come on, move over.'

Kathy put down two gin and orange, two glasses of stout and two packets of crisps. The men drained their pints and left, but not before sending over another two gins. The girls looking at each other, grinning widely. It was going to be a good night.

It was well past midnight when they arrived back at Rooken Road. Mary was giggling while trying to have a serious discussion with Kathy; her voice was loud, her words slurred.

'Why can't I pick up my bag from the pavement? My arms have shrunk, Miss Kathy. Are your arms longer than mine?'

'No, Mrs Mary, but I'll bet Gerry from the pub would help ye, he has longer arms.' Both girls roared with laughter.

Mary quickly stood up looking straight at her friend. 'Oh Kathy, I'm going to be in big trouble with Archie, but I don't even care. Will you come in with me when we get up the stairs, will you? You know what he's like. If you're there, he won't say as much. Oh God! I hope he's fed Scot.'

Kathy staggered slightly. 'Too right I will, pal, don't you worry about Archie. I'll soon put him in his place.'

Mary quickly regained her humour and carried on laughing and singing as they staggered up the stairs into the close. She banged on the door, calling out, 'Helloooooo! Hellooooo, open the door please, Mr Bray, it's your wee wife.'

Still laughing and singing they fell over each other against the stone wall. The door opened slowly. They jumped to attention like soldiers at muster.

Squinting into the dark, Mary could see nothing but black.

Suddenly, a striped pyjama-clad arm reached out and grabbed her roughly by the shoulder.

'Right, you! In here, the noo!'

Archie's stubble appeared; red, glaring, and angry. He dragged her inside the door, banging her head on the wall till she lost her footing and fell. Still trying to smile, she called out to Kathy, 'See you tomorrow, Kathy. Thank you for my birthday.'

Archie was silent as he pushed her further into the room. Turning back, he scowled at Kathy as she defiantly glared back. He tried to slam the door on her, but she was too quick and put her foot down on the floor inside. Archie lurched forward and raised his arm to strike out at her, then stopped. She moved her foot looked at him with a thin smile and a wiggle of her raised fingers. 'Now, now, temper, temper, Archie boy.' She leaned forward, inches from his nose, and said, 'Goodnight. Fuckface!'

Kathy King ran down the stairs, her loud high-pitched laughter resonated throughout the quiet close and into the gas-lit street. She slowly walked home.

Chapter 8

Christmas arrived wet, windy, and cold. Mary loved this time of year, from the faces of the children to the Christmas Carols, the nativity scenes, hot chestnuts, the coloured fairy lights. All that was missing was the snow. Last year's white covering had been magical.

She managed to save some of last year's decorations to brighten the room. Silver tinsel draped from the fireplace next to one of Archie's well-scrubbed socks that Alice had attached to a nail for a Christmas stocking.

On Christmas Eve, when she was sure the children were asleep, Mary stood on a chair to reach the high cupboard in the hallway and bring down the toys she had gathered throughout the year. First, she stuffed the stocking for Alice with an apple, an orange, some nuts, a penny dainty toffee, a polka dot hair clasp, and a small box of liquorice allsorts. She then laid out Santa's presents. There was a small compendium of games, the Dandy and Beano annual comic books, a cardboard doll with lots of cut out clothes, and a small bat and ball. Mary found a brightly coloured spinning top in a toy shop. It was a bit faded in parts and the handle had lost a screw. The woman behind the counter had given it to her for a shilling. It was almost new and could hum beautifully.

Alice had desperately wanted a big walkie-talkie doll with eyes that opened and closed, but Mary told her that Santa was not able to get one for her this year, though she was sure that he would have one next year. Scot was still too young to understand all the Christmas excitement, nevertheless Mary still managed to buy him a string of small rattle balls from Woolworths that she could hang either side of the hood in his pram. They made a happy sound.

All was quiet. Archie was still at the pub. Mary had stoked the fire high with coal dross, making sure it would last until morning; the kettle puffed and shook on the grate.

She made a pot of tea, nursing the cup and saucer in her lap as she sat by the fire. Her eyes closed as the back of her neck dropped comfortably onto the curve of the chair. She was in another place; it was another Christmas. It was the first time she had ever laid eyes on him ... her Charlie.

In 1944 she was seventeen. The war was dragging on. London had survived the blitz, but at a massive cost. Lives were lost, homes demolished, and injuries were catastrophic. In June of that year, thousands of British and American soldiers died on Normandy Beach in France. The impact on those left behind brought immeasurable grief.

The young people of Britain were tired of fighting, death, and hunger. News from the front declared that the war would not be over by Christmas. Although restrictions on the black outs had eased, it was not enough. The young craved excitement, colour, and laughter; they wanted music, dancing, company ... and peace.

There was a gathering at the local community hall three days before Christmas day.

Lettie, a friend from the ammunition factory where Mary worked, said there would be music and lots of GIs there, another influx of

American soldiers had just landed in London. Lettie desperately wanted to meet a GI, and quickly organised a group of her fellow workers to go with her to the gathering.

Mary had been saving a tan-coloured woollen dress, given to her by a friend who could no longer wear it. It hugged her curves perfectly. She had also been saving the last of her pink lipstick, only just managing to scrape it out of the tube with a hairpin. Her hair shone, thanks to a vigorous wash with the last scrap of precious Lifebuoy soap, then she swept it back into a French roll secured by a brown tortoiseshell comb.

They met outside the hall. Everyone was in a happy mood, shouting, laughing, and stamping their feet to keep warm. It was snowing, but no one cared. Lettie beamed as she gathered her group around her.

'Come on girls,' she said. 'We're all here now, so let's go. The Yanks are coming!'

Everyone laughed as she led them through the door and into the warmth of the hall. It was softly lit and welcoming. She ran ahead, claiming ownership of a table, quickly beckoning to her friends. 'Look! Let's sit here, it's close to the band.'

Mary followed them all to the front of the hall and sat down next to Lettie, facing the music. Silver balls hung from low lights, red and green coloured squares of crepe paper decorated the tables, there was a small Christmas tree in one corner of the room.

A table of American soldiers had watched them as they came in, and they began to whistle and wave. Lettie, in her element, winked and waved back.

The room was filling as Mary and her group continued to chat and laugh. The band had set up and started playing their first number. She sat back in the chair, resting her eyes, listening, and concentrating on the soft jazz sound. She had never heard a live band play before and the feeling was intoxicating; she was drifting and slowly moving her head and shoulders in time with the music. When she opened her eyes she saw him.

He was standing at the edge of the stage, quite apart from the rest, playing the saxophone. She was hypnotised, watching intently as he pressed down on the buttons, amazed at the sounds of each note gliding out and filling the room with happiness. His body moulded to the sax; his eyes closed as he swayed in perfect time to the melody. Afraid to taint the moment, Mary didn't move. The music rose to a climax, and with a sudden roll of drums and clash of cymbals it stopped. He opened his eyes, immediately locking onto hers.

It was an unforgettable split second in time.

The music played on, the moment shifted, and Mary chatted with her friends, still mesmerised by the sound. She tried desperately not to sneak glimpses of the saxophone player. At the end of each number he would smile at her, she looked away, embarrassed but exhilarated.

The band announced they were taking a break. The GIs roared, stamped their feet, stood up and applauded, yelling for more. The dancers left the floor, clapping as they went. The room was buzzing. A tall, broad-shouldered and tanned GI approached their table. With an outstretched hand, he made a beeline for Lettie.

'Mam, can ah have the honour of offerin you a glass of soda. Ah got some nice Wild Turkey Bourbon here in ma pocket that will sure as hell hot up yo soda, jist givin you a little taste of The United States of America.'

Lettie looked up at him open mouthed.

He touched her arm and smiled. 'Mam?'

As Lettie got up, she nudged Mary, whispering out the side of her mouth, 'My luck's in, and so is yours.' She laughed. 'Look out! He's coming over. You're blushing, … don't look up yet.'

Lettie smiled discretely as she vacated her chair and walked away hand-in-hand with her GI.

He came over to their table. Mary raised her head and everyone else melted into the floorboards. There was only him, and he was looking at only her.

'Hello, my name's Charlie.' He turned to the other girls before sitting down at the empty chair next to her. 'May I?'

They nodded, smiling warmly at Mary.

He looked at her intently. She had never seen such eyes, never such a blue, his dulcet English accent was soft, his smile, haunting.

'Can I play something for you tonight? I noticed you singing along to some of the Benny Goodman numbers. Do you have a favourite song?'

Mary opened her mouth to say he could play anything, anything at all, she didn't mind what it was, but instead she smiled enthusiastically. 'Oh … yes, yes, I do have a favourite. Do you know *As Time Goes By*?'

He frowned slightly, raised his eyes and smiled.

It went deep into her very soul.

'Yes, I do, and I'm sure the boys know it too. What's your name?'

'It's Mary.'

The boys in the band ribbed him when he went back to the stage. At the microphone, he looked back at her and smiled. 'Ladies and gentlemen, this next number is for Mary.'

Lights in the old hall dimmed, the room chatter lulled, couples on the dance floor moved around cheek to cheek and a young girl named Mary, oblivious to everything around her, hung on every note of the melancholy *As Time Goes By* as it drifted through the air and into her heart.

Later that night they talked, laughed, and made memories. Charlie told her about his sister and her family and his faithful old dog Monty. His voice lowered and his eyes glazed over when he told her while fighting at the front in Normandy he had witnessed horrors of destruction and death and as a result he suffered blackouts and dizzy spells. Medically downgraded, he had to return to base camp in England, and it was there he joined the army band. He smiled, telling her of the happiness that his music brought to those left behind. Mary was mesmerised by his sensitivity. She tried to capture every detail of his face, those amazing eyes, his square clean-shaven jaw, how he bit down on his bottom lip as he listened attentively to her.

The snow was falling lightly that night as he walked her home. The street trees were draped majestically in a fine ice lace. People were congregating on the church steps, talking, laughing, hugging, and kissing, rejoicing that the blackout restrictions had at last relaxed. The church lights were on for the first time in four years. They could hear the organ from inside playing with great gusto *Hark the Herald Angels Sing.*

Charlie said goodnight to her at the front door of her boarding house. He bent down, tilted her head with his cupped hand, his lips slowly threading her cheek until he found her lips, then he kissed her tenderly. With a hoarse voice buried into the nape of her neck, he whispered, 'Goodnight, lovely Mary.'

She would remember that night for all time.

Christmas dinner that year was at Leighton Avenue. Mary, Archie, and the children arrived late. Everyone was seated, including Peggy and her friend Morag from work, and Sadie's widowed brother Frank, who sat next to Sadie. It was his first Christmas without his wife.

Sadie and Peggy had gone to great trouble to make cakes and shortbread. A traditional Clootie dumpling embedded with silver-threepenny pieces, made weeks ago, sat regally all skinned and plump on a round silver platter. They had chicken. Mary smiled at a sullen Peggy, calling out to her, 'That was lovely, Peggy, thank you. I know you and your mother went to a lot of trouble today. We all appreciate it, don't we, Archie?'

'Aye, aye, lovely thanks, Peg.' He looked over to his wife. 'Hey Mary, can you no make somethin like that? I mean its only chicken and vegetables and a wee bit ah gravy?'

Mary nodded and smiled, thinking to herself where in heaven's name did Archie think she was ever going to get money to buy chicken?

After the meal, while Mary fed Scot, Uncle Bob called out to Alice, 'Come on now, Alice, can ye give me a hand with handing out the presents, wee lassie? I will read the tags and ye can hand them out. Would ye like that?'

'Oh, aye, Uncle Bob, I would love that so I would. Is that all right, Mammy?'

Alice looked at her mother, her eyes bright and shining, Mary nodded and laughed. 'Of course you can, pet, off you go.'

Under the tree, the gifts had been placed carefully, all wrapped nicely.

For a short time, there was animated conversation, laughter, and an excited sense of anticipation from everyone.

Alice would fetch each present then ask Uncle Bob to read the label. She would then hand it over ceremoniously with the greatest of reverence. She was thrilled to play such an important part in the day. There were gifts for everyone.

Archie was given handkerchiefs, work socks and cigarettes. Mary, a paisley patterned headscarf, and for the children, socks, mittens, and underwear.

Mary had given the family a colourful Christmas tin of plain biscuits; she had taken great pains to wrap it nicely with silver ribbon and a bow she had been saving.

No one commented.

Bob and Frank cleared the table, then went to the kitchen to do the washing up. Archie disappeared upstairs with Peggy and Morag, and the old man snored in the armchair. Sadie had been sitting on a stool by the fire; she got up slowly and reached round to the back of the tree. Between the folds of the heavy textured curtains, she brought out another parcel wrapped in bright red reindeer paper with a big green tinsel bow. She handed it to Alice.

'This is for you, Alice. Santa left it here because he knows ye have been very good and that ye were coming here today.'

Her little face lit up. She looked at her mother, then at Sadie.

'Oh, Auntie Sadie, is this really for me? Can I open it Mammy, can I?'

Mary nodded as Sadie laughed. 'Yes, yes, it's for you, wee lass, go on, open it.'

'My goodness whit is it? Can I keep the paper too, Auntie Sadie?'

She didn't wait for an answer, just quickly took the parcel, holding it gingerly. The excitement was all too much for Alice, she pulled off the tinsel bow and tore the paper at the last corner. Her little mouth opened, drawing in a deep breath, she let out a squeal. The paper and ribbon dropped to the floor, forgotten.

Alice held on tightly to the little doll in a pink knitted dress. It had a mop of blonde nylon curls tamed by a pink knitted bonnet, blue eyes, and perfectly shaped bow lips.

'Oh! Auntie Sadie ... she's gorgeous, so she is. I really wanted a big walkie-talkie doll, but Santa couldnie bring me a big one this year, he must have given me this wee doll because he knows I've been a big help to Mammy. I'm getting a walkie-talkie next year, sure I am, Mammy?' Her voice was getting louder with excitement. 'Look Mammy, her eyes open and shut and her arms move.'

Alice jumped onto the couch, clutching the doll to her chest, then she started to lovingly dress and undress her new treasure.

Mary's eyes filled with tears. She couldn't find her voice, but she quickly looked at Sadie in gratitude and mouthed, 'Thank you.'

No words needed.

A few days after Christmas, Mary became unwell. She coughed constantly, her back ached, and she had no energy nor appetite. Archie was more irritable than normal and understood even less. She was exhausted, trying to feed and sooth a tired and hungry toddler after another sleepless night. Archie was sitting at the table wearing a dirty vest and pyjama bottoms; he had a three-day beard growth.

'Can ye not shut that wean up, Mary, he's bawled aw day. Take him for a walk or somethin ... and does Alice need to play with that baw in here? Send her oot the back to play, for Christ's sake! I'm trying to read the paper.'

Mary sat Scot down on the floor and went over to the sink to peel potatoes. As she held onto the draining board, she felt her legs give way, she reached for the chair, looking wearily at her husband. 'Archie, for goodness' sake, it's too cold to send Alice outside and I'm too tired to take Scot for a walk. He will fall asleep soon. Please, can you just pick him up for a few minutes. I'll need to sit down.'

Mary slumped down at the kitchen table. Archie stood up, dropped his paper, and started to pace around the room. He snapped back at her, 'I don't have the time tay pick him up, Mary, I'll need to leave for work, and I've got a meetin with the union in twenty minutes. Jesus, Mary, get it through yer heid! I've got enough to dae wi work, and the union. Gie me a break, eh! Yer always moanin.'

He stood up, pushing his odorous feet into heavy steel-capped boots. 'I'm away for a pee. Make up ma piece for work, will ye? And don't put jam on it again. I'm sick of fuckin jam.'

He grabbed his old army coat from the hook and opened the door; a gust of cold air swept into the room. Alice ran to close the door as Archie turned back, scowling at her. 'And you listen to me, Alice, if you wet the chairs in the night again, ye'll sleep stawnin up in that corner. Do ye hear me?'

Alice looked at Archie wide-eyed and terrified. 'But, Da, I don't know I'm doing it, I canny help it, honest.'

The door banged and Archie was gone. Alice trembled. Her bottom lip shook. 'Mammy, I canny help it. Don't let him put me in a corner, will ye?'

'Of course, he won't, Alice. Your Daddy doesn't mean that. I will never let that happen, pet, now come here and give your Mammy a big cuddle.' Mary's heart was breaking as she held her daughter close trying desperately to comfort her.

Archie had never accepted Alice. Mary's heart ached that her young daughter never had the chance of growing up with her father Charlie. She wouldn't remember sitting on his knee, being fed solids, or singing her to sleep with lullabies. She would explain when she was older how much he loved them both and how happy they were. She wrestled with guilt every day, her past constantly haunting her. One reckless moment and her life dissolved into a cesspool of despair forever.

Her head ached, her chest hurt, her legs were weak, she was exhausted. She would go and see Dr McMillan, he had given her a tonic once before and that seemed to help, only this time the coughing was relentless, the breathing more difficult. She thought she might need an X-ray. She had three days off work, it would give her time to recuperate.

Dr McMillan's surgery was very busy that night. Mary pushed Scot in his go-chair and Alice skipped along behind. They found a chair at the back of the waiting room. She caught sight of Bella.

'Oh, hello, Mary, how are ye, hen? Are ye here to see the doctor about that cough of yours? Is it any better? I'm here for ma varicose veins. They're giving me hell so they are; it took me twenty minutes to walk doon the street this mornin. Where is that lazy, good fur nothin man of yours? Can he no mind these weans while ye come here? Lucky, he's no ma man so he is, I would kill him so I would. Ye shoudnie be putting up wi it, a lovely lassie like you.'

Bella hardly drew breath. Mary smiled patiently at the feisty old woman. 'He is working, Bella, doesn't finish till ten. I'm only here for a tonic, been feeling a bit tired and can't shake this cough, just need a pick-me-up.'

Bella shook her head. Looking away, she muttered, 'Bloody lazy swine.'

Dr McMillan came into the waiting room and called Mary's name. She left the children with Bella and followed him into his surgery, sitting down on the chair. He had become a confidante to her ever since her pregnancy with Scot. She told him how tired she was all the time. He leaned back in his chair nodding his head knowingly.

'It's been a while since you had a full examination, Mary. Let me give you a good check-up and take things from there. You're looking pale and tired.'

Mary stood up quickly and went behind the screen to get undressed. She lay on the table, trying desperately to cover her modesty with a thin blanket while looking up at the ceiling.

The doctor began his examination. He didn't speak, except to say, 'Just relax, Mary.'

When he had finished, he left her to get dressed. She slid off the examination table, hastily collecting her clothes. The doctor was sitting at his desk, head down, one hand pressing against his temple, the other writing furiously. She sat quietly opposite him, closing the buttons on her coat, at the same time watching his face. There was a long silence, interrupted only by the scratch of a fountain pen.

Dr McMillan continued scribing, then he slowly capped his pen, placing it neatly in its holder. His face was expressionless as he adjusted glasses that needed no adjusting. Mary suddenly had a feeling that something could be wrong. She felt uncomfortable, should she speak? Her words came out unrehearsed and quickly.

'What is it doctor? Is it my lungs, will I need to go to hospital? I know it's getting worse but if I need to go to hospital ...'

The doctor raised his eyebrows, very slightly shook his head then leaned over, laying one hand gently on her shoulder.

'Yes, yes you will indeed need to go to hospital, but not yet, congratulations, Mary. You're pregnant.'

Chapter 9

It had been a hard week for Archie. Mary's constant whinges and complaints were getting him down, the weans were always greetin, and his dinner was never ready. It was Friday,
5 o'clock, pay day, and he had just clocked off at work. He needed a break, a few beers at the pub to let things settled at home. Mary would have the weans in bed and his tea ready. Smiling to himself, he thought, aye that's whit I'll do.

Pulling his cap down over his ears and fastening the top button of his jacket, he stepped through the factory's narrow wooden door into the street. The cold blast of air took him off guard, as he walked quickly to the pub.

The barman greeted him warmly. 'Archie, how's it goin, son? Yer usual?'

Archie was craving that first taste of heavy beer. 'Aye Jimmy, line em up.'

Two hours later he felt warm, comfortable, and lightheaded. The beers, followed by whisky chasers, gave him a lift. Pushing his empty glass along the edge of the bar, he called out, 'Hey Jimmy, gie us wan for the road, eh?'

By this time, Jimmy had lost his sense of humour with an inebriated Archie. He didn't look up, but his booming voice spoke volumes. 'Maybe no, Archie, I think ye've had enough, eh? It's way past seven o'clock. Away hame to yer wife before I throw ye oot and bar ye from ever coming back here again, do ye hear what I'm saying, eh, do ye? Well, fuck off!'

Archie's vision was clouded. Stepping down from the stool, his foot slipped on the broken wooden rung and he crashed heavily to the floor. Lying there in a heap, he swore, while thrashing around trying to get up. No one moved or made any effort to help. Standing up with clenched fists he defiantly faced the bemused drinkers.

'What are yous lookin at? Want to have a go at me, eh?'

Staggering to the door and lurching himself onto the pavement, he mumbled out loud to anyone within earshot. 'Ma wife is a fuckin cow, you know, she disnae give a dam aboot me, too busy mollycoddling they weans, the bitch! It's her bloody pal Kathy so it is; too much to say for herself that yin, always fillin Mary's heed full of fancy ideas. She had better watch oot, one of these days I'll gie that bitch a piece of ma mind. I'll show her who's in charge here. Aye I will, I'll show er, so I will, I'll fuckin show her.'

The deserted street was a silent audience for Archie's tirade, the only onlookers being rummaging rats and scurrying mice.

By the time he reached the bus stop it was dark. The half empty bus crawled slowly then stopped for him. He made a grab for the rail, pulling himself up and flopping down on the first window seat. Looking out into the blackness was all consuming; it was hard work. His forehead pressed slowly against the window as he slid down and fell asleep.

The ageing bus continued to crawl and rumble along the narrow streets, forging into the night, eventually coming to a halt at the terminus.

The middle-aged conductor at the end of his shift was tired and anxious to get home. He shook Archie roughly.

'Hey, you, come on, we're at the terminus. Get aff, ye havnie paid yer fare, so gie me it before ye go, aw right?'

Archie, trying hard to focus, looked up at the conductor with bloodshot eyes. Saliva had escaped his gaping mouth leaving shiny thin streaks down the front of his coat. He dug deep into his pocket until he found a shilling wedged in the corner. The conductor quickly snatched it from his numb fingers. Archie missed his footing, sliding off the bus platform onto the cold, hard pavement.

Sitting up and looking around he realised he had gone way past his stop; he had no idea where he was. As the taillights of the bus disappeared, in the distance he saw the flashing neon sign of a garage.

Right then he knew exactly where he was, and he knew exactly who would be there. Staggering over to the wire fence he undid his fly and had a pee.

Kathy took her apron off and hung it on the back door of the café. She was exhausted after being on her feet since early morning. Tally Tony had asked her to work some extra shifts at the cafe whilst he had time off with family. She didn't mind, he was good to her, and she needed the money, plus she liked to be in charge. Helping her that night was a young student called Andrew. He had been a real help.

'I'm off home then, Kathy, okay?' Andrew called out from the front counter. 'Will you be alright here by yourself?'

'Sure, son, away ye go. Thanks for tonight. Just watch goin doon the hill, somebody's smashed the light bulb and its pitch-black till ye get onto the road. I'll bring in the signs in a minute, ma bus leaves at half past.'

'Righto then, cheerio.' Andrew waved.

Kathy closed the door behind him and watched from the window as he confidently stepped out into the darkness.

The cafe was three hundred yards from the main highway. Most of the lorry drivers were regulars and day-trippers. Kathy knew most of them and their routines. There was never any overnight transporters, so no more custom tonight.

When reaching into a drawer for the key to lock up she heard it, a loud noise, then a crack. She froze, holding her breath.

It came again, followed by the snap and crack of dry twigs. Fumbling for the key in the packed drawer, Kathy remembered news on the radio had mentioned an outbreak of foxes in the area that were slowly edging their way to civilisation in search of food. Her shoulders dropped in relief. Peering through the window into the dark, she heard it. This time it was louder.

'Fuck,' she said aloud, half-smiling. 'They must be wearin steel-capped boots.'

Kathy continued her regular routine of locking away the receipts and cash, then she checked all the switches and heaters before coming back to the kitchen. The sounds continued outside; they were getting closer. They came in short bursts. There had been no drones, no headlights, no signs of passing trade, so it wasn't foxes. Whatever it was, had walked. She was scared.

Pressing her face hard against the window she peered out. All she saw were shadows ... shades of black.

If she could reach the main door to lock up, she would be safe. The key clutched in her hand was reassuring. The closest sign of life was the distant hum of traffic on the motorway. A phone call wouldn't help either. Tony, with his penny-pinching ways, only allowed incoming calls, putting a ban on staff making outgoing calls.

She tiptoed silently through the kitchen to the main door;

her heart was racing, her knees buckled beneath her as she tried desperately to put the key into the lock.

Without warning, the door broke from its hinges slamming heavily against her. She fell backwards, hitting her head on the stone floor, and blacked out.

Seconds later she opened her eyes and shook her head, trying to focus.

A dark bulk looming over her filled the doorframe. She felt the collar of her cardigan tighten as she struggled for breath. She was choking. All she could see was black, all she could feel was rough, and all she could smell was filth.

Reaching out to the table, she tried to pull herself up. Someone or something was dragging her back down. The breathing was close, the smell repugnant; her hair was wrenched back as she screamed in pain. Her eyes cleared, and in the dim light a face slowly materialised ... the black stubbled-face of Archie Bray.

His eyes were half-closed, a stream of saliva dribbled from a mouth of yellowed teeth, and the overwhelming stench of alcohol made Kathy retch. His face was inches from hers, his voice slurred and almost inaudible.

She was trapped.

'You, ye fucking cow, think ye can turn Mary against me, tryin to gie her big ideas, eh? I'll show ye, ye slut, don't gey me any of this smart alec know all fuckin attitude, okay? Do ye hear me, ye bitch? Are ye listening?'

He staggered slightly, losing his balance, but his grip on her cardigan was strong. Before she could recover, he was on top of her, gripping her arm like a steel vice. His whole body lay across her as he pushed his groin down deeper and harder onto her pelvis. She felt him go rigid, panting like an animal, forcing his hand between her tight thighs, his words coming quick and fast between heavy breathing.

'I'll show ye what a real man is, ye whore. Ye've been asking for this for years, yer a fuckin tease that's whit ye are. Open yer legs, ye slut.'

He undid the buttons on his trousers, his hard penis throbbing as it splayed against her thigh.

Kathy was terrified. It was no comfort that she knew her attacker; she had never seen him this disturbed, never this drunk.

The voice that she heard must have been hers because there was no one else there. It was calm and strong; her laugh was loud and high-pitched. 'Archie, c'mon, don't be daft noo, ye've had too much to drink. Don't do anything stupid, get up aff me and go away hame to Mary. We'll forget this ever happened. I'll no say a word to anybody.'

Archie didn't answer, he just kept grunting and pushing her harder. His belt was undone, his trousers were falling. She tried to stop him from yanking up her skirt, but he was too strong. She panicked as his rough hands grabbed at her bare thighs. Kathy desperately attempted to appeal to his memories. It was her last card. 'Come on now, Archie, we go back a long way, you and me. We have a special secret, dae we no, eh? Do ye mind aw those years ago when things were different, eh? When we went to that school camp? If you're worried about Mary ever finding oot about what happened, well, don't. She'll never know, naebody will ever know, honest to God I'll never say a word. Just let me get up and we'll have a wee cup of tea before ye go hame, and we'll no mention this again, awright?'

Kathy's voice was calm, but Archie wasn't listening. He snapped back at her with glazed eyes. 'Naw, it's no fuckin all right! Yer getting it right up ye; ye've been asking for this for years and I'm the very man to gie it to ye. I'll show ye what a real man is made of, noo ... open they fuckin legs, ye bitch.'

His face was a breath away from hers, his odour unbearable. He was too strong. She pleaded with him coyly, 'Aw Archie, what would Mary say if she thought that ye were putting the hard word on her best pal? She would be mortified, would she no? C'mon noo, let me up.'

Archie's eyes narrowed, his words came from a gap at the side of his bottom lip. 'Ye'll never tell her, ye whore. When I tell her what a slut ye are she'll dump ye right away.'

Kathy cringed and held her breath as she felt Archie's warmth on her thighs getting harder in his push to penetrate her. She closed her eyes and prayed.

Then it happened!

The bell on the back door rang. It was the sound of salvation.

'Hello, Kathy? Are you still here? It's me, Andrew, I forgot my timetable. I'll just take it from the front counter, is that okay? Are you there, Kathy?'

Archie's body went limp. She pushed him away, surprised how little resistance there was. Reaching out she grabbed the chair, dragged herself up and pulled down her skirt, calling out, 'Aye, aye, Andrew, nae problem just take it. Sorry, son, I'll be there in a minute. I'll just change ma shoes. Can ye bring in the sign? We can catch the ten past bus the gether.'

'Aye okay, nae problem, Kathy.'

Archie's eyes were pools of panic. He struggled getting his trousers up whilst grappling with the buckle on his belt. Running blindly to the door, he pushed it open, scurrying into the night like a petrified rat.

Kathy closed her eyes. She was weak with relief, but strong with anger. Walking through to the front of the café, she muttered to herself, 'He'll pay for this, the bastard. I'll tell the polis. I'll tell Dave, he'll crucify the fuckin loser, he'll be done when I'm finished wi him.'

Even playing out this revenge in her mind, Kathy knew she would not report him. How could she hurt Mary? Her dearest friend didn't deserve it. This would only bring up his dark past and Mary had suffered enough. Archie Bray was safe for the moment, but only just.

After locking all the doors and switching off all the lights, she linked arms with Andrew as they ran down the dark path through the clearing and toward the comfort and glow of civilisation.

Chapter 10

Daylight had all but disappeared as Mary approached the bus stop. She desperately needed to sit down. The string bag holding potatoes, milk and a few more essentials was cutting into her arm as she wrestled with both hands trying to balance it with the bag of damp washing. At the bus stop Mary waited in line. Eventually, the bus groaned slowly along the road, arriving at the stop. The conductor on the platform had his hand on the aluminium pole, the other hand holding up one finger. He shouted over the cries and curses of the long queue of weary locals.

'Only wan! Only room for wan inside.'

Trying to pacify them, he added positively, 'Hush yersel, there's another wan fifteen minutes behind, don't panic.'

Mary's heart sank. She was near the start of the queue, but there was an elderly man before her. She waited and watched silently while he shuffled along the pavement. He stopped suddenly, turning to Mary. 'Away ye go, hen, you look dead tired with that bag and yer washing. I can wait till the next one, I'm in nae hurry.'

Mary, limp with relief, turned to the old man with a weak smile. 'Oh, thank you so much, you're very kind.'

The old man nodded and tipped his hat. 'God bless ye, hen.'

The conductor took her washing and the shopping bag from her, placing them in the luggage space under the stairs. She struggled to sit down on a low stair.

The bus moved slowly, creaking with its heavy load, the conductor standing beside her, checking his tickets started talking to her. He was very dark skinned, almost black; he told her he came from Jamaica. Mary listened intently, almost reverently.

'Jamaica, where is that? What is it like there? Is it warm?'

The conductor's round face opened up; he was beaming.

'Oh missus, it's the most beautiful place in de whole of de Caribbean. The sun always shines, beaches are so clean, and water? Well, de ocean, it just runs between your toes, tickling your feet.'

His big lips opened wide with a loud laugh, revealing the whitest teeth Mary had ever seen.

'Oh, and you should taste the mangoes! Man, they are so ripe and sweet ... and dancing? Oh, missus, everybody dances everywhere, de whole family from de Mama to de babybee.'

He stood to the side, swinging his hips and waving his arms, his silver ticket machine banging against his ribs. The other passengers laughed and cheered, egging him on.

Mary smiled at his antics, but she wondered why, after living in a magical place like Jamaica, that anyone would want to live in Glasgow ... and work on the Glasgow Corporation Buses.

She wanted to live in Jamaica. She wanted to feel sun on the back of her neck and sand between her toes, she wanted to taste a mango, sit on a beach, and dance to calypso music. She wanted to live anywhere, *anywhere* in the world but the rat-infested hovel that was Rooken Road.

The bus continued along the narrow streets and stopped at the corner of her road. The conductor carried her washing out to the pavement then helped her off the bus. He waved, calling out, 'See you in Jamaica, missus.'

Mary waved back then slowly walked the short distance to the close.

The gas lighter was leaving. 'Hello there, darlin,' he called out in his Irish brogue. 'Are ye wanting a hand up the stairs now?'

'Oh, thanks, Paddy, that would be great.'

Mary's hands were cold, her knuckles white and stiff. Paddy leaned his long lighting stick against the wall and took the heavy washing and bag from her. He balanced them comfortably on his hip, then, with no effort, carried them up the first flight of stairs.

'You take it easy there, Mary love, yer not looking too good. Is yer man home?'

'Yes, Paddy, he is. Thanks so much, that's been a great help. Goodnight now.'

Whistling softly, Paddy skipped down the stone stairs, on his way to light up the lives of the tenants in Rooken Road.

Mary stood at the door, leaning against the wall, holding her stomach. It was only a niggling pain, but she knew what it was. Archie opened the door to her gentle knock as Alice ran past him and tugged at her coat, calling out excitedly.

'Mammy, come in quick! Look, Auntie Sadie's here.'

The room was very tidy, and Archie was putting the kettle on, being unusually pleasant. Mary struggled for breath, feeling another pain shoot low down. She frowned, looking round the room.

'Sadie, what are you doing here?'

Sadie got up from the fireside chair, pulling her cardigan around her body. 'I just had to come. I had to come and tell ye, I have some news!'

'News? What do you mean, what kind of news?' Mary was breathing heavily.

'A letter came in the post today addressed to me, but it was about you and Archie. It said that ye have been on the waiting list long enough and ye have been given a brand new two-bedroom flat in the new Bethblair estate.' Sadie was smiling and waving her arms about. 'Brand new, Mary, brand new! Is that no great, eh?'

Sadie's face, flush with enthusiasm took one look at Mary. 'Mary, Mary? My God, are ye alright?'

Mary doubled over, holding her stomach. She tried to hold the pain at bay, but it was pulling her down. Her thighs were wet.

The baby was coming.

Billy was a big baby, round-faced and fair-haired. Although he came two weeks early, he weighed eight pounds and had a strong, healthy cry. Mary stayed in hospital for ten days, she was exhausted. The birth had drained her. Sadie was minding Alice and Scot.

She imagined that this was what it would be like being on holiday: no cooking, no cleaning ... and no Archie.

'Mrs Bray, Mrs Bray, wake up! Here's a wee cup of tea.'

Mary sat up and rubbed her eyes. A young, freckled-faced nurse was placing a cup and saucer on her bedside locker. She smiled fondly at Mary, quickly stacking the pillows behind her head.

'Oh, thank you, nurse. Sorry, I was so tired. How is the baby? Can I have him now?'

'Oh, Mrs Bray, the wean is fine, he's asleep in the nursery. Doctor says ye must have as much rest as possible because yer gonna be so busy when ye get home. Come on now, drink yer tea then have another wee nap. Visiting time is ages away yet, yer man will likely come to see ye.'

Mary smiled and nodded, leaning back on the pillows she closed her eyes. Oh yes, her man was coming to see her all right, but she was the only one who could see him. She closed her eyes, and he was there. 'Mary, Mary are you awake, I've seen the baby, I've seen Alice, she's lovely, I ...'

Charlie's voice broke as he bent down to kiss his young wife. Mary put her arms around his neck, fading into his shoulder. She gathered his smell, the feel of his skin, his touch. The rough wool of his army uniform brushed her face as he looked down at her.

'I love you, Mary.'

'I love you, Charlie.'

She was complete.

Chapter 11

Rooken Road was now a miserable memory for Mary Bray. Since moving to Bethblair she had come alive, motivated for the first time in many years. Knowing that her efforts were at last taking shape gave her confidence and strength to take a viewpoint, to make decisions and to have an opinion. Little education and a lack of finance was no barrier for Mary. She would learn, she would prevail, and for her children she would flourish.

Bethblair was a new estate. The flats were new, bright, and big. They were on the ground floor with a small garden. There were two bedrooms, and for the first time in her young life, Alice would have a real bed. The room was large enough for Scot to have his mattress in there. Billy had his cot in the bigger bedroom beside her and Archie.

Their living room was almost as big as the whole house at Rooken Road. Mary loved it. A large window looked out onto a small oval, skirting a fast-flowing burn. The kitchen was small with a stove, a pantry, and just enough room for a table and four chairs, but it was the bathroom that Mary prized most of all. An inside toilet, a blue hand basin and the greatest of luxuries, a bath! Mary was elated.

Whilst still in hospital following Billy's birth, Sadie and Archie had moved their few possessions to their new home. Sadie had given them an old sofa; although showing signs of a long-loved past life, it was still solid and very comfortable. Mary found a floral-patterned cover in a second-hand shop. She gave it new life. After a good washing and the torn fringes were sewn back on, it fitted perfectly over the sofa. The vinyl chairs were refreshed with colourful cushions and chair back covers, the old dresser was now standing to attention against the wall shining, and smelling of lavender polish.

Money was still tight in the household. Tally Tony had told Mary that he would have to replace her because now that she had another wean and lived further away from the cafe, she would be too much of a risk. Although bitterly disappointed, she understood. She hadn't seen much of Kathy, their shifts always seemed to clash, but her sister Yvonne came to the hospital with a note and a two-shilling piece wrapped in a pristine hankie. A keepsake for the baby she said.

Billy was six months old when Mary went looking for work. She was indebted to Sadie, who always seemed to have time to look after the children whenever there was a need, and the children loved her.

She set out early one Monday morning in the best outfit she had. A well-worn belted trench coat given a lift by a turquoise chiffon scarf and some silver ball earrings, a pair of down at the heel black peep-toe shoes, and a black vinyl clutch bag. A touch of pale pink lipstick, perfectly groomed eyebrows, and a high curled ponytail completed her ensemble. She was ready.

She began at one end of the long main shopping street and called in on all the shopkeepers with the same polite request. Responses were mostly sympathetic, but no work was available. After finishing one side of the street she was getting tired and her feet ached, so she leaned against a wall and slipped her shoes off. There was the start of a blister on her heel.

Crossing to the other side of the street, Mary glimpsed a well-lit shop down a long dark laneway. Approaching two large glass doors, she could hear laughter and loud voices. Inside was a worn wooden counter, a glass display case underneath was bulging with fish. A sign on a large bright-eyed salmon read, 'Feed yer man salmon'.

The smell of the sea filled her nostrils as she walked confidently through the sawdust scattered over the wooden floor.

A tall solid, bald man, wearing a bloodstained apron with his shirtsleeves rolled up above his elbows, came out from the back of the shop as she came in. He looked at her and frowned. She was nervous but smiled confidently.

'Hello, my name is Mary Bray. I was wondering if I could speak to whoever's in charge.'

The man stared and growled back. 'Aye that would be me, Johnny! Whit are ye after?'

'I wondered if you needed any staff. I'm looking for work and don't live too far from here and—'

He cut her off. 'Aye, as a matter of fact I'm in desperate need of sumdy to work full-time, but it's hard work.' He looked at her and frowned. 'Ye don't look too strong to me, darlin. Where have ye worked before?'

Mary straightened her back and talked quickly. 'I've worked for Tally Tony in his transport cafe out on the main road. I am very reliable and punctual. The only reason I left is—'

Johnny pushed the palm of his hand forward to quieten her. 'That's enough, lassie. I know Tony Tally and if ye worked for him that's good enough for me. When can ye start?'

'Oh, straight away! I just need to arrange for my children's care. Is the day after tomorrow alright?'

Johnny went back to his order sheets and without a glance answered, 'Aye, right then. 9 o'clock on the dot, okay?'

Mary smiled. 'Thank you, Johnny.'

Walking quickly back down the lane she did a light skip on the cobblestones; her tired feet were forgotten. When the bus arrived, she went straight to Sadie's to collect the children and give her the good news. Mary had grown closer to Sadie over the years.

Whilst in hospital, Mary had told her of Archie's abuse, and how afraid she was for the safety of her children. Sadie was shocked at first, and tried to defend him, but as Mary detailed past incidents she could no longer protect him. Sadie promised Mary that things would change.

And some things did change. Since that day, the physical abuse had stopped, the fear of constant punching gone, and the bruises healed. But the mental torture was ongoing.

Mary liked working in the fish shop. It was constant, she was on her feet all day, but the hours allowed her to take the children to Sadie's before work in the morning. Johnny was a fair boss and the girls who gutted the fish were friendly and chatty. They were rough and ready, swore a lot and made her laugh. A bit like Kathy.

She missed her friend. Mary never really understood what went wrong with their close friendship. She had tried over the years that followed to meet up with her, but it never happened, there always seemed to be some excuse. Now that she lived so far away, and with a young family and work taking up her time, it was even more difficult for Mary to keep up the contact. She missed Kathy and longed for their friendship to be as it once was.

It didn't take Archie long to settle into Bethblair. He discovered someone living nearby with an illegal phone betting system where he could bet on every race. The overtime he was getting at the power station meant more money for him to gamble and less time to help with the children. When Mary complained and stood her ground, he would head for the nearest pub.

With all the problems that had shadowed her from Rooken Road, Mary still embraced life at Bethblair. Over the years since their move the children had thrived. They had made new friends, were healthy, and the freedom of the park and playgrounds gave them a new focus. The boys, in particular, loved to kick the ball around the grounds. There was always food on the table, and they rarely went hungry. When funds were low, Mary bought food on credit from the local co-operative society. When the coal ran out, she had the luxury of an electric heater that would tide them through until payday. Yet life was still a battle.

Johnny was paying her well, but it was physically challenging work picking up crates, sorting fish, cleaning, and gutting and preparing fish for sale. She also realised that since starting work, she was paying for almost everything at home. Her patience with Archie was waning. She was working tirelessly at the fish shop then coming home to clean and cook. They argued constantly about money, his drinking, gambling, and his absences. Many rows were about Alice. By the age of twelve she was getting more vocal and defiant. When he tried to enforce boundaries, she would provoke him and the situation would escalate.

Mary longed for peace, for the happy family life she had once known. Often when alone, sitting by the fireside, she would close her eyes and his dear face was always there for her. She remembered their first home.

'Do you really like it, Mary? Is it big enough? It's close to my sister, so while I'm away you can visit her. I thought you'd like the kitchen—it's got a new stove.'

Mary stood there with baby Alice in her arms. Charlie had found them this place. Now they wouldn't have to stay with his sister anymore.

'Charlie, it's lovely. I don't know what to say. Look at that beautiful big bay window. It even has a box seat, and the blinds are almost new. Was it expensive? Can we afford it?'

'Don't you worry your pretty head about money. The army will look after us. I can't be England's best soldier if my family are not taken care of, now can I?'

Charlie laughed, wrapping his arms around them both. They moved in straight away.

Alice loved being picked up by her daddy. When he came home on leave, he played with her endlessly, changed her nappy and sang softly when tucking her into her cot at night. Then he would pull Mary down onto the cushions on the floor.

'This is forever, Mary, just the three of us.'

'Forever, Charlie,' she would say. 'Forever.'

Chapter 12

Alice was bored. It was school holidays, she at was home alone looking after her two brothers. Scot was outside on the street playing football with his best pal Keith. Billy had been so tired from walking with her to the shops he had fallen asleep on the floor. Alice put a cover over him then sat by the window.

It had rained heavily; the streets were shiny and clean. She watched as Scot kicked the ball to Keith, who dived to catch it but slipped and fell over into a puddle. Both boys roared with laughter as Keith's pants, shoes, and socks got a soaking, while the ball continued its merry way to the next street.

Alice smiled at the antics of the boys. She loved living in Bethblair, despite her father. The only thing she remembered about Rooken Road was those awful vinyl chairs where she had slept. She smiled at the memory of them, often parting ways, with her landing on the cold floor.

In the six years they had lived in Bethblair, she had made many friends in the street, she had a bedroom to put up her posters, and she had a small record player that could play her Elvis records. Although she shared the room with Scot, he was always out playing football with his pals and was almost never there until bedtime. Her best friend Rena lived only a few doors away and they saw each other every day.

Alice had noticed changes in her mother. She was different somehow, stronger, perhaps, and more determined. Her views were often very opinionated, something that would never have happened in the past. There were many times she raised her voice to disagree with Archie and that would lead to heated altercations. She was frequently tired, falling asleep on the couch or the chair after tea. When she coughed it was loud, long, raspy, and frightening.

Archie seldom disciplined her brothers, but she didn't mind. They were good boys and she loved them dearly.

Alice stood back from the window, abandoning her memories. The rain had stopped. She could hear the boys' laughter while chasing the ball. In the kitchen where she had prepared tea, the potatoes were peeled and chopped, sitting in a pan covered with water. She would fry the six sausages, add an onion, a beef cube, and a cup of water. Maybe open a tin of beans. The boys loved her sausages.

Fighting hunger pangs, she took a crust of bread from the bread bin, spread it with margarine, dipped it in sugar and ate it quickly.

The weekend was going to be exciting. Peter McPherson, who lived in the next estate, had spoken to her on the school bus every day of the previous week. She really liked him, but no one knew that, only Rena. He had thick black glasses and brown hair and looked a bit like Buddy Holly. He said he was going to the pictures on Saturday to see Tommy Steele in *The Duke Wore Jeans*. Alice was a big fan of Tommy Steele, so she persuaded Rena to come with her, hoping she would see Peter there.

Alice wanted to look her best, but she had no idea of what to wear. Her mother had a white mohair jumper that she rarely wore, only for the best occasions. It was kept in a clear plastic bag in the bottom drawer of her dressing table.

She knew her mother wouldn't mind if she tried on her clothes when she was not there. Gazing around the neat room, she saw the many personal touches she loved so much about her mother. On her bedside table was a pile of books on history and travel, and a black-and-white picture of Alice and her brothers was in a wooden frame on the dressing table, sitting on a large-embroidered doily.

Alice crouched down on the floor and slowly dragged out the bottom drawer of the dresser. It was heavy, packed tightly with documents, papers, and clothes. She pulled out a pile of rolled up socks, some papers, and tightly packed envelopes, laying them carefully on the floor. Reaching at the back of the drawer, she felt for the jumper. It was folded carefully in a clear plastic bag; the little pearl buttons shone through the plastic. It was her mother's favourite jumper. Lifting it gently, she removed it from the plastic, spread it out on the floor to admire it and then slowly pulled it over her head. Her arms slid down the soft sleeves. It was light and fuzzy, sitting around her neck and waist perfectly. How lovely it felt! She could even smell her mother's special rosewater soap. Closing her eyes and rubbing her cheek down one shoulder she sighed, happy that her mother was small. They were almost the same size. Alice took the jumper off with great care, placing it back in the plastic bag, being careful to fold the sleeves exactly as they were.

All the papers and documents she had pulled out to get to the bag were scattered on the floor, she gathered them up and put them back. A few old, torn manila folders seemed to be full of receipts and official looking documents. Alice placed them into the corner of the drawer where they had been.

It was then she saw it, an old grey scratched leather folder tucked into the corner.

It was very thin, the stitches on the edges had come loose and it had a loop fastener. Alice knew she shouldn't pry, but it was set apart from all the other documents, almost as if it was of singular major importance. Slipping off the leather loop she opened the folder. Inside was one yellow-tinged sheet of paper folded neatly in half. She lifted it out gently and opened it.

On the top right-hand side there was a washed-out looking stamp bearing the British Royal Crown. Underneath it read:

In the Aldershot and Farnham County Court
Between Mr Charles Lambert – Petitioner and
Mrs Mary Lambert –Respondent.

Some legal terms followed, words that Alice had never heard of and did not understand ... except for the last line: <u>that the marriage be dissolved</u>. The date was two years after she was born.

She could hardly breathe.

It read that the court was satisfied that adultery had been committed and the marriage had broken down irretrievably. After six weeks, a decree would be final and absolute. <u>They would be divorced.</u>

She read it three times.

Her hands shook as she turned the paper over repeatedly, trying to comprehend what it all meant. Her mother had been divorced from a man called Charlie. What did all this mean? She had never heard her mention this name, not once. If it was two years after she was born, then this Charlie had to be her biological father.

Her father?

The thin paper left her hands and drifted plume-like onto the floor.

Her hands were shaking, her breath coming in short gasps, Alice was frightened, she was confused. She was wracked with feelings of shock, disbelief, and betrayal.

Suddenly, all the years of Archie's behaviour and his bad temper made sense. Of course, he didn't have time for her; of course, he had never shown her any affection; and of course, he favoured her brothers. Of course, of course. She was not his daughter at all. He was not her father. She had endured the wrath of Archie Bray all these years and only now did she understand why he could barely be civil to her.

Leaning back on the base of the bed, she closed her eyes and let out a long, heart-rending scream.

'Alsi Alsi!' Billy was awake and crying. 'I need the lavy, quick!'

Alice wiped her eyes. 'Coming, Billy, I'm just coming.'

Jumping up quickly, she slowly folded the paper, placing it carefully back in the shabby wallet before closing the drawer. Her anger dissolved into surprise, relief, and a desperate curiosity. Who was her father and why had he abandoned her?

Billy jumped up and down, holding his crotch and calling out, 'Quick! Quick!'

She opened the bathroom door for him as he ran in, chatting all the way, but Alice was only half listening. How could her mother have kept this from her for so many years? What could she do? Who could she talk to? Who could she tell?

Rena, she could tell Rena! Rena would know what to do.

When Billy finished she cleaned him, holding his hand she walked quickly down the road to Rena's house. On the way, she told Scot and Keith not to leave the street.

Unexpectedly, she was exhilarated.

Mary stepped down from the bus, carefully negotiating puddles on the pavement as she walked quickly home. At the front door, all was quiet. In the distance, she could hear children playing football in the park nearby, but there were no signs of her children. She rattled the letterbox and pulled the key up from a string hanging behind the door. It was cold inside the house. The fireplace was grey and unfriendly. Alice had not set it as she normally did. The previous night's ashes were scattered mournfully in the bottom of the grate.

Dropping her shopping bag, Mary knelt down and began to screw up newspapers and lay sticks. Sitting there amongst the paper she had a flashback. It was the old place again and the old fire grate. The sadness of Rooken Road loomed, the desolation, the hopelessness, and the constant cold and hunger. She felt comforted now knowing that she had moved on from that time and that her secret plan was beginning to take shape.

The outside door flew open and banged against the wall. Scot ran down the hallway into the living room with Keith behind him. His boyish face bright with excitement, his nose and cheeks bright red.

'I'm starving, Ma, when's tea?'

Mary ruffled his hair. 'Won't be long, son.'

In the tiny kitchen Alice had prepared everything, but where was she?

'Scot, run to the corner and see if Alice is coming down the hill. That's a good boy.'

Chapter 13

Rena opened the door to a distraught Alice, who ran past her upstairs to the bedroom then threw herself onto the bed. Billy raced outside to play with the dog, while Rena followed Alice and stood at the bedroom door.

'Are you okay, Alice? What's the matter? Have you been crying? Is it your ma?'

Alice closed her eyes, shook her head, and said quietly, 'No Rena, it's no my ma, it's him, its Archie.'

Alice was shaking, going through a nervous ritual where she would pull down and crack each finger of both hands. She started to cry. 'Yer no gonna believe this, Rena, I can hardly believe it myself. It's a nightmare.' She sobbed and dabbed at her eyes. 'I just found some papers in my ma's dressing table drawer that said, that said … that …' She began to tremble.

Rena sat down and put her arm around Alice's shoulder. 'What? What did it say, Alice?'

Alice took a deep breath and looked directly into Rena's eyes. 'He's no my dad, Rena. Archie Bray is no my real dad.'

Rena sat upright. 'What are you talking about, Alice? Of course, he's your dad.'

Alice shook her head. 'It's true, honest, Rena. When I was looking for the jumper, I found a divorce paper saying my ma was divorced from a Charlie somebody, and it was dated two years after I was born.

All this time and she never told me.' Alice was shaking. 'What am I gonna do, Rena? I can't stand him; he can't stand me, but at least I know why now. We are no even related, he is nothing to me. I don't have a real da, and I don't even know if I ever had one. Ma never ever mentioned this Charlie person. I just canny believe she would keep this from me for all these years.'

Alice started to sob and groan. She pulled a handkerchief from her sleeve and blew her nose.

Rena put her arm around Alice's shoulders. 'Don't say that, Alice. You have so got a da, everybody's got a da. Go and talk to your ma about it, but maybe no the night. Do it when you feel better. You are just too angry the night, pal. Away and take Billy home and come back here for the night. We'll make cocoa and listen to Radio Luxembourg, okay?'

Alice nodded knowing her friend was right, but it didn't change her feelings of being lost, sad, and deceived. She called out to her brother. 'Come on noo, Billy, Ma will wonder what's happened tae us. She'll have started the tea by now. Its sausages, yer favourite.'

Mary heard the door open. As Billy raced down the hallway, she gave him a hug then looked up as Alice quickly turned and ran back out the door again. Mary ran after her.

'Alice, Alice? Where are you going? What's wrong?' she called out, but Alice had gone.

Billy called out to his mother from the kitchen. 'It's okay, Ma, she's staying wi Rena the night.'

The next morning, Mary was up early waiting for Alice to come home. There was something very wrong. Archie was at work and the boys were playing football in the street. Mary began to lay the table. As she turned the kettle off, the front door slammed. She had an overwhelming sense of foreboding.

Alice came into the room, without a glance at her mother, and sat down by the fireside, staring vacantly at last night's cinders in the grate. Mary sat opposite her. 'What's wrong, pet? Is Rena okay? Can you tell me what's upsetting you?'

Alice looked straight into her mother's eyes. 'Why did you no tell me? Why have ye lied to me awe these years? Have ye any idea what this has done tay me, and how I feel? Ye don't do ye, do ye? Well, I'll tell ye; I feel cheated. I have been lied to for years by my own mother. My own mother! How could ye, Ma?' Alice started sobbing loudly, covering her face.

Mary was bewildered, her heart in her throat. 'Tell ye what, Alice? What is it? What's wrong? What have I done?'

'Ye know what ye have done, Ma, so stop kidding on.'

'What are you talking about, Alice? What's the matter with you?'

'Archie Bray is no ma' da, that's what. I found out last night when I was looking for yer jumper to borrow. I found the divorce papers in yer drawer. Ye have kept this from me all these years. Who is ma da anyway? Have I even got a da?'

She began to cough, crying uncontrollably.

Mary flinched, fighting back the urge to scream out to her daughter, 'Yes, yes, you have a father, and you had another brother, and I had a wonderful husband, we were so very happy, and I live with shame and regret every day of my life'. She wanted to say all of that, but she didn't. Instead, she spoke softly to her daughter.

'Alice, calm down, of course you have a father. He was a wonderful man and he loved you so very much. I made a mistake, a big one, and I have regretted it ever since. I hurt him badly and he has never forgiven me. I had to leave with Archie; I had nowhere else to go. Please believe me, Alice. I have wanted to tell you so many times, but I was so scared. I felt you were too young. I thought you might understand better when you were older, but I was wrong, and I am so sorry, so very sorry. It has been difficult, I know it has, but you and the boys are all that matter to me, and I promise you that there will be a better life for us all and—Alice! Alice? Where are you going?'

Alice turned her back on her mother. She ran up the hallway and out into the street.

Mary ran after her, but she had gone. Slowly closing the door, she went back to sit by the cold fireside to sob, loud sobs, then wails. Wrapping both arms around herself she began to rock back and forth, trying to stop the aching and the remorse. The coughing and wheezing came on quickly, she struggled to breathe. Holding on to the walls in desperation she reached the bedroom, found her inhaler, and held it to her mouth, the lifesaving vapours finding her throat. She lay on the bed exhausted, closed her eyes for a few minutes, and let the memories engulf her.

After a few minutes, she stood up slowly and reached for an old wallet stored beneath some boxes at the back of the wardrobe. It had an invisible side pocket. Here was her only photograph of Charlie in his army uniform. He wore a hint of a smile, his tight crinkly hair and laughing blue eyes gazing out at her. The photographer had touched it up with colour. Holding him close to her heart, she lay back down on the bed as tears pushed through closed eyelids.

'Mary,' Charlie whispered. 'Mary, our son has been born, Jonathon is here. They have taken him to be weighed Oh! Mary I can't find the words. Our family is complete, thank you for our beautiful children.'

Charlie kissed Mary gently on the forehead, then covered her arms gently with the sheet, she closed her eyes and smiled. She was tired. He was still at her bedside when the doctors told him that his wife had eclampsia, and a very low blood count. The baby had shown signs of foetal distress, his tiny lungs deprived of oxygen. The doctors were concerned for the welfare of both mother and baby.

Charlie was distraught at the plight of his family; he stayed three more days with Mary, nursing his son for a few precious minutes before leaving for a posting in France.

Jonathon never left hospital to join his family. His little lungs and heart gave in, his struggle for life just too much to ask. His time on earth, only six weeks. Mary would take months to regain her health. Both she and Charlie were inconsolable.

'Ma, Ma ... wake up.' Billy jumped on the bed. 'Whose picture are ye holdin?'

Mary opened her eyes slowly and sat up. 'Oh, son, it's just somebody I knew years ago. I was going to put it in that old album that Auntie Sadie gave us, but I can do it later. Go and tell Scot to come in and get something to eat.'

'Okay, Ma.'

Mary rose and watched Archie from the window as he crossed the bridge to their home. He looked angry and disgruntled and was sure to have been at the pub after work. She waited for the key; it turned abruptly as he walked into silence.

'Mary, where are ye? Where the fuck is ma tea? Is anybody here?'

'Yes, Archie,' Mary called from the bedroom, as she gathered up what was before her, 'I was just looking for something. I'll be there in a minute.'

Agitated and angry he called back, 'God help us, Mary, can a man no have a meal ready when he works overtime? Here ye are just poking aroon lookin for things. Whit's the matter wi ye, for Christ's sake?'

Mary went to the kitchen and looked at her husband despising him by the minute. 'Archie, sit down I need to talk to you.'

He ignored her.

Mary undeterred, continued on. 'Alice knows you are not her father. She found the divorce papers and she's taking it very badly. She is very upset and I don't know where she is right now, but when she does come back can you please show her just a little understanding? It's been a terrible shock.'

Archie began to unlace his boots.

'Understaunin, are ye kidding me, Mary? I have taken her on when I took you on, and I didnie huv tay. She's no even mine, but I gave her ma name and put a roof over her heed. She is the wan that should understaun, I'm no taking any cheek fray that yin … none.' He looked up, calling out, 'Do you hear me, Mary? Where are ye? Are ye listening to me? Where the fuck is ma tea, Mary? Mary?'

Mary had left the room.

Chapter 14

In the six years since Alice had discovered Archie was not her biological father, Mary had seen many changes in the dynamics of her family. During that time, her relationship with her daughter had improved, they were now closer than ever. She explained to the boys that Archie was not Alice's real father, but the only one that she had known. They barely responded, nothing had changed for them. They both had busy lives with school, football girls. Much to Mary's relief, this family revelation seemed to be accepted, without being questioned.

Scot, at fifteen, was very relaxed and sociable, charming both teachers and classmates. Billy, at twelve, was a talented football player who idolised his brother. Both boys had a good relationship with their father, who was supportive and proud of their football skills. They would listen intently to his advice before every game.

Mary's relationship with Archie was distant but cordial. She was relieved he had taken such an interest in the boys, not only with football but with their homework. Not so with Alice. He had no time for her nor she him. Whenever they were together it was constant turmoil with shouting, arguing and always present was the threat of physical violence.

Alice had been expelled from school for unacceptable behaviour— smoking marijuana in the boys' toilets. Mary's hopes of her daughter embracing a good education and finding a career were dashed.

Alice had various jobs as a waitress, shop assistant, factory worker and even a short stint at a vet practice cleaning cages and feeding animals. Mary worried constantly about her restless daughter. When she was almost eighteen, she started going out dancing with her pals. The most popular dance hall with the best bands was the Palais. They had strict rules of not allowing any alcohol on the premises. One Friday night, as Alice and Rena stood in the queue for entry, a leather-clad man holding a smouldering cigarette swaggered over.

'Hey, good-looking, ma name's Robbie. Any chance of yous taking in my half bottle in yer bag? They're dooin a search on aw the boys.'

Alice looked at him blankly. 'It depends,' she said boldly.

'Oh aye, on whit, darlin?'

'On you givin me a wee drink from yer bottle.'

He grinned and handed over the bottle, which Alice deftly slipped into her bag. The girls waited patiently before confidently walking into the ballroom. Once inside, Robbie led them to an empty table. He sat down as Rena left to dance with one of his friends. Alice bent down, passed the whisky to him from her bag under the table, where Robbie skilfully and discretely topped up two glasses of Coca-Cola. They sat together, talking, and laughing, and when he asked to take her home on his bike later in the evening, she agreed enthusiastically.

On the back of his Harley Davidson, Alice came alive, roaring through the streets with her arms around his waist, her face pressing against his back. She inhaled the heady smell of old leather. It was the start of their relationship. They saw each other often; she went on rides with him on weekends and spent time at his club. The members were a loud and aggressive group of riders called 'The Green Arcs', feared by many and well known to the law. It meant that Alice was in a circle very new to her, and it was exhilarating. She wore a leather jacket and tight jeans. Robbie bought her a helmet, and in her naivety, Alice never fully comprehended that whilst desperately trying to escape her problematic life at home, she was nurturing a very unpredictable and risky situation.

Constable Jock Sinclair braced himself before knocking at the door. Families were never prepared when they opened the door to his uniform, always fearing the worst. Archie answered the knock.

'Mr Bray?'

He stood there in bare feet with the braces on his grey work pants hanging loosely over an egg-stained navy-blue vest. His stubble was heavy, his eyes half closed, a cigarette jammed tightly between thin lips.

'Aye, officer, that's me. Whit's the problem? Did I not pay my union dues?'

His smile was forced and crooked, his attitude sarcastic, he looked uncomfortable. Jock made a mental note.

'No, not at all, Mr Bray, it's about your daughter, Alice. Is she home now? Can I have a wee word with her?'

Mary stood behind Archie, clutching at the sides of her apron. 'Oh my God, what's happened? Is she alright?'

Archie slumped against the door while looking over his shoulder. 'Get back inside, Mary, I'll handle this.'

Mary didn't move.

Archie slowly pulled the cigarette from the side of his mouth speaking with an unusual and theatrical eloquence. 'Eh, no, she's not here at the moment officer. Can I be of any assistance?'

Jock cleared his throat. 'We've had a complaint that your daughter and her pals were involved in a bit of a scuffle in the street next to the Mecca skating rink last night. One of the onlookers said she recognised her from school days. She was with a group on motor bikes. The neighbours said that they had terrorised the street, revved their bikes, drank copious amounts of alcohol, and used bad language. An elderly man from the corner house had come out to try to reason with them, but he became agitated, speaking loudly, then collapsed. He has had a major heart attack and is now in intensive care fighting for his life in the Royal Hospital. It's not looking good, Mr Bray. The family want answers. I'm hoping Alice can help.'

Mary's hand flew to her mouth as Archie relaxed slightly.

'It appears that your daughter tried to administer first aid but was pulled away by a man in grey leathers.'

Archie sighed and shook his head, leaning back against the door with a smug expression, while stubbing his cigarette out on the wall. 'Oh, right then, I get the picture. Is she charged with an offence, officer?'

Jock was quick to assure them. 'No, no, we just want to ask her a few questions. Can you ask her to call into the station as soon as she can?'

Archie stood up straight with his hand on the doorknob, speaking through a crooked smile. 'Certainly, officer, just you leave it with me. I'll make sure she gets in touch.'

Jock tipped his hat, smiled at Mary and said goodnight. Striding briskly down the street, he reflected on this family. The mother seemed a nice enough woman, it looked like she cared for her daughter, but what hope did she have with a father like that?

Alice arrived home just after midnight. The living room light was still on. She rummaged in her bag for the key, opened and then closed the door silently behind her. She paused. Mary and Archie were sitting by the fireplace. The fire was almost out, the air was chilled. Mary was holding a cup with both hands as though trying to extract the last trace of the heat. The beer Archie was drinking had missed his mouth, making jigsaw patterns on his navy work vest, the buttons on his fly were half-undone and a hideous smell likened to stale milk emanated from his bare feet. She stood with her back to the wall, drawing in a deep breath. 'Still up?'

Her mother nodded. 'Yes, pet.'

Archie's eyes glazed over, his voice was slurred. Laying back on the chair, his hands were clasped under a bloated belly. He sneered. 'The polis were here lookin for ye, Alice.'

'For me? what fur?'

'Like, ye've been involved in causing an auld bloke to have a heart attack. He's gonna die!'

Mary jumped up, shouting, 'That's not true, Archie, you know it's not! Don't frighten her.' She spoke softly. 'A very nice police officer called in earlier on tonight asking about a fight in the south side. Someone mentioned that you had been there. He said one of the neighbours collapsed with a heart attack. Do you remember that, pet? Were you there?

Alice looked sadly at her mother. 'Ma, it was a terrible night. Me and Robbie were sitting on a bench near the bus stop when it happened. I ran over and started CPR to help revive him, but Robbie tried to drag me away. Everybody else just stood there making derogatory comments and laughing. I started CPR until the ambulance came. They all had been drinking, Ma, and Robbie had smoked marijuana. I hate to tell ye this, but he is already on probation for being drunk and disorderly, and didnae want to be seen anywhere there was trouble, so we left as soon as we could. I'm really sorry.'

Mary listened in silence,

'Ye believe me don't ye, Ma? I did try to help, honestly, I did, but there was that many people there and Robbie was scared to stay. We didnae hurt anybody; we just got caught up in the whole mess of it all.'

Mary looked into her daughter's tear-filled eyes and then put her arms around her. 'Of course, I believe you. You did the right thing, pet, you probably saved that man's life. I am very proud of you.'

Archie stood up, muttered, and glared at Mary. Walking past Alice, he swayed slightly, then grabbed her arm. 'Yer an embarrassment tay this family. Ye brought the law to this door. You and yer lead-footed pals, yer never to go near them again, dae ye hear me?'

Alice wiped her tears and pulled her arm away. She faced her stepfather defiantly. 'That's the pot calling the kettle black if ever I've heard it. It's only by the grace of God ye've no been nicked by the polis. My ma deserves better than you, ye pathetic swine. Why don't ye dae us aw a favour ... fuck off and top yersel.'

There was deadly silence. Archie's eyes narrowed; his breathing laboured. Throwing his right arm out, he took a swipe at her. 'Ya bitch! Who do ye think yer talking to, eh? I'll gie ye something to wipe that smirk aff yer face.'

Alice ducked and laughed aloud as he punched at thin air before falling to the floor.

Mary jumped between them, throwing her arms around her daughter. 'Please, Alice, please, just let it go. He's drunk. He'll forget by tomorrow.'

Her voice was thick; she struggled and coughed, her mouth filling with phlegm. She spat into her handkerchief before wiping her eyes. Archie lay where he had fallen. His mouth was wide open, displaying a chasm of yellow teeth and dribble. Alice hugged her mother, stepped over the pathetic soul snoring beneath her, and quickly walked out the door.

There was a slight improvement after that night. Both Alice and Archie still seemed to avoid each other whenever possible. Mary, deeply affected by the altercation, was more than ever determined to change the destiny of her family.

Her plan was progressing.

Two months later, Mary was at home in the kitchen when she heard the postman's heavy boots as they climbed up the outside steps, dropping the letters through the letterbox. Drying her hands, she moved quickly and silently up the hallway, being careful not to wake Archie, who was sleeping late after a night shift.

There were three open-faced envelopes. A postcard addressed to Scot and a letter for Alice, but it was the large manila envelope with a majestic crest in the corner that Mary had been waiting for. It was addressed to her, handwritten in scrawled letters. With a pounding heart, she grabbed it, folded it in half and went to the kitchen, closing the door behind her. Propping it up against a milk bottle on the kitchen table, she sat down with a strong cup of tea. She was having a week off from work and the children were all out. It was peaceful.

Lifting the documents out carefully, she laid them on the table. There was a long letter addressed to her and five lots of stapled pages. Reading the letter slowly, she absorbed every line.

Would she be able to do this? It was overwhelming. Her family needed to understand all the positives of her motives for taking this drastic step. She had to convince them that there was a better life outside of Glasgow. She had to say they could have a healthier, happier life, earning more than they would ever earn here. She knew the boys would be cautious at first, but they would adapt well, seeing it as an adventure. Alice would be a problem; she was very headstrong, and so attached to Robbie, her first real boyfriend. Mary knew there would be issues.

However, the biggest challenge would be Archie. He would be furious, seeing this as a conspiracy. He would demand to know how she had the nerve to make such a drastic move without consulting him. Nevertheless, Mary was adamant. She was no longer being dictated to; she had made a major decision that was all her own. The slight emotional connection she had felt for Archie in their early years was long gone, but she knew she could not travel anywhere outside of Britain with her boys without his consent.

Archie had barely travelled anywhere, apart from England, when he was in the army. How would he ever consider a move to the other side of the world?

How would Archie Bray ever contemplate ... Australia?

Chapter 15

Mary folded the letter and the five stapled pages of application forms, placing them in a shoebox at the bottom of her wardrobe. She was chasing a dream, a new start, hoping that her children would grasp with both hands the opportunities that Australia had to offer. It had been an impossible vision in the beginning, but as the years passed the dream had taken on real possibilities, it was when Mary remembered that her mother had a brother called Ralph in Australia, someone she had spoken of fondly. She discovered his name and address in the pocket of an old handbag, which had been abandoned in a cupboard after her mother died. It was also the last time she saw Ellen and Jack, the memories of her siblings so vivid. Uncle Ralph could be the answer for her family, for a completely new life in a new country. It was a drastic step, but she had to try.

Finally, plucking up courage she went to the post office. She had never used an aerogram before, but sat down confidently and wrote to her uncle. Mary told him about her life in Glasgow, about her family, and how much her mother had cared for him. She asked if they decided to immigrate on the government's ten-pound immigration scheme, would he be able to sponsor them. She gave her mailing address as the shoe shop where she now worked. The manager was an elderly man who had taken a liking to her and said that he was more than happy to receive her mail.

'Aye, Mary,' he had said. 'Whatever it is, lassie, yer secret's safe wi me.'

To Mary's joy, Uncle Ralph replied immediately. He was elated, saying how overcome with emotion he had been on receiving her letter. He said he had been very close to her mother, but after she got married they moved away and over the years they had lost touch.

His wife had died ten years ago and they had no children, so hearing from his beloved sister's first born was like a miracle.

He told her he would be delighted to sponsor them to start afresh in Australia. He owned his own home with enough room to accommodate them all, there was a very good school nearby for young Billy, and that for twenty-five years he had been a supervisor in a biscuit factory and was sure he could secure a job for Archie. Since his wife's death he had been very lonely and would welcome the company, bringing life back into his home.

When she received Uncle Ralph's letter, Mary lost no time. She contacted Australia House in London for the application forms straight away. Now that they had arrived, she was both excited and hesitant with the task ahead ... to convince her family.

Archie came home late from work that night. They sat together at the table eating in silence. He devoured his meal, belched loudly, then pulled the newspaper from his hip pocket and started to pencil notes in the racing guide for the next day. Mary finished, wiped her mouth with a paper serviette, then placed her knife and fork together in the centre of her plate. She coughed and pushed the plates over.

'Archie, I need to talk to you about something.'

He looked up in anger. 'What is it? Can ye no see I'm busy?'

Ignoring him, she brought out the letter and application forms from the folder and spread them on the table.

Archie looked at her. 'What the fuck's this?'

Unperturbed Mary said., 'Do you remember some time ago we read about the Melbourne Cup, a big horse race in Australia? I told you about my mother's brother who was a jockey and had raced at Ascot?'

'Eh? What are ye talking about? What uncle? What the fuck is Ascot?' He caught sight of the forms on the table. 'What's this?'

She spoke quickly trying to get as much out before he exploded. 'Well, Archie, you see, my Uncle Ralph is now living in Australia. I have managed to locate him and asked if it was possible for him to sponsor us all to live there. The forms and information have just arrived from Australia House in London. The government have a great immigration scheme, it's only ten pounds each and—'

Archie stood up, pushing out his chest and breathing heavily through his nostrils. 'Awstraliya! Awstraliya! Are ye daft in the heed, Mary? What's aw this aboot? Where did aw this come fae?'

Mary didn't falter; she held the forms in her hand, pointing out the headings to Archie. 'Look, the Australian Government have an immigration scheme for British citizens. It costs just ten pounds each and you only have to agree to stay there for two years. Uncle Ralph has agreed to sponsor us all, provide accommodation and help us to get jobs. The opportunities for the children are—'

'Shut up! Shut up!' Archie pushed her arms off the table and the forms fell to the floor. 'No way, Mary, no fucking way! I was born in Glesca and I will die in Glesca. I have a good job here and I'm well respected.'

Mary listened to his ranting with no reaction.

'And another thing, the boys are happy here! Look at Scot, the coach wants him for the first team. Billy has been telt that he shows a lot a promise as well. There is no way am ah leaving the fitba here, get that straight, Mary, just get that fuckin straight!'

Archie threw his knife and fork at the plate. It broke. He cocked his head from side to side and glared at her. 'And by the way! I have a responsibility at work in case ye've forgotten. I am the shop steward for the union. The men aw rely on me tae dae what's right. I am no a troublemaker, I huv got influence and I make sure we aw get wir rights. I huv a clean polis record, ah have never had a summons, been caught receivin, or sellin stolen goods, or even for peein in the close. Awstraliya, Mary? Aye! You and Alice can fuck off there to that daft auld man, but the boys are staying here, okay? Wi me!'

He left, muttering under his breath, and slamming the door.

Mary knelt on the floor, gathering up the forms. Archie didn't like change, she knew there would be resistance, but she didn't expect this outburst of anger and finality. He was stubborn, angry, and adamant that he would never leave Glasgow.

Her years of dreams and hopes lay scattered on the floor. She was defeated and trapped, with nowhere to turn and no other plan.

He had won.

Tears ran freely down her cheeks. The realisation that her chance for a new life was thrown out like murky dishwater left her feeling lost. Mary Bray had played her last card.

It was two weeks later when Archie was clocking off from work. It had been a difficult day with management, arguing then losing the fight for a pay raise for the night-shift workers. The workers had walked away from him, disappointed, and although they didn't say it, they thought he could have tried harder. He was angry and frustrated and in no mood to go home. Mary had barely spoken to him since the night he had quashed any ideas she had about going to the other side of the world. At least he had won that battle.

Putting his card back in the rack, he left the power station and walked over to the bus stop. A long queue was forming, only fuelling his anger, knowing that he would have little chance of getting on the bus and would have to wait for the next one. 'Fuck it,' he mumbled. 'A few beers are right in order the noo.' He walked quickly away and down the street to the welcoming arms of the local barflies.

The pub was busy. The air was filled with laughter, swearing and jibes from workers just in there for a quick pint after work before heading home. He heaved himself onto a stool at the bar, pushing a pound note over to the barman.

'A pint of bitter, ma man, and a wee hauf when yer ready.'

Archie relaxed. He pulled out a cigarette and a box of matches from his coat pocket, lit up and inhaled deeply, stretching his legs. He smiled. This was his life ... the pub, the fags, the beer, the pals, the singsongs ... what more could a man want? Fucking Awstraliya, he thought. The wuman's demented, no way would he leave Glesga.

From behind came a muffled voice from the throng. The voice got louder; it was calling his name. Sitting up straight, he reached for his glass and took another gulp.

'Archie Bray, the very person I was looking fur.'

Archie turned to face his fears.

Dave Taylor strode up to the bar, swinging his arms loosely. He grabbed Archie's shoulder roughly and shook it. With partially closed lips and an unswerving stare, he said, 'Hello there, wee man. Did you know that Stan King was getting oot of Barlinne prison in six months?'

Archie's face stiffened, barely managing to hide his terror. Dave Taylor was bad, very bad, a retired heavyweight boxer with a left-hand punch that could land a man in hospital. Stan King was Dave's best pal.

Archie, with mock surprise answered, 'Naw, naw, I didnay know that. It's been a while, eh?' He didn't blink. The only sign of internal terror was a paling of skin under his thick stubble.

Archie was sure that Stan would be behind bars for many years after he was given a heavy sentence. He had no idea that he was getting an early release for good behaviour. Knowing that it would happen sometime, but not this soon, he wasn't prepared.

Fuck, he thought to himself, I'll need tay disappear afore he gets oot.

Dave Taylor's waterproof jacket brushed past Archie on his way out the door. He slowly turned back, calling out, 'Aye, we'll 'need to have a wee night oot the gether when he gets released, Archie, for auld time's sake! Whit dae ye think, son?'

Archie raised his eyebrows and nodded. 'Aye, Dave, that would be great. Let me know when, okay?'

Archie Bray twisted back around to the bar, picked up his pint and reminded himself of the cause of Stan's imprisonment all those years ago. How could he ever forget it? He was only a teenager, but some memories never fade.

It was a cold night and everyone was on a binge. When the pub shut, the late drinkers spilled out onto the street. There was an argument about religion and football.

A scuffle led to a fight. Men and boys, all inebriated, the aged and the young, attacking each other at random. As the sirens got closer the group scattered. Archie, drunk and paralysed with fear, stood back in a doorway. He saw a shiny switchblade knife appear from the sleeve of Stan King. It struck only once, ending the life of a young man.

Archie and Stan both ran, leaving a lifeless soul to bleed to death, while a family's very existence would change forever that night.

Someone's father, someone's husband, someone's son, struck down ... his last breath inhaled from the filthy gutter of a dim Glasgow Street.

Archie had witnessed it all. The drunken young man had threatened Stan with a knife to his throat. Stan was in fear of his life and had retaliated in self-defence; the shiny blade appeared from nowhere and fatally pierced a loved one's heart.

Archie was the only witness.

He could have reduced the sentence Stan received had he given evidence to say that the young man had goaded Stan and was about to slit his throat, that Stan had indeed acted in self-defence. Instead, the coward that he was, he ran and hid, leaving behind a trail of devastation.

Later that night when police interviewed him, Archie said that he had never been there when it happened; he said that he had walked home alone before the fight started. Youth, guilt, and fear all contributed to his decision to remain silent that night. A decision that would haunt him forever.

Archie was terrified of Stan King. He knew that someday he would be looking for revenge and answers as to why he was abandoned that night. Dave Taylor also wanted payback for his best pal.

Archie was a coward. He would have to disappear, to leave

Glasgow; he had to go to ground for a long time. Somewhere where no one would know him, somewhere far, far away. Somewhere like ... Awstraliya!

Mary had unknowingly given him the perfect solution. He would tell her that he had changed his mind, he had spoken to someone in the pub who told him that good fitba players were just taking off in Awstraliya and players and coaches were desperately needed, they would be well paid. He also knew that if you had a criminal record of any kind you could not immigrate. He had no criminal record, but Stan King did, as did Dave Taylor, so here was the answer. Awstraliya would be his salvation.

Mary would never know the real reason behind his change of heart. He would tell her that he was only doing this to help the boys and their fitba career. This would be the story he would tell anyone who was in the least interested in his departure. He called out for another beer.

Chapter 16

Kathy sat alone by the fire in her living room. It was almost dusk, and the flames cast a shiny mosaic of orange and red over the room. Kathy was reminiscing about her friendship with Mary. She should have told her years ago, that time in the pub for her birthday was the perfect opportunity, but it was lost. Now that Mary and her family were leaving Scotland for Australia, she felt a desperate need to talk to her, to tell her of her daily heartache and remorse. She had carried this burden alone and desperately needed to off-load what happened all those years ago. She had avoided Mary from the time that Archie had tried to rape her at the cafe. She was too embarrassed and too consumed with guilt, afraid that something might slip during their chats. The close relationship they once had was gone; it was her fault, she knew that. From the very start of their friendship, she should have told Mary the truth.

How could she ever have foreseen such a strong and close friendship would develop with this unworldly young English girl? A girl who only ever wanted to rise above poverty to give her children everything that she never had. Mary didn't deserve Archie Bray. No one deserved Archie Bray.

Kathy lay back, it was cosy sitting there in the big armchair, gazing at the hot and deadly flames as they disappeared up the chimmney. All was quiet. She lay back, allowing her eyes to slowly close. She willed herself to remember.

She was fourteen years old, leaving on a school camp for a rural area on the outskirts of Glasgow, a striking contrast from the ageing, grey Glasgow tenements.

The whole class set off in a school bus full of excited pupils, slowly zigzagging its way along the narrow roads. The trip was an hour and a half of mayhem, the students interacting loudly with each other, changing seats and throwing paper darts.

Climbing to the top of a hill, the camp finally came into view. There was a raucous chorus of, 'We're here!'

The old bus ground to a halt on a dirt road, the driver trying his best to be heard above the excited students as he called out. 'Calm doon, the lot o ye, and be careful getting aff! Don't leave anythin on the bus, awrigh?'

They all cheered the patient driver as they disembarked and he waved goodbye. A bespectacled middle-aged teacher appeared, giving them permission to go, to run, and to explore the grounds.

Kathy stood back, taking it all in. The compound was a basic assortment of buildings and huts; there were two long fibreglass single-storey dormitories clearly marked one male and one female. A small brick administration office, a large dining room and kitchen, and a recreation hall were close by. In the near distance was an overgrown football pitch with a small, covered stand and bench seating.

Nearby, horned black faced sheep carrying heavy coats could be seen wandering around aimlessly, invading the rolling hills, dales, and fast running burns.

Like most of the class, it was Kathy's first time away from home. The first time away from her family and her first time experiencing total independence.

Archie Bray was in her class at school. He was good looking and smarter than the rest of the class, he had a great sense of humour and made everyone laugh. He was afraid of nothing. She had been sitting in front of him on the school bus. He had started to kick the back of her seat, and as she turned around, he leaned forward and whispered in her ear, 'Ah huv got a half bottle of whisky in ma duffle bag. Fancy a wee taste later on?'

She was flattered and exhilarated that he had chosen her to confide in, to share his forbidden whisky. She could only nod and smile.

On the second day of camp, they got together and decided to meet secretly after lights out in the dining hall. Kathy had saved two paper cups and a packet of crisps from the picnic that afternoon.

Well after midnight she slipped silently out of the girl's dormitory to rendezvous with Archie Bray. It was dark in the dining hall except for a small floor light. They both squeezed into a narrow alcove reserved for cleaning materials.

Archie poured her a full cup of whisky. Kathy took a gulp; it tasted bitter and she gagged. He laughed, telling her that after a few mouthfuls she would relax, and she did, the brown liquor slid easily down her throat. She felt a warm glow in her cheeks and an ecstatic tingle in her stomach. They sipped the whiskey slowly, laughed quietly whispered, and giggled as they refilled the cups.

It was cold in the alcove. They lay on the floor and clung together, trying to keep warm under the tarpaulin that Archie had found folded on the corridor trolley, ready for the next day's clean. They were both virgins.

She never resisted when he kissed her. His lips were soft and tender as she felt his tongue slip slowly through her parted lips. He had a little stubble that tickled her cheek. His kisses were long and sweet. She didn't object when he pulled down her knickers, nor did she cry out when he entered her, not even when it hurt. His touch on her skin was like a moth's wing. It was euphoric; she forgot the pain. It was comfort; it was the best part.

Archie had panted like a dog as she tried very hard not to laugh. Her knickers were at her ankles, entangled in her pyjama pants. Her top was up under her chin, almost choking her. That part felt a bit ungainly and awkward. The whisky made them both feel silly and numb. He really liked her, she knew that. He had said so when he was bucking like a horse. He told her she was the only one for him and she didn't have to worry, that it was okay to 'do it'. Much later, Kathy tried, with great difficulty, to recall any intimacy or tenderness that she had read about in magazines.

She didn't see him around very much after that, but he did sit behind her on the bus on the way home and put his feet on the back of her seat. She could feel the force of it on her back. She knew that he was trying to send her a message, of that she was very sure, he would want her to be his girlfriend at school from then on. They would go to the Christmas school dance; she would hold his hand in the gym hall in front of the whole school. All those girls in her class would be jealous. Kathy had no doubt that they would be a couple, they were without doubt 'going together'. They had done something secretive, something very special, something that only they knew.

It never happened again after that.

Archie had acted very strange; he hardly spoke to her. Whenever she saw him, he always seemed to be busy or had to be somewhere else in a hurry. It took a long while for her to realise that he had, in fact, made every effort to avoid her. It continued for weeks until one morning before class she bailed him up at the school gate.

'Archie, I need to talk to you.'

'Aye, whit is it?'

She started to shake and pleaded for him to look at her. 'Archie, can ye look at me, eh? And please don't be mad, it's just that I'm really worried. I've missed two periods and I've never missed before, my bust is really itchy, and I was sick this mornin in the toilets. I think I might be pregnant.'

Archie looked at her in horror shaking his head. 'Come aff it, whit are ye tellin me fur? It's no mine, ye canny pin anything like that on me, and don't try either. I'll deny it. Everybudy knows what yer like, just easy meat. Naw, naw, Kathy, nuthin to dae wi me. Yer on yer own there darlin, cheerio!'

'Archie, that's no fair and ye know it. I have never, ever—'

But Archie wasn't listening. He carried on his way, then he turned around and called out to her, 'Fuck off, ya slut. Keep awa fae me.'

Kathy sat on a quiet street bench and cried, vowing to tell no one about her predicament. Right there and then, she swore that one day he would regret this ... one day Archie Bray would get his just rewards.

When she finally told her parents she was pregnant they were shocked and ashamed. Her mother cried, while her father who had a temper, punched the wall in anger. They never asked who the father was. They were in denial and covered it up, preferring to think that it had never happened. Acting quickly, they took her far away from Glasgow to a country home for unwed mothers, telling everyone that she had gone to Edinburgh for a few months to take care of an elderly aunt.

The home was a crumbled old stone building, isolated from the community and far from the nearest town. The Catholic Church had built an old convent during the eighteenth century, with cold stone floors, brick walls and no heating. The nuns who ran it referred to their charges as fallen women, or prostitutes. They slept in dormitories.

After joining in daily prayers, everyone had to help with domestic duties. Kathy scrubbed toilets and floors, collected and washed sheets and towels, cleaned the silver and served meals to the nuns.

There were many girls in the same position. None of them were allowed to talk to one another or even have meals together. At night after lights out they would whisper and try to generate some comfort and support for each other. The nuns, who were harsh and judgemental, told them constantly how they much they had sinned and were destined for damnation.

Kathy cried every day, watching her young body blossom. She cried for the situation she was in, she cried for the disappointment and sadness on her mother's face, and the rage on her father's. She cried angry tears for the betrayal of Archie, but most of all she cried for her child. That beautiful feeling of life moving within her was a tragic reminder of what she was about to lose.

The night her daughter was born Kathy tried desperately to lift herself up to see the baby, but a large sheet was held in front of her as the umbilical cord was severed, robbing her of the life that she alone had cherished for nine months. She sobbed when she heard her daughter's first cries, they were loud and lusty. The nuns said it was for the best that Kathy did not hold her daughter, that she should not become too attached. They said that her baby would go to the home of a good Catholic family. A childless couple who would be able to give her child a good Christian life.

The night following the birth of her daughter, Kathy lay awake, staring at the bare globe on the ceiling. It was late. A young novice nun slipped into the sleeping dormitory. She stood at the door and whispered quietly 'Kathy, Kathy, come here quick, hurry up. Sister has gone for a break. Would you like a quick look in the nursery to see your wee girl?'

Kathy looked at the young fresh-faced nun in amazement and stumbled out of bed. 'What? Oh yes, yes, I would, thank you.'

In her billowing nightshirt and bare feet, she followed the nun down the corridor into a sparse room with six cots and two tables. The young nun walked briskly, stopping at the cot nearest the wall. 'Here she is.'

Kathy drew a deep breath and walked reverently over to the cot, holding her hand over her mouth she looked down at her daughter swaddled in a tight pink shawl. The tiny face had fine features and a scattering of fair hair.

Kathy was trying to stop the tears, her hands trembled. 'Oh, she's perfect. Can I hold her for just a minute please?'

The young nun shook her head sadly. 'I'm awfi sorry, Kathy, we need to get back. Sister takes just short breaks, but here, I'll loosen the shawl, hold her wee fingers ... quick.'

Kathy put her hands down the shawl and placed her finger into the baby's palm. The grip was instant. Mother and daughter had briefly bonded. Kathy sobbed; a flood of tears escaped her closed eyes.

The vision of that perfect little face framed by fine fair hair was etched into her memory from that moment.

Later, knowing exactly what she was about to sign, Kathy gave her daughter away to strangers. She told herself she was doing the right thing, that her parents would be saved the embarrassment and disgrace of having their daughter give birth to an illegitimate child. She could finish school, have a career and no one would ever know. She named her daughter Grace. Kathy never knew if she kept that name.

The next day from a secluded balcony at the front of the old building, she watched as her daughter's new family walked to their car, holding a large part of her heart wrapped in white. The car edged slowly out of the driveway as Kathy strained in vain for a glimpse of her baby. She stood back, leaned against the wall, and let out a soulful scream, followed by the unrestrained sobs of a discarded mother. The following day, her parents were waiting for her in the foyer of the home. They showed no emotion and did not speak on the long drive home. She knew that life would be not be the same for her now; the schoolgirl that had left home six months ago was now a mother.

Neither her father nor her mother ever spoke of it again. Life continued as before for the family. Sadly, not for Kathy King.

Kathy never forgave Archie Bray. As the years passed, she would hear stories about him and his flirtations with the local girls and the adoration of his conservative family. Like a local hero, Archie went off to the armed forces. Kathy was astounded when two years later she heard he had returned to Glasgow with a wife: a pregnant divorcee with a two-year-old daughter. Her loathing for him was all-consuming. She had never seen his wife, and had no idea what she looked like.

The first time Kathy set eyes on Mary Bray she had gone to the local Bag Wash with her laundry, something Kathy did every week. She stood at the counter waiting and watching her washing going through its cycle.

At the other end of the counter, she caught sight of a young woman in a well-worn khaki raincoat, her hair covered by a floral turban scarf. This woman was wearing lipstick. No one came to the Bag Wash wearing lipstick!

She was trying to push her wet washing into a pillowcase. Catching sight of Kathy, she smiled. Kathy smiled back. The young woman, with great difficulty, heaved the load off the counter. Kathy came over. 'Let me help ye wi that, hen. You take the top and I'll grab the bottom.'

Mary laughed apologetically. 'Oh, thank you so much. It's my first time here. I didn't realise it would be so heavy when wet.'

Kathy grinned then nodded while they both manoeuvred the heavy bag into an old pram. 'Don't worry, ye'll get used to it. Remember to bring yer ain powder next time. It's cheaper.'

'I will. Thank you so much.' Mary waved goodbye.

After that Kathy would see Mary regularly at the Bag Wash. They would chat laugh and sometimes have a cup of tea at the café next door. She recalled her rarely mentioning her husband, but she talked endlessly about her daughter and her dreams. When Kathy finally discovered who her husband was it was all too late.

Chapter 17

It had been eight weeks since the letter arrived telling Mary and her family of their acceptance to immigrate to Australia. After weeks of interviews, medicals, uncertainty, second thoughts, and tears, now their departure date was imminent. The last few days in Glasgow were busy with last-minute packing, farewell drinks and parties to say goodbye to their friends, school friends, work friends, and football friends, with promises to write and come back after two years for a holiday.

It was Mary's second last day in Scotland. She wanted to go back on her own to Bethblair one last time to relive the memories, good and bad. She had to do this by herself to reflect on days gone by and the life she was about to leave behind, to ponder on what lay ahead, and regardless of what it was, to be determined to take every opportunity offered by this new young country.

Stepping carefully off the bus, Mary quickly walked the short distance to the flats. Climbing the three well-trodden steps, she stood for a moment at the faded blue front door. The brass letterbox was shining, just as she has left it. She recalled that first flush of excitement when carrying Billy as a baby in her arms across the threshold of a real home, and a new phase in her life. Pushing the door open, she slowly walked down the long empty hallway, her footsteps echoing around the walls. Standing at the kitchen door and gazing into the tiny room, she choked back a tear. The round table and chairs that had kept her family together at mealtimes were now gone, given a new life by a neighbour. The walls, once a brilliant white, were now a sickly yellow and peeling at the corners. Mary smiled at the memory of Scot helping his father paint this room. He was so excited at discovering a new skill, picturing himself as a budding painter and decorator. She shook her head and smiled slightly. Whoever moved in would have to paint it all over again.

The living room was empty. The pink shell wall lights that Archie had complained about shone brightly, Mary had polished the chrome surrounds until they sparkled. The vibrant flocked striped wallpaper was only slightly faded but still intact. She hoped the new people would keep it for a while; it had taken them three years to pay off the instalments on the wallpaper and the paint. She had scrubbed the fireplace tiles and surrounds until her fingers were red but still failed to remove the singe marks from the wall, or the cigarette burns from the mantelpiece. Both bedrooms had been stripped bare, except for the double bed in the room she had shared with Archie. The local Catholic Church had asked if they could have it for a large, needy family. Archie had complained to anyone within earshot that giving anything to Catholics was not on. Mary happily agreed to donate it to the church. It was one aspect of Scotland that Mary detested. Many Glaswegians, just like Archie, were opinionated and hypocritical although they never went to church. It was all about football to them. He was a protestant, a Glasgow Rangers supporter. Catholics supported the Celtic football team. It was passionate rivalry; she would not miss this bigotry at all.

In Alice's room, the walls still showed signs of impossible to remove yellow tape and faded patches. She could still visualise 'Elvis Forever' emblazoned in every corner.

It was then that sadness overcame her. Standing with her back against the wall, she slid down onto the cold floor, cloaked in grief. Tears rolled shamelessly down her cheeks. They were leaving for a new life the following night, but they were leaving without her daughter, her first-born, who wanted to stay behind with Robbie. Alice promised that they would both follow later. Mary doubted it.

She had not seen her for a few days, but was hoping for a visit from her daughter before they left. A letter arrived in the mail that morning. She pulled it from her coat pocket, reading it for the umpteenth time.

Dear Ma,

I know this is not right. I should be coming to say cheerio to you, I'm sorry, but I just can't do it. I am going to miss you and the boys something terrible. I never thought I would feel this bad. I know I have not been the best daughter these last few years, worrying you and bringing you so much trouble, and it is only now when you are all leaving me that I realise how much family means. I really am sorry, Ma, for all those wild years, and I promise to make up for it and make you proud of me. Please kiss the boys and tell them I love them, tell them to behave, be good, and that I'll see them soon. All my love to you always, Ma.

Alice xxxx

Mary folded the letter, put it back into her pocket, and dabbed at her eyes with the end of her scarf. She went into the bathroom and splashed her face; the cold water refreshed and revitalised her. She splashed again, wiping herself dry with a handkerchief. Looking down at the bath she smiled, recalling the first time she had laid eyes on it all those years ago, and the unimaginable pleasure of having her first bath.

The letterbox rattled loudly, encroaching on her reverie; it resonated down the empty hallway.

Mary quickly patted her hair, and straightened her coat. 'Coming!' she called. 'I'm just coming.'

Rena stood at the open doorway. Mary smiled and reached out for her. 'Rena! Oh, come in, your mother said you were away at your auntie's house. I am so glad to see you. Don't stand there, pet, come in, come in.'

'Oh, Mrs Bray, I've just come to say cheerio. I'm sorry I've taken that long, but honest, I was really just puttin it off. I hate goodbyes.'

'Oh, Rena, I would have been so sad not to have seen you before we left. You have been part of our family for many years. Thank you, thank you. Come in, Rena, come on in.'

Rena stood on the doorstep, twisting the end of her cardigan round and around, then moving from one foot to another she followed Mary into Alice's room.

'Alice said that you might be here today on your own, so I just thought I could see you, and tell you by myself that that I'm going to miss you all, I really am.' Her voice broke. 'I'm sorry, Mrs Bray, I wisni gonna cry honestly, it's just that you've always been really nice to me and we have known you all for such a long time, even my Ma was havin a wee greet thinking that you'll no be here anymore.'

Mary put her arms around Rena and they cried together, sitting down on the bare floor talking about the past, the school days, the boy crushes, the Elvis pictures, and the strong friendship that Rena had developed with Alice.

'Don't worry, Mrs Bray, Alice will be fine wi us. You know how my ma and my sisters feel about her. After aw these years she is one of our family.'

Mary nodded. 'I know, I know, Rena, but she is my only daughter.

It's just so hard leaving Scotland without her. I will miss her so much.'

Rena's words comforted Mary, but the feeling of desolation still lingered. They stood up and hugged each other, then walked to the front door whispering lingering promises of never losing touch. Rena ran down the stairs, turned back and waved again.

Mary knew it was time to leave. She walked slowly down the hallway, picked up her shopping bag and left, pulling the door behind her for the last time.

She ran down the steps to the street only pausing at the bridge. Bending over the rails, she watched the course of the burn as it continued its race over shiny stones on a frenzied quest for the open waters of the river.

That burn had brought so much pleasure to her boys when they were young. They had paddled across its shallows many times, squatting down to catch minnows in their cupped hands. They would keep the tiny fish in a jar for days on end then let them go, only to repeat the process all over again. She recalled the freezing winters and the not so pretty predators of the burn. Those very early days when she left for work, and the snow was thick and pristine on the ground, untouched, but for the lonely tracks of rats as they ran from the icy burn to the back of the flats to scavenge in the dustbins that had overflowed.

Mary left the burn and walked quickly, catching the bus as it pulled up at the stop. She sat down on the first seat inside, her eyes fixed on the window, taking in every glimpse of the housing estate she knew she would never see again. Feelings of sadness surprised her. There had been many wonderful times here; there had also been great challenges, conflict, and heartache. The neighbours had been kind and supportive and she had made many good friends. Her children had thrived growing up in this environment and never complained.

Now nearing forty, Mary felt she had grown stronger and was no longer a woman overlooked, downtrodden or disregarded. Much to Archie's annoyance she had grown, she had views, opinions, beliefs and intelligence and she didn't hold back.

The years had been kind to Mary; her pale English skin was almost unlined, with only the faintest touch of silver threads through her hair. Her dress size had barely changed and she took great pride in her appearance. She could never have imagined her life would lead her to Scotland, but it did, and she survived.

For her children, there were many traditions that Mary upheld in Glasgow. Guy Fawkes Night and the giant bonfires built on any vacant land or park area. Neighbours would throw bits of old furniture on to the fire, and cheers would erupt as an effigy of Guy Fawkes was tossed into the flames.

Halloween was another custom celebrated with great gusto. It brought anticipation and excitement from the children. They would dress up in hand-me-down adult clothes, cowboy suits, masks, or pirate patches. They would spill out onto the streets laughing and calling out to each other as they knocked on the doors. A song or a rhyme was rewarded with sweets, an apple, or a penny.

Hogmanay (New Year's Eve) was the year's highlight for Glaswegians. To many, it was more important than Christmas. Celebrations began at midnight with feasts of steak pies, potatoes, shortbread, and whisky. Homes were scrubbed and cleaned scrupulously to be rid of the old year's dirt, and New Year resolutions were made.

Although she upheld these traditions, she wouldn't miss them at all.

Arriving back at Leighton Avenue, where the family had been staying with Sadie, it was almost dusk. The noise level was escalating as everyone was talking, laughing, calling out and arguing. Everyone was busy, excited, and noisy ... everyone but Alice.

Sadie was fussing around organising sheets and blankets, changing pillowslips, and moving furniture. She looked up as Mary came in. Sadie's face was flushed with beads of sweat that had collected on her top lip, wisps of hair drifted from under her hair net. 'Mary, I'll make up the bed settee for you and Archie, the boys can sleep on cushions on the floor. I'll give them an eiderdown; will that be okay?'

'That is just fine, Sadie. Please don't worry, it's only one night and we are all so tired we could sleep on a bed of nails.'

Sadie pushed her hair back under her hairnet and smiled wearily. Leaning against the wall, she sighed. 'I will miss ye, Mary, yer such a good wife and mother. Archie just disnae know he's born, honest tay God. Ye have put up with so much over the years, we all know that, and we want for ye to realise all yer dreams in Australia. Nobody can deny that ye have come a long way since that first time we saw ye, scared, pregnant, and unsure of everything, holding onto yer wee lassie's hand. I remember that so well, Mary. I know ye will make it work, this new life. Yer strength and determination will make sure of that.' She took Mary's hand and squeezed it. Mary wiped a tear.

They had one large suitcase each, packed and stacked against the door. The trunk with household possessions and mementoes was the last to be locked, it lay open on the floor. It was being collected and going by ship. The atmosphere although noisy was happy. Scot was keeping everyone amused by doing card tricks and telling jokes.

Bob and Frank were delighted to take them all into the train station by taxis the next day, for their rail trip to London, then on to Heathrow ... Australia bound!

After supper, they bedded down for their last night in Scotland. It had been a long day; everyone was tired and sleep came effortlessly.

Mary was first to wake. Outside it was raining steadily. Daylight cast its comfort onto their surroundings; suitcases, a trunk, coats, jackets and hand luggage, all remnants of Mary's lifetime of living in a country she hated.

She knew that Archie was going to be a liability. She didn't question his change of heart on immigrating, she didn't even care, all she wanted was his consent for the boys to travel. She so desperately wanted to get away from Glasgow, yet she surprised herself by having twinges of guilt that she was taking Archie away from his secure neighbourhood. He was so set in his ways and would be at a loss in unfamiliar surroundings.

He had made her life unbearable at times over the years, particularly when the children were young. She knew that she was using him now, but she didn't care. This was survival and moving forward for her children, this was part of the bigger plan. She knew that Archie would struggle with anything new, such as a new lifestyle, a different accent, different currency, and different food. Archie Bray was a creature of habit, nevertheless, Mary did not let her conscience or her heart cloud her vision. She listened to her head, knowing that her heart would follow. It was the right thing to do. She was excited at the challenge and the chance to explore a new world. To give new horizons to her children, and to give them a license to dream.

Billy woke up and slipped his feet under her blanket at the foot of the bed settee.

'Billy, your feet are freezing.'

Archie's head appeared from beneath the sheets. 'What's all the fuckin noise about? We've got hours yet.'

'We can't sleep down here anymore, Archie.' Mary snapped back 'Everyone will be up soon, and I still have a lot to do. I have to go and say goodbye to Kathy. I sent Billy around with a note yesterday to say I was coming. I haven't seen her in such a long time and her father is getting out of jail in two weeks. Did you know he was getting out early?'

Archie pulled the blanket up to his chin, turned to the wall, and mumbled, 'That slut, whit are ye botherin wi her fur? Aye, I heard aboot Stan getting oot early, somebody mentioned it in the pub last week. It's a shame I'll just miss seeing him, eh?'

His words lost to Mary as she quietly closed the door behind her.

Chapter 18

Behind the door, Kathy was biting her nails again. That youthful habit she had conquered long ago was now resurfacing. It had been so long since they had seen each other and she was nervous. This would be the last chance for Kathy to offload her conscience. She desperately wanted Mary's response, her approval, and her forgiveness, but she was scared. If she rejected her or dismissed her, or, worse still, did not believe her, Kathy would be distraught. Worrying had kept her awake the previous night. At dawn, she decided to tell her everything and the consequences she would have to accept. It was the right thing to do.

She had tried with her appearance, hoping to capture some of the magnetism of her youth, but it was not working. She still looked tired. Her once sparkling green eyes were now flat and dull, the thick red bouncing hair of her youth now flecked heavily with grey and hanging in lank strands behind her ears.

Kathy's life was not as she would have hoped. Her fantasy of leaving Glasgow on a white charger with a handsome knight had long ago dissolved. She had hoped for a new life far away from poverty, from the hurt and from the memories. Instead, she had stopped working and was now a recluse, having withdrawn from friends and the social life she had once known. Her sisters had left home. Helen was happily married with a young family, and Yvonne was a nurse, living in at the hospital that had so lovingly cared for her when she was younger. Kathy, imprisoned by memories and plagued by guilt, was now very much alone.

Mary gazed vacantly at the panelled door with its tartan-backed nameplate, her eyes rested on the brass letterbox and solid doorknob that she remembered so well. Why was she here? Why had she come? How would Kathy greet her? Would she even answer the door? She thought about turning around and running down the stairs to the safety of the busy pavement, but she had come this far. There was no going back. Instead, she stood back from the door, knocked gently and waited. Her heart was thumping. Drawing in a deep breath she knocked again, this time straightening her skirt and pulling down on her heavy cardigan. There was no response, no movement, nothing.

As she turned around to leave, there was a faint shuffle from behind the door, followed by the drawing of a bolt and the slow turning of a latch. The heavy door drew back slowly.

Kathy emerged from the shadows. Turning her head to the side and narrowing her eyes, she struggled to focus on her old friend. 'Mary,' her voice a whisper. 'Is that you?'

'Yes, Kathy, it's me.'

'Oh, oh. I... I don't know what to say.'

'No, no ... neither do I.'

Mary reached out, Kathy did too, they both fell into an embrace no one spoke. An entire conversation unravelled before them in utter silence. They cried and then laughed then held hands, standing for a moment just looking at each other.

Suddenly, Kathy became animated as she took Mary's hand and

half pulled her into the room. 'Come in, come on in, Mary, oh ye look great. It's so good to see ye. Here, sit in this chair by the fire, I'm that glad to see ye so I am.' Kathy began to cry.

Mary reached out and hugged her old friend. It was a soundless moment, no one spoke. Kathy stood back, holding Mary at arm's length.

'I canny believe yer leaving Glasgow, Mary. I wanted to speak to ye that many times before ye left, but couldnie find the courage, I could have kissed wee Billy yesterday when he gave me yer note. Thanks, pal, I'm that happy, so I am.'

Kathy sat down beside he friend. The years melted away; they were young again.

They talked and laughed loudly, recalling the days at the transport cafe and how timid Mary was, and the night of her birthday when neither of them could stand up straight after having too many gins. Then there was the time that Kathy tried a home perm on Mary's thin hair and it fell out in clumps, and another time when Mary had to hide Kathy in her coalbunker from the jealous girlfriend of a good-looking body builder she had been flirting with.

As Mary sat back and watched her friend come alive, boosted by memories, she saw glimpses of the old Kathy, but all the laughter and re-telling could not disguise the reality that the vibrant young girl she had known and always remembered was now a tired and prematurely aging woman.

Kathy dabbed at her eyes, then stood up and reached for a package that lay at the end of table. She held it with two hands and then gently handed it to Mary. 'I want ye to have this, Mary. My ma made it years ago when we were aw wee. I know by ye havin it ye will no forget me, and part of me will always be a part of you and yer new life in Australia.'

Mary shook her head and looked at her 'What is it, Kathy? Honestly, you didn't have to give me anything. Having this time together is gift enough for me.'

Mary took the package and slowly untied the white ribbon, releasing pale blue tissue paper.

A burst of colour unfurled on to her lap and over her knees. She held her hand to her mouth and muffled a scream: it was a quilt. Kathy, wide-eyed and trembling, watched her response then immediately explained. 'My ma started it when I was born, Mary, then she added bits and pieces when Yvonne and Helen came along.' Kathy's voice was breaking with emotion as the patchwork came to life.

Each square told a story of Kathy and her sisters. A piece of flannelette from her baby blanket, a checked square from her school dress, a piece of her Girl Guide tie. Brightly coloured taffeta squares and pieces of fine lace added with trinkets here and there. A silver threepenny bit from a Christmas pudding, a medal won at a sports day. Three little baby teeth encased in chiffon securely sewn into the satin. Kathy had kept it in perfect condition. Mary lifted the quilt and gently caressed the squares with her fingers.

'Oh Kathy, I don't know what to say. It is the most beautiful present I have ever had. I will treasure it always Thank you. Thank You.' Mary closed her eyes and gently rubbed the quilt on her wet cheek.

Kathy smiled and nodded, then braced herself. It had to be now, she had to tell her now, she had to unload and to relive that nightmare from all those years ago. She waited until Mary had folded the quilt and placed it tenderly into its wrapping. 'I still canny believe I might never see ye again, Mary. I've wanted to talk to ye about something so many times, but instead I just ignored it. I was waiting fur it aw to disappear, but it never will. Ye see, Mary, there is something ye need to know. It happened a long time ago. I mean long before we even met.

I'm scared that once I tell ye, ye'll really hate me and never speak to me again. It's no nice and I am no proud of it, but it's in my past and I canny deny it. It's something that needs to be told, something that ye should know.'

Kathy was looking down and biting her lip. She swallowed hard and started to shake.

Mary leaned, over forcing Kathy to look directly into her eyes, then she took hold of both of her hands and squeezed them. 'Kathy ... Kathy, look at me. Nothing you can say will ever change the way I feel. You are the best friend I have ever had. I have missed you, and so have the children. I should have taken notice of you all those years ago when you would argue with Archie. Now I see the man that he is, and why you reacted to him the way you did. I have always thought that you had something between you both in the past, but that is what it is ... the past. I have wanted to talk to you so many times about him, his attitude and temper. Had it not been for the boys, I would have left years ago. Things might be better in Australia, who knows? Whatever it is that has bothered you, Kathy, is history ... and that's where it stays. I don't want to know. If there is anything you want me to forgive you for, I do. I forgive you, honestly, I do. I want to leave Scotland knowing that our friendship is still solid and unbroken.'

Mary sat back and let go of Kathy's hands.

'But Mary—'

'I mean it, Kathy. It's history, it doesn't matter and I don't need to know.'

Kathy stared at her and shook her head. She had tried, but Mary had given her an out, had insisted that it was in the past, it was finished, it was gone. Her need to be relieved of this burden was over, but not in the way she had thought. After years of mental torture, Kathy was free at last. It was cheating, it was the easy way out; nevertheless, it was forgiven ... Mary had said so.

Surprisingly, Kathy felt much better. She was relieved. Her past with Archie had weighed heavily on her for so long. She had suffered the loss of a daughter and the humiliation of Archie's denials. If Mary ever did find out, then at least she would know that she had tried to tell her. Mary would know that.

Kathy stood up, wiped her eyes and went to the dresser shelf. She took down two glasses. With her back to Mary, she half turned her head and raised one eyebrow: 'Fancy a wee drink then, eh, Mrs Bray?' It was the old Kathy.

With her soft English lilt and best Scottish brogue, Mary smiled and replied, 'Aye, nae bother, pal.'

Arriving back at Leighton Avenue, Mary was feeling lightheaded and happy. Knocking the door, she leaned against the wall, smiling to herself. There was mumbling from behind the door as it creaked open.

'Where the fuck huv ye been? Ye've been away for hours.'

Archie's face was red, his eyes were bulging, and his breath came in short gasps. Siding up to her he said, 'Yer breath's rotten. Have you been drinkin?'

Mary, flushed, happy, and unsteady on her feet, burped then giggled. 'Yes! As a matter of fact, I have. So what?'

'So what? Like the taxi's gonna be here in an oor and ye've no finished packing that hand luggage yit, that's what.'

Mary walked to the door, picked up a towel and headed for the bathroom. Throwing the towel over her shoulder, she turned to her husband. 'Archie?'

He glared at her.

'It's your hand luggage. Pack it your fucking self!'

PART TWO

AUSTRALIA: 1965

Chapter 19

'Ladies and gentlemen, we are now on our approach to Melbourne. The captain has turned on the seatbelt and no smoking signs. Please bring your seats to an upright position, ensure all cigarettes are completely extinguished, and that your seatbelts are securely fastened. All hand luggage should be stored in the lockers above your head, or placed securely in the seat in front of you for your arrival at Essendon airport. The temperature in Melbourne today is a very warm 36 degrees Celsius. On arrival, disembarkation will be by the forward and rear doors, a crew member on the tarmac will direct you to the terminal building. On behalf of Ansett ANA, we would like to thank you for your company today and look forward to welcoming you on board when next you fly. Good Morning.'

Mary turned to Scot and shook him gently. Billy was already awake, his nose flat against the window. 'Scot, Scot, wake up, we're nearly here. Put your seat up, quick.'

'Here, where, what? Oh, aye great. I'm awake, I'm awake.' He sat up quickly, looking down the isle of the aircraft. 'Have I time for a pee, Ma?'

His mother glared at him, shaking her head vigorously.

Across the aisle, Archie lay slumped in his seat with his mouth open, snoring loudly with his head leaning on the shoulder of the woman next to him. Mary shook him gently, he recoiled and grunted. She looked at him with disgust. He had not fared well on this long journey at all, offering complaint after complaint from the time they had left London. He had been even worse on this last leg from Darwin to Melbourne. Seated in a non-smoking row and without a cigarette, Archie was unbearable.

Although the aircraft cabin was air-conditioned, he could not cope with the heat, the thick woollen trousers he had worn since leaving freezing Scotland were causing him great discomfort, as did the heavy brogues that were lost amongst papers and blankets under the seat in front. Archie had found fault with everything: the food, the seats, the tea, even the hardworking cabin crew. When he did sleep, it was only in short naps, his loud snores and foot odour was an embarrassment to them all. He picked up a toothpick from his tray table and started to poke inside his ears, a habit that had never waned since his youth. Stretching his legs out into the aisle he farted, then he bent down, mumbling and whinging whilst groping around his feet.

Mary was embarrassed. 'What is it, Archie? What are you doing?'

'What the fuck do ye think I'm doin? Lookin for my fuckin shoes.'

Mary cringed. The woman seated next to him, with nowhere to move, just closed her eyes and tried with great difficulty to turn away.

Mary sighed and looked away in disgust. Although tired and jet-lagged, she wanted to look her best when meeting her uncle. Reaching down to the side pocket of her travel case, she pulled out a small compact and lipstick, deftly applying it to her lips. Her heart was racing. She knew that whatever lay ahead for her and her family in this new world would far exceed the challenges she had endured in the old.

The drone of the engine lulled, the aircraft appeared to stop mid-air, the giant wheels slowly groaned and lowered in preparation for landing. Mary watched the landscape fly past. Matchbox houses with patches of blue. She heard someone in the seat behind say they were swimming pools.

They landed with a bump, then a roar, as the aircraft careered along the tarmac, slowing down as the terminal building came into view. Noise in the cabin intensified and the hostess making an announcement for them to remain seated went unheard. The passengers had started to climb over one another, retrieving bags and overcoats from the overhead lockers and under the seats.

The tarmac propelled waves of heat rising up from the hot cement. Tanned airport workers in tight shorts and white short-sleeved shirts laughed and joked with each other as they sidled up to the belly of the plane with empty luggage trolleys, taking control of the life's possessions from a throng of new Australians. The tired and bewildered group struggled slowly through the glass doors of the terminal building, struggling with their hand luggage, whilst directing confused and tired children. Mary wiped the perspiration from her brow as she walked briskly ahead of her weary family. Her energy was now rejuvenated. She was on the other side of the world ... at last.

Uncle Ralph stood against the back wall of the arrivals lounge in the sweltering heat, scrutinising the passengers as they alighted from the plane. He was a small, thin spritely man in his seventies with bright blue eyes radiating from a tanned, lined face, and a shock of thick white hair. He smiled and frowned in regular sequence; not exactly sure who he was looking for. He had only ever seen a small black and white photograph of his niece Mary, taken when she was just six years old. Her mother, Ella, had been his only sister and when she died he lost touch with Mary and her siblings. He was to discover later that Mary went to an orphanage whilst her siblings went to foster homes.

The crowd thinned as Uncle Ralph wiped the sweat from the back of his neck with a large handkerchief. He was anxious and worried that perhaps he had missed them in the initial rowdy throng. But he needn't have worried; it turned out he would have known her anywhere.

She walked through the revolving door, straight and confident, scanning the waiting crowd, then she stepped with care into the small, carpeted lobby.

It was his sister Ella, just as he remembered her. Mary was her mother's mirror image. Standing back in the shade of a large concrete pillar, Uncle Ralph wiped his forehead, then dabbed at his eyes before pushing through the crowds to the barrier, calling out her name. 'Mary, Mary love.'

She saw him immediately. 'Uncle Ralph?'

Dropping her belongings at her feet she held out her arms. The old man's eyes clouded over, the weathered skin on his aged face disappeared into deep furrows as he embraced his niece, his voice breaking as he held her at arm's length. 'Aye, lass, I'd know you anywhere. You're your mam all over.'

Between sobs she whispered in his ear, 'Oh Uncle Ralph, at last, at long last.'

Archie and the boys stood back, giving Mary her emotional moment, then grasping her uncle's hand, she led him over to her family. 'Uncle Ralph, these are my boys, Scot, and Billy, and this is my husband, Archie.'

Uncle Ralph grabbed their hands and shook vigorously. The boys shuffled their feet and looked down in embarrassment. Archie held out his limp hand, and Uncle Ralph smiled broadly and grabbed it with gusto in both of his. 'Aye, welcome lads, welcome.'

Archie's contorted face looked away, planting both hands deep into his trouser pockets.

Uncle Ralph walked ahead to fetch his old car from the car park while Archie and the boys pulled the cases from the luggage belt. They carried them to the kerbside outside, loaded up, then they all squeezed into the old car as it chugged slowly away from the airport.

It was early January and very hot. Inside the car it was stifling, everyone was clammy and uncomfortable. Despite this, the boys seemed eager to explore. Before the eyes of this excited family the suburbs of Melbourne unfolded, like the golden petals of a sunflower, Billy letting out cries at every turn.

Archie was dishevelled, still wearing his suit and tie; it was crumpled and grubby. When he left Glasgow, it had been three degrees Fahrenheit and raining. Yet he insisted in not removing his suit, but he continued to complain. As the old car laboured along the road, Mary and the boys chatted nonstop, and pointed and laughed at almost everything. Archie lay against the window with his eyes closed and mouth open, too tired and too disinterested to note anything on the first day of their new life.

Essendon was a nice suburb with lots of trees and houses set wide apart from each other with gardens, fences, and garages. Majestic churches with open doors were set back from the road. Swing parks were teeming with bronzed children wearing colourful shorts and rubber foot thongs. Mary absorbed everything: the space, the sun, and the bright summer clothes of the passing public. The car slowed down as it turned into a wide street with broad nature strips and high trees, shading neat, uniformed verandas and picket fences. Uncle Ralph, with anticipation and excitement in his voice, drove slowly into the driveway of number twenty-eight.

'We're ere, Mary love, we're ome.'

The boys and Archie unloaded the bags and cases and brought them inside. Mary was exhilarated.

'Oh, Uncle Ralph, it's lovely, and so big ... look, look, Archie, isn't the garden lovely? The daisy bush, and all those fruit trees, and, my goodness, just look at that shady porch and those wooden chairs and table.'

Archie didn't answer. Uncle Ralph said that before they opened any cases or bags, they must have a cup of tea and some chocolate chip cookies he had made.

Mary loved the old house at first sight. Uncle Ralph's wife had died ten years prior, they never had any children, and she had been the gardener. There was a plethora of fruit trees: lemon, orange, grapefruit—even peach and plum.

The home was on a large allotment. It was an Edwardian weatherboard with a wooden veranda all the way around. The baskets that hung from the wooden slats off the veranda cascaded with colourful petunias and yellow daises in large clusters. The white paint had peeled in places off the house and the flywire door had acquired large holes, but Mary thought this all added to its charm. Uncle Ralph made it very clear on that first day that they could have the run of the house. He would live most of the time in the front room where his bedroom and living room were. He didn't always have cooked meals, but when he did he would eat early so that Mary could have the kitchen to herself. It was a big kitchen with plenty of cupboards; she was amazed at the size of the fridge. She had never owned a real fridge.

The boys had homemade lemonade. Archie just grabbed two cookies from the plate, saying that he had to have a lie down. Mary raised her eyes to the ceiling in disgust. Uncle Ralph led them into their room.

The windows had white venetian blinds with green floral chintz curtains hanging either side that almost touched the floor. The matching chintz covered pelmet gave the window a larger aspect. The wardrobe was dark brown walnut with a full-length mirror in the middle. Underneath were four large drawers all with brass ball handles. Two single twin beds with cream quilted eiderdowns perfectly covered the brown chenille bedspreads. On top of a small cabinet, Uncle Ralph had placed some colourful petunias in a small vase beside an oval sepia picture of Mary's mother. She went to thank him for being so thoughtful, he was touching the bedheads and apologising.

'Sorry, lass, we only ever ad single beds in this room. For when we had visitors, you know. Ope it will be alright.'

Mary could hardly contain her delight and relief. 'That's perfectly fine, Uncle Ralph. It's a good idea in hot weather anyway.'

Archie sat down on one of the beds, taking off his shoes and biting into the cookies. Speaking with a mouth full of biscuit and dropping crumbs on the carpet, he nodded to Uncle Ralph. 'Aye, this is fine, Ralph. Don't mind if I have a wee kip, do ye? I'm dead tired.'

Mary glared at him.

'No, lad, that's alright. It's been a long flight for ya, just take yer time.'

The boys had single beds in the sleep out, a room with large windows that had been an addition to the old house. They had their own beds, bed lights, a chest of drawers, their own back door, even a small transistor radio. They loved it. It looked out onto the back lawn that had an outside clothesline. They discovered later that it was an Australian icon, a Hills Hoist. It was a circular clothes line that turned with a push and came to you, instead of having to walk up and down lines of rope. The boys were fascinated.

On her first night in Australia, Mary and her uncle talked nonstop about England, Scotland, her mother, the life she had lived, and her sorrow when she died. She told him how hard she had tried to find her brother Jack and sister Ellen, but they had both been adopted, the details of which were confidential. She was only told that they were adopted together; this alone gave her some peace knowing at least they had each other.

They cried and laughed until very late. Mary stood up and yawned, stretching her back before hugging her uncle. 'Uncle Ralph, I feel I have known you all my life and for the first time in … oh! I can't remember how long, I feel so connected to my mother's family, something that has always been missing. I want to thank you from all of us for being so much a part of our small family, and for giving us the chance of a new life in Australia.'

Uncle Ralph took her hand 'Mary, love, I av lived a very good life ere and av done alright for meself, but I av never ad family, something I wanted all of me life, and now I av it. So, lass, I av been blessed too. I am sure our Ella is guiding us. Goodnight, luv.'

'Goodnight, Uncle Ralph.'

Mary watched as he slowly left the room, closing the door quietly behind him. She locked the back door and switched off the lights before silently slipping into her own single bed.

Oh, the joy of it all! The space, the freedom, the weather, even the nasal snorts and grunts in the next bed did not tarnish her contentment.

During their first week in Australia, Archie criticised everything. He couldn't sleep at night for the heat; he muttered under his breath that the ceiling fan was too noisy, that the mosquitoes targeted him, and that the hollow cry of the cicadas at the end of the day drove him crazy. Mary loved the haunting chirp of the cicada, feeling comforted by their chant. She didn't mind the heat. Keeping the blinds down and the curtains closed during the day gave shelter from the hot sun, the ceiling fans kept the place cool and bearable.

At night, the temperatures lowered, and often a light breeze would flow through the house. The boys never seemed to feel the heat; they adapted quickly only wearing shorts and rubber thongs on their feet. When it was very hot, they would turn on the garden sprinkler and run under it. Often, they would lay down on a plastic tarpaulin and do belly flops on the wet plastic. Mary never tired of hearing their screams of laughter.

The abundance of fresh fruit and vegetables in Australia amazed her, and as the weeks passed, she cooked, baked, or bottled something every day. The family revelled in her newfound cooking skills, even Archie complimented her occasionally.

Uncle Ralph told them previously that he had spent the last years of his working life in a biscuit factory, and he told them that management had said they would be happy to help his family with employment. True to his word, he secured a job for Archie in the storeroom; however, Archie told Mary he felt that to work in a storeroom was beneath him and after a few months he would sort things out, he would nominate himself for a union role. After all, he said, he was well qualified in this area.

A few months later, Scot celebrated his sixteenth birthday. He decided that he was finished with school and planned to be a plumber. Mary objected strongly, but Scot was having none of it. 'Listen, Mum, I want to do an apprenticeship to become a plumber and one day have my own business.'

'Your own business, really? I didn't know you were thinking of owning a business, son. All the more reason to do another two years at school. It will open many doors for you.'

Scot put his hand on his mother's arm and smiled patiently. 'Mum, Mum, my mind is made up. I can look for a job. I have been looking at the job ads in the paper every day, and there are plenty of jobs for apprentices. Trust me, it's the right thing for me.'

Mary raised her arms, shaking her head. Scot winked and leaned over kissing her cheek before leaving the room.

It was late on Sunday afternoon. Scot was tinkering in the shed with S-bends and cistern plugs, when Uncle Ralph called out from the house. 'Scot, lad, got a minute?'

'Sure, Uncle Ralph, what's up?' He came in through the flywire door, wiping his hands on a dishcloth before pulling out a chair.

'I've just been talking to an old pal of mine from the bowling club. His son has a small plumbing business over Moonee Ponds way, and e told me that e is looking for an apprentice. I told im about ye and what a good fixer upper you was and e is very keen to have a chat, e pays apprentice wages and there is overtime plus a Christmas bonus. Would you be interested, lad?'

Scot jumped up from his chair. 'Would I? Aye, Uncle Ralph, I would that. When can I see him? What do I need to do?'

Uncle Ralph smiled. 'Leave it to me, lad, I'll make a time for ye to meet im. Now go tell your mam, she's in the kitchen.'

Scot rushed into the kitchen. His mother was singing quietly to herself, peeling vegetables at the sink. He grabbed her around the waist. 'Guess what? I'm getting a job!'

She turned around to face him. 'A what?'

'A job.'

'Slow down, what kind of job?'

'A plumbing job, well I haven't exactly got it yet, but Uncle Ralph is sure this man in Moonee Ponds will hire me. Isn't that great?'

Mary laughed aloud and hugged her son. 'That's great, Scotty, you'll get it, I know you will. You'll just charm him.'

Turning back to the sink she smiled, knowing that Scot would make his way in the world. He had such a gift of connecting and always made her laugh.

Mary didn't have to rush out immediately to look for a job. Uncle Ralph was not charging them any rent, and so far, Archie was giving her most of his wages from the biscuit factory, but of this she was never sure because he never divulged exactly how much he earned.

She had navigated her way around Uncle Ralph's house very quickly and mastered his aged, workable kitchen gadgets. It allowed her to experiment with different recipes. She began pottering in the garden too. The tired tomato vines were now thriving and had started to produce. The little row of lettuces all stood to attention, alongside the solid colours of red and green capsicum. The pumpkin leaves had started to spread, hiding the rapid growth of their bounty. Mary had also experimented by potting herbs from seedlings and rejoiced as each one grew and flourished, giving more ammunition to enhance her recipes.

The opportunities that Australia gave to the Bray family were life-changing; however, a dark and heavy cloud hovered over Mary. Alice was not here, sharing this new life with the family.

Every day Mary would listen for the postman's whistle as he cycled up and down the street. She relished getting letters from home, hearing news from her old neighbours and friends and Sadie, but what she yearned for most were letters from Alice. She heard from her regularly, but it was never enough. She always wrote how positive and happy she was, talking about Rena and her family and how kind they were to her, and the fun times she and Rena had, now that she had broken off her relationship with Robbie.

Mary heard the postman's whistle and hurried outside to the gate. He waved from across the street, as Mary lifted the letters from the mailbox.

'G'day, Mrs Bray, bonza day!'

'Hello there, Barry, yes, isn't it just?' She waved back.

'All right, Mary, love?' Uncle Ralph came from behind the house. He had been working in the back garden all morning and was now pushing his wheelbarrow out to the front gate. It was loaded with lemons, grapefruits, and oranges ready to go to the church hall. 'Anything from ome?'

Mary shuffled the letters while mumbling to herself. 'Just one for Scot from his girl, he'll be pleased. I shouldn't really look for one from Alice again. I did hear last week, but I don't think she is happy. Reading between the lines, things have not gone well with her boyfriend. I miss her so much.'

Uncle Ralph was hard of hearing, and quite often got things a bit muddled in his response. In all the years he had been in Australia, he still maintained his strong north country English accent. His eyes glazed over. 'Don't worry, lass; it'll all work out in the end.' His wiry little arms strained under the wheelbarrow's weight. 'Why don't you pop kettle on and we'll ave a cuppa after I deliver this lot to the church?'

Mary smiled nodding absentmindedly while walking back to the house. She put the kettle on and laid two cups and saucers on the kitchen table.

It was times like this that she missed Kathy, the Kathy of long ago. She missed the confidences shared and the secrets that would forever stay buried. She had only heard from her once in the six months that they had been here. It was only two pages, mainly about her father and how good it was to have him home. He had managed to get a job in the power station where Archie had worked and was trying to put the last twelve years behind him.

Yvonne was now a nursing sister at the hospital, and Helen was pregnant again. Mary felt how sad it was that Kathy never had a child. She was so good with children. She would have made a wonderful mother.

Chapter 20

Skirting the city on a fast-growing industrial state stood an old, entrenched bluestone house, a blatant contrast from the more recent additions of pink brick buildings and aluminium sheds at the rear. The tiny wooden windows were all still intact; the glass panes sparkled in the hot sun. There was an old square stone surrounded by overgrown tufts of grass near the entrance, the writing on it was just legible. It read 'Baker's Family Biscuits'.

The Baker family had built their business from humble beginnings during the late 1800s to a successful company of the day. When Mr and Mrs Baker passed away, the first-born grandson inherited the business. The old bluestone building became offices. The introduction of conveyer belts, moulds, flour bins and machinery housed in two massive tin roofed buildings saw an increase of productivity and therefore the staff at Baker's escalated to over three hundred.

Uncle Ralph had spent twenty-five years of his working life there. He had befriended the Baker family and they regarded him as loyal, hard-working, and honest, and therefore had no hesitation in offering Archie, sight unseen, a position in the supply store of the factory. He started work straight away. The work itself was not labour intensive, all he had to do was make sure the stock was up to date, record it, order equipment, and liaise with suppliers. He kept to himself in the factory, with the exception of Sid, a Londoner. They became best mates. When Sid discovered that Archie had been a shop steward in

Glasgow, he immediately suggested that he should nominate for the vacant position of shop steward at Baker's. Archie felt he was well-qualified for the shop steward position and was more than happy to nominate. The blue-collar workers at Baker's were unanimous in nominating Archie Bray as their representative.

The week after his appointment, he was strolling through the workshop with operators on the machines acknowledged him enthusiastically with cheers and thumbs up. 'Good onya, mate.'

A stilted voice from behind one of the conveyer belts rose above the clatter and calls from the workers. 'Archie ... got a minute, mate?'

Archie had been wary of Steve, the supervisor from day one. He didn't trust him, he asked too many questions, and he made him accountable. He sauntered over to the solidly built Steve. 'Aye, Stevie, son. What seems to be the problem?'

Steve glared. 'No great problem, mate, it's just that the steel press I asked you to order four weeks ago hasn't turned up. The girls are nagging me to death. The old one is on its last legs and getting harder to operate.' His eyes narrowed. 'I thought you said it was to be an immediate delivery, mate?'

Archie didn't flinch. 'Oh, aye, it was. In fact, I spoke to the supplier yesterday. He said the gear was still on the docks, waiting for the labour to come and move it. There was a bit of union bother doon there, ye know whit I mean? I'll gie him another wee phone awrigh, eh? Tell them to get aff their arse, eh?'

Steve answered with an expressionless, 'Okay, mate. Make it happen, it's very urgent.'

'Fuck's sake,' Archie muttered as he walked away. He had forgotten all about the order. Steve would be livid if he knew, maybe he would call the supplier and tell him that if he got the press here early next week, he would get preference when his supply contract was up for renewal next month. Aye, that's what he would do. That would shut that smart arse up for a while. He headed for the lockers.

'Allo, allo, me old son, fancy a pint then?' Sid called out to Archie as he passed him on the way to the social club in the basement.

Archie turned, grinning broadly. 'Aye, okay then, pal, I'll be there in five minutes.'

Mary was careful as she stepped down from the bus and crossed the unmade road onto the narrow footpath. This was her first interview in Australia, and she was nervous. The advertisement in the local paper was for a waitress in a small restaurant. It said that experience was preferred, but not essential; however, a strong work ethic was compulsory. She was worried that never having worked in a real restaurant it would be a disadvantage, but hoped she could convince them of her dedication and willingness to learn.

Dressing carefully that morning, she wore the smart green light wool coat that Sadie had bought her just before leaving Scotland. It was double-breasted with black buttons, wide lapels and slit pockets slightly fitted at the waist, showing off her slim figure. The Melbourne winter was colder than she had thought, and the coat was warm and comfortable. Adding black patent Cuban heel shoes, a small chiffon scarf around her neck and a black patent clutch bag gave Mary an air of elegant confidence. Her shoulder length dark blonde hair was brushed back neatly behind her ears, revealing a delicate profile.

Mary rarely wore makeup, only lipstick and a touch of blush, but today her eyebrows were shaped and touched up lightly with brown pencil, framing her bright eyes. She recalled all those years ago how they would make a very young Alice gaze in wonder. 'Mammy, why do you draw on your eyebrows?' she would ask.

'To show off my eyes, Alice. They're the windows to the soul,' she would tell her daughter. 'Always keep them bright.'

The restaurant was in a small group of shops slotted between a milk bar and a real estate agency. It was painted dark brown with a striped red and green awning over the door. The name 'Ronaldo's' was scrawled across the window in bright red script. Through the shopfront window, Mary could see tables and chairs set up with white tablecloths, wine glasses and stainless-steel cutlery. Each table had a little centrepiece of yellow and white artificial daises in small glass vases. She could just see the statue of David towering over a dry fountain in the small reception area at the entrance. The sign on the glass door said 'closed', but Mary pushed the door very gently anyway. She stepped inside as it opened.

It was dark, and she was instantly aware of a sweet smell, like melted toffee over tart apples. It seemed to come from somewhere down near the back. Lifting a small bell from the table, she rang once.

All was quiet, then came a shuffle. A door opened, allowing a slither of light revealing a man slowly emerging from the source of the toffee apple aroma. Mary thought he could have been in his late thirties; he was tall and thickset with a head of dense black hair heavily injected with strands of silver. He walked with a slight limp and puffed slightly as he came toward her with an outstretched hand and a broad smile.

'Hello, you must be Mary. I'm Vince. Sorry I wasn't here when you came in, I have only just finished with the plumber outside. Please sit down.'

He pointed to one of the newly laid tables. Mary sat down and crossed her legs at the ankles, being very careful not to put her handbag on the white cloth. Vince sat opposite her, pushing his chair back to accommodate a bloated girth. He looked up at her, smiling.

'Did you find us alright? We are just a bit off the beaten track here, but most people know where we are, word of mouth is a wonderful thing.'

Mary swallowed and shifted in her seat. 'Yes, it was easy, really it was, the bus driver knew exactly where you were. I think he must have been a customer.'

They both laughed.

Vince drew in a deep breath then tapped his pen on a blank notebook in front of him. 'Well Mary, before we discuss your application, I would like to give you some background on who we are. We are a small family business specialising in classic homemade Italian dishes. My brother Max and I hope to expand the business. We have longed to have our own restaurant ever since we were at high school.' He grinned almost apologetically. 'Our father passed away some years ago and our mother is elderly but still active. She likes to be involved, helping in the kitchen. Nothing too stressful, you understand. No heavy lifts or hard scrubs, mainly she tidies and stacks the shelves.'

The smile faded and his shoulders dropped. Looking down at the tablecloth, he shook his head. 'Until last week, Max's wife Selena worked in this room. She managed all the table service and attended to everything front of house. She was such an asset, the customers loved her. Now, after almost fifteen years of trying to have a baby, she found out that she is pregnant and resigned immediately. Don't get me wrong, Mary, we are all thrilled to be having a baby in the family and just delighted for them, but it's the worst time for us here at the restaurant to lose her. She was the face of our business. She knew all the regulars, and many came here just because of the way she looked after them. We have only recently established a regular clientele in this area, and I need an urgent replacement for Selena.'

Mary listened closely to Vince as he explained his predicament and detailed what was required in the position.

'We open four days for lunch Wednesday to Saturday, and we are hopeful of extending that to Friday and Saturday night dinner. We also cater for small functions; we have customers from a large company on the estate and have just secured our first private function. Selena's great news couldn't have come at a worse time for us.'

Vince then opened the folder with Mary's application. Turning the flimsy paper, he pointed to her references. 'Your past experience and recommendations from Glasgow are very impressive, however, working in a small restaurant serving a corporate clientele is not the same as a motorway transport café, filling the bellies of hungry truck drivers. If you were to be successful, I would need to be convinced that you could adjust to serving a different type of customer.'

Mary, engrossed by his story, had listened attentively. He had good eye contact and didn't stand on ceremony, and she could see that he was dedicated with a strong work ethic and real family values. Here was someone just like her with high standards, someone who sought from life only what hard work would bring. Mary wanted to work for Vince. She really wanted this job. She sat up straight on the wooden chair, uncrossed her ankles then looked directly into Vince's eyes.

'Yes, Mr Ronaldo, I know that both positions seem to be worlds apart, but in reality they're not. Ravenous transport drivers deserve the same good food, good service, and good manners as the corporate clientele that you serve here. The food they pay for, the courtesies and smiles are free. I am a hard worker and a fast learner. I am punctual, with an eye for detail, and I work well under pressure. I have no doubt I would be an asset to your business. My references, as you can see, speak highly of my loyalty and honesty. I only ask that you try me. I promise you, I can do this job and I guarantee you will not be disappointed.'

Mary leaned back, taking a deep breath, surprising herself at such a confident and opinionated outburst. She dropped her shoulders, relaxing with the knowledge that she had spoken clearly whilst masking her insecurities and inward turmoil. Her knees trembled slightly, but only for a moment. The air resounded in silence.

Vince had listened closely. Resting an elbow on the edge of the table and rubbing his knuckles under his chin, he looked up. 'Mary, I'll tell you what I'll do. I am very impressed with your integrity and work ethics. I don't have time for any more interviews, especially with a function on Saturday night. I'll start you on a three-month trial and see how we go, then take it from there. It will be four days a week. Wednesday until Saturday lunch from 11 am until 3 pm. In addition, we have private functions. We pay above award wages and share tips. This will be a permanent part-time position. You will have holiday pay, sick pay, work autonomously, and we expect 110 per cent effort. How do you feel about that?' Vince raising his eyebrows, looked at Mary.

Smiling nervously and talking too fast, she could barely hide her relief. 'Oh yes, Mr Ronaldo, that sounds just fine, I am very happy with that. When would you like me to start?'

'Tomorrow 11 am. Is that all right with you? There are only a few tables booked for lunch, but it would give you an idea of where everything is in readiness for the following night, which is a private party for eighty people. It's a golden wedding anniversary. They are the parents of a regular client here, and I promised the family we would make it very special. Most of the prep has been done, but we will need fully committed staff as it will be very busy. Do you think you can manage?'

A flicker of terror crossed Mary's eyes. Eighty people? And she couldn't even fold a cloth napkin. It would be a challenge. She had a sudden flash back to the transport cafe in Glasgow, when an army personnel truck loaded with hungry young soldiers unexpectedly charged through the door. Tony was at a meeting, Kathy had been sick that day, and the kitchen staff were part-timers. Mary had to take control. It was frantic, she went into overdrive and surprised even herself, feeding and satisfying them all. They left happy, no one complained.

'I certainly can, Mr Ronaldo.' Mary looked at him and beamed. 'I promise you that you won't be disappointed. I won't let you down.'

They walked together to the glass entrance door. Vince shook her hand again and laughed aloud. 'Welcome, Mary. Just one more thing … please, please, call me Vince.'

Mary smiled back. 'Right! Vince.'

Crossing the road, she walked quickly to the bus stop, humming to herself as she went. She would have to practice napkin folding tonight, Uncle Ralph's handkerchiefs would be perfect.

Uncle Ralph pulled off his heavy boots, leaving them on the doormat as he came in from the garden. He looked at the clock, it was almost 5.15 pm. He knew that Mary should be home soon from her interview. He had been thinking of her all afternoon, anxious to know how it all went. How lovely she looked when she left earlier in the day, he thought how proud his late sister would have been. Not so with Archie, her daughter's choice of husband.

In the many months that they lived together, Uncle Ralph had tried very hard to get along and be friends with Archie. He secured him the job at Baker's and advised him on all manner of things, including insurances, banks, real estate, and community-minded clubs.

There were many times when Uncle Ralph tried to engage him in conversation, but Archie would get side tracked, go to the toilet or head out to buy the paper. More than anything else, Uncle Ralph felt let down. Archie was the most ungrateful man he had ever met. Had it not been for Mary and the boys, he would have put him out of the house long ago.

The back flywire door flew open and banged against the outside wall. The loud banter of his two great-nephews filled the kitchen. Uncle Ralph lit the gas under the kettle.

'Scot, you promised to take me with you,' Billy wailed. 'You said if I went to the milk bar for you yesterday that you would take me to the concert! Come on, Scot, that's just not fair.'

Scot looked sympathetically at his younger brother, shaking his head, half-smiling. 'Sorry, Billy. I only have two tickets and I forgot that I'd asked Carol last week. I promise you I'll take you to the next one, okay?'

'No, it's not okay.' Billy tossed his schoolbag onto the floor in a tantrum.

The Vinyls, an English pop group, were having a performance in Melbourne the following week. It was the talk of the school. Billy had told them that his brother was taking him to the concert. He was the envy of the whole class. Billy was a loner, he was still having trouble settling in at this new school, struggling to make friends, preferring the company of his older brother to that of his schoolmates who made fun of his accent, despite the fact it was starting to fade the longer they were in Australia. He missed Scotland and his friends from the street, and he missed football. Very few boys in Australia played the game. They called it soccer. Aussie Rules was the Australian code, and it was altogether different, he didn't even want to try it. This concert was going to give him status in his class, as no one else had been able to get tickets. What would he say at school now? They would laugh, and say that he had been making it all up that he was a pathetic liar. He stormed out of the room and headed for the sleep out, banging the door behind him. Scot shrugged his shoulders then turned to his uncle unperturbed.

'Hi, Uncle Ralph. How was your day?'

Uncle Ralph nodded; Scot certainly was such a relaxed boy. Nothing seemed to upset him. He had a beautiful nature, just like his mother. He smiled at his nephew. 'I've been pretty busy, lad. I cleared down the back, then turned the compost heap ready for the vegie planting. Your mam should be ome any minute. I'll wash up and peel the potatoes. Would you lay the table, son?'

'Sure thing, Uncle Ralph.'

The nights were getting colder, summer was long gone, and autumn was fading. Uncle Ralph pulled up his jacket zip and called out to a silent Billy.

'Come on now, Billy lad. Don't be sulky, tea's nearly ready.'

Billy didn't look up as he came to the table, sitting down quietly on a chair. The boys chatted awkwardly whilst Billy pulled out pencils and project material from his schoolbag and began to write.

Mary's heels clicked loudly on the stone step. She called out, 'Halloo ... I'm home!'

The flywire door slowly creaked then flew open. Her face was flushed, her eyes shone, and she smiled broadly.

Uncle Ralph dried his hands on a tea towel, and frowned slightly, looking to his adored niece.

'Mary, lass, ow was it? Ow did ye get on?'

The boys looked up expectantly. 'C'mon, Mum, how did it go?'

Mary, hardly able to contain her excitement a minute longer, dropped her bag to the floor and threw her arms into the air. 'I got it! I got the job. I start tomorrow.'

Scot jumped up and gave his mum a hug. Billy banged his hand on the table. Uncle Ralph just grinned from ear to ear. 'I knew you would, lass. I just knew it.'

The table was laid, the room was warm, and the boys were immersed in homework. Uncle Ralph stood at the stove with his apron on. Mary embraced the whole scene.

Chatter in the kitchen that night was animated and loud. Everyone was giving advice and support on how to tackle the intricacies of folding a cloth napkin.

As Mary's fingers struggled to fold a large handkerchief, she stopped suddenly, looked around the table and grabbed at her open mouth in horror. She looked at Scot sheepishly.

'Oh Scotty, I am so sorry, I forgot to tell you. I bumped into Carol's mum at the bus stop earlier. She asked me to tell you that she was sorry that Carol was not able to go to the Vinyls concert. She has an extra class at night school that night, and she said to say she hoped you could get rid of the ticket.'

Billy jumped up from his chair and punched at the air. 'Whoa, yes! Yes! Yes!'

Mary looked at Uncle Ralph. 'What was that all about?'

'Don't ask, lass.' He laughed as the boys fell into a friendly wrestle on the carpet. 'Just don't ask.'

Later, when they were clearing the table and chatting, no one mentioned the untouched table setting or the vacant chair. Archie's absence was always a relief for Mary, it meant less tension and less arguments.

Mary began clearing the table, humming as she went. Life was gradually morphing into the Australian way for her and her boys, whilst Archie continued his rants and complaints, comparisons and vulgar language.

She realised that her uncle was getting very weary of Archie, and of the living arrangements. The old man never complained, but she watched as he walked around the house slowly, his ageing body now more bent than when they had arrived. The shelves on the dresser were crowded with pictures of his late wife Gwen, and of the glory days when he was a jockey. He dusted them religiously, picking each one up and caressing it with a soft cloth. Mary knew he was enveloped in a time when it was just the two of them.

She was grateful for his patience, and for sharing his house of four very different personalities. Mary knew it was time now for them to move on. Time to pursue their own part of Australia. Getting a job meant that she would earn a wage, she would gain more independence, her dream was progressing. While stacking the dishes she closed her eyes and smiled, whispering reverently to herself, 'A home of our own.'

The hot water burst from the tap and the liquid soap melted the gravy streams from the dinner plates, and she began to sing softly.

She washed. Uncle Ralph wiped. No one spoke.

Chapter 21

On her first day at Ronaldo's, Mary arrived early. She had dressed carefully, making sure there were no creases in her crisp white shirt and that her black pleated skirt had been pressed to perfection with a damp cloth and a hot iron. She had hung it outside on the clothesline that morning to make sure that there was no smoke odour from Archie's late-night cigarettes.

Vince greeted her warmly. 'Good morning, Mary. Come through and meet Max and my mother.'

Max shook Mary's hand and smiled. 'Welcome, Mary, very happy to meet you.'

His mother reached out excitedly, kissing her on both cheeks and speaking rapidly in Italian.

Mary blushed, nodded, and smiled. 'Thank you.'

Vince walked Mary through the restaurant showing her where everything was neatly stored. The tables had to be set up for the afternoon diners and Vince explained that he was very particular in the positioning of the tables. He didn't want diners to be too close and invasive of the next table. He also insisted that the white starched tablecloths must be perfectly laid, ensuring that all corners were folded and the same length.

Mary nodded positively. 'Yes, yes.'

When Vince retreated to the kitchen, Mary quickly went to the bathroom to wash her hands thoroughly and began laying the tables, making sure she followed Vince's explicit instructions. She wiped down all the chairs with a damp cloth and polished the glasses.

That afternoon, there was one table of eight and four tables of two already booked. Vince said they often got 'walk ins', especially towards the end of the week.

As the patrons arrived, Mary greeted them and chatted warmly. The large table was a birthday celebration for a regular customer; she was a local businesswoman accompanied by a host of female friends. There was lots of loud laughter and screams of delight. The orders were taken swiftly, the meals served hot and collectively. Bottles of Spumante were emptying at high speed, escalating the noise level further. A beaming young woman walked out from the kitchen, majestically carrying a large birthday cake covered in candles. The guest of honour screamed in disbelief, and though looking awkward and flushed, she appeared to be enjoying every minute whilst attempting to blow out the candles. Mary swiftly provided small tea plates, forks, and serviettes for everyone to enjoy a slice of cake.

As the celebrations wound down, the guests gradually left, all of them singing the praises of the restaurant, of the food and of the service.

The birthday girl threw her arms around Mary and sang very much out of tune, 'Thank you, Mary, pretty, Mary. Thank you for my lovely birthday.'

It was well after three o'clock when Mary called out her goodbyes to the kitchen, put on her jacket, and walked quickly to the bus stop. Clouds of dust in the distance heralded the impending arrival of the bus, as it pulled in slowly on the side of the road.

Uncle Ralph was in his lounge eagerly awaiting to hear all about Mary's first day. A pot of tea, covered in a woollen tea cosy, and a poppy seed cake were on the table. The boys were not home and Archie had taken a day off work. He was snoring loudly in the next room.

Mary called out from the door, 'Halloo! First day over!'

Uncle Ralph looked up, bright eyed and expectant. 'Oh, Mary, luv, ow was it, lass? I've been thinkin about ye all day. I've made yer a pot o tea.'

'Oh, Uncle Ralph, just what I need, thank you.'

Standing on one leg and removing first one shoe, then the other, she slumped down on a chair. 'It was a really good day. I really like Vince and his family, and I think they were happy with me, but I am feeling a bit weary now. My feet are killing me. Can we sit in your room over by the window, please?' Mary made an exaggerated pout and laughed.

Uncle Ralph leaned over and lifted the tray. 'Aye, lass, we certainly can!'

The following day, Vince closed the restaurant in preparation for the function that evening, which was a three-course dinner for eighty guests to celebrate a family golden wedding anniversary. Profits from the night would help the planning of an extension at the rear of the building, something that Vince and his family had talked about endlessly. The prospect of further bookings from this group was high. They were all very socially connected, they expected good food, comfort, value for money and top service.

His thoughts turned to Mary. She had handled her first day with finesse and professionalism. She had coped well, very well, in fact. She had initiative and drive, was calm, approachable, and very friendly; however, he was concerned how she would handle tonight's function. There would be a lot of pressure, both back and front of house. He had concerns. Could she manage it? As he looked up, she came into the room.

'There you are, Mary. Did you recover from last night?'

Mary laughed. 'I think so, Vince, not sure about my feet though. I've brought another pair of shoes to wear for set up, keeping the low heels for table service. I should have thought of that yesterday.'

Hanging up her coat and bag in the cupboard, she put on an apron and began polishing the glasses.

The phone rang, Vince answered it quickly. There was a long silence after hello. He sat down slowly, pushing his hair back and rubbing his forehead. His voice was stilted, as he struggled to stay calm. 'Well, then … is she alright? What? How long? Oh God, I am so sorry! What can I do? Are you sure? He looked at Mary and shook his head, then threw his hand up into the air. 'No, no! We will be fine really; please don't worry. Just do what you have to do. Yes … yes … alright, bye.'

Vince sank into a chair and started wailing like a wounded animal. His big hands spread-eagled over his brow, shielding his face, and mumbling in Italian. He looked at Mary, raised his eyes upward and dragged a shaking hand through his hair.

'It's Selena, she's in premature labour, she could lose the baby. Max is out of his mind with worry and so is Mother. They are both at the hospital. Selena is in emergency; it's touch and go.' Vince looked down, wailing again. 'God, I am so sorry for Selena, really, I am, and I know Max and my mother want to be with her, I understand all of that, but please, I ask you, what am I going to do with eighty people coming here to my restaurant in under eight hours, all expecting good food and first-class service? What can I do with no staff? Can you please tell me that? I am finished, Mary, I am finished!' Vince's eyes welled up, looking to the ceiling, begging for an answer.

Mary stood by silently, waiting until his rants finished. Sitting down quietly next to him, she took both his hands in hers forcing him to look at her.

'Vince, Vince! Look at me. We *will* manage, we have to. We don't have a choice.' Her voice was strong as she spoke to her new boss gently but firmly. 'Tears and curses won't change the situation and we can't cancel at this late hour; it has to happen. We need a plan to work with what we have, and to do it quickly. Do you agree?'

Vince did not look at her, his eyes had glazed over.

'Vince! Vince, please. Do you agree? Will you help me? I know we can do this. It's a private function and a set menu so that's good. When I spoke with Max yesterday, he told me he had already done most of the preparation and—' Mary stopped mid-sentence, pulling Vince's head up to face her. 'Vince, please look at me. We are not finished. All is not lost. We will do this together, and we will do it as a team. I can run the kitchen with a little support. Can you ask Helen from the petrol station across the road if her daughter can come in and help me? Tell her it's mainly washing dishes and plating up. You did mention that she has worked in a café before, is that right?'

Vince nodded.

'Good! I'll call my son Scot at work right now. He can explain the situation to his boss, and I am sure he will be able to get here straight away. He can help with the prep, and then work front of house with you.'

Vince bent over, his head in his hands moaning and espousing Italian expletives.

'Vince, are you listening to me? Do you have any other ideas? If you have, now is the time to tell me. Come on, pull yourself together, we can do this.'

Vince raised his head and looked at her. 'No Mary, I have no other ideas. I am gutted really. It's all in your hands now.'

'Good! Now go and wash your face and bring in that sack of potatoes from the shed.' Mary went straight to the fridge to check on the plastic tubs of minestrone soup that Sofia had made the previous day. That would be easy to just heat and serve, and osso bucco was the main course. There was masses of it in varying sizes of pots and containers marinating in a savoury sauce in the second fridge. The vegetables would take more time. Potatoes in tin foil would replace the fancy potato gratin that Max had planned, but he hadn't started it. Tinned baby carrots and frozen peas could be dressed up nicely with just a sprinkle of fresh garden mint, growing wild at the back fence.

Sofia had only managed to make half of the cakes needed for dessert, but Mary was not fazed. She would get ice cream from the corner milk bar and open some of the large tins of fruit salad stored in a back cupboard.

Vince was getting more and more agitated. He didn't interfere, only watched from the shadows as her hands and head moved in different directions at a rapid pace. Like a laser beam she flashed in and out of fridges, cupboards, and shelves; called out orders, sorted pans, plates, cutlery, and improvising when necessary.

Scot arrived in record time. His boss had whisked him home to change into a white shirt and black pants before dropping him at the restaurant. Vince met him with a much-loved bow tie.

Mary, her cheeks shining with perspiration, caught sight of him. Rushing over, she wrapped her arms around him. 'Oh Scotty, thank you so much for this. You're a lifesaver, really. Vince will give you a quick run through and a five-minute lesson on laying down and taking away. You will be great, I know it. Just be the charmer that you are.'

'That's alright, Mum, you can flatter me all you want, but you still owe me big time.'

She stood on tiptoe and kissed his cheek. 'I always pay my debts, son.'

It was almost 7 o'clock. The restaurant was now completely transformed and ready for its first guest. The overhead lights were turned down low, allowing low lamps to beam circles of radiance onto the high gloss side tables. Simple polished glassware and rattan tablemats set an elegant tone on the tables. White serviettes, folded and slightly pleated, were placed alongside the dinner forks. Tea light candles in small clear glass cups had a makeover.

Mary had raced to a nearby small goods factory supplier and begged for a can of quick drying gold paint and some packets of tiny gold hearts and glitter. She sprayed the glass cups gold, adding a sprinkling of hearts to the wet paint. At the back fence of the restaurant, a large clump of ivy had escaped from the overgrown vacant block. She curled a piece of this around the base of each cup before placing them in the centre of every table. The gold glitter was scattered lightly and randomly onto the tablecloths.

Before the first guests arrived, Vince walked into the room and sat down at one of the tables shaking his head. 'Mary, what have you done? This is magical!'

Mary nodded and smiled. 'It's imagination, boss ... only imagination.'

By 7.30 pm, everyone had arrived. Meeting and greeting friends and family in the reception area took some time, time that was a godsend for Mary and her staff. Helen's daughter Anne had jumped at the chance to earn some pocket money and had been diligently concentrating on the job at hand. Mary and Anne plated up the soup served to the tables with sticks of French bread cut in uniformed slices stacked high in chequered-lined wicker table baskets. Everyone was in a jovial mood, enjoying the company of friends and relatives they had not seen in years. No one noticed the nerves, improvisations, and lengthy delays from the staff. Compliments for Sofia's soup radiated from every table.

Mary had cooked the main course to perfection. Colour and presentation were high on her priority list. The veal on the osso bucco was parting from the bone slowly on every plate, juices from the meat enhancing the rich brown gravy. Complimenting this was the brilliant bright green of young peas and vibrant orange of freshly dug carrots. Silver foil on the split potatoes encased a bed of soft flesh bathed in thick sour cream, delicately veiled with finely chopped mint. It was a kaleidoscope of colour. Mary checked every plate as it left the kitchen, making sure that no sauce drips or misplaced content marred her masterpieces.

The serving of the desserts and coffee went smoothly. The fine Italian wines that Vince had bought in for the occasion were subjected to much discussion and comparisons of regional Italian vineyards. Talk and laughter filled every corner; it was warm and comforting.

It was time for the speeches. The guests of honour, seated in the middle of the longest table at the back of the room, sat quietly. They listened and smiled shyly as friends and relatives stood up to praise and congratulate them on their long and happy marriage.

A large wooden-framed sepia wedding photograph placed on a side table in the corner of the room showed a slender girl unsmiling, with large, dark scared eyes, wearing a calf-length cream satin gown, white stockings, and white buckled heeled shoes. A profusion of translucent veil, secured by two large net rosettes above each ear, billowed around her. One arm struggled to balance a massive flowing bouquet of roses and fern. She rested her other arm stiffly on a young man in a close-fitting serge suit with a high-buttoned waistcoat, bearing a long silver chain fastened to both side pockets. A white bow tie rested beneath a stiffly starched collar. He carried white gloves, and was also unsmiling. The photograph was crystal clear, in perfect condition. Over the years it had been protected, having pride of place in their home. It was only right that today, fifty years later, it should be part of the celebrations.

The couple hesitated; both looking uncomfortable and self-conscious. They stood up, he put his arm protectively around her, as would a mother to her child. She lay her head on his stooped shoulder. His voice cracked with emotion.

'Thank you for coming here tonight. My Maria, she is a so shy and cannot talk, so I am agoona talk for us. Her and me that is, isa okay with you?'

Everyone laughed, cheering him on.

'You forgive my English, okay? My Maria hasa brought me so much happiness from when we gotta married in Napoli. I want to say grazie for our two beautiful girls and two beautiful boys; they have make us a very happy Nonno, and Noona, with their little bambinos. I am also saying a biga grazie for her, for her patience for all ofa these years, and for her special pasta ... I think I love-a the pasta as much as I love-a her.'

This brought great hilarity, many tears and resounding applause. The old woman lifted her glasses and dabbed at the corners of her eyes. The man put both arms around her and they cried together.

Mary stood back out of sight against the wall. Her eyes stinging at the love and emotion she had just witnessed, knowing this would never happen to her. She could never be free of her loveless marriage. Archie had been a mistake from the start. It was an impossible life commitment and she was trapped by guilt and regret, pining for her lost love Charlie, a love so strong and alive, deep within her. Closing her eyes, his eternally youthful face was before her.

It was a bombsite, a casualty of the London Blitz. They were sitting on a patch of green grass raised up from the mass of rubble that had survived the blast. Charlie had taken off his jacket and laid it down for them to sit on. He put his arm around her shoulder and whispered in her ear, 'Mary, I have a surprise!'

He opened up a brown paper carrier bag and carefully produced two pickled eggs, two spam sandwiches and two toffee apples.

Mary threw her head back and laughed. 'Oh, Charlie, how wonderful, but you must have used up all your coupons. How did you manage to get toffee apples?'

'I have been saving coupons for weeks. I had to eat bully beef and biscuits for months, then promise a sax lesson for the sergeant in the quartermaster's store to get the apples.'

They both laughed and hugged each other.

Eating heartily, they consumed the eggs and sandwiches in between discussions of the war, and the tragic loss of lives. They talked about a world without war, without pain and without struggle. They saw pictures in their minds of sunshine drenched gardens with white picket fences, of food in abundance, and of music ... lots of music.

Charlie stopped talking as Mary continued with her verbal dreams, then she too stopped. Charlie had taken hold of both her hands, clenching his fingers around hers. She lifted her head and looked into his eyes. He didn't blink, looking deep into her very soul.

'Mary. Oh! Mary, I want all of those things we have dreamed of, I want them all for both of us, I want to take care of you always. Mary, my lovely, Mary … I want you to be my wife. I want you to marry me. Will you, Mary? Will you marry me?'

Charlie unclenched his hand stretching it out. In the middle of his palm lay a small gold band with two little hearts entwined around a tiny blue stone. With a sharp breath and moist eyes, she nodded. Charlie picked it up threading it gently on to her finger.

'For always, Mary.'

'For always, Charlie.'

After the speeches, claps and cheers echoed around the room, Mary looked away, rummaging in her apron pocket for a handkerchief.

She could have had speeches on her wedding anniversary.

She could have had a photograph on a side table for all to see.

She knew she could have had all of that … all of it, with her Charlie.

With a smile she congratulated the couple, then retreated to the kitchen and wept.

Chapter 22

It was 1966. The Bray family had been in Australia for almost a year. It had been a time of change, making new friends, discovering a new way of life, a life of sunshine and plenty. Mary had embraced everything in their new homeland. She had blossomed. Her pale skin, now tinted lightly by the sun, had a healthy glow. Much to the delight of her family, she had been taking cooking classes. She had no shortage of willing tasters.

Scot was thriving, relishing in the challenges of his apprenticeship, always keen to learn of advances in the plumbing trade and showing a real knack for communication with customers. Outside of work, most of his time was spent with his girlfriend Carol.

Billy had taken longer to settle into this lifestyle. He didn't have the social skills of the brother he worshipped, but was slowly integrating into his new school. The boys were starting to lose the sharp edges of their Glasgow accents. The more time passed, the more they were sounding Australian.

Archie, however, was very unhappy in Australia. He knew that life in this new country was the only way to escape his past, and his tormentors. He struggled to let go of old ways and traditions. Mary knew that taking him away from Glasgow would be difficult. She didn't count on him being this difficult.

In his workplace, Archie had managed to make many enemies, mainly those in authority. He was forever testing the patience of his boss, having the unfortunate skill of being disruptive and argumentative. To the workers he was a hero, but none of this escaped the ears of Uncle Ralph. He still had many friends who worked at Baker's telling him of the comings and goings of the arrogant Scot. They said they didn't like the man.

In February of that year, Australian currency had changed from pounds sterling to dollars and cents. Uncle Ralph found this new currency confusing and hard to grasp.

The boys were a great help, constantly singing the advertising jingle, doing little sums on the kitchen table, and taking him to the milk bar on the corner to buy the newspaper, milk, and bread, all with the new currency. He slowly adjusted.

It was mid-morning in late autumn. Mary had just finished sweeping the front porch. She came in and sat down at the kitchen table holding the mail, calling out to Uncle Ralph.

'Two for you Uncle Ralph.' She put them to one side, flipping through the rest. There was a card for Scot emblazoned with hearts (no doubt from Carol), two for Archie from his worker's union, a letter addressed to them both from the bank and the last one was from Alice. She opened it straight away. Uncle Ralph came in from the garden, washed his hands and sat down beside her.

'Oh, Uncle Ralph, Alice has finally gone for her medical to immigrate. She has actually done it! That must mean she is serious doesn't it? I mean, she will be accepted won't she? I mean going for her medical ... won't she?'

Uncle Ralph nodded and grinned back. 'Well, lass, if she is ealthy and all, and is sponsored, it's definitely looking that way, but don't get your opes up yet, lass. Let's just wait till the results come through, eh?'

Mary wasn't listening; she was too elated and continued reading. 'She sounds so happy, saying she is going away with Rena for a few days next month now that Rena has passed her driving test and got her licence. They are going to listen to a band in Edinburgh.' Mary turned the pages and continued on reading quickly, her voice high pitched and excited. 'Oh, Uncle Ralph, listen. She says she wants to get her driver's license when she comes to Australia, she really does sound like she's over Robbie and wants to be with family again! It's just the best news ever! I am so, so happy, Uncle Ralph. I know I can get her work in the restaurant for a while until she settles. She doesn't want to work in hospitality for a career though, she told me that, her heart is with children and childcare. She has such a natural rapport with them.' She smiled. 'You know, Uncle Ralph, when Billy was little and I had to work, Alice, who was still a child herself, did so much in the raising of her brother. I still feel guilty about those times. Billy was so close to her, but she never complained. If there was any comfort for me at all, it was that I had no choice.'

Mary read the letter, wiped a tear, then folded it and neatly put it back into the envelope. She would read it again later when she was alone. Lifting the loosely gummed flap on the envelope from the bank, she read the letter. It was addressed to both herself and Archie.

Dear Mr and Mrs Bray,
Thank you for your enquiry regarding a housing loan, our apologies
for this late response. We would be delighted to discuss further
with you the possibility of support with finance from this bank

for your proposed plan of building a home. We are a community minded bank, and welcome enquiries from new Australians such as yourself. Please contact our office as soon as convenient to set up an appointment.

Yours truly,

J. Rowntree

Manager

Mary read it again. She had written to the bank weeks ago making an initial enquiry. Not hearing anything for a while, she thought this was because their savings were not vast. Thanks to the kindness of Uncle Ralph allowing them to stay rent-free, they had managed to save enough for what they hoped would be a deposit. Uncle Ralph told Mary quietly that he would go guarantor for them if it would help get their own place.

She had seen an advertisement in the local paper for house and land packages. The estate was a long way from Uncle Ralph's house, but closer to Archie's work and she could easily catch a bus to her job at the restaurant. The land was cheap as there were not many facilities in place. New immigrants were encouraged to apply.

Mary began to dream. Could this be it? Could this be possible? Could they afford it after such a short time in Australia?

That night she sat down with Archie at the kitchen table to discuss the budget. Although she was the driving force and desperately wanted this, she was having second thoughts. She was concerned about the repayments. As much as she loathed Archie and his habits, she admitted that he had a good head for figures and could talk the talk with the bank. He would be able to convince the manager that they could afford the repayments on the land and house.

'Och! It's a piece a cake,' he said confidently

Later that night, after a few beers, Archie was his aggressive self. Mary knew there would have to be a second mortgage, stamp duty, solicitors, conveyancing and more. She rubbed her forehead. 'I think we are over-committing, Archie.'

'Jesus Christ, Mary, don't be so fuckin negative. You were the wan that wanted this, I've already told ye we can easily do it. With the overtime at work, yer extra days and Scot paying more board, it's no a problem.'

Mary looked at him with disgust. In between drags of nicotine and drinking from a longneck beer bottle, he was scribbling with a stubby pencil.

She spoke calmly. 'Archie, I want this so much, but I think it is a bit soon. Maybe we should wait a bit longer until we get more of a deposit together. I'm sure Uncle Ralph won't mind us staying on for another year.'

Archie stood up and banged his fist on the table. 'Well, I mind. We are no stayin here. Silly old git canny even be civil to me.'

Mary realised as soon as she said it that another year would be a terrible strain on her uncle. The old man was almost at the end of his tether. He had been a blessing since their arrival, but even angels have their limits. 'All right, Archie,' she said. 'All right.'

Two weeks later they were on a train to the city. The station was busy, people were everywhere. Mary rarely went to the city, but when she did, she made a special effort with her dress. She wore a smart navy suit with matching shoes, a white bag and gloves Archie, straight from work, was wearing grubby grey overalls and heavy boots. After walking three blocks they arrived at the impressive glass facade of the bank. An express lift whisked them up to the 21st floor where a well-groomed, sharp-suited young man greeted them at the door.

'Mr and Mrs Bray, I presume. Welcome to our city office. Please come this way.'

They followed him down a passageway, stopping at a large oak panelled door, knocking quickly and then ushering them in.

Mr Rowntree was short and red-faced, and a wispy grey border fringed his shining bald head. His suit jacket buttoned in the middle, straining over a swollen girth, and a shirt collar tortured his bulbous neck. A brown-checked faintly stained tie had comically slipped slightly around his neck. He was perspiring and puffing as he stood up, directing them to the straight-backed chairs facing his desk. 'Please sit down. Excuse the mess, I just don't know where the day has gone. How was the train trip?' He didn't raise his eyes. 'Can we get started?'

Mary and Archie quickly outlined their finances, explaining to him that they were very reliable, hardworking, and honest new Australians, very keen to be homeowners and contribute to the growth of this wonderful young country.

Archie leaned forward and pushed out his chest whilst taming his course vocabulary. 'Eh, Mr Rowntree, don't take too much notice of the wages figures and pay slips there, I have more slips in ma locker at work that would help, and I will get extra overtime so the repayments are not a problem at all. Mary works as well. She makes good money and gets loads of tips.'

Mr Rowntree interrupted, abruptly tapping his fingers on his desk. 'Mr Bray, under no circumstances can we consider your wife's wages. She may get pregnant or sick at any time and that would be loss of an income. You do not appear to have a decent savings record with the bank. We would have to be convinced that you could manage the weekly repayments.'

Mary sat stoically in her chair, feeling completely ostracised. She disliked this man. He was not in the least interested in their plans to build a new life. He seemed to be preoccupied and in a hurry to leave their meeting. He certainly was not interested in what she had to say. Archie was the object of his entire conversation. She was greatly offended and felt she may as well have been in the toilet. Her husband was unperturbed and smiling.

'Don't worry about that, Mr Rowntree. Mary cannot have any more weans and she is the healthiest person I know.'

Mary stifled a cough in response, looking at her husband expressionless.

Mr. Rowntree was now perspiring and scowling. He stood up, sorting papers into piles on his desk, at the same time nodding to Archie. 'Well, I'll have a look at it. I understand that you want to settle in Australia with your family, but we do have guidelines to follow. I am sure you understand, so again, Mr Bray, I am sorry, but I do have to leave.'

He moved from behind his desk, puffing and tapping his foot, whilst waiting until Mary had picked up her handbag and Archie had tied his bootlace, and then, with no eye contact, he led them out to the lifts.

'Well goodbye, Mr and Mrs Bray. Thank you for coming in, we'll get back to you within two weeks.'

Mary turned to respond as his back rapidly disappeared through the glass doors.

Archie walked confidently into the empty lift, followed by Mary. He was smiling, hands deep in his overall pockets humming an indefinable tune.

Clinging to her bag, Mary looked down, she stepped out of the lift, and walked quickly along the city pavement. The bare heads and blank faces of the mannequins in the high-end shops of Collins Street in the city gazed out vacantly as they passed.

Archie, strutting along the pavement behind her, lit a cigarette and inhaled deeply, cocking his head slightly as he grinned broadly.

'I think that went quiet well, eh? I think he was very impressed wi me, do you no?'

Chapter 23

Alice slowly folded the letter neatly back into the envelope before placing it in the top drawer of her dressing table. It was from Australia House saying that she had passed the medical examination for eligibility to immigrate to Australia. Within the next two weeks, she would have her departure date.

That time had finally arrived. Now she would be saying goodbye to the only country she had ever known, leaving behind friendships that had become family. Alice sorely missed her own family, especially her mother, but it was time for her to embrace a new life and a new land. She looked out the window at the neighbourhood below. It was a dull, grey day. The rain had ceased and left the rooftops buffed. Chimney pots were leaking thin ribbons of smoke, snaking slowly up to the sky then quickly vanishing.

Alice had relished her two years with Rena and her family. During that time, she had managed to get Robbie out of her life. The handsome leather-clad bike rider she had fallen in love with had turned nasty. His dark jealously scared her, so she ended the relationship. The time away from her mother had made Alice realise just how much she meant to her, she had come to recognise her strengths and determination. She had always thought of her mother as downtrodden and sad, and only now could she appreciate what stamina and planning it had taken to uproot her family from the only home they had ever known and move to an unfamiliar life on other side of the world. Knowing how much her mother had embraced Australia made Alice determined to be part of her mother's dreams.

Over the years, she had experienced fleeting thoughts of her biological father. Why had he deserted her, and why was she resenting someone she had never known? Whenever she asked her mother about him, her head would shake slowly, she would say it was the happiest and saddest time of her life. Every now and then, when all was quiet, Alice would catch her mother looking intently into her eyes, or lovingly reach out to touch the ends of her hair. It was then she knew that her mother was with her father.

In the kitchen downstairs, Rena was getting impatient, calling loudly, 'Come on, Alice! Come on, hurry up, hurry up! I don't want to catch all that peak hour traffic on the motorway. I'm going out to the car. I'll see you there.'

Alice quickly slipped on her shoes, grabbed her jacket, and stumbled downstairs while checking her bag for her lipstick and comb. 'I'm coming! I'm coming, sorry.'

She slid into the passenger seat of Rena's new sports car. It was pillar-box red with shiny chrome trim and a soft black roof that slid back in warm weather.

Rena was petite and pretty with long, straight black hair and the biggest bluest eyes peering out from under a thick dark fringe. She wore tight jeans, a big jumper, and high-heeled boots. Her part-time work at a children's nursery helped to pay off her car while she studied at college to be a primary school teacher.

Alice looked over at her friend, who was touching up her lipstick in the rear vision mirror. She desperately wanted to tell her about the medical results and her imminent departure for Australia, but not now, it would cast a shadow over their night. She would wait until tomorrow. Right now, they were relaxed and carefree, later they would be laughing and singing with the band.

'Midnight Mayhem' was the only reason they were going to Edinburgh. They were a great London rock 'n' roll group with a massive following. Alice had all their records. She leaned forward, whispering secretively to Rena, 'If we get up to the front of the stage, Rena, that wee bass player you fancy will blow a fuse when he sees ye, ye look fantastic.'

They both whooped and laughed.

Rena slowly edged her car away from the pavement. The rain had held off all day, but now it was slowly rolling in through the distant dark clouds. She switched on the wipers as the tiny drops and rivulets quickly came into view, then disappeared. As the tenements and narrow streets of Glasgow slowly slid away behind them, the road ahead became clear and the countryside opened up like rejuvenated flowers. Rena, with a rush of adrenalin, pressed down on the accelerator and smiled. It was going to be a great night.

The music was exploding from all four speakers in the car. Together they sang every lyric along with the band.

As they raced around the bends on the narrow road, Rena called out to Alice, 'Can you light me a cigarette? The packet is in my bag with the matches.'

Alice took a cigarette from the packet, lit it, then inhaled slowly. Roy Orbison came on the radio, he was singing *Blue Bayou.*

Rena called out excitedly, 'Oh, I love this song, Alice. Turn it up, turn it up.'

Alice quickly reached forward with one hand, searching for the volume control on the dashboard. She laughed, calling out, 'Alright! Alright!'

At the same time, with the other hand, she blindly passed the lit cigarette to her friend. Their hands collided. Rena's outstretched hand took the full force of the red-hot cigarette as it landed in her palm. She screamed in pain. Her eyes left the road, her grip on the steering wheel slipped, she lost control, her body arched forward. There was a bus stop up ahead.

The wipers came to an abrupt halt as the rain's fury battered against the cracked windscreen. The music had stopped.

The amber and red road lights were blinking continuously through the steady light rain, the sirens were silent. Two police cars had parked at an angle, trying to protect the little red sports car from prying eyes. Both headlights wrapped around the pole. A two-way radio crackled with toneless voices relaying messages and giving direction. Many cars had slowed to a crawl to watch the gruesome scene.

The seasoned ambulance officer wearily wiped his face, slammed the vehicle's door, and turned the massive lever. 'Another one,' he said to his partner, 'and another one too many.' For a few seconds he stood with his back to the door and closed his eyes. He turned to the young police officer standing beside him. 'She was a young lassie, not a scratch on her. God help us all, this is gonna be a sad night for some family, so it will.'

The young rookie police officer stood there with rain dripping slowly from his new police cap. He shuffled his feet uncomfortably. With an ashen face, he looked at the older man. 'Many injuries, Bobby?' he asked hesitantly. 'I didnae see much blood.'

The ambulance officer didn't answer right away. He walked quickly to the front of the ambulance, jumped into the driver's seat, and turned on the siren.

The young policeman had sidled up to the open driver's window of the ambulance, his face intermittently lit by the police car's hazard lights.

Above the noise and the flurry of drizzling rain, the ambulance officer called out, 'Not visibly, son, but just the same ... only one will make it.'

Chapter 24

Mary sat at the kitchen table; it was late. She was going over the figures that Archie had worked out for their budget. On paper, it looked like they could manage the mortgage, but it would be very tight. There would have to be sacrifices.

It had been nearly six weeks since the meeting with Mr Rowntree, and still no approval of their loan. Archie was confident, he kept telling her that it was 'in the bag', that he had connected 'man to man'. Mary ignored him.

They had been looking for weeks at homes they could afford, deciding on the cheapest, most basic home there was. Mary had walked through the rooms trance-like. Three bedrooms would mean the larger one for her and Archie, a shared room for the boys and a smaller room for Alice at the back of the house with a view to the back garden. She would love it. The kitchen extended out to a dining room; it was larger than the whole of the single room that four of them had endured in Rooken Road all those years ago. Glass sliding doors from the kitchen opened out to the back garden. The living room was wide with a large window on one wall looking out to the street. There was a gas heater resting below the wooden mantelpiece on a tiled hearth. The bathroom had a blue bath and wash hand basin. The toilet was next door in a small separate room. Mary had cringed when Archie said to the salesman that this was the best thing about the house. Now he could lock the door and sit down undisturbed to read the racing form whilst having a smoke.

The clock on the dresser chimed softly it was 11.30 pm. The boys had gone to bed long ago. Mary gathered the documents together, placing them neatly back into a thin brown cardboard concertina file. Archie got up from his chair, yawned, pulled down on his braces as they slapped onto his bare chest, like dead fish hitting a steel sink. He stubbed out a cigarette, leaving the remainder to smoulder and foul the air. Mary looked away in disgust. She quickly removed it, doused it with water, then washed the ashtray.

He ambled into the bedroom mumbling as he went. 'I'm away tay bed then.'

'Goodnight, Archie.'

As he left the room, she surprised herself at her complacency over these last months. Life in Australia had given her independence and confidence, she would no longer be treated as a doormat. Archie was her husband in name only. How lovely it was now to have single beds. The spare room was a godsend. Unbeknownst to him, those bed arrangements were here to stay. Tiptoeing quietly into the room, Mary pulled back the eiderdown, slid between the cool sheets and fell into a deep sleep.

A soft tap on her door went unheeded. It was the gentle shaking of her shoulder that aroused her. Sitting up, she tried to focus. Through the blind slats there were stars, the bedside clock was glowing green. It was 2.35 am. Uncle Ralph stood by her bed in the dark, only illuminated by the kitchen light, his voice was barely audible. 'Mary, love, sorry if I gave ye a fright, but ... but there's somebody at door for ye.'

'For me? Who is it at this time for goodness' sake?'

'Best you come, soon as ye can, lass.'

Mary started to cough. Her hands shook as she switched on the bedside light. Uncle Ralph slipped silently out of the room.

Archie woke up and mumbled under his breath. He looked over at her, screwed up his eyes and spluttered, 'Put the fuckin light out, will ye?'

Mary ignored him, put on her dressing gown and slippers, and opened the door. Uncle Ralph was standing there, wringing his hands. His face was ashen.

'I don't know what's wrong, love, but there's two policemen at the door wanting to talk to ye.'

'Two policemen? My Lord, what do they want with me?'

Pulling the lapels of her dressing gown closer to her throat she instinctively patted her hair, then quickly followed Uncle Ralph to the front door. Two young officers stood outside in the dark porch. They nodded as he beckoned to them, 'Would ye like to come in, lads? C'mon, this way.'

Mary's heart was racing, watching them follow her uncle into the front room. 'What is it? What's wrong? What's happened? What have I done?'

The police officers looked apprehensively at each other. One of them said, 'You've done nothing wrong, Mrs Bray. Best if you sit down.'

The taller one pulled out a chair from under the table. Mary stood erect and looked directly at the older officer. 'No, no, I'm fine, thank you, I don't want to sit down,' she said, pushing the chair back under the table then leaning on it with trembling hands.

'Mrs Bray, we need you to come down to the police station to take a telephone call from Scotland.'

'Scotland? Has something happened to Alice?' Mary's voice rose to a high-pitched shrill. 'Tell me, is it Alice?'

'We don't know, Mrs Bray. We got a call from the Glasgow Royal Hospital. There has been an accident and—'

Mary's hand flew to her mouth; a wail escaped her clenched fingers. 'No, no! What accident? Is Alice all right? Oh my God! What happened?'

Mary swayed slightly, holding firmly onto the back of the chair. The young officer was calm. 'Yes, Mrs Bray, it was an accident, a serious one. Your daughter was a passenger in a red sports car, and the driver—'

'Yes, yes, I know the driver, it's her friend Rena ... are they alright, are they hurt?'

The young man spoke quietly. 'The car missed a bend and hit a bus stop.'

Mary reached out, grabbed his uniform sleeve and started to shake it. 'And the girls? What about the girls? Are they alright? Please, please officer, tell me that the girls are all right.'

'Mrs Bray,' he said, gently removing her hand from his arm. 'They were both taken to hospital, one is in a serious condition, and the other, well ... I am so sorry, Mrs Bray, sadly the other didn't make it.'

Mary's hands flew up to her mouth, trying to stop screams that wouldn't come. 'No, no,' she cried.

Uncle Ralph quickly put his around her trying to comfort her; Archie appeared at the door rubbing his eyes.

'Whit the fuck's goin on here?'

Seeing the police uniforms, he immediately stopped, stood quietly, and listened as the police officer briefed him. Archie was out of his comfort zone, awkward attempts at patting her shoulder went unnoticed. Mary was in shock—she didn't move.

Uncle Ralph was struggling trying to find the words as his ageing heart broke for his beloved niece.

The boys, quickly out of bed, were briefed by the sympathetic police. Billy cried and Scot held his mother.

The police officer spoke softly to Mary. 'Mrs Bray, why don't you get dressed and come with us to the station.'

Mary gazed vacantly at the door and nodded. Lifting her coat from the hallstand, she put it on over her dressing gown. She was still wearing her slippers.

Sitting in the back seat of the patrol car with a screwed-up handkerchief wedged into her tight fist, Mary found her voice and started to cry loudly whilst talking nonstop to the two officers trying to extract information. No matter how many times they told her they knew nothing more, she kept badgering them, continuing to cry, and repeating herself, begging for more information. The police officer in the front passenger seat turned to her tearstained puffed face.

'Mrs Bray, I don't know how else to tell you, please believe me. We have no more information. We were only advised it was a fatality.'

'I'm sorry, I'm really sorry, but you see Alice is my only daughter. We're very close, she will be here in Australia very soon to join us. I have missed her so. She can't leave me, she can't.' The sobs continued as the officers drove on in silence.

It never gets any easier, they thought. Tragedy is such a cruel courier.

Archie sat in the back seat, muttering to himself. 'Bloody Alice, nothing but bloody well trouble!'

The car pulled up at the police station, Mary opened the door, jumped out quickly and ran up the steps of the station. The night sergeant was waiting at the front desk for them. He stood up as she rushed in.

'Mrs Bray, please come through.'

Taking Mary's arm, he gently steered her into his office. Archie followed them. She sat down as the sergeant lifted the receiver and started to dial; he spoke gently.

'Mrs Bray, I have been asked by the Glasgow Police to contact the hospital once we have located you. I'm doing that now; it shouldn't take too long.'

She closed her eyes, her voice stilled, her hands firmly clasped in front of her.

Alice's lovely face flashed before her it was when she was young. She was laughing at the antics of her brothers as they splashed in the waters of the burn, her blonde hair shone and bounced on her shoulders as she jumped off a rock. It was her father's hair.

The sergeant's voice quietly seeped through her reverie. 'Mrs Bray, Mrs Bray, I have a Dr Taylor on the line from Glasgow. Do you feel up to take this call or shall I give it to your husband?'

Unblinking and dry eyed, she looked back at the kindly sergeant, held out her hand and with a controlled soft voice answered.

'No thank you, sergeant. I'll take it.'

Chapter 25

Summer had arrived with revenge. Vince had grudgingly installed air conditioning to replace the old ceiling fans that he insisted were still effective. Mary had convinced him that they would increase business and make for happier staff.

Their relationship was now on another level. She would constantly remind him of her gratitude and appreciation for the compassion and understanding he had shown when Alice had the accident. She had taken so much time off work that Vince had to hire two casual staff to replace her. She was highly stressed, lost weight and grief stricken; it had been a traumatic time for everyone.

The relief that her daughter had survived was immense. The inconsolable grief that Rena had perished was beyond measure.

Alice had sustained many injuries, shattered bones, and torn skin. She was unconscious for two days with a fractured skull, broken limbs, and short-term memory loss. Rena had died on impact with massive internal injuries. Her beautiful face was untouched. Alice was hospitalised for three months; Mary was constantly in touch with the medical staff for updates. She wrote to her daughter every day.

Alice left Glasgow as soon after the accident as the hospital would allow. She had endured months of pain and physiotherapy and had cried endlessly for the loss of her best friend. All that she wanted was her mother.

During the weeks before she was due to arrive in Australia, Mary spent hours decorating the old, oversized storage room. She bought a new bed with a thick purple bedspread, adorned the little white Queen Anne dressing table with family photos, then she added fresh flowers. The drawers were filled with toiletries, brushes, and 'girlie' things that Mary had been collecting for months.

The morning her daughter was due to arrive at the airport she had been awake for hours. Archie was at work, saying that he couldn't possibly take time off to come to the airport.

After breakfast she woke the boys, then went to check again on Alice's room, adding yet more fresh flowers to her bedside table.

'Come on, Scotty, hurry up, we can't be late.' Mary was on edge, calling her son from the bedroom.

Scot was unruffled. 'Mum! The plane won't land for another hour and we are only fifteen minutes away. Don't worry, we'll be there in plenty of time.'

True to his word, as Mary and her sons walked quickly into the terminal building there was an announcement saying the aircraft from London via Darwin was about to land. Mary shook Scot's arm.

'Oh, Scotty, I'm so nervous. I'll just duck in to the toilet to freshen up.'

As she walked quickly away, Scot couldn't resist nudging Billy and laughing, calling after his mother, 'Mum, you look fine! Alice won't care how you look, come back here.'

The aircraft came to a stop on the hot tarmac, steps were pushed to the front door and the weary passengers slowly disembarked.

Mary saw her straight away at the top of the stairs. She was wearing a heavy coat and carrying two bags, her hair was a lighter blonde than it had been in Glasgow and was tied back in a low ponytail behind her ears. She seemed to struggle with the stairs a bit. When reaching the bottom, Mary let out a soft cry, her daughter was limping slowly, as she headed towards the terminal building. She quickly wiped her eyes. Billy squeezed his mother's arm. The crowd of dazed passengers began to trickle through the tarmac doors. Pushing forward to the front of the barrier, Mary called out, 'Alice, Alice!'

Alice saw her mother immediately. She dropped her bags, opened her arms, and let out a heart-rending, 'Mum!'

They cried and clung to each other whilst still separated by the airport handrail.

Alice was home.

Vince was more than happy to give Alice work at the restaurant on busy days. He said that she had many of her mother's qualities and was a welcome addition to his small business. She worked the dining room with competence and courtesy, always with a smile and eager to please.

Mary had an eye for colour and style and found herself taking on a prominent role with the new renovations, selecting colours and materials. She was delighted to be involved, trusted to deal with the painters and decorators who were more than often unreliable. Business at Ronaldo's had escalated, they had extended their trading hours to lunch five days a week and dinner two nights a week. Everyone agreed that Mary was the open secret that made it all happen. Over the previous two years, she had worked tirelessly, giving 150 per cent to every project, rejoicing as the business grew. She handled everything: the menu, the functions, the suppliers, the decor, the cooking, plus endless fresh ideas. Nothing was problematic for Mary Bray.

It was mid-morning. Vincent arrived late at the restaurant. His biggest customer, a national car company had a meeting the night before. Vince and Max had served drinks and snacks and then a late supper. They had stayed late, drinking, and arguing until well after midnight. Max left to go home to his family while Vince saw the last customer out and locked up, deciding to leave the clean up until the next day. Now he regretted it. He was feeling tired and breathless, the childhood injury to his knee was aching more than normal, making him sit down frequently to regain his breath.

Sofia was in the kitchen. She had slowed down in recent months. The mild arthritis she had suffered for years was now more severe, affecting her legs and feet. She was also getting frailer and more forgetful. Nevertheless, she loved being around her boys. Sofia was sitting, quietly humming to herself whilst cleaning and polishing the blades of her precious pasta machine. It sparkled and shone; she would not allow anyone else to clean it from the day her late husband had given it to her.

Mary and Vince often had long chats together. Vince would confide his private thoughts, something he said he was never able to do with any other woman or man. He trusted her completely. Mary, too, felt very much at ease with Vince, but anything more than that was just not possible. Her heart was in England always and forever ... with her soldier.

Vince was almost finished reorganising the room, placing chairs neatly under pre-set tables ready for the afternoon trade. Picking up three stacked chairs, he lifted them above his waist before lowering them slowly to the floor. Without warning, they slipped from his hands with a loud crash. Unsteady on his feet and breathing heavily he called out, frantically tearing at his shirt. Falling sluggishly onto a chair, he grabbed the end of a tablecloth before crashing to the floor, showered by a profusion of glass and silverware.

In the kitchen, Sofia had just finished polishing the handles of her pasta machine. She folded her cloths into a small leather pouch, then washed her hands. Then she heard it, the sound of falling cutlery and broken glass, resonating around the room. She shuffled with her walking stick into the dining room.

It was then that she saw him, her beloved son lying on the floor between two tables, a dark red circle slowly seeped out from beneath his hairline. His limp legs curled backwards.

The old woman hobbled clumsily to the table, calling her son's name. 'Vincenzo! Vincenzo, my Vincenzo!' Bending down awkwardly between the tables she took his hand, while screaming and ranting in Italian. Alone and frightened, Sofia had no idea how to use the telephone to call for help or ring for an ambulance. She could only sit on the floor and cry, too afraid to leave him.

Mary stepped off the bus and waved to the conductress, a middle-aged woman, whom she frequently had on her bus to work. They regularly had long chats. It reminded her of a life long ago, when she depended so much on the arrival and departure of buses, and the friendly chat of a conductress. She decided to come to work early, knowing that Vince would be tired from last night and in need of an extra pair of hands.

Slipping her cardigan off, she laced it through the handles of her handbag. It was getting warmer. She loved feeling the sun's little heat waves on her arms and the back of her neck. Walking quickly on the new bitumen pavement, her mind was crammed with tasks that needed doing that day.

The sound didn't register at first. It was a siren she heard it in the distance, perhaps it was a bushfire in the hills, or police after a young heavy-footed driver.

By the time Mary had turned the corner at the top of the road it had stopped. There was an ambulance in the distance, it was outside the restaurant. She ran.

At the restaurant, she was confronted by the stark white of the ambulance, flashing blue and red lights, and men running inside with equipment. Strangers stood on the footpath, watching and whispering. Local shopkeepers in their doorways frowned, shaking their heads. The doors of the restaurant were open; she could hear wailing and crying.

Mary looked frantically at strangers, begging them for answers. There was no response just a shrug and a morbid curiosity at what was before them. Huddled into a corner, partially obscured by an elderly man was Sofia, being comforted by a stranger. Mary ran to her, holding out her arms.

'My God, Sofia, what happened? What happened?'

Before Sofia could answer, a young boy in grubby overalls came over. 'I'll tell you what happened, Mrs. I was delivering bread next door when I heard this terrible scream, howling and crying. I mean *really* crying. I thought somebody was being killed, she was hysterical, this old woman here, and the man on the floor ... shit! He was not looking too good. I rang for an ambulance right away from that phone over there and they came really quick. I hope he's gonna be okay.'

Mary quickly looked over at the unconscious Vince before managing a winded, 'Thank you very much for your kindness,' to the boy.

Kneeling down, she put her arms around Sofia's thin frame, holding her close. Her moans and howling in garbled Italian were heartbreaking. Two ambulance officers were bending over Vince, taking it in turns to perform CPR. Sweat beads formed on their brow as they tirelessly continued the regular rhythm on his big chest. Mary cried as she watched. She could see his face. Both eyes were closed, his lips were pale and parted and a grey pallor. The side of his head rested in a circle of blood stemming from somewhere underneath his matted hair. She tried not to let the shock of it all show on her face. All she could do was stand aside, let the ambulance officers do their job and support the distraught Sofia.

After what seemed like forever, one of the officers shouted out the blessed words, 'Got it!'

Vince was still here. Slipping an oxygen mask over his face, he was placed gently onto a stretcher before the doors of the ambulance closed and locked securely. With sirens blaring and lights flashing, it sped down the road, disappearing round the bend.

Max and Selena heard the sirens on their way to the restaurant. They pulled over to the side of the road to let the ambulance pass. Turning the corner they saw the crowd on the pavement, Max screamed out to his wife, 'Selena, my God, what has happened here? It must be Mama.' Getting out of the car, he ran inside.

Seeing her son, Sofia's wails escalated. 'My Vincenzo! My Vincenzo!'

Max put his arms around her, talking in soft Italian. Selena came and sat down beside her, stroking her arm. She looked over at Mary, frowning. 'What happened?'

'They said it was a cardiac arrest,' Mary said through tears, 'but he has stabilised.'

Max nodded, too emotional to speak. Placing his jacket around his mother's shoulders, they all left quickly for the hospital.

There were four bookings for lunch that day. Within ten minutes, Mary had cancelled them, put the closed sign on the door and rescued some of the food. Tomorrow they were full for lunch and overbooked for dinner. Vince would not be around for some time, so she needed a plan. Suppliers had to be paid, so a cancelled day was out of the question. She couldn't ask Vince's family for help; they were all too distraught and emotional and could only manage to focus on their much-loved Vince.

By the next day, Mary had recruited a first and second chef from an agency, her children all rallied to help on the day too. It was hectic but successful, and every customer left feeling happy and satisfied, with no complaints. There were four return bookings.

Vince survived the heart attack, thanks to the speed and skills of the ambulance officers. He suffered setbacks and complications, a lengthy stay in hospital, then two weeks in rehabilitation. He was paralysed partially on the left side and unable to walk any distance without the aid of a walking stick. The family focussed on his recovery and barely gave a thought to the restaurant. They knew everything would run smoothly; they knew there would be no disasters.

They knew that because they had Mary.

<h1 align="center">Chapter 26</h1>

It was Sunday morning. The letters on the hall table had gone unnoticed, buried between junk mail and the local paper. Scot was helping Uncle Ralph repair the fence out front. Walking in through the front door, he caught sight of the unopened mail.

'Any of this for us, Uncle Ralph?'

The old man came in behind him, shook his head in disbelief and muttered, 'Oh, aye, lad, I clean forgot about it. All of it's for your mam.'

Scot smiled and put his arm around his great-uncle's shoulders. 'No problems, Uncle Ralph. Nothing looks urgent, fancy a cuppa?'

Uncle Ralph nodded and sighed with relief then headed for the kitchen. Scot picked up the letters, dropping them on the kitchen table. 'Mail for us, Mum.'

Mary was at the sink drying her hands. 'Thanks, son.'

There was an open-faced envelope that looked like a bill, advertising material and two letters. One was for Alice from Rena's mother in Scotland, the other was for her from Sadie. It was not her usual flimsy aerogram, rather a thick envelope with an array of stamps and stickers. Taking a fruit knife from the kitchen drawer she slit open all the letters, reading Sadie's first. As always, it began by saying how much she missed the boys and their banter, and the nice little chats that they had when they were on their own. Her father had been very sick. The doctor said that it was his age and it was only a matter of time now. She said that Bob and Frank had the usual aches and pains, but overall, they were both well and kept busy in the potting shed. Peggy had a promotion at work; she seemed to be a lot more relaxed, smiling more these days. Sadie put in brackets that her daughter had been keeping company with a man in her new department. She had enclosed a few photographs of when they had gone on a boat trip on the river Clyde. Peggy was standing by the boat rail, the wind catching her hair that looked much longer now. She was wearing a close fitting zipped waterproof jacket and was smiling broadly while waving at the camera. Mary hoped that she had now found happiness.

Opening the window-faced envelope expecting a bill, she let out a scream. The chair crashed to the floor behind her as she jumped up from the table.

'Uncle Ralph, Scotty, come here quickly!' She couldn't wait, running outside and waving the letter above her head. She grabbed Scot by the arm.

'What's up, Mum? Where's the fire?'

Mary was shaking her head and laughing. 'Look! Look! It's our loan application! It's been approved! They have approved our loan application, saying we can start building right away.' Mary looked at her son in amazement. 'Did you hear what I said? We can start building right away! We are going to have our very own home ... at long last, our very first home.'

Mary, holding back tears, sat down on the garden bench as Scot and Uncle Ralph began to yell, scream, and dance in circles around her. Just then, the side gate creaked open as Billy, followed by Archie, came into the backyard to a scene of bedlam. Mary ran over to them, and, between laughter and quotes from the letter, shouted, 'Look at this! The bank has approved our loan! I can't believe it we're going to have our very own home.'

Billy threw his arms in the air and joined in dancing with his brother and uncle.

Archie said nothing, only shrugging his shoulders and shaking his head. He went into the house followed by Mary. He sat down and took off his shoes, lit a cigarette, exhaling slowly and looked at her with a smirk. 'Ah well, that's it then, eh? Up to wir eyes in debt. I thought that stupid bank manager had given us the flick after aw this time. Well, ye wanted this, Mary. Don't blame me when the money disnae come in. There is nae guarantee I'm gonna get overtime, just remember that.'

Mary looked at him in disbelief. 'Archie, what are you talking about? We sat down weeks ago and you said it would be difficult, but we could manage if we all helped. You said you expected to get more overtime, now you have changed your mind.' Mary stood up and slammed the letter down on the table in front of her husband, with blazing eyes and an unwavering voice, she pounced. 'Well, you have failed, Archie Bray. Get ready for commitment. I am building a home for this family with or without you. You can sink or swim, Archie Bray ... sink or swim.'

Mary turned round and stormed out of the room. Archie started to speak, but he changed his mind and slumped back in his chair.

Scot had heard it all. He came into the kitchen and ruffled his dad's hair. 'Oh, come on now, don't be like that. You've already said it would work, and Mum has wanted this for as long as I can remember. What's happened now? How come you've changed your tune?'

'I havnie changed ma tune, son, I never thought we would get it, that's aw. I only went wi yer ma to shut her up. It's been three months and we never heard a thing. The situation is different noo. I'm no getting the overtime, its aw drying up, and noo this.'

Pushing his chair back, Archie lit another cigarette from the one he was about to extinguish. Scot left the room half smiling, shaking his head.

That weekend Mary and Archie formally committed to the building of their new home. After signing the contracts, they went again to look at the display home, this time knowing it was soon going to be a reality.

The house was very basic, the cheapest in the range, but Mary loved it. It was her dream, a home, another milestone accomplished.

The estate was new and well outside of town. Many amenities were still in the pipeline, but Mary was not deterred, the thought of being a homeowner still surprised her. They had come a long way from a condemned building in a Glasgow slum to owning their very own brand-new home on their very own small part of the Australian landscape.

However, happiness came at a cost to the Bray family. The building of their home would take many months, almost a year. Unions, weather, and incompetent tradesmen held up progress and frustrated the family.

Debts were mounting, with Archie's promised contributions as predicted, getting less each payday. Mary worked extra days and the children helped, ensuring their commitments were met.

Uncle Ralph had mixed feelings. Apart from Archie, he would miss the family sorely. It had been wonderful having Mary close by, and his nephews lit up every day with their chatter and jokes. Nevertheless, the strain of sharing his home was taking its toll and he was tired. It had been a long three years and now it was time for him to have his old life back. Although still very spritely and fit, Uncle

Ralph was nearing eighty, and age and its ailments had caught up faster than he would have liked. He longed to be alone again with all the memories of life with his lovely Gwen. He wanted her paintings around the house again. Her framed tapestries back on the shelves and her embroidery once again gracing the kitchen chair backs. He wanted peace.

The day finally arrived for the move to Broadfields Estate. It was a sweltering 38 degrees Celsius. Archie had arranged for someone he knew at work with a small truck to help them. In the three years they had been in Australia, they had accumulated quite a bit, mainly clothing and personal effects. Mary had been buying kitchen utensils and crockery in preparation for the move to their very first home. Much to her annoyance, the old truck had broken down three times over three trips to move their belongings. There were suitcases, boxes, and bags, plus the unopened trunk they had sent from Scotland the day that they left. It contained mostly bedding, sentimental keepsakes and ornaments. None of it was needed whilst living at Uncle Ralph's home.

It was early in the evening when the truck finally coughed and spluttered slowly away from their front door. Everyone helped with unpacking. Alice was overjoyed at having her own room overlooking the garden. Although barren and full of weeds and thistles, with only the rotary clothes hoist in residence, she had promised her mother that she would be preparing the soil as soon as possible to plant flowers and shrubs.

The boys jostled on the floor in their room and argued about whose bed would be by the window. Mary had taken time off work to arrange utility connections and other necessities.

All of the extra bills from the bank, government charges, and moving expenses were taking their toll. Mary reluctantly secured a line of credit at a local furniture shop for beds, a kitchen table, and chairs, plus a lounge suite. Sadly, the credit did not extend to the purchase of a fridge, which was a huge expense and a big problem in the scorching Australian summers. Scot found an old meat safe in a junk yard, which many years ago in Australia served as a fridge. It was made of wood with metal shelves and drainage holes, and when placing a solid block of ice on the shelves it would keep milk meat and butter cool temporarily in the searing summer heat. It seemed primitive, but it worked.

The first weeks at Broadfields Estate was an adjustment for the family. It was a new area with new neighbours, with new challenges to find their way around shops and the limited public transport. Everything was new and fresh in the house, but the garden desperately needed to be cleared. Weeds and thistles were scattered in large clumps, and the ground was hard. Billy and Scot had volunteered immediately to do clean up; Archie said he would get around to it very soon.

One evening, a few weeks later after tea, Billy came out from the room he shared with Scot. He called out to his mother at the kitchen sink. 'Hey, Mum, what exactly is in that trunk in our room? Can we move it? It's taking up too much space. Can it be emptied?'

Mary smiled. 'Its winter blankets, ornaments, and keepsakes, Billy. I suppose we can empty it now that there is room in the hall cupboard. Ask your dad to help you bring it in to the lounge room, will you?'

Archie and Billy managed to lift and half drag the trunk into the lounge room. The heavy padlock and side locks were unlocked and prised open. Mary, Archie, and the boys gathered round and met the full force of a strong, musty smell as the lid creaked open. The newspapers covering the top had yellowed. Their name and Uncle Ralph's address was scrawled in heavy black marking on the outside and inside top cover. Mary recalled the night they had done that. Billy had insisted he was the best writer so was allowed to write the address and was chuffed. Looking now at his young, childish hand, made Mary smile.

'It's like Christmas, Mum, isn't it? Look at all this.' Billy was pulling out the treasures one by one: blankets, sheets, boxes of ornaments, brass candlesticks, brass Spanish Galleon wall plaque, games and books, old report cards and treasured teenage love letters. Every package brought cries of laughter from them all.

'What's this, Mum?' Billy asked, holding up a large black plastic-covered parcel sandwiched between two pieces of cardboard and secured with tape.

Mary frowned. 'I've no idea, son. Get the scissors and open it.'

Billy carefully cut the tape and split the sides of the black plastic. As the bag and tissue paper fell away, flashes of colour fell onto the table. Mary's hand flew to her mouth. 'Oh, my Lord! It's the quilt, it's the patchwork quilt Kathy gave me. Here, give it to me, quickly please.' She held out her hands.

Billy gently picked it up and handed it to his mother. Mary reached out, held it with both hands and pressed it to her face. There was no musty smell, just Kathy's smell, a very faint whiff of the Norman Hartnell *In Love* perfume she always wore. Mary's eyes filled with tears as she burrowed deep into the soft cotton and cried.

Everyone was silent, until Archie broke the mood. He shuffled his feet and raised his eyes to the ceiling. 'Jesus, Mary, ah don't know why yer greetin over that slut, she disnae even write to ye. Some pal she is!'

Mary ignored him. Touching the quilt and all the little mementoes of Kathy's childhood overwhelmed her. She would always miss her first real friend, something that Archie would never understand.

Chapter 27

The early years living in Broadfields were a challenge for the Bray family. The new suburb had slowly advanced, providing more bus routes, shopping strips, primary and secondary schools, and a large industrial estate assuring job security for the locals.

Although the isolated position of their home put pressure on the family, Mary remained focussed, recalling where she had been, where she was now, and where she had yet to discover.

The restaurant was expanding and increasing clientele. She was taking on more responsibility working longer hours and being paid accordingly. There were new trappings for the home, a sparkling new electric fridge, replacing the old meat safe, built-in wardrobes with drawers, and a sliding mirrored door had replaced the hanging rails in her children's rooms. An additional room was built on to the back of the house for Scot to give each of the boys their privacy.

New twin beds for Mary and Archie were gifts to herself. How she revelled in her own night space, her own bed lamp, and her own luxurious quilt.

Gradually, families moved in as the suburb grew around them. The extension of the railway line meant that public transport now gave them more options. Street trees began to flourish around the neighbourhood, as did Mary Bray and her family.

Archie maintained his job working in the biscuit factory storeroom, still managing to irritate anyone in authority. His position as shop steward for the workers made him a local hero; however, there were many resenting his arrogant ways.

As the years had passed, Mary found herself drifting further away from him. He often stayed at the social club after at work, not coming home at all. She was never worried or even cared. She was always pleased when he was out of the house. Conversations between them were limited. The boys tolerated and humoured him, mostly because he had always supported them in maths at school or in sport. He enjoyed going to their football club every weekend, cheering them on then staying back to socialise in the clubrooms after the game.

Mary was relieved that he had done this one decent thing in his life, spending time with his sons. His relationship with Alice had improved slightly since the accident, they were now civil to one another other, albeit only when necessary.

Alice had thrived in Australia. Like her brothers, she was slowly losing her Glaswegian lilt. She pursued her love of children by enrolling in night studies for a diploma in Early Childhood Development. She passed her course with high distinctions and was furthering her studies to be a kindergarten teacher. The injuries from the accident had healed, leaving only scarred limbs. The emotional scars would never heal.

Mary worried more than ever about her attractive daughter. Since arriving in Australia, she rarely socialised. She seemed content to stay home to read or write, always giving the same answer to her mother. 'I'll be fine, Mum. I just want to be here with you and the boys right now.'

It was no consolation for Mary.

Ronaldo's Restaurant was getting another overhaul. This time with a more modern look and cleaner lines. Mary had replaced much of the equipment that was outdated or obsolete; she added three staff to her team, including a second chef. Every fortnight the enticing and creative menus were updated. The new chefs were young and not afraid to attempt anything new.

Vince had never fully recovered from his heart attack. The paralysis down one side of his body was evident. His face was slightly twisted; his left hand curled back into a claw and his voice had a distinctive slur. He depended heavily on a walking stick. Nevertheless, with all these obstacles, he could still help Mary with the accounts and her business dealings with the suppliers. Sofia was very frail and only visited the restaurant on occasions, preferring to stay home. Max came in from time to time as a courtesy and as a partner, but he had other financial interests and a young family. He was more than happy for Mary to handle everything; he trusted her completely.

The day would stay with Mary forever. She was sitting at a table in a small storeroom behind the main building doing a stocktake. Vince was at the typewriter in the office next door. Before looking at any paperwork she slipped a cassette into the player, it was the overture from *Swan Lake*. Laying back, she closed her eyes. It was the first ballet she had ever seen on television, many years ago. She became lost in the purity and emotion of the music, her mind's eye vividly seeing every detail. The ballerina pirouetting on her toes, circling the boards like a bird in flight, her slender arms raised waving in pain, she began floating to the edge of the stage then gliding down slowly to rest on her limp legs. All four limbs caressed the stage as she embraced her feathered head. The music intensified as she rose up in triumph, then slowly faded as she lay down in defeat. All was quiet. The swan, now stilled by death, lay centre stage. The haunting strains of violins rose to a crescendo then gradually faded. The backlights dimmed, the spotlight on the swan revealed only sorrow. The curtain came down.

Mary opened her eyes. The magic had gone, the swan had gone. Vince stood before her, leaning heavily on his cane. His face twitched slightly, grabbing his arm and shaking it, Mary pleaded, 'Vince, what's wrong? You look terrible. What is it? Tell me, sit down, please tell me what's wrong. I'll get you some water.'

Vince held up his cane to stop her. 'No Mary, please no water, just sit down, I have some sad news. There's been an accident. You need to go to the Royal Melbourne Hospital right now. It's Uncle Ralph.'

Mary screamed, 'What? What happened to him?'

'They wouldn't tell me much because I'm not family. What they did say was that you had to get there as soon as possible.'

Mary swayed then crumpled onto the chair, holding her ears, trying to block out what Vince would say next. He lifted the phone to dial his brother.

'I'll call Max to see if he can drive you there. Get your coat, Mary, and try to reach Alice.'

Max answered almost immediately. 'It's me, Max, where are you?' Vince didn't wait for an answer. 'There's been an accident. No, no, not Mum, nor Mary, it's Mary's Uncle Ralph. Can you get here straight away and take Mary and Alice to the Royal Melbourne?' Turning away from Mary and holding the mouthpiece closer, he whispered, 'He's in a bad way.' He hung up. 'Max is on his way, Mary. He can take you to the hospital. Where's Alice working today? Is she still nearby at that kindergarten?'

Mary nodded, sobbing, 'Yes. Oh, I can't believe this. Only yesterday we were chatting. What could have happened?'

Within minutes, Max pulled up at the restaurant door and helped Mary into the back seat of his station wagon. 'Just direct me to Alice's work, Mary. Is it near the old Queens Arms pub?' Mary nodded as they sped off. Alice was waiting at the kerbside.

Both women sat close together in silence in the back seat of Max's car, Alice with her arm protecting her mother. The daughter, now the carer.

The car pulled up abruptly at the emergency entrance of the hospital. Mother and daughter rushed inside to the intensive care unit.

Mary had never been in an intensive care unit. She expected everyone to have glum faces and talk in hushed tones, but it was quite the opposite. People were talking normally, and staff were smiling and chatting to relatives as they adjusted tubes and needles. Taped music was drifting from every corner. There were monitors wired to beds with tubes extending to various parts of human forms, many of whom appeared comatose. Constant regular beeps were hearts under pressure, maintaining and monitoring precious life, some louder than others. The nurses' station was lively, with doctors, nurses, and interns all checking charts, conferring with colleagues and talking on phones.

One room was tucked round a corner, it had glass walls. A man and a woman moulded together were sitting on a steel bench. She sobbed, he stared into space. A tall, imposing man, his face drawn and wearing a white coat with a stethoscope hanging limply around his neck, was leaving the room. He closed the door quietly behind him.

Mary and Alice were ushered into the next room. A young nursing sister introduced herself and then closed the door. All three sat on hard plastic chairs. The nurse leaned forward looking, directly into the wide and hopeful eyes of Mary.

'Mrs Bray, please prepare yourself. I am afraid your uncle has been put into an induced coma.'

Mary gasped. 'What?'

The experienced young nurse braced herself for the inevitable. 'He had a nasty fall from quite a distance. He has a fractured skull and traumatic brain injury causing swelling of the brain. We have made him comfortable, and he is no pain, but I'm afraid—'

The young nursed stopped as she saw Mary's eyes roll back, managing to grab her just before she fell. She called out, 'Porter! Water, quickly!'

When Mary recovered, she learned that her uncle had fallen heavily on his head. He had been on the roof cleaning out the gutters. She knew this chore had been long overdue; he had told her many times that when the heavy rains came the water just cascaded from the gutters and flooded his backyard. Mary had told him then that a man of his age should not be climbing up ladders and working on roofs; she said that Archie would do it. She begged him not to use the stepladders, they were not quite tall enough and he was just a bit too short to reach up to the gutter. Archie had promised to do it as soon as he had a minute. That minute never came.

Mrs Jessop had found him. She had called in to give him some of her quince jam. Getting no answer at the front door, she went round the back. He was lying on his side on the concrete path, unconscious and bleeding from the back of his head. She had screamed out for the next-door neighbour to call an ambulance. None of the neighbours knew how long he had been lying there. The bucket, half-full of branches and leaves, lay upturned on the path; the trowel was still in his hand, caked in mud.

The hospital report said that he had fallen heavily on his head, fracturing his thin skull. There was also swelling to the brain and internal bleeding. He was unlikely to recover. Mary and Alice sat by his bedside until the end. Mary liked to think he knew she was there. She held his old, worn calloused hand in hers and spoke softly to him. She told him how much she loved him and how her children loved him, that she would always be grateful for his help in getting them all settled in this country, and how happy her mother would have been that they had reunited. She cried silently whispering to him, 'Please come back to me.'

Mother and daughter sat quietly together one either side of the bed, the only sound penetrating their thoughts was the constant beep of the monitors letting them know that Uncle Ralph was still with them. They stayed until the beeps slowly faded then finally stopped. Despite all the medical efforts, Uncle Ralph's fighting spirit had surrendered and he lost the battle.

Alice moved first, hardly breathing. She came around to her mother, lifting her hand gently away from Uncle Ralph's forever-still fingers. 'Come on, Mum. He's at peace now, it's time to say goodbye.'

Mary slumped back, letting out a sob, then she slowly stood up, straightening the sheets and placing his still warm hands over them. She kissed his forehead as tears fell to his cheek. A nurse standing by the window came to Mary, who had started to cough and wheeze, and led her gently outside. Sitting in the nurses' station, she was comforted by the staff, telling her that Uncle Ralph would have been in no pain. With Alice by her side, they left the room and walked down the deserted hospital corridors in silence, leaving behind the lifeless body of Uncle Ralph.

Outside, the air had chilled, Alice gently steered her mother across the road to the large wooden arched doors of the Catholic church. Mary didn't object. They were met inside with calm and peace. Two women, heads covered and dressed completely in black were absorbed in front of an alter laden with fresh white lilies. They were deep in prayer. Low lights above the imposing stained-glass windows told stories of the crucifixion and the sorrow of dedicated disciples.

Alice sat her mother down at the end of a pew close to the door, then she walked up to the racks of small glass containers beside the alter. She lit two vigil light candles. One for a great uncle who had lived a long and fruitful life. The other for a dear friend, eternally robbed of that chance.

Chapter 28

Uncle Ralph had been well known and respected in Melbourne. The funeral drew a large crowd who gathered in groups outside after the service. Mary and her children were well received and comforted by many. Not so Archie, who lurked behind a concrete pillar for most of the service, cunningly avoiding eye contact with anyone in his line of vision. Later, at the wake in the church hall, he made weak attempts to speak to mourners about Uncle Ralph and what great mates they had been. These were met with civil nods. Although unsaid, it was widely known that if Archie had cleaned the gutters as requested Uncle Ralph would still be here.

The clean-up began two days after the funeral. Mary as his next of kin, and her children, accepted that responsibility. Like so many of his generation, Uncle Ralph was a hoarder. Mary, Alice, and the boys spent many days filling bags and boxes with old newspapers and magazines dating back to the 1930s. He kept race books and programmes from every track he had raced, Gwen's patterns and recipes were neatly folded and stored in plastic bags, and his household receipts catalogued, labelled, and folded neatly in cardboard boxes. Mary was very subdued in the beginning, but as time wore on she rejoiced in much of her dear uncle's long life. The boys and Alice kept her spirits up by recalling many happy stories about him; how he would get confused when he was excited, relating stories of his youth and getting his words and sentences mixed up. This eased the tension for Mary. She laughed with tear-filled eyes, the job no less painful, but the burden on her heart had been lessened.

Two weeks later, Mary was in the shed sorting out the many glass jars to give to Mrs Jessop. Billy came to the shed wearing grubby jeans and a T-shirt. He stood at the door, wiping his brow. 'Mum, someone here to see you. He's in the front room.'

She straightened her apron. 'Who is it?'

Billy had already left, calling out, 'Don't know, Mum.'

Reverend Bryce from the church was standing in the middle of Uncle Ralph's upturned front room. He was a tall man with broad shoulders, an open, smiling bespectacled face, and a thick head of greying hair. Mary came through the house to the front room, fighting her way through half-filled boxes, plastic bags, and piles of neatly tied old newspapers.

'Mrs Bray, so good to see you.' The Reverend laughed, holding out his hand. 'You look like you are in the middle of a mammoth task. I hope I haven't come at a bad time.'

'No, no, not at all, Reverend. It's lovely to see you. Please sit down, if you can find a chair.' She laughed. 'Would you like a cup of tea?'

'No ... no thank you. I won't hold you up. It's just that I need to talk to you about a matter that is rather sensitive.'

Moving a pile of magazines from a corner chair he sat down, Mary pulled out a chair and sat opposite him. She frowned, thinking for a moment how uncomfortable he looked.

'Mary, as you know Ralph and Gwen were long time parishioners of our church. Actually, from the first week they arrived in the neighbourhood they came to our Sunday sermon. When Gwen died some years ago, Ralph decided that, as they had no family, and when it was his time, he said that he would leave his house to the church when he passed away.' He continued quickly. 'He had a will made and left a copy in our vault. I'm more than happy to show it to you. He said he was always grateful for the love and friendship that we at the church had, and that—'

Mary interrupted shaking her head. 'No need to go into detail, Reverend. I had a good idea that this was his intent. He would often make little comments to me about the comfort and support he had over the years from his church and in his own words would say that he would 'see them alright'. These were the actual words he used; I remember very clearly. This is what he wanted, so therefore Reverend, this is what I want. His gift to you comes as no surprise to me. When Gwen passed away, he was so grateful for the comfort and support he received from you and your congregation. Having her name engraved in gold on your honour board in the vestry made a significant impact on him all those years ago.'

Reverend Bryce drew a deep breath. 'That is such a relief, Mary. I had no idea how you would feel, being his closest relative and knowing that he thought the world of you. I thought that perhaps he would have wanted you to have it.'

Mary again assured him. 'Not at all, Reverend. Please don't concern yourself. My uncle made this decision many years ago. I am very happy for you and your church.'

The minister smiled and doffed his hat to her as he turned and walked out the door.

'Oh, Reverend Bryce,' Mary called after him. 'Would you like the furniture and kitchen crockery?'

Looking back, he nodded gratefully. 'We would indeed, thank you, Mary. Many of my parishioner's struggle with the basics of living. I'll send someone round with a van whenever you're ready.'

They smiled at each other and waved goodbye. Closing the door, Mary returned to the clean-up and her thoughts of Uncle Ralph. How happy he would have been to see all his beautiful furniture and crockery going to needy families.

In his bedroom, Mary was subdued and melancholy. It was just as he had left it. The single bed was neatly made up with the burgundy silk eiderdown placed squarely at each corner. His bedside table was crowded with a small wooden-based lamp, his reading glasses, the current *Readers Digest*, a folded newspaper with the previous month's horse racing tips, the stub of a blunt pencil, a jar of vitamin tablets and a small, framed sepia photograph of his Gwen. With tears welling, Mary picked up the newspaper and pencil, putting it safely into her apron pocket. The old oak-mirrored wardrobe standing solidly against the wall was packed tightly with clothes, all hanging neatly. Suits and jackets brought across from England all those years ago, never worn, the beautiful, heavy Harris tweeds with caps to match. The local charity shop were delighted to come and collect them, together with bags of linen and ornaments.

Mary was saddened to see the remnants of her uncle's life leave the safe haven of his shelves, but she was realistic enough to know that she just could not keep it all.

Sitting down on a padded stool she wiped her brow and smiled, recalling the antics of her sons. They were such a tonic during this sad task by keeping her and Alice amused. They would try on clothes and hats, then make jokes about Uncle Ralph's souvenir teaspoons. He had over two hundred, all collected over the years by himself and Gwen. They had both been enthusiastic members of a club. Scot could hardly contain himself. A teaspoon collecting club was just too hysterically funny for words.

From her seat on the stool, Mary caught sight of something dark and bulky under the bed. Getting down on all fours, stashed neatly against the wall, was a narrow light brown heavy cardboard suitcase. She pulled it into the middle of the floor. It was very grubby. A thin leather belt with a broken buckle secured the case; there was old and torn travel labels threaded through the handles with elastic bands. Releasing the belt buckle, she pressed with both hands to open the rusty locks on either side. The springs were still strong and snapped back when she released them. Lifting the lid, the smell overwhelmed her. Old newspapers, dissipated mothballs, and labelled envelopes containing photographs, of which there were many. The photos were mostly sepia; some were black and white. Few were coloured. Mary gathered them all together.

'I'll keep these,' she said out loud. 'Every single one.'

At the bottom of the case was a large package wrapped in torn-yellowed tissue paper. It was protecting a square bag with a brown-tasselled drawstring. Mary gently removed the tissue. Inside the bag was a thick leather-bound book. The front cover had an insert scrawled in faded gold script and embellished with flowers reading: Family Album.

Tentatively, she opened the cover then let out a feeble cry. The pages were of a thick card, with all images glued into tightly fitting pre-cut oval shapes. Every photo was in sepia. There was a beautiful picture of her mother as a child, sitting on a high stool with Uncle Ralph, only a few years old, standing beside her. Both children were dressed in sailor suits. She was wearing a pleated skirt that dropped below her knees, the bloused top had a large, square striped collar. Her hair hung in loose ringlets captured by a giant satin bow, she wore long white socks, and black patent buckled shoes. He wore short pantaloons with a similar top and lanyard. His hair was long, thick and wavy. He was holding a wooden toy boat with a big sail. Both children, although fine-looking, were very sullen.

Closing the book that had protected its contents for so many years, Mary placed it carefully back into the green velvet cover. Holding it close to her chest for a moment, she sighed, then slumping forward she quietly wept. The door opened, Alice came silently into the room and wrapped her arms around her mother.

'Come on, Mum, that's enough for today. Let's go home.'

It was just too much for Mary. She looked at her daughter with tears in her eyes and nodded wearily. 'Apart from you kids, he was all the family I had. I will miss him so much.'

After a sleepless night plagued by memories, Mary returned to the old house early next morning. The shed was the last major clean-up left. It had been Uncle Ralph's domain. All his life he had loved to potter around in there, where he made and fixed things. There were many tools, and although Uncle Ralph had labelled everything neatly in little drawers and boxes, they all had to be distributed. The neighbours were all declining, passing away, moving into retirement villages, nursing homes, or selling up, making way for a younger generation. There was no call for old clamps and cumbersome saws. Mary knew of a sheltered workshop that Vince had mentioned. She would give them a call and offer his beloved tools. She was sure that Uncle Ralph would have given his stamp of approval.

The house was bare, in the front lounge room the old floral carpet was still in perfect condition, showing indents of legs and heavy cabinets, and there were faded spots where the sun had rested. The windows adorned with the netting and drapes that Gwen had sewn, were now torn in parts, hanging in shreds. A four-inch nail bolted in halfway to the window frame two inches from the bottom acted as a lock, allowing the room to breathe.

Sadness overcame Mary. There was no need for her to come back here again; the boys could finish clearing the shed. She only had to collect the mail. It was closure on a chapter of her life. The man who had given her and her family so much, was no more. It was time to move on. Closing the front door gently behind her, she walked down the path to check for mail. The little tin box with its peeling white paint and rusted hinges was bulging with advertising material, the local paper, and three envelopes. One from a local charity looking for support from her soft-hearted uncle, one for the next-door neighbour put there by mistake, and the other was a long-cream stiff envelope. She turned it over slowly, letting out a heavy sigh. It was addressed to her.

The return address was a post office box in Melbourne. Sitting down on the wooden steps, she gently slid her fingers under the gummed envelope. The letter in thick parchment paper was folded lengthways. It was very short and straight to the point.

Dear Mrs Bray,
I act for the late Mr Ralph Clark. It would be appreciated if you could contact my secretary as soon as convenient on the above number to make an appointment. Sooner rather than later would be preferable. I look forward to meeting you.
Yours faithfully,
Andrew Secombe
Secombe & Thomson Solicitors

Mary had never heard of an Andrew Secombe, or his company of solicitors. Uncle Ralph had never mentioned this name. She would call as soon as she got home.

The next day Mary found herself standing on the wide city pavement of a multi-storey office building in the heart of the city. She rarely came to the city. The lift went straight up to the sixth floor. Secombe & Thomson Solicitors glass-fronted office was straight ahead. The smiling young receptionist looked up from her typewriter, welcoming her warmly. 'Good afternoon. Can I help you?'

Mary smiled. 'My name is Mary Bray. I have an appointment with Mr Secombe. I am a bit early, but I don't mind waiting.'

'That's fine, Mrs Bray, please take a seat. He's on the phone right now. I'll tell him you're here as soon as he's free.'

She pointed to a seat by the window then resumed typing. Mary picked up the *Financial Times* from the table, the only reading matter offered. The headlines were full of the 1974 economic recession and the failure of the Whitlam Government to manage the Australian economy. The receptionist's voice interrupted Mary's interest and concentration.

'Mrs Bray, Mr Secombe will see you now. Please go through.'

The young man seated behind the large desk stood up as she came in. He extended his hand, good morning, Mrs Bray. I'm Andrew Secombe. Thank you for coming in so promptly; please, sit down'.

Mary shook his hand warmly then sat down, her handbag on her lap.

'Mrs Bray, I'll come straight to the point. Were you aware that your late uncle was a client of ours?' Andrew Secombe looked intently at Mary.

Mary frowned and shook her head. 'No, no I wasn't. We never discussed his private affairs.' 'Well then, you see he first came to my father's office over fifty years ago, and my father gave him advice. Our business in those days was in its fledgling era. We offered advice on legal issues, and investments. This was around the time that your uncle got his first promotion at the biscuit factory. He had been budgeting and saving every week and had accumulated a small nest egg. He wanted some advice on stocks and shares. It was the start of a very unusual friendship. Both men were from very different backgrounds, but both had a love of horses and investments. Your uncle was a canny man, Mrs Bray. He made some very good choices over the years, and these have paid handsome dividends. Did you know that he owned outright a block of six flats on the edge of Melbourne?'

Mary whispered, 'No, no, didn't know that. I had no idea, I—'

'He also owned the house where a Mrs Jessop lives. As you know, she was a lifelong friend of Gwen Clark your late aunt. Your uncle promised his wife that her friend could stay in that house until the day she died. He and my father also jointly invested in stocks and shares. Some of these shares are now out of the buying power of the average investor. Your uncle bought many hundreds. He also had a major financial interest in the stables of Liam Haggerty, and I don't need to tell you how successful that man is.'

Mary was looking intently at Andrew, unable to form words, unable to comment. She began coughing and wheezing and wiping her brow. Andrew Secombe quickly buzzed through to his receptionist.

'Emma, can you bring Mrs Bray a glass of water right away, please.'

The water was hurried in. Mary took a long drink before looking directly at the young man opposite her. 'Mr Secombe, I'm lost for words. He never mentioned any of this, even when I went through all his papers; nothing gave any indication or suggestion that he had so many investments. In fact, there was not even a single letterhead from your company.'

Andrew Secombe leaned forward and clasped his outstretched hands in front of him.

'That was because your uncle realised that he didn't have the skills to manage his investments. They were getting too big. He and my father had a long history, a very close bond. I can remember as a young student seeing your uncle in Dad's office on many occasions having a coffee and a laugh together. He asked my father to manage his affairs. They had a gentlemen's agreement. Everything was in my father's files; no correspondence left the office. They had the odd phone call and coffee catch up and that was it. My father died two years ago, so I combined my law practice with his investment business and moved it all here, to the city. Your uncle came to see me twelve months ago. He asked me to update his will. As you can imagine, this was no easy task. His investments had grown to such an extent that I had to allocate another staff member to work solely on his account. He wanted to keep this part of his life private, and we gave him that assurance. His documents are all up to date with signatures and instructions for when the inevitable happened, and of course it has.'

Mary's eyes never left the young man's face.

Andrew continued. 'As you are surely already aware, your uncle has left his residential home to the church. In the scheme of things, this is but a very small portion of his estate. He had favoured many charities over the years, they were always going to benefit from his generosity. However, when you and your family came into his life it changed everything. He thought the world of you, Mrs Bray. He sat where you are sitting now, his eyes brimming with tears, telling me how you were the living image of his late sister and what joy you and your children were bringing him in his later life. He was most definite that you should be well cared for when he was gone, so I am delighted to tell you that apart from the church, you alone are the major beneficiary of Mr Ralph Clark's estate. In round figures, we would estimate your assets to be well over $500 thousand dollars. Mrs Bray, you are a very wealthy woman.'

Chapter 29

Black clouds had gathered in the skies above an isolated country club on the outskirts of Melbourne. A chill wind whipped through a half-eaten hay bale, scattering plant heads, leaves, and stems around the patchy paddock, much to the delight of a flock of white cockatoos. It was late afternoon. A lone figure sat scowling out from a large bay window of the prestigious club.

'Bloody Awstraliya,' he mumbled, stubbing out his cigarette on the highly polished wooden floor. 'Might as well be in Glesga with this fuckin weather.'

Archie Bray stood up and pressed his face against the windowpane, trying to see round the corner. 'Where is she?' he muttered. He had been waiting for over an hour.

Years ago, he would never have ventured into a place like this: A grand lounge with deep comfortable armchairs, polished tables with glass tops, and a long mahogany bar with bottles of spirits and liquors resting on glass shelves fronting a massive mirror.

He would have been more comfortable in the back nook of the local pub getting abusive, dribbling beer over the soaked beer mats while he ranted, giving the barman his life story. Times had changed. When Mary came into money three years prior, he stopped handing over his pay every week. She paid for everything except his beer and smokes. Had he known that silly old Ralph was loaded, he would have been nicer to him. Mary was being a right smart arse; never discussing things with him, knowing that he was so good at managing money. She had gone to see some financial person, got herself involved with different things, and was always away out somewhere: at the restaurant, at meetings, or on the phone. He had no idea how much Uncle Ralph had left her. Probably a couple of thousand dollars. He didn't care. He had fag and beer money. Stupid bitch!

Archie had reluctantly accepted the Australian lifestyle. Sitting in the sunshine of the beer garden in his local pub he could drink without reprimand, laugh loudly, swear and spill beer. The summer weather was great, and the steaks were unbelievable. Even his bit on the side, Cheryl, was a bonus, he mused.

Behind the stone wall at the gates was a plethora of bushes dotted randomly over the sloping hills. They led to large, swaying grey gum trees with veiled shards of water glinting through the branches. The occasional wayward sheep would stray into the fields from surrounding farms. She had thought it was idyllic, out of the way. They had met here many times. He ordered another beer ... his third.

The screeching of tyres signalled Cheryl's arrival as her car raced into the car park, narrowly missing an ornamental tree on the centre garden strip. He watched as she quickly checked her appearance in a small hand mirror, throwing her hair back then checking her teeth for lipstick smudges. Sliding awkwardly out of the seat in high stiletto heels, she struggled to negotiate the pebble pathway leading to the club foyer. Her short, tight skirt bound together two of the loveliest, longest limbs that Archie had ever seen. Minutes later, she was in the lounge heading straight for his table. Her face was sullen, her forehead knotted, full painted lips puckered. He had a sudden rush of lust as she brushed against him whilst sliding into the padded seat. Turning to face her, he quickly decided that chastising her for being late was not a good idea. 'You okay, darlin?'

She glared at him, snapping back, 'No, Archie, I'm not okay.' She put her elbows on the table, rubbing her brow in rotation. 'He knows, Archie,' she mumbled to the table. 'Steve knows about us and he's gunning for you. I'm fucking terrified.'

Her words hung heavily in the air whilst Archie looked at her in disbelief.

'What?'

'You heard me.'

'Okay, okay, I heard ye, but how do ye know?'

'His brother was here last Tuesday night. His work had a presentation dinner or some bloody thing in the function room. He came through here on his way to the toilet and saw us dancing, dancing close, Archie, you know, the way we do. He told Steve this morning and we had a massive fight. I denied it, of course, told him it certainly was not me. He said he was going to check up on my Tuesday night sewing class. If he finds out I have been lying, he said he would kick me out and would make sure I would lose the kids.'

Her voice broke and she started crying into her handkerchief. 'My God, Archie, I have never seen him so fired up! I am so scared, he'll come after you, my God he will, I know it. He has friends who you would not want to mess with; they are dangerous and could maim you for life. What are we going to do?' Cheryl was shaking Archie's arm. 'Archie, Archie, are you listening? What the hell are we going to do?'

Archie's face had paled, his trembling hand raising his glass. He made no effort to comfort her. 'Well then, where is he the noo?'

'He's taken our youngest to footy training. I'll need to get back before he does.'

Archie banged his fist on the table, jumped up, and walked quickly away in the direction of the toilet.

Cheryl lay back on the seat, closed her eyes, resting her head on the back wall. What had she been thinking of? Allowing this coward, this man to seduce her and jeopardise her family. How did it happen?

It was three years ago, a time when she and Steve were having money problems and constantly arguing. He was always tired, always working late. They hardly spoke to each other and the kids suffered, they missed him. She felt neglected, worthless, and alone.

Archie was such a boost. Whenever Steve was out of sight at work, he would chat her up. She found his Scottish accent and sense of humour magnetic.

He was smart too. She had watched him take on management whenever the workers had a grievance. He was the workers saviour, and she was in awe of him.

The night it happened, they had both been working late. Steve had already left the factory to pick up the kids, and everyone else had gone home. Archie was locking up. She was cleaning out the flour bins at the back of the room when she slipped and twisted her ankle. Sitting on a stool and rubbing it, she let out a mouthful of expletives.

He heard her cries, came over quickly and knelt down to remove her shoe. While reaching under her wide overalls, he rested his hands on her bare skin. The exhilaration she felt from his touch was powerful. Moving up to her face, he put his hand behind her neck, and brought her to him. She didn't resist.

His kisses were long and tender, and made her feel wanted, loved, important and beautiful. She gave in to his passion. Everything that really mattered to her was forgotten at that moment.

Later, as they held each other close undercover of the massive flour bins, she felt warm and wanted. From then on, there was no turning back.

Cheryl opened her eyes to the deserted room. Where had he gone? She needed support, he had to tell her it was all okay, that they would get through this together. She needed him to say that he would confront Steve and tell him that they had just fallen in love. It was not planned; it had just happened. As much as she needed this assurance, Cheryl knew she would never hear it from Archie. She realised now that he only ever wanted her for one thing. He was a weakling, and a liar, and she knew for certain it was all over with him now.
She desperately did not want it to be over with Steve and her children.

Archie walked past the toilets into the public bar. He ordered a whisky and sat down at a corner table. He felt physically sick. He had to disappear before Steve caught up with him, but where to? He was a big man with a violent temper. Archie had only seen him lose it once. It was last Christmas at a barbeque at the factory. One of the contractors, after too many beers, had made a playful pass at Cheryl's tits. They were almost hanging out of her white laced-up peasant blouse.

Steve, who had been drinking nonstop for a few hours, quickly spotted the interaction between them both and asked the man to step outside for a minute. It was a noisy encounter, with bangs, crashes, and screams, but no one intervened. The man's sight was saved thanks to the ambulance that got him to the hospital in record time. His story to the doctors was that he had one too many that night and had fallen from a balcony. The last Archie heard was that he was left with low vision in one eye and having trouble finding work.

He came back to the table, but didn't sit down. He knew what he had to do. He needed to leave, now, but Cheryl beat him to it.

She stood up holding her bag close to her chest. 'I suppose it's cheerio then, Archie, eh? Nothing else to say, is there?'

'Aye, yer right there, hen, its fur the best, eh? Away ye go then, aw the best, darlin, cheerio!'

Cheryl let out a whimper, wiped her eyes then staggered quickly through the mahogany doors. He watched as she stumbled across the pebbles, tripping and falling over in her stiletto heels. Throwing herself into the driver's seat she reversed, hit a garden gnome, and sped off. As her car disappeared into the distance, Archie lay back, closed his eyes and mumbled to himself, 'Thank God fur that. She was a hopeless fuck, anyhow.'

Chapter 30

It had been three years since Uncle Ralph's passing. During that time, Mary's life had moved to another plateau. Both her boys were now married and living in their own homes, and both had successful careers. Scot had his own thriving plumbing business, and Billy's career in finance made him the youngest credit manager of a major city bank. Alice still lived at home. She became a kindergarten teacher, working part-time at a nearby childcare centre, in addition to working with Mary in the restaurant.

Thanks to Uncle Ralph's generosity, Mary didn't have to work, but she wanted to work. She was still at the helm of a restaurant that was thriving, now with a staff of nine.

In her mid-fifties, active and well-groomed, she was revelling in her successes at Ronaldo's. Sadly, however, she still suffered bouts of ill health—coughing, wheezing, and shortness of breath—but she never complained or made a fuss, always appearing to be in control. Vince and Max were now silent partners of the business, giving the whole operation to Mary, with their full support.

The dark shadow in her life was Archie. Three years earlier, he had suddenly left Baker's with no explanation. Mary didn't exactly know why. He wouldn't talk about it and she didn't pursue it. He had quickly taken an out-of-town job as a clerk on the construction site of a new estate. It was many miles away from her home, so there were times when he went to the pub after work and he would stay overnight in a nearby boarding house. Their relationship was in name only. When the boys had left home, she moved into the spare bedroom, rarely seeing him. Sometimes he would stay away for days at a time; hence it came as a complete surprise to Mary one morning when the phone rang while she was working at the dining room table.

'Hello?'

'Hello, Mary? This is John Talbot from Lomond Constructions here. Is this a good time to call?'

'Oh John! Hello, what a surprise. My goodness, I haven't heard from you in a long time. How are you? Yes, it's fine, I am just working from home.' Mary put her pen down, puzzled as to why he was calling.

'I'm fine, thanks, Mary. Sorry to bother you, I was wondering if Archie was there.'

'Well, no, John, sorry he's not, I presumed he was at work. I haven't seen him for a few days. As you know, he often stays at the boarding house. Is everything okay?'

'Well, I hope so, it's just that he didn't turn up here yesterday when he had to join us in a meeting with the auditors. Actually, it was a crucial meeting. He had to go over some accounts with us. There seems to be a discrepancy; the auditors couldn't account for some missing entries. A sizeable amount really, over $2,000. I'm sure it's just been overlooked somewhere, but we need Archie to validate it.'

Mary was speechless, but not surprised. 'Oh John, sorry, I don't know where he is at all, honestly, I don't, but I'll make a few calls and get back to you later if I hear anything. Is that alright?'

John said that was fine and they said their goodbyes.

Mary dragged her hand over her face. She closed her eyes. 'Oh God, please, please make him gone.'

The landlady at the boarding house was very brisk. 'No, darl, haven't seen him since last week, no idea where that one is ... bloody drunk! When you do find him, tell him he owes us seventy dollars, will ya?'

Mary thanked her, apologising for her husband's behaviour.

His bedroom was chaotic, clothes everywhere, drawers opened and upturned, dirty crockery and glasses by the bed. His sports bag, runners, t-shirts, and jeans were missing. A joint savings account bank book with a balance of $520 had also disappeared. Joint signatures were no problem for Archie; he was an expert at forgery. A small wooden framed photograph of the boys when they were young, posing in their football strip, was also gone.

Right at that moment, Mary grasped that he had left the family home, and left quickly. He had simply disappeared. The boys hadn't seen much of their father of late, and didn't seem too surprised. Scot laughed when she told him, with Billy in the background calling out, 'Don't worry, Mum, he'll be back. Probably just gone walkabout!'

In 1980, Prime Minister Malcolm Fraser governed Australia, and baby Azaria Chamberlain disappeared at Ayes Rock, Uluru, reportedly taken by a dingo. Australian Aboriginal Evonne Goolagong Cawley won her final grand slam match at Wimbledon, and for Mary Bray it was decision time.

Now that Archie was gone, it was time to move from the home that had given her and her family so much pleasure when it was built all those years ago. Rather than sell it, she decided to keep it as an investment, renting it to a young family who had just arrived in Australia from England. She wanted a new home for her and Alice, somewhere with space, light, and views; a place she could savour peace, quiet, birds, flowers, and trees. She basked in the successes of her children and quietly rejoiced at the hasty departure of her husband. The restaurant was exceeding all her expectations with happy staff and satisfied return customers.

It was only when alone, she let the memories take over, allowing her to go back in time to her soldier Charlie, the happiness of living with him, and the guilt of losing him. She welcomed the relief of tears.

Within weeks of her decision to leave Broadfields Estate, and after many house inspections and discussions with real estate agents, Mary found the home she knew would be her forever home. It was a sprawling property in a semi-rural belt of Melbourne with too many rooms and bathrooms for two people, but she loved it instantly. It had belonged to a New Zealand stonemason, a master artisan. He had built it of natural bluestone in a labour of love for his wife. The driveways, paths and retaining walls, the fireplaces, and birdbaths, were all carefully crafted in stone, a testament of his skill and devotion. Sadly, his wife died unexpectedly from an undiagnosed illness before they ever had a chance to enjoy the peace, ambience, and spectacular views from their new home. He was a broken man.

This tragic love story had immense appeal for Mary, knowing that every stone placed carefully and retained throughout the home was motivated by a man's love for his wife. He had named the house in memory of her. 'Huhana', Māori for 'Susan'. Mary kept the name.

It was an open plan and airy house, with floor to ceiling windows that were enhanced by heavy satin drapes for winter warmth. The wide-open fireplaces with cast iron surrounds were the feature points in two living areas, stacked with firewood in large copper buckets either side of the grate. The main family room had three steps leading down to a sunken lounge embellished with large rust-coloured soft sofas and gigantic multi-coloured cushions. Secured in the centre was a massive cedar wood coffee table holding four heavy wooden candleholders and a large, highly polished oak fruit bowl. The bathrooms and kitchen areas had grey slate floors with chrome fittings and marble benches. Comfort was in every room, regardless of the weather.

Mary's sanctuary was her bedroom. It was spacious and decorated in light pastel colours with delicate Victorian furniture sitting on light, pine polished floorboards. A large floor to ceiling window with two sizeable outward opening French doors led to a secluded veranda. Beyond that was the courtyard and stone steps leading to a garden decked out with statues, paths, and climbing rose vines, all from another era.

It was the view that sold her. The house sat comfortably atop a gentle sloping hill, peppered with native Australian gum and bush trees. Hidden from view was a dam with overhanging eucalyptus trees, attracting an abundance of birdlife. At dusk and late into the night, the faraway twinkling lights of the nearest town would assure and comfort her.

Mary and Alice settled quickly into their new home, both contented and happy. It was barely an hour's scenic drive from the restaurant.

It was late one afternoon. Mary changed into a heavy cotton dress and light cardigan, in preparation for dinner that evening with Vince and his family. The summer weather with its unrelenting heat was now becoming the golds and reds of autumn. How she loved autumn in Melbourne; the trees surrounding her gave so much pleasure as she watched them turn gracefully from verdant green to burnt hues. The days were still warm, but the cool nights warned of imminent colder days. It reminded her of a late English summer, an English park, and a young English soldier, some decades ago.

Slipping off her sandals, she lay on top of the bed and closed her eyes; it was all so easy to recall. Contentment and peace washed over her.

'Come on, Mary, you can do it, it's only a little stream. Jump! I'll catch you.' Charlie stood barefoot with outstretched arms on the other side of the river. His striped shirtsleeves and trousers were rolled up, waiting for her to land on the rock in the middle.

'No, Charlie, I'm scared! It looks too deep there; I can't do it.'

'I promise I'll catch you. Come on, I'm here, look!' Charlie laughed, trying to persuade her, but she couldn't move.

'Well, all right then,' he said, 'just stay there. I'll come over ... and don't look so scared! I won't let the fish bite you.'

He paddled through the water, knee deep, and turned to the rock so she could climb onto his back.

'You mad thing!' Mary yelled between squeals of 'don't you dare drop me' and 'help, I'm going to fall!'.

On the other bank they fell on to the soft grass, laughing and clutching each other. It was a shaded spot, the only sounds being the ripple of the water as it toiled its way down stream over the shiny stones and the intermittent melodic mating call of sparrows. The bank turned slowly to a sanctuary of falling leaves and thick perennial bushes. The late afternoon sun sparkled between the branches of the old elm tree high above them. As they stretched on the cool soft ground, their heads fell together on a cover of green. They stopped laughing.

Charlie pushed himself up onto his elbow and looked down at her loveliness. Their eyes were reading each other's innermost thoughts.

He leaned forward and kissed her softly on the cheek. She closed her eyes, savouring the moment. She felt the brush of his lips on hers, so gentle at first, then deeper and more passionate. His strong arms enveloped her. Mary felt warm and safe. All her senses were numb, time was without end, she was powerless, completely lost in him. He was in control of her body and of her mind. He had captured her and taken her on a journey of discovery and fulfilment ... a euphoric voyage into her very soul.

Much later, they lay on the bank in silence, still wrapped in each other's arms and feeling the other's heartbeat, knowing that what they had was something far greater than special. Mary lifted Charlie's hand to her lips and kissed each finger then laid her head on his shoulder as he stroked her hair. Later, they would recall it was at that time they had created Alice.

Mary opened her eyes, catching her reflection in the wardrobe mirror. She was smiling. Reaching reached down to the drawer of her bedside table she pulled out a worn leather folder. The stitching was frayed and the leather thin and faded. The black stud button had lost most of its paint and was silver in parts, but it was still strong enough to protect the precious contents. She slowly pulled out the photograph. It was a head and shoulder shot the size of a postcard taken in a studio.

He was wearing a heavy khaki uniform with brass buttons, his side cap worn at an angle over his tight blonde curls. The photograph, touched up with colour, did not detract from the fine features of his handsome face. On the back in flowing scribe, he had handwritten: *To My Mary – Always, Charlie.*

She brushed the tips of her fingers tenderly over the image before returning it to its secret place. Mary closed her eyes again and started to doze off. The phone by her bed rang. It was Max.

'Mary we are at the door, are you ready?'

Mary jumped up quickly, still half asleep. Picking up her earrings from the bedside table, she dropped one. It rolled under the bed.

'Yes, yes, I'll be right there, Max, just looking for my earring. It rolled under the bed. I won't be a minute.'

The wayward pearl was lying on the floor, far under the bed. She pushed her head forward almost touching the bed base and grabbed it, then she started coughing and inhaling dust and fibres from the carpet. Coughing turned to wheezing, her throat tightened, breathing became difficult, and she just managed to push herself back from under the bed.

Mary grabbed at her throat with two hands, squeezing and pulling, gasping for air. She crawled to the bedside table, fighting to stay alert, nausea and dizziness took hold. Lunging at the bedside table, she grasped her inhaler. Releasing the lifesaving vapour, she inhaled, hunkering over, praying for relief.

She sat on the bed exhausted. Her cheeks were wet, her breathing now regulated. This was occurring with too much regularity. It was only a matter of time until the children found out how serious it was. She would discuss a plan with her doctor.

Mary stood up and looked in the mirror. Her face was ashen, her eyes red rimmed. Brushing her hair and touching up her makeup gave a glow to her cheeks. The lipstick was a bit bright, she thought, and then she smiled to herself. Selena would like it.

As she opened the front door, Max held out his arms. 'Oh, Mary, here you are, you look beautiful as always. Give me a hug. I swear your years are going backwards.'

Mary laughed and hugged him. She hooked onto his arm and walked to the gate, treading slowly on the paving. Max put his arm around her as they neared the car parked outside her gate. 'Vince is so excited to see you, Mary, he's been talking nonstop so please, when you get in the car, can you tell him his new haircut looks great, that it takes years off him?

Mary laughed at the devoted brother. 'Of course, I will, Max. You know me!'

Climbing into the back seat of the car, she leaned forward to kiss Selena, then gave Vince a peck on the cheek. 'Vince, let me look at you. You look great, so different. What is it, is it your hair? It is your hair; I can see that now. It's so short, so fashionable. You look younger, it really suits you.'

Vince, with a tinge of blush, looked away and smiled. 'Oh Mary, thank you! I am glad you like it, I thought you would.'

Max and Selena sat quietly in the front seat, looking straight ahead.

They were going to a favourite restaurant. Vince had been very evasive on the phone. Mary put it down to his medication. He was often forgetful.

The restaurant owner knew of Mary and her reputation. He had reserved a table in the farthest corner overlooking the pond. Vince could manoeuvre his wheelchair to the edge of the table, Mary sat close to him.

The menu was a point of great discussion. They all had opinions, all choosing a different dish. Mary smiled to herself thinking this was good market research.

Max had been sitting quietly throughout dinner not saying much, while Selena and Vince kept up a constant stream of conversation. After their plates had been cleared and the table brushed down, Max leaned forward with one hand resting on his chin. He coughed and cleared his throat, looking at Mary intently.

'Mary, we are always so happy to see you and tonight is no different. However, there's something that we have been thinking about for some time now and would like to discuss with you. It's something that we couldn't really talk about by phone, and to be honest, Mary, it has been bothering me for some time.'

Mary frowned slightly, then with a half-smile shook her head, looking firstly at Selena then at Vince. They waited for Max to speak.

Alice was at home, writing reports for the parents of her charges at the kindergarten. She put down her pen, stretched her arms and leaned back on the chair. Looking over at a painting on her wall of Glasgow in the fifties, she reflected how different her life was now, and how it would have been, had she stayed in Glasgow.

She would almost certainly still be living on the estate, possibly working in a factory or a shop, and probably always short of money. The accident might never have happened, and her beautiful best friend Rena would still be alive. She would be a teacher by now and they would still share confidences, perhaps both would have husbands and children. No matter how she tried to diminish those thoughts, they remained so vivid in her mind, still bringing unbearable pain, remorse, and immeasurable guilt. Rubbing her forehead, she forced the recollections. Closing her eyes, she went back.

That night—the rain, the speed, the music, the volume—all contributors.

Although it was a tragic fatal accident, she felt guilty knowing that she had concentrated more on tuning the radio than passing the lit cigarette cautiously to Rena.

It was a moment of guilt that would stay with her forever, a moment when her best friend paid the ultimate price. Alice blamed herself for what happened that night. She told no one.

Settled on the other side of the world with her family had eased the pain, but only to an extent. She took little solace in the knowledge that it was an accident, but she alone knew what a tragic part she had played in Rena's short life. Rena loved children, and had studied to be a primary school teacher. In memory of her closest friend, Alice would aspire to work with children.

'Alice, can I come in, pet?' Mary tapped gently on Alice's bedroom door.

'Oh, Mum, yes, please come in. I have finished now. My eyes are failing, I could not look at another page.' Alice's laugh was so infectious.

Mary sat on a stool at the end of her daughter's bed. She braced herself. 'Alice, I need to talk to you about something ... something very important. It's a decision I need to make, and I need your advice, your support and your blessing.'

Alice looked at her mother and frowned; she quickly closed her desk drawer and sat down cross-legged on the striped cushions on the floor.

'What's the matter, Mum? You look like all of Australia's problems have just landed on your shoulders.' Grabbing her mother's shoe, she shook it, trying to ease the mood.

'Last night I went out for dinner with Max, Selena, and Vince. They wanted to tell me that they have decided to move interstate. They are going to Queensland to live.'

'Queensland?' Alice screwed her eyes. 'Why Queensland?'

'Because Selena's family are there. Her parents are getting older and frailer and want to see more of their only grandchild. With Sofia passing away, Max is now Vince's primary carer, and he won't leave Melbourne without him, so have decided they will all move to the sunny state before winter.'

'What? Vince leaving Melbourne? Does he want to go?'

'It's not a matter of wanting, the alternative is to put him into a nursing home, and none of us would allow that. He is still so mentally active, it's his body that is wasting away. Selena's sister is a nurse and very supportive of the whole idea. They will all live near each other, so as sad as it is for us this is the best option for Vince, and he agrees.' Mary cleared her throat, speaking too quickly. 'Alice I am so scared.'

Alice sat up looking directly at her mother. 'Scared, Mum? What are you scared of? What is it?'

'Well, you see, the dinner was lovely, and we all chatted, but the real reason for it was that they wanted me to ...' Mary stood up smiling and talking faster, she blurted out, 'They want me to buy the restaurant!'

Alice, wide eyed, looked at her mother. 'What?

'You see, Alice, they feel it's more my restaurant than theirs anyway.' She laughed softly. 'They said they would give it to me at less than market price and with no agents involved. It would be financially beneficial for all of us. As you all know, I do love being there. I just don't know if I can do it.' Mary's eyes glazed over briefly, as she looked to the ceiling and smiled. 'Did I ever tell you about the time when Selena got sick, and I had to cater for eighty people on my third day?

Alice smiled. 'Yes, Mum, many times.' She pulled her mother up from the stool and hugged her. 'Whatever you decide to do, you know we will all support you. I am just worried that you should be slowing down a bit now, not starting out on a new venture. Not with your bronchitis and chest the way it is. I know you said you have felt better these last months, but winter is not a good time for you. You should take it quietly. Have an early night tonight and we'll get the boys together later for a family discussion.'

Mary nodded. 'Yes, darling, you're probably right. I do need to sleep on it, but I just had to tell you.' She hugged her daughter, said goodnight then headed to her bedroom.

Undressing in the dark, she quickly slipped on her nightdress then climbed into bed under a thin cotton blanket. The garden lights were still on, the moon suspended beneath the stars high above the willow tree. It came to her at that moment, an idea, and it was a great idea. Quickly switching on her bed lamp, she reached for a pen and pad and started making notes, scribbling at high speed.

Much later, the bedside clock said 2.30 am. The moon had faded and the only lights in the garden were from the tiny solar glows edging the stone pathway. Mary switched off her bedside lamp, the cicadas soothing her senses. She snuggled into her blanket and slept until morning.

Chapter 31

Scot at thirty was tall with strong, chiselled features and a thick head of dark brown hair that was starting to recede. Giving up his soccer training four years ago, saw him gain quite a few pounds. He attributed this to Carol's cooking. Scot was popular with his customers, friends, and colleagues.

He relished in the plumbing industry, acquiring skills that would eventually see him open his own business in domestic and commercial plumbing. A huge showroom in a semi-industrial area presented the latest in bathroom colours and styles such as Hollywood type make-up mirrors, blocked glass walls, etched glass shower screens, lime green bathroom suites, teak kitchen cupboards, and wide single sinks with faucet handles made of glass. He was thriving, and in great demand for his up-to-the-minute designs and knowledge.

It was a day that had been particularly busy for Scot. The staff had left at 5 o'clock, whilst he stayed back writing notes for a meeting the following afternoon. Placing them in a folder in the top drawer of his desk, he got up to leave, put on his jacket, and reached for the light switch ... then the phone rang.

He was tired and thought about letting it ring out, realising it was late for a business call and that emergency plumbing went through to the agency on another number, so it must be personal.

'Hello.'

'Is that Scot Bray?' It was a woman.

'Yes, it is. Who am I speaking with?'

'You don't know me. My name is Anne Sullivan I am a social worker at the Casuarina Hospital here in Darwin. Are you able to talk to me at this time, Mr Bray?'

Scot pulled a chair over and sat down. 'Well ... yes, but Darwin? Yes, okay then, that's fine.'

'Mr Bray, I don't want to alarm you but we have a patient here at the moment, his name is Archie Bray. We think he is your father. He is a very sick man.'

'What?'

She continued talking. Scot, in a haze, was struggling to concentrate. It was a difficult conversation. Anne was short on pleasantries, getting straight to the point. He listened patiently and interjected only to ask her to repeat and clarify something. They talked for twenty minutes.

Hanging up, he leaned back, gripping the armrests of his chair trying to stop his shaking hands. He couldn't comprehend it, but he knew exactly what he had to do.

He called his brother. The phone rang twice, Billy answered.

'It's Scot ... yeah, not bad.'

Billy began to relate his mundane day at work.

Scot quickly interrupted. 'Billy, Billy, sorry to stop you there, mate, but we need to talk. I've just had a disturbing phone call from a woman, a social worker, from a hospital in Darwin.'

Billy stopped and drew in a deep breath. 'Darwin? Who do you know in Darwin for God's sake, Scotty?'

'It's Dad. He's in hospital, been there for two weeks.'

'What? Dad in Darwin? What do you mean how did he get there? Is he ... was he? My God, have you spoken to him? I mean how do you know this Anne woman is genuine?

'Billy, Billy, hold on, I have no idea. I have only just spoken briefly to her, and I do believe her. They found my name in a bible, of all things, in his possessions. They tracked me down through that.'

Scot paused, waiting for a response, but his brother was silent.

'The drink has finally caught up with him. It's his liver, Billy, he's delusional. She told me that he would not last much more than a couple of weeks. She said he was ranting and calling out for all of us. I can't tell Mum; her conscience will tell her she should be there, but I don't think she should. She's not strong enough. No point in telling Alice, of course. She couldn't care less. So, it's up to us. We have to go to him, Billy. He's our father, and he's dying.'

Billy's voice came from a tunnel 'I can't believe it. Are you sure? I mean, who is this social worker is she—?'

'Yes, I'm sure and yes, she is genuine. Now, get organised. I'll try to book a flight for tomorrow, okay?'

'Yes okay, but what will we tell—'

Scot's voice was specific. 'It's a business trip, Billy, alright?'

'A business trip, but ... what the? I see, right! Good idea, Scotty, you're right.'

The plane touched down at Darwin Airport late in the afternoon. It was hot, dusty, and oppressive. They brothers hurried across the tarmac, both men had backpacks. A lone taxi was sitting outside at the rank. Hailing it, they asked for the motel. The driver, a middle-aged aboriginal, sat up straight, smiling at them, showing off a row of half-missing yellow teeth.

'Where you wanna go, brudder?'

'To the Windar Motel, mate, how far?' Scot asked.

'Oh, him not too far, brudder. We soon be dare.'

It was only a short distance along a wide, dusty road. The driver waited as they briefly stopped at the motel to check in and drop off their backpacks.

Neither Billy nor Scot had been to Australia's top end, nor did they have any idea of what life was like there. At any other time they would have been fascinated, keen to learn more about the land, the community, and the direct contrast with Melbourne, but not today. These were sorrowful times.

Casuarina Hospital had only recently opened its doors to the people of Darwin. It was the territory's much needed pride and joy and the locals loved it. They had embraced this new, modern high-rise structure and all the facilities it offered. The building towered above a large car park dotted with palm trees. For two brothers from a faraway eastern city, it was a place of sorrow. A place to make peace.

At the reception desk, a young woman stared intently at her typewriter. Scot waited until she looked up.

'Hello there, I'm looking for my father, his name is Archie Bray. He was brought here very recently.'

She smiled and flicked through the pages in front of her. 'It's on the first floor, Mr Bray, but it may be quicker to take the stairs.'

Scot thanked her, and the brothers walked briskly up the stairs where they were met by the duty sister, who introduced herself. 'Mr Bray, I am Sister Baillieu; how do you do.' Extending a limp hand to each brother, she looked directly from one to the other.

'I'll come straight to the point. Your father is in the advanced stages of ALD, that is Acute Liver Disease, or cirrhosis of the liver. He has been here for the last two weeks, brought in by a pastor from one of the settlements near the riverbed. He has been in and out of consciousness, and at times not making much sense; however, we did manage to find out that he has a family. Your name and suburb were written on the inside back cover of an old bible.' Picking up a small book from beneath an envelope on her desk she handed it to Scot. 'I think this belongs to you.'

Scot frowned, taking the tattered leather pocketbook from her. The gilded lettering of The New Testament was long gone, only a thin imprint remained; the gold edged pages were faded and torn. He shook his head.

'No, sorry, I can't recall this and my father is not religious, or I should say he never used to be. Perhaps the pastor gave it to him.'

Sister Baillieu's tone softened as she spoke. 'No, Mr Bray, the pastor only became aware of him just over two weeks ago. He was dirty, matted, and delirious when they found him. He had sheltered in the wreck of an old utility near the settlement. One of the elders helped revive him and then sent for the pastor.'

Scot stared at the woman. His voice incredulous. 'Are you telling us that our father lived as a homeless person in the wreck of a car?'

'It certainly appears that way I'm afraid. I'm sorry.' Clasping her hands together at her waist she sighed. 'Mr Bray, I think you should look at the inside cover of the book.'

Scot looked down at the little book nestled in the palm of his hand and gently opened the flimsy cover. Billy leaned over his brother curiously, it was a bookplate. The once vivid dark blue and gold scrolls were now sadly faded, but the cursive writing was still legible. It made the hairs on Scot's neck rise: *Presented to Scot Bray for Excellence in Reading.*

The brothers then followed Sister Baillieu down the long, empty corridor leading to the ward. She stopped at the last bed completely encased in thin white curtains then turned to face them.

'Just a word of warning to you both, your father may not look like the person you remember. He has deteriorated in the time that he has been here. The combination of alcohol abuse and poor nutrition is lethal. Right now, he is asleep. There is a chance that when he wakes up he may not recognise you, so please, be prepared.'

The brothers looked at each other in dread. Standing together, they watched her spin around reaching for the middle of the curtain. Hesitating briefly, with one great swish, she pulled it back … exposing what was left of Archie Bray.

Billy made the first move to the pristine sheets. His eyes widened in disbelief, looking down at the heartbreak before him. Whatever form of life this was, it was not his father. He was sure of that. Scot stood behind him. Reaching out, he gripped his shoulder.

Archie's shrunken, pitiful form lay wrapped under taut white cotton; his motionless arms lay outside the sheets. His face, skull like, was thinly covered by a yellow-tinged skin tone; long stringy strands of thin grey hair fringed his forehead. His eyes were sunken and closed; a gaping mouth revealed discoloured and rotted teeth.

Billy stood back and held on to the bed rails. Looking to his brother, he whispered, 'God Almighty, Scotty, what happened? What in God's name happened here?'

Scot, seeing his brother slump forward with both hands covering his face, gently sat him down on a chair away from the bed, realising right then just how vulnerable his younger brother was. It forced him to relive the past. Billy had never experienced the early years of Archie, the years that could easily have split their family and destroyed their mother. When Billy had reached school age, Archie had mellowed slightly and Mary had grown stronger.

He spoke softly to his brother. 'Billy, he's done it tough these last few years, and wherever he's been it hasn't been easy. He gave Mum a terrible life, we all know that, but look at him today. My God! I think he's paid for it, don't you? We're here for him now and that's all that matters.'

Billy didn't answer, he was absorbed with the form on the bed. Apart from the distention in his abdomen that rose like a pregnancy, it was a strange stick man that lay under the immaculate sheets. His breathing was alarming, laboured and crackled.

'I know, Scotty, I know that. I just find it hard to accept that this is him, that's all.' Billy was wringing his hands and shaking his head. 'I mean, he did do his bit at the football club, didn't he? He was as proud as anything, coming to the games. Do you remember those times, Scotty?' Billy's voice broke. Both fell silent, swathed in their own memories.

It was two days before Archie opened his eyes. The medication had given him relief from pain, but little ability to communicate. Scot and Billy were there most of the time, holding his hand. Sharni, the young aboriginal nurse who looked after him, bustled around, changing his water and straightening the bed sheets.

It was early evening when Archie finally opened his eyes. He blinked a few times, then shook his head. Looking first at Scot then at Billy, he tried to speak but coughed instead, phlegm filling his mouth. Sharni was there and quickly lifted his shoulders, holding a silver spittoon dish to his mouth, before laying him back on the pillow.

Shaking his head, he tried hard to focus, first on Scot then Billy, but he couldn't lift his arm so Scot moved forward and gently gripped what resembled a shaved stick. Archie tried to smile but wept instead. His voice was rough and grated, the Glasgow dialect was as strong and evident as it was that day in 1966 when he walked onto the hot tarmac at Essendon Airport with Mary and his boys. His words came in bursts.

'Whit are yous doing here? How did ye know I was here, eh? Christ, I'm that pleased tae see the two of ye. How's the fitba goin, eh? Still got Norrie, that fuckwit of a coach?'

Archie had gone back twenty years.

Trying to clear his throat, his emaciated body heaved, his bloodshot eyes shed tears of exertion. Sharni was again at his side, holding him up as he struggled to spit into the dish at his chin. With closed eyes, he fell back onto the pillow, exhausted.

'Scot?'

'I'm here, Dad.'

'Son, tell your ma that ...' He was struggling to breathe. 'Tell her that ...'

'What, Dad? What will I tell her?'

'I know I've been a right bastard to her aw those years ago, she never deserved it. Tell her I'm sorry for aw that. She's a good woman, Scot, and a great mother. Naebody in England, Scotland or Australiya could staun in her shoes. Will ye tell her that, son, will ye, eh? Tell her that frae me, okay?' The tears flowed freely down his cheeks.

'I'll tell her, Dad, I'll tell her.'

While holding a damp cloth to his father's brow, Archie drifted into a drugged sleep. In all his years Scot had never heard Archie say a kind or complimentary word to, or about, his mother. If only he could have said that years ago. If only he had given her a little praise or thanks. If only he had supported her a little ... 'if only' was now, sadly, too late.

Sister Baillieu slipped silently into the confines of the bedside.

'Mr Bray, I'll have to ask you to leave now. I'll call if there is any change.'

Scot nodded, then leaned down to kiss his father's cheek. Billy did the same, leaving the ward in silence. Both men were resigned, ready to accept the inevitable.

As they left the hospital, the clear Northern Territory sky put on a display, a sky sprinkling with millions of stars. It was a spectacle. It gave the brothers momentary comfort, a distraction from what lay ahead.

Back at the motel a four-wheel drive had just pulled into the parking space in front of the reception area. A young couple were dragging out backpacks and pillows from the back seat, at the same time struggling to calm the cries of irritable children worn out from the day's drive. The baby had just thrown up on his father's shoulder and the toddler had woken grumpy. The young father smiled wearily at the fellow travellers getting out the taxi.

He called out good-naturedly, 'G'day, mate. Look at this, will ya? Wouldn't be dead for quids, eh?'

The brothers smiled and waved back.

Billy went on ahead of Scot and opened the door to their room. The phone was ringing.

Looking anxiously at each other, Billy lifted the phone. 'Hello?'

The voice on the other end was quiet and subdued. 'This is Sister Baillieu. Am I speaking to Scot or Billy?'

Chapter 32

Sister Baillieu explained that their father had deteriorated rapidly after they left the hospital, saying that they should get back quickly if they wanted to say their final goodbyes. With no hesitation and heavy hearts, the brothers returned. Again, they walked down the deserted corridor only this time the closed curtains were open. Sharni stood stoically by the bed like a guardian angel. It was another agonising encounter.

Sitting down either side of the bed, each took hold of a skeletal hand. Billy gently dabbed his father's parched lips with a sponge whilst softly speaking words of love and support, hoping that his hearing was still intact. Sharni said that of all the senses hearing was the last to go in the death process. When guttural choking sounds arose from Archie's emaciated body, they looked at Sharni in alarm.

She half smiled and quickly waved her hand, telling them, 'Don't be alarmed. This is the death rattle. Your father can no longer cough or swallow He's in no pain; the time is very close now.'

Scot was concerned about his brother fixating at the rise and fall of the bed sheets, half expecting him to break down. Billy stayed silent and strong.

Archie's mouth was gaping. The rattling sound from his throat slowly diminished until it gradually stopped. He had slipped away. His face relaxed. Resting on the pillow, he looked remarkably at peace.

Sharni dimmed the lights before quietly leaving the room. Scot and Billy sat with their father in silence, both grieving for a man who at the end of his life had tried in the only way he knew to right his wrongs and seek forgiveness. Neither of them had experienced anything so profound. Scot kissed his father's head, reached into his pocket, and brought out the small, well-worn bible his father had treasured all these years. Bringing Archie's hands together, he pressed the book between them.

'It's yours, Dad.'

There was a short service at the hospital chapel performed by a local pastor, followed immediately by a cremation. Only the brothers and hospital staff were there. Leaving the room, a young nurse who had been lingering outside in the corridor hesitated before coming forward to speak to Billy.

'Excuse me, Billy, can I talk to you for a minute? Your dad asked me to write this note for him a few weeks ago and he signed it. It wasn't addressed to anyone in particular, but he was adamant that this was what he wanted to be done when he passed away.'

Billy thanked the nurse for her kindness. It was one page written in small, neat handwriting.

'I want my ashes spread in the middle of the fitba pitch at Ibrox Stadium in Glasgow, home of the world's best fuckin fitba team.'

An almost illegible scrawl resembled Archie's signature. Billy's eyes filled, trying hard not to blink, and allowing himself to smile at his father's loyalties, expletives, and the improbability of his request. Folding the note, he placed it securely in his wallet, then went over to the nurse's station, a middle-aged woman looked up and smiled as he approached.

'Excuse me, but can I ask a question?' Without waiting he continued. 'We're leaving tomorrow night for Melbourne and were hoping we could take our father's ashes back with us. Would that be possible?'

The nurse nodded. 'Well, it's not standard procedure, Mr Bray, but under the circumstances we have already had permission. They can be collected here late tomorrow afternoon here at our station, and again, our condolences to you and your family.'

The following night, Scot and Billy boarded the plane bound for Melbourne. The captain's voice smoothly narrated their departure from the Northern Territory. The aircraft lifted off calmly, taking to the air and soaring upwards, reluctantly leaving behind a part of the Bray family history. When the seatbelt signs went off, they reclined in their seats. The hostess offered them a beer each, which they accepted willingly.

Billy lifted the glass to his brother for a toast. 'To Dad,' he said.

'To Dad,' Scot responded, as their glasses touched.

'You know, Scotty, he wasn't all bad. Well, not to me, anyway. He did teach me how to play football, he always came to watch me at training, and he fought my battles when the referee was being unfair. He helped me with maths too. God, he was smart at maths. You know, there were times when I was young and I shouldn't have laughed, really, but when we were on our own, he did tell me some very funny crude jokes.'

Scot laughed out loud, then ordered more beers. He turned to his brother.

'I know he had a lot of good points, Billy, and I know he helped us both when we were growing up. I really hate to tell you this, especially now. Maybe the beer has loosened my tongue or maybe I'm just tired, I don't know, but I remember many sad and painful times. Not so much for me, I mean, but for Mum. She really did suffer. Listen, I have never really told you this before and I don't want to taint your memory of our father, but you need to know what Mum had to endure for many years. I know it was a long time ago and to see her today you could hardly believe that she would have accepted such treatment. I can tell you now that he constantly criticised and shouted at her, and he would beat her up for no reason, but she never complained. That, of course, was in the early days. She would cry a lot because she had no money to feed us, no money for coal to keep us warm. She would patch up holes in the soles of our shoes with cardboard insoles. There were times, before leaving for the pub, he would watch as she wheeled your pram down the street through the snow and sleet, with Alice and me tagging, along following the coal lorry. She would wait for the loose bits of coal to fall off the back of the truck then take them home to warm us. It's hard to believe, isn't it? Nevertheless, it's the truth. I am only telling you now so that you have an accurate picture of how it really was at that time, and how Mum overcame so many obstacles to give us what we have now. There were many more times of hardship, Billy, that you don't really need to know, but do you know what? We all came through it. Thanks to Mum. She always fought back. She never forgave him for those early years.'

Billy was quiet, listening intently to his brother's emotions taking over. He looked down at the wooden urn at his feet, whispering just loud enough for Scot to hear.

'But I still loved him.'

Mary woke late. She looked at her bedside table. It was 11.30 am in the morning. Leaping out of bed, she opened the blinds. The morning sun had long gone. The sky was an enormous patch of blue. The parrots and lorikeets dotted throughout the foliage of the gum trees screeched, waiting for seed. She grabbed her gown and heeled slippers, then opening the French doors, went to the birdhouse on the edge of the patio. Standing on the stone steps she filled the feeder and within minutes, they descended. Parrots, lorikeets, and rosellas. Mary sat back in the covered swing and watched. It was one thing she truly loved, wild birds. So colourful and active, listening to their mating calls and melodic chirps gave her endless hours of pleasure.

The phone by her bed rang, she let it go to the answering machine. It was Max, gently probing if she had decided yet to buy the restaurant. She hadn't. She had to speak to her boys first. Mary dialled Scot's number.

'Darling, there you are. Did I wake you?'

Scot answered with a husky voice. 'Oh, hello, Mum. No ... no, it's alright! I have overslept, should have been up hours ago. Sorry I haven't called, I had to go to the Northern Territory for a quick trip, Billy came with me. I need to go into the office for a while today. Can I come over late this afternoon for a chat?'

'Of course you can, son. I am home all day today, just catching up on some bookwork. Will you come for dinner?'

'No, not for dinner, Mum, we are going to Carol's parents. Been planned for some time. Sorry, hope that's alright?'

'Of course, it is, see you soon.'

Mary hung, up baffled. Scot seemed a bit distant and evasive. Perhaps something was wrong with Carol? She hoped not, Carol was a lovely girl.

It was late in the afternoon when the front doorbell rang. Marlene had just finished for the day and was about to leave. She answered the door.

'Oh, Mr Bray, hello. Mrs Bray's sitting outside on the decking.'

Scot liked Marlene. She came to his mother twice a week as a housekeeper. They had a wonderful rapport. Marlene came from an Irish background; she was born there but immigrated when very young. She and Mum would talk endlessly about the old times, the similarities in their upbringing, and the wonderful world that was Australia.

Mary was sitting on the decking reading; a tray of tea and biscuits lay untouched on the glass side table. Hearing the door close, she got up to welcome and hug her son.

'Why didn't you tell me you were going away? Didn't know you were taking Billy with you. Is everything alright?'

Scot sat down on the cane chair facing his mother. He avoided her eyes, but he had to tell her straight away. Holding her hand, he spoke quietly. 'Mum, Billy, and I had to go to Darwin, but it wasn't for business. It was private.'

Scot coughed, struggling to speak.

Mary's eyes widened, she leaned over and grabbed his arm. 'Scot, what is it? Tell me what's happened. Who do we know in Darwin? Why on earth did you go there?' Mary tightened her grip on her son's bare arm.

Scot looked directly at her swallowed, then he licked his dry lips, and because he could think of nothing else to say, he hung his head and blurted it out. 'It's Dad, Mum, he's dead.'

Mary's grip loosened on Scot's arm as she slumped back in the chair. Putting her hand over her eyes, she coughed slightly, then she sat up asking Scot in a low voice. 'What happened, Scot? How did you find him?'

Scot sat down beside his mother and told her how it had all unfolded. He didn't elaborate on his father's condition or appearance, only that the alcohol had finally caught up with him. Mary listened intently without interruptions, nodding, and shaking her head with each revelation.

When he had finished, she stood up, nodding her head sadly. 'The worst times were a long time ago, Scotty. I hope, somehow, in the last years your father has found some peace, somewhere.'

Kissing her son lightly on the cheek, she then went inside, closing the door. She walked through to the dining room. Everything was quiet, suddenly, and with no warning she was consumed with nostalgia. A strange aura enveloped her. From below the bar, she brought out a bottle of liqueur. Taking a small handful of ice, she poured the clear liquid halfway up the glass. Nestling into a large leather armchair in a nook by the window, she dimmed the lamp and gazed out into her floodlight garden. She closed her eyes.

'So, your name's Mary then, eh?'

'Yes,' was all she could say.

'Fancy goin to the pictures wan night, eh?'

'Oh, I don't think so. I mean, I'm not sure. I don't think I should because I'm married and—'

'That's no a problem tae me, but don't flatter yersel, hen. I'm just asking ye tay go tay the pictures, awright?'

'Yes, alright then.'

Mary was trying very hard to be casual. She hoped that her voice did not give away too much. She had noticed Archie over many weeks at the recreational cafe at the barracks. He was so cheeky, always winking and laughing at her. He was so good-looking and had everyone around him laughing. She knew it was wrong. She knew she should never have encouraged him, but Charlie was always away. She was so lonely sometimes, especially when Alice was asleep, and the night was still young. She was tempted, sure that nothing would happen, that Charlie would never find out. But something did happen, and Charlie did find out.

It was the end of her world.

Chapter 33

Alice waited patiently as the security gates to her mother's home opened slowly. She stood back as the large gates swung toward the house, swaying gently, coming to rest near the flower borders. Since learning of Archie's death, her mother had asked for privacy. It had been almost a week of mixed emotions not only for her mother, but also for Alice. When she was younger, she had prayed for the day he would never wake up. Now, all she felt was a great sadness. Her brothers were more compassionate. They had a different relationship with him during life, and a surreal bond with him at death. Billy asked Alice to remember her stepfather as he was when she last saw him. Cocky, confident, and manipulative. He told her that the Archie they cremated was a shell, a sorrowful end for the man he had once been, and a vision only the brothers could share.

Alice worried about her mother. Mary had insisted on spending time alone. She didn't want company, comfort, or consolation; she grieved in her own way.

It was a welcome relief for Alice, that tonight her family and Vince's family were getting together at their home. Her mother had been very mysterious as to the reasons why, but she insisted, as she always did, that everyone be on time.

Alice had come straight from work and was searching for her key when she heard the click of her mother's sandals on the tiled hallway. The door opened.

'I heard your car, darling. You're the first to arrive as always, so punctual.'

Alice laughed. Her mother looked so slim and refreshed in her beige tailored pants and white open neck shirt. Her hair, although showing touches of grey, had been expertly coloured and blended. Her girlish face belied her age. She wore little makeup just a touch of blusher on her cheeks and a very pale tangerine lipstick.

'Oh, Mum, you look great.' Alice hugged her mother tightly. Mary responded by kissing her cheek. They linked arms and moved to the dining room.

'I thought we would all sit here. The table can be extended, and that way Marlene can bring in sandwiches later.'

'Good idea, Mum, but this is about buying the restaurant, is it not?'

Mary smiled and nodded. 'Yes, that too!'

Alice laughed aloud and spun her mother round to face her. 'What do you mean "that too"?'

Before Mary could answer, the front doorbell rang.

Alice called out to Marlene that she would get it and walked down the hallway followed by her mother. Her brothers and their wives came in first, followed closely by Vince, Max, and Selena.

'Whoa, I'm being invaded!' Mary laughed as everyone congregated in the hallway, kissing and talking loudly, before moving through to the dining room. Marlene came out to take their jackets and flowers then discreetly disappeared into the kitchen.

After condolences from Vince and family, and quick family updates, it was time to talk business. Mary had put her plans on hold while dealing with her past. She was now ready to talk enthusiastically about her project. She had decided to go ahead with the sale, but she wanted the endorsement of her family.

Sitting at the top of the large dining room table, she accepted the teasing from her sons that she was Chairman of the Board.

'Well, we are all here … this is not too official, I hope,' said Mary with a nervous laugh. 'I wanted to discuss with you all a dream, and a vision I have harboured for many years.' She paused. 'I'll get straight to the point. Max and Vince have asked me, or I should say offered me …' Mary's voice broke as she held her mouth for a moment. 'Oh, sorry everyone, I am a bit overcome.'

'Come on, Mum, spit it out!' Billy laughed.

Mary then sat upright and looked directly at everyone around the table as she spoke. 'I want to buy Ronaldo's. Max and Vince want to sell the business and have given me the first option to buy. They have offered me a very good price and we can negotiate extras, set up contracts ourselves with the lawyers, and avoid the agent's fees.'

Mary waited as the surprise looks of the table turned to frowns. 'I want to buy it; I desperately want to buy it, but it wouldn't be under the present arrangement.' Mary was getting excited. Her voice was getting louder. 'Many times, over the years, I have had discussions with diners young and old. They all love the experience of dining out. They enjoy coming to a place where they feel comfortable, have good food and great service, and they relish in being spoilt. They want to feel special. Many of them enjoy a big night out with other family members, but for some in the family it's just not possible.' Mary was talking too fast and repeating herself too often.

'Hey, Mum, slow down. What are you getting at?' Scot laughed.

'Let me finish, Scotty.' She wasn't going to slow down now; she was on a mission to sell her idea to the family.

'Well, sometimes during personal conversations, I have discovered that often, particularly with a family get together, someone misses out as they have to stay home with the children. You would be amazed at how many families don't have friends to babysit, or will not go to an agency. Instead, they stay home and miss out altogether. Now, the land alongside the restaurant has been vacant for years and is now in the hands of an agent. I think I should buy it. I called him and he thinks the owners would be very interested in talking to me. It has been on the market for some time, and they would consider a reasonable offer for a quick settlement.' Mary swallowed and looked around swiftly at the expressionless, upturned faces of her family and friends, waiting for her to continue.

'I think we should add a childcare room.'

'A what?' Alice frowned and looked at her mother.

Mary continued. 'This area around here has built up over the years with a strong mix of young families and young professionals. These young professionals have young families, families who want to dine together, but also to have time on their own knowing that their children are cared for nearby. Being cared for in a room with qualified, expert supervision means the parents could relax and enjoy fine dining without constant interruptions. We would cater for children from three months to twelve years. The room would be equipped to the required laws and standards; they will have an appropriate creative child's meal prepared by young Toby in the kitchen who loves a challenge. There will be a range of suitable toys and books in a specific play area. Beds and cots would be available, pending the needs and age of that child. This is the perfect solution for parents who want to enjoy a relaxing meal and know that they can check on their children at any time. Alice and her staff will, of course, run the room. Her expertise in childcare will ensure we have the right permits, equipment, and age-related nutritional know-how.

'There will be no additional expense for the diner, apart from a small cost for the food. I think the novelty will attract more custom which will then give us a springboard to display our produce and seasonal menu. We can also close one night a week for private functions or staff training. The corporate area around Ronaldo's, as you know, has expanded over the years. Rooms for private functions in the area are scarce. We have needed this facility for some time. We'll start from scratch with new kitchen staff. Vince would be more than happy to guide us in that area ... by phone of course.' Mary laughed nervously and smiled at Vince.

Then it was over, her proposal complete. She was breathless and smiling, sitting back and relaxed, the deal was on the table. She looked around at her nearest and dearest. No one spoke. Mary coughed and leant forward, nodding her head. 'Well, what do you think?'

Alice jumped up. 'Mum, I love it. Yes! Yes! I want to do it. It's a great idea.'

Alice was, as Mary fully expected, full of enthusiasm.

'I know exactly who could help me. Karen from the course has had heaps of experience and she is a trained nurse; she is looking for a new job. Oh! This is a great idea.'

Alice's face was pink and as she stood up straighter, almost as though being taller would help her voice carry and get a stamp of approval sealed from a great height. She continued to praise her mother for her entrepreneurial flair and insight. The room started to buzz with chatter. Scot and Billy had their heads together and were talking quietly. They were nodding and smiling, and then Billy looked up and spoke directly to his mother.

'Mum, you always amaze us with your vision. Always positive and full of ideas, workable ideas, that we all embrace. Our only concern is that you are taking on a major project at a time in your life when you should be taking things easier. I mean, you're not twenty anymore, and you don't need the money. Why not just sit back and do the silly thing everyone tells you to do ... tend to those bewitching roses in your garden?'

Mary politely ignored the last comment and smiled instead. 'My darling boys, I have been in the workforce since I was 14 years old. I have never been out of a job, and I have worked at whatever jobs I could get. Shops, factories, cafes, anything I could get—it was called survival. I have never had a proper education. I have been poor, I have been cold, and I have been hungry. However, I have always had a vision. I have always moved forward and worked toward a better life for you three children, and for myself and, well, I am not finished yet, young man!'

Billy half-smiled at his mother almost chastising her. 'Oh! Come on, Mum, we *are* comfortable. We do have security. We have good jobs and Scot has a thriving business. We do not need to take on new ventures. Especially not you.'

Mary looked to her son, her last-born and the most sensitive. She desperately wanted him to embrace her vision; she wanted him to be part of a family business.

'I know, son, but please, just think about it.'

Vince was sitting quietly in his wheelchair, listening attentively to the family as they bantered, agreed, and then disagreed with Mary. If she did not buy it, he would be devastated; it would be betraying a family institution by selling to a stranger. He knew that Mary would retain many of the Italian touches that had been there for years, like the old pristine black and white prints now hanging evenly in their shiny black frames, side-by-side around the restaurant. The statue of David, all those years ago, squeezed into their small reception area, was now holding its own in an alcove specially built at the last renovation. Besides, the family dynamics had changed over the years. He was getting more dependent on others and needed more care. No longer could they afford the luxury of running a restaurant successfully if it was at the expense of his health and the family lifestyle.

After much discussion, Scot and his brother finally embraced Mary's dream. This was their mother, and it was what made her tick. They agreed that Scot, having his own successful business, would be there initially to help them set up. Then, later on, as an advisor. Billy, after much discussion with his brother, was very happy to be involved, giving them the benefit of his business experiences to assist with the set up and initial management. Alice was the most enthusiastic, spruiking her ideas and plans for equipment, meals, colour schemes, educational toys, and books. She was her mother's daughter.

It was time for celebrations. Scot had disappeared into Mary's bar fridge; alongside the orange juice and soda water was a bottle of French Champagne that he had bought her for the previous Christmas. It was chilled, and still in its wrapping. He signalled to Marlene to bring some glasses, then he stood ceremoniously behind the bar, tearing off the gold foil.

He popped the cork and made an announcement. 'I am taking it upon myself to officially seal this agreement,' he said ceremoniously.

Marlene re-appeared with a tray of saucer champagne glasses. Scot poured the golden bubbles into each glass as Mary watched, holding back a tear.

Scot raised his glass high. 'To Mary!'

'To Mary!' they said in unison.

Chapter 34

It had been three long months of negotiation with builders and contractors. Three months of argy-bargy, as Alice would say. The owner of the property next door had been stubborn, telling Mary that he had refused better offers, could she up her price. She stood her ground, called his bluff, and walked away. Within hours, he had called back and said that he had reconsidered her offer, providing she could settle in 30 days, grudgingly adding that she had a bargain.

Building got underway four weeks later. Scot had supervised all the building works with saving massive on labour hire. After his original fears, Billy agreed that there were definite profitable possibilities in this venture. He worked with Alice on the books and together they put together a business plan. They budgeted and sourced materials for the decor. Billy, out of his comfort zone, surprised himself on his colour co-ordination skills.

Mary was happy to sit back in the comfort of her own home, reading and working on her new hobby of watercolour painting. She had almost completed her first picture of a Japanese garden to give to Alice. Rather than watch the building works in progress, she was content to wait until it was almost finished.

Alice had grasped the whole project with both hands. Her friend Karen had jumped at the opportunity to be able to work in a field where she could not only use her new skills in early childhood development, but she could administer nursing care if needed.

Rebecca was a young, eager and enthusiastic childcare student who was thrilled to be working on this innovation.

The months rolled on; it was the day before opening. The restaurant was almost fully booked. The childcare room had bookings for eight children. Alice was relieved, as it was just enough for the first night. Everyone was frantically adding all the final touches. The bright yellow walls with shiny white skirting boards was the happy shell of the room. Large wooden characters appeared to jump off the walls. Colourful animations of Donald Duck, Goofy, Mickey Mouse, Tinkerbell, and Snow White all smiled for the young guests. Two rows of brightly painted rainbow pegs at child height zigzagged along the wall. Various building blocks, picture books, storybooks, teddies, dolls, and soldiers were stacked neatly, ready for eager little hands. A large wooden doll's house, a replica of an Australian homestead, intricate in its detail and complete with miniature furniture, stood against the wall. Parked beneath a shelf weighed down with games and age-appropriate books stood two green and yellow ride-on tractors with giant rubber wheels. It was a room of love and laughter.

The phone rang in the restaurant next door. At the reception desk, Scot was doing last-minute safety checks. He reached for it with one hand whilst checking with the other, agitated at the interruption.

'Yes, yes this is Scot Bray. Who's calling?' There was a slight pause. 'Hello? Look, who is this?'

'Mr Bray, my name is Dr Kruger from The Royal Melbourne Hospital, I—'

'The Royal Melbourne Hospital?'

'Yes. Mr Bray, I am calling to let you know that we admitted your mother here about two hours ago. She presented with severe obstruction of the respiratory tract; she had stopped breathing.'

'She what? No, that couldn't be right. She was fine this morning, I talked to her on the phone. She stopped breathing? My mother?'

Dr Kruger interrupted gruffly. 'Yes, I am sorry. We performed a tracheotomy to help clear her airways and managed to resuscitate her. We now have a respirator in place to aid her breathing, and her heart has stabilised in the last hour, but I do have concerns, Mr Bray. I think you and your family should get here as soon as you can. I'll see you soon.' Dr Kruger hung up quickly.

Billy, working in the dining room, had heard his brother on the phone. He heard the strain in his voice, and he heard the word 'hospital'.

'What is it, Scotty? Did you say hospital?'

Scot, still holding the phone, looked wide-eyed at his brother. 'It's Mum. She's in the Royal Melbourne. The doctor wants us all there as soon as possible, he said she's in intensive care and that she's stable. My God. Oh! My God.'

Scot put the phone down, buried his face in his hands and then dragged them through his hair. 'It's serious, Billy. Oh God!' He wailed like a wounded animal. Billy put his arm around his brother.

Alice had gone looking for Billy to help in the childcare room. She came through to reception, and seeing both brothers pale-faced and leaning against a wall she rushed over.

'Scot, Billy, what's wrong? What's happened? Look at me please. What is it?'

Billy lifted his head slowly. 'It's Mum. She's in hospital, she's having trouble breathing. We have to go there right away, right away, Alice. Now!'

Her hand went to her mouth, biting down on one finger,

smothering a scream. No, no, her head cried, but her lips were silent. 'Give me the keys to the station wagon, Scot.'

'But Alice, you won't be able to drive.'

She snatched the keys from him. 'And neither will either of you. Let's go.'

After a frantic drive, the car screeched to a halt outside the hospital. They rushed inside to the foyer. Totally lost and distraught, they eventually located the intensive care ward. An elderly, weary-looking ward clerk looked up from the desk.

'Yes, what is it? Can I help you?'

'My name is Scot Bray. We are looking for our mother, Mary Bray. She was admitted here earlier. Can you tell us which ward she is in?'

The clerk lowered his glasses. 'Please sit down, Mr Bray, I'll check. It could take a few minutes.'

Scot was adamant. 'No, I'm sorry we won't sit down. We will stand here for however long it takes. We need to know where our mother is, and we need to know now.'

The desk clerk didn't look up, nor did he answer.

Alice managed to calm her brother. She held his hand and steered him to a corner bench seat. Without warning, a side door flew open, a distressed woman came rushing out of a corridor. It was Marlene. Seeing them she ran over, talking quickly, and crying.

'Oh, Scotty, I'm so sorry, but your mum had a bit of a turn. She couldn't breathe. The phone rang out every time I tried to call you, and your mum was getting weaker. I thought the ambulance would take too long and I only just managed to get her into the car. I drove straight here. I hope I did the right thing, I'm so sorry; she's not in a good way, really, she isn't.'

Marlene was getting upset, dabbing at her eyes.

Billy hugged her. 'You did the right thing, Marlene. The phone has been busy all morning, so sorry. Thank you, thank you so much for bringing her here.'

Marlene walked quickly down the corridor, in between sobs calling out her goodbyes.

The siblings sat down quietly, shaken after Marlene's outburst. This hospital scenario was all too familiar to them all. Alice, when she sat with her mother as Uncle Ralph was dying, and Scot and Billy only months ago as they said goodbye to their father. Now this ... their own mother, clinging to life.

It was all too much for Alice. She had been strong in getting them all to the hospital so quickly, but now they were at a standstill, unable to see their mum and not knowing her condition was just too much for her. Staring at the bare cream walls was taking its toll. Her shoulders shook as the tears let loose, rolling down her gaunt cheeks. Billy put his arm around his sister as she closed her eyes and sobbed aloud.

'Please God, please not my mother, I will do anything, anything. Please do not take her yet. I need her. We all need her.' Alice burrowed her face into Billy's shoulder as he laid his wet cheek on her hair.

Just then, a nurse came out from the side door and walked briskly toward them. She had a soft voice, laced with comfort. 'Excuse me, you can see your mother now, but before we go in the charge nurse would like to have a brief chat. Please follow me.'

It was a bland, cold room. There were no pictures on the wall and no windows, only a brown wooden table with six chairs. They sat down to face a small, mature-aged nurse.

'My name is Hilary. I was here when they brought your mother in. I am not sure if you know what happened, but—'

Scot stood up, agitated. 'No, no we don't, nurse, we don't know a bloody thing. We got the call from a Dr Kruger less than an hour ago telling us it was urgent. I want to speak to Dr Kruger, but before I do, would you please take us to see our mother.'

Hilary was calm. 'Yes, shortly, Mr Bray, but first I think I'd better tell you what happened. It appeared your mother had a bad attack at home earlier today. She—'

'Attack, what sort of an attack?'

'Well, an asthma attack, of course. You know she's a chronic asthmatic, don't you?' Without waiting for an answer, Hilary continued. 'Her housekeeper Marlene found her in the bedroom; she was struggling to breathe and was distressed. She had reached for the telephone, but she collapsed and fell over the table. Marlene heard the crash and managed to lift her into the car; she brought her here straight away. You are very lucky that she found her when she did or we could have been having an entirely different conversation now.'

Alice interrupted. She sat upright in her chair, looking directly at Hilary. 'What do you mean an asthma attack? What sort of asthma attack? And no, no we didn't know she was a chronic asthmatic. What exactly is that?'

Hilary made eye contact with them all. 'Your mother has suffered from bronchitis for many years. Over time the bronchitis developed into asthma. She is, in fact, a bronchial asthmatic. Her lungs are damaged and are very weak. Your mother is a very sick woman. I am so sorry. I thought you knew.'

Alice looked at Scot then Billy. They were speechless. Scot was the first to speak.

'We knew she had bronchitis, that's what she always told us, and we knew she often disappeared into her bedroom or out to her car to have a few whiffs of her inhaler. I mean, she never made an issue of it and always seemed to bounce back. She never mentioned anything about her lungs. Excuse my lack of knowledge, but how bad exactly are her lungs? Is it curable? Is she going to be alright?'

Hilary had been in the nursing profession for twenty-two years. Nothing phased her. She was a very patient and understanding nurse, but these instances with families who were unaware of their loved one's illness was always upsetting. 'Mr Bray, I think this is something you have to discuss with the doctor. He's here in the ward now, expecting to speak to you all and give more detail on her condition, but first let me take you to your mother.'

Her smile faded as she led them out of the room, walking quickly down the corridor and through a swing door into an assortment of clinical machinery that surrounded beds. She stopped at the second bed.

Another familiar scene for the siblings—monitors, tubes, white sheets, and chrome. Only this time the patient was different. This was their mother. This was their nightmare.

Alice moved closer to the bed and drew in a short breath, looking down at her mother. Her eyes were closed, her mouth open, and her pallor was pale, almost a delicate blue. Her chest heaved, as tubes and machines made connections with her body, steadily monitoring her. Alice looked in disbelief... this could not be her mother. That untidy, lank hair and cold to the touch pale brow was of a much older and thinner woman.

Billy stood on the other side of the bed and held his mother's thin, almost transparent hand. It was cold; a needle was taped into one of the veins. Scot stood behind him, dabbing at his eyes.

Dr Kruger coughed and closed the door quietly as he penetrated the space of this family. He was a short man with a round face, black-rimmed glasses, and brown receding hair. He wore an open neck shirt and a white coat with his hospital ID card swinging from a lanyard around his neck. He exuded a confident no-nonsense air as he approached the bed. 'I'm Dr Kruger,' he said looking at both boys. 'I think we spoke on the phone.'

'Yes,' said Scot, quickly shaking his hand. 'This is my brother Billy and my sister Alice.'

Dr Kruger asked them to move away from the bed to the corner of the room. He spoke quietly, directing all his conversation to Scot.

'Mr Bray, I am sorry to have to tell you this, but your mother is a very sick woman. She has what is called Chronic Obstructive Pulmonary Disease.'

'What?' they said in unison.

'What is that?' Alice asked.

'It's a lung disease that typically occurs in heavy smokers. Now, I know that your mother has never smoked, and this may seem a bit unfair; however, air pollution is also a high-risk factor, and I believe your mother's early years were spent in a coal mining village, so—'

'Well, yes, they were, Doctor,' Alice interrupted, 'but not for very long.'

Doctor Kruger's voice softened. 'She also suffered pneumonia, Alice, which left her with little resistance and prone to chest and lung infections. She was never fully prepared for the cold winters of England and Scotland. What I am trying to say is, discussions that I have had in the past with your mother made me think that not having enough warm clothes or heating made her ill prepared for those winters. Another significant fact in the deterioration of your mother's health is that she was exposed to passive smoking for many years—that is, inhaling another's cigarette smoke, particularly in a confined area—and—'

'Dad's smoking, you mean, Doctor?' said Scot.

'I would say so yes.' There was an uncomfortable silence.

Alice looked directly at the doctor. 'So, tell me please, what exactly is the prognosis for our mother? Is she going to be okay?'

Dr Kruger braced himself for the inevitable question. He looked kindly at her troubled face. 'Alice, your mother has been treated off and on at this hospital for many years. I know that she kept this hidden from her family because she told me. She also asked me to respect her confidence, which I have done until now. She has good days and bad days. She has always managed her illness, and if I may say, always presented here very well, being smartly dressed and perfectly made up. Sadly, no matter how much makeup your mother applies and how outwardly well she appears, it will never hide the fact that she is a very sick woman and has been for some time. We lost her for almost three minutes this time and had to vigorously apply CPR. Unfortunately, in doing so we have cracked three ribs, so when she wakes, she will be in a bit of pain.' Dr Kruger drew a deep breath. 'In answer to your question, Alice, the answer is no. She is not going to be okay; there is no happy ending here. This is a progressive disease which worsens over time. People with COPD have a poor quality of life. I'm sorry.'

Alice swayed and closed her eyes. Scot managed to grab her just before she fell to the floor. He sat her on a chair then addressed the doctor. 'Thank you, Doctor, for explaining Mum's situation and for your sensitivity. I know you understand how shocked and confused we are. We will confer as a family and take the appropriate steps to ensure her wellbeing, and that she has the best quality of life possible. We are all so very grateful to you and your team for bringing her back to us.'

The doctor nodded and left the room.

The young, intensive care nurse who had been standing motionless behind Dr Kruger had quickly disappeared and returned with a glass of water for Alice. She spoke to them all almost in a whisper. 'Your mum will sleep for some time now. She has been heavily sedated and is in no immediate danger. She will be given painkillers for her ribs when she wakes up, but I am afraid she won't be able to laugh too much!'

Billy smiled at the young nurse, appreciating her humour and attempt to lift their spirit.

'I think you should all go home now and get some rest.'

The siblings, all in turn, kissed their mother's cool, damp forehead before leaving her bedside and the hospital for the long drive home. Tomorrow was going to be a big day. The restaurant and new childcare facility was opening for business, but their mother wouldn't be there to see it.

Mary felt the heat on her face. She opened one eye and closed it again. Everything was bright, but this was not her bedroom. This certainly was not her bed. My Lord! she thought, what was sitting on her chest? It was so heavy, she needed to cough. She tried, but it was too painful.

'Mrs Bray! Here you are.' A smiling, bespectacled nurse held a silver dish to her mouth. 'Spit in here if you have to.'

She tried to say she would like to, but nothing came out. She was feeling like her throat was on fire. The nurse said her name was Jennifer. Mary's voice was barely a whisper.

'What am I doing here, where is this?'

'You're in hospital, Mrs Bray. Your housekeeper brought you in late yesterday. You collapsed at home.'

'Collapsed?'

'Yes, you had an asthma attack.'

'I can't remember, I—'

'Don't worry, Mrs Bray, you're fine now. Just lay back and rest. The doctor will be in later this morning, so save your energy for then.'

Mary lay back on the pillow and closed her eyes. The pain in her chest was not too bad if she didn't have to cough. Then she remembered, today was the big opening day. She would have to get up and help Alice ... but first a nap, then a nice cup of tea.

AUSTRALIA: 1982

Chapter 35

The restaurant was a great success. Three months after the re-opening, Alice was taking bookings for a month ahead. They were serving breakfast and taking on more staff; some days she had to be on site almost eighteen hours a day. The long drive home and back was taking its toll. She decided a small apartment close by was needed.

Two extra rooms had already been added to the recent renovations, the wiring and plumbing already installed. This was somewhere she could stay after late night functions or before early corporate breakfast meetings without having the long drive home.

Scot and Billy were less involved in the everyday running of the restaurant now. Alice had complete control. The additional staff allowed more time for her to be with her mother.

Mary recovered slowly. Her bruised ribs throbbed with every cough or exertion, causing great discomfort. The doctor said there was no quick cure.

'Rest, Mary. You must rest,' was all he would say.

Her medication was increased and the doctor provided a nebuliser to help clear the airways. She was under strict instructions to cut back on her many physical chores. A week later, she left hospital for home. Dr Kruger, although rather guarded, was very pleased with her progress.

Mary desperately wanted to help in the restaurant, but her children were adamant. She had to be content with tending her flowerbeds, reading, painting, and keeping in touch with friends by letter and telephone. Over the next months, Mary regained her strength and kept to her daily routine.

It was a warm morning in March the following year. The weather was perfect; the radio had called it an Indian summer. Alice had just left her mother, who was busy planning surprise birthday party for Billy. Her health was now stable, and she had taken on Billy's birthday with great gusto. Alice could not be happier. Apart from giving her mother a purpose, it gave her motivation and energy.

Before going directly to the restaurant, she quickly called into the apartment to change her shoes. The phone was ringing as she fumbled for her keys. Alice quickly grabbed at the receiver.

'Hello?'

No one answered.

'Hello? Hello?' Alice repeated.

The line crackled with intermittent pips.

'Oh, hello. Can you hear me now? I'm not sure if I have the right person, but is this the number for an Alice Bray?' The voice was soft and unfamiliar.

'Who is this?'

'My name is Jean Hazelwood. I am from the Salvation Army, the Family Tracing Services Division. Have you heard of it?'

'Family Tracing? No, but if you're looking for a donation, we don't donate over the phone. We usually—'

'No, no, I'm not looking for a donation. I am calling with some information, but first I must make sure I have the right Alice. Is your mother's name Mary?'

'I beg your pardon, who are you exactly?'

Alice was agitated. She had to be at the restaurant before the lunch crowd arrived. Who was this woman? Just as she was about to hang up, Jean Hazelwood persisted.

'I'm sorry, but if you'll just bear with me a little longer. This may sound intrusive, but it's a very sensitive situation and I have to make sure I am speaking to the right person. Would you mind giving me your birthdate and that of your mother?'

'What? Oh! This is ridiculous. This is not information I give over the phone, particularly to a strange—'

Jean Hazelwood expected this reaction. She had been contacting people like Alice for years and knew exactly how to handle it. 'I failed to mention that I'm calling from our office in London, England.'

'England?' Alice muttered.

'I'll come straight to the point. We have a client, a man. He has been searching for his first wife and their daughter without success. He is desperate to find them and has contacted us for help. The reason I am calling and not writing is that there is some urgency with this case. If it helps in the identification process, we are acting on a discussion we have had from a Kathy King in Glasgow, Scotland. I understand she was a great friend of your mother.'

Alice withdrew, her voice a whisper. 'Auntie Kathy? How do you know her?'

'Kathy has been a great help with our search. She spoke very fondly of Alice and her mother and of the early years with Archie Bray.'

Alice held her mouth, stifling a scream. Jean Hazelwood continued, revealing little known facts about her, her mother, and their time in Rooken Road. She knew then that this woman must be genuine.

Jean's voice came over strong and gentle. 'Your birthdates, please.'

Sitting down, Alice gripped the phone like a lifeline. She spoke in a clear, steady voice, giving both dates. Then repeated it. The line went quiet.

'Thank you, Alice. We are acting on behalf of Charles Lambert. Does that name mean anything to you?'

'No, I can't say it does, I—' Alice froze, her stomach churned, her legs lifeless.

'He's looking for his first wife and daughter, last seeing them in England in 1948.'

Alice could hear Jean's voice growing softer and sensed her smile.

'I think it could be you and your mother.'

Alice didn't speak, her grip loosened on the phone, her white knuckles regained colour. She had a sudden urge to drop it into its cradle to silence that strong, gentle voice, a voice telling her something implausible. She must get to the restaurant to continue her workday; she had customers, she had staff, she wanted to do anything that would erase what she had just heard. Coughing slightly, she stood up. 'Look, Jean, I'm really sorry to disappoint you, but I don't know anyone by that name. I never knew my father, my mother never discussed him, and to be perfectly honest, I don't want her to recall that time in her life. She has been very ill and something like this would be detrimental to her health. Please, tell your client that unfortunately we are not who or what he is searching for. I have to go now, goodbye.'

Jean's raised voice was pleading. 'Please, please, wait. Can you reconsider? I do think we have found his family. The dates you gave me correspond exactly with the dates he gave us. He is desperate to find them. Can I leave my telephone number and ask that you contact me should you change your mind? I promise, we will not make contact again.'

Alice reluctantly wrote down the telephone number on her pad, but even then, she knew she was in denial. Jean Hazelwood knew so much about them, it was unnerving.

Jean spoke gently. 'Please believe me. I feel strongly that this is the right match. I do hope I hear from you. Goodbye, Alice.'

Alice leaned back and closed her eyes. Her mother rarely discussed her biological father. He was a stranger to her. Whenever Alice asked about him, Mary would get a lost look in her eyes and say, 'He never wanted me to take you away.'

When her mother had married Archie Bray, he agreed that she would take his name. There was never anything official. She had only looked at her birth certificate once, when she first discovered Archie Bray was not her father. The name 'Charlie' materialised from her memory.

Lifting the phone, she called the restaurant next door. 'Hello, David. Can you tell the staff that I won't be in for the lunches. I am going back to be with my mother for a while.' She nodded. 'Thanks, David. Bye!'

Alice drove back to her mother's house with a mind clouded by doubt, trying to think of the best way to talk to her about what had just occurred. Perhaps she shouldn't mention it at all.

Going to the back of the house, she walked slowly down the stone path to the gazebo where her mother was reading, just as she had left her earlier that day. For an instant, Alice contemplated turning around, sliding back behind the wheel of her car to her daily ritual, to forget the call, pretend it never happened. She coughed. Mary dropped her book and looked round, startled.

'Darling! Back so soon. Did you forget something?'

Alice smiled and shook her head. 'No, Mum. They didn't really need me, so rather than eat there, I thought that if you have not already eaten perhaps Marlene could make me a sandwich, if that's what you're having.'

'Yes, yes, darling, it is. This is lovely. I'm glad you're here because I thought that for Billy's birthday cake we could have dark chocolate and orange icing then perhaps add some caramel somewhere. What do you think?'

Alice and her mother continued where they had left off, chatting, and organising. Alice was waiting for the right moment to mention her father. That moment came when Mary said that the band she wanted must have a saxophone player. It was the opportunity Alice needed.

'A saxophone player? Mum, didn't you mention to me once that my father played saxophone?'

Mary was leaning forward, writing notes. She didn't look at her daughter, only nodded. 'Yes. Yes, Alice, he did,' she continued 'I have found a four-piece band, it's—'

Alice interrupted, seizing the moment.

'Mum, can we talk about him for a minute? I don't want to upset you, but there are times when I just feel I would like to know a little more about him. You know, did he ever, oh! I don't know, you know ... take me out in my pram or change my nappy? Do I look anything like him at all?'

Alice was nearing her 36th birthday. She was still single, very attractive, and was still prone to blushing when told that she didn't look her age.

Mary carefully packed her notes away, then held out her hand.

'Hold on a minute, darling. Help me up. I have something you should see.'

The two women returned to house. Alice sat back as her mother rummaged around in her bedroom. She came back, handing her a picture.

'This is your father, Alice.'

Alice looked at her mother's face. It glowed with a look she had never seen before. It was pride, it was relief, it was love ... a shared love.

Alice looked at the man in the army uniform. He didn't smile with his lips, but his eyes laughed, and his hair was fair and curly, identical to hers. The black and white picture, touched up with a hint of colour, showed an unmistakable burnished blonde. She was surprised at how handsome he was. Quite unexpectedly, her eyes filled with tears. Mary put her arms around her daughter.

'I have never forgotten him, Alice. In all the years I was married to Archie I never stopped loving your father. I was unfaithful and I have always regretted it. I have deprived you of a wonderful father, a man who loved us both dearly. I will carry this guilt in my heart until the day I die. For years I have hidden him from the world, now I feel I can talk to you about him.'

Mary reached for her handbag, took out a handkerchief and wiped her eyes, looking lovingly at her daughter. 'Charlie was a one-off, Alice. Your father could get a conversation out of a wooden chair, and he loved you very much.' She leant over, and hugged her daughter: 'I'm sorry, darling. I feel a bit tired now. I think I'll just lay down for a while.'

Following her mother into the bedroom, Alice covered her with a cotton blanket and kissed her forehead. She left feeling unusually calm and slightly elated, but she was not ready to tell her mother about Jean Hazelwood's call; she would speak to her brothers first. Now that her mother had finally talked about her father and said how much she loved him, she was unsure what to do. Jean Hazelwood had her information right; Alice knew that for certainty.

Her brothers came to the restaurant late that night. When most of the diners had gone, they sat down at a corner table, listening intently, saying nothing as Alice went over the events of the afternoon.

Headshakes and frowns were the only reactions, neither of them had any idea about their mother's early life.

They said goodnight, agreeing to meet at Billy's home the next evening. Alice went back to her apartment, got undressed in the dark and slipped underneath the covers. Sleep only came at dawn.

Billy's home was in a new suburb not far from the restaurant. It was contemporary, modern and spacious. His wife, Anna, had left earlier that day for a two-day visit to her mother in the country. The timing was perfect for sibling time.

Sitting in Billy's lounge room, the conversation had been awkward in the beginning but had now dried up completely; each struggling with their thoughts and feelings. Billy went over to the settee and sat down, putting his arm around his sister.

'Alice, I really do think that you should make the call. You should speak to him before Mum does, sound him out a little bit. You know how she would react to his voice. If you like the sound of him then, that's it. Decision made!'

'I can't, Billy. Honestly, what would I say? The man's a perfect stranger.'

'I know he is, but by doing it this way you'll be able to soften the blow a little for Mum.'

'But I might get angry and ask why, after all these years, why he is trying to find us now, and why did he wait so long? I might spoil everything for Mum.'

Alice was speaking faster and getting angry. She had thought a lot about this man since Jean's call and had started to feel pangs of resentment at this sudden intrusion in all of their lives.

Scot sat down on the other side of the settee and put his arm around her. 'Alice, for Mum's sake you must speak to him. Just make the call to the woman from the Salvation Army. Sound her out. Tell her you want to make contact first then decide if it is right for Mum. She would understand that. Alice, are you listening to me?'

'Yes, yes, I am listening. I know you're right. I'll call her; in fact, I'll call her now. What time is it in England?'

Jean Hazelwood answered the phone after the first ring, surprised to hear back from Alice so soon. Listening patiently about her brothers, and sensing the tension in Alice's voice, she stopped her mid-sentence.

'Alice, listen, I have just had a thought. Charlie is coming in here to my office in two hours' time. Would it be all right if he called you from here on this number? I know he would be very keen.'

Alice looked at her brothers. 'Oh, I'm not sure, it's so early. I don't think I'm ready. I mean, I'm not prepared, I don't know what to say. Really, can't we wait for a few days until—'

'He's really very nice, Alice. You'll find him so easy to talk to. I do think the sooner the better, don't you?'

'I suppose so. Yes, you're right. Hold on, I'll just check with my brothers.' She held her hand over the mouthpiece of the phone. 'She wants him to call back on this number in two hours. What will I say? I'm terrified!'

'Do it, Alice. Do it now while we are here to support you.' Billy assured her and Scot nodded.

'All right then, Jean.' Alice confirmed her number. 'I'll hear from you, or should I say *him* later. Goodbye.'

Chapter 36

It was two hours of deep thoughts and reflections with the siblings. There were tears, laughter, and memories, with everyone discreetly glancing at the wall clock.

'Thanks for staying, you two.' Alice laughed nervously.

'Well, where else would we be when our big sis needs us,' said Billy. 'Plus, it *is* my house!' He laughed. Billy moved to the bar. 'Come on, Ali, you need a heart-starter. What will it be?'

'Just a white wine would be great, thanks. To the top if you like!'

The boys laughed, trying to lighten the tension in the room. Scot raised his beer. All three clinked glasses. 'To Mum,' was the unanimous toast.

Two hours had flown by. The phone rang. No one moved. It rang four times before Alice grabbed it. 'Hello.'

The boys got up from the table and crept quietly out of the room to the backyard. Pressing the phone to her ear, Alice waited.

'Hello? Hello, is that you, Alice?

She could hardly breathe. 'Yes, yes, it's me. Hello, how are you?' It was all she could think of to say. 'I mean, I don't know what to say. It's all a bit awkward really, all a bit of a surprise.' She knew she was talking too fast.

'I know, Alice, but I have imagined this moment so many times over the years, about how I would react, and what I would say to you when I heard your voice. Now, as I listen and hear your voice, I just can't believe it. I have never stopped thinking about you and your mother. It's like a miracle. I love you both so very much. Alice, I ...' Charlie's voice broke.

The line went quiet. Alice was silently sobbing into her handkerchief, savouring his soft, emotional voice.

They spoke hesitantly at first, then the words flowed easily. They talked about regret, sorrow, love, happiness, and the miracle of reconnecting. Time was irrelevant. He was so close, his voice so very clear, and him, so very far away.

Almost an hour later, Alice gently laid the phone back in its cradle. She didn't want it to end. She wanted to see him, to talk to him again, and to love him.

Outside, she sat down with her brothers. They both waited for her to speak.

'He said he has lived with sadness and regret for almost 38 years,' she said. 'He told me how Mum had been lonely when he was away so often. He knew how she loved company, and how much she missed him when he had to leave her. He said he lost his mind when he found her with Archie, telling her to go but to leave me. Mum, of course, wouldn't hear of it. He said he was young then, heartbroken, and couldn't forgive her. It was the last time he saw either of us.'

Billy and Scot could only listen.

'He married again but had no children. His wife died four years ago. He said the marriage was comfortable and he felt he was quite happy, but there was only ever one woman in his life. He said every birthday he would try to visualise how I had grown and what I was doing at school. He kept repeating that he had never forgotten me.'

Scot, continuing to drink with Billy, was looking restless and agitated. 'What else did he say about Mum, Alice? What did you tell him? Did you say that she was in poor health now, and a shock like this could be fatal for her? What does he want from you both, and why has it taken so long? This person means not a thing to neither Billy nor me. He comes on the scene after more than three decades to turn your world upside down, not to mention the effect it could have on the fragile life of our mother.'

Alice stood up from the table, shaking her head and begging her brothers to try and understand her father's reasons. Verging on tears, she clasped and unclasped her hands. 'No, no, Scotty. He said he doesn't want to upset Mum, he just wants to know that she is happy. He said he has been very sick, but he didn't go into detail. I honestly don't know how I feel. It was very easy talking with him. He talked about when I was a baby and how proud he was. He said he has a picture of the three of us that he has hidden away from the world all these years. He said it was in front of him as we were speaking.'

'Alice.' Billy stood up, interrupting. 'Where did he leave the conversation? What did he want you to tell Mum, and what are you going to tell Mum?'

'He didn't say anything, Billy. He gave me a phone number and said we could call any time, night or day. He said he doesn't go out much these days. His health is not good; he gets tired easily and prefers to stay home.'

Alice followed her brothers inside and sat down, taking a large mouthful of wine. Scot poured himself another beer. The room was dark and chilled. Billy turned on the overhead down lights and the underfloor heating. No one spoke. All three sat quietly. The hallway clock melodically chimed ten times.

Alice stood up. 'I guess I'd better be going. Big day at work tomorrow, and I don't think I'll be getting much sleep.' She picked up her bag, half-smiled and headed for the front door.

'I'm going too,' said Scot, wobbling slightly as he followed her out.

'No, you won't,' Billy said. 'You have had enough to drink. Stay here tonight; I'll call Carol.'

Alice leaned forward and hugged her brother. 'Stay here, Scotty. I just need some time now to digest all of this. I have to figure out how I am going to tell Mum, pick the right time, you know what I mean?'

Alice was looking down as she spoke, the conversation was more with herself that her brother.

'Yes, Ali, I do understand. Call me tomorrow, okay?'

'Sure.' She kissed his cheek and blew a kiss to Billy. 'Talk tomorrow.'

That night, the past, the present and the unknown future created a kaleidoscope slideshow behind her closed eyes. At 7.00 am she turned off her alarm. She had not slept at all. Later that morning her mother called.

'Hello, darling. Just wondered how you are today.'

Alice braced herself forcing a positive response. 'I'm really good, Mum. How are you?'

'I have spent an hour in the garden whilst the sun was out and did not used my puffer once. Then I tidied the cupboard under the stairs. After that, I went with Marlene to the market and bought fresh whiting for tea. I was wondering if you were coming home for dinner tonight. We could watch *Sons and Daughters* on television later, if you feel like it.'

Alice laughed. 'You and your soapies, Mum. All right then, that would be great. It might be just after seven. I have a few things to tidy up here, but don't start without me.'

She laughed and hung up, thinking this would be a perfect opportunity to tell her mother that she had actually spoken to her father and what it had meant to her, but how she would react? Alice's joy was tinged with fear.

Mary was busy in the kitchen when Alice let herself in.

'I'm here, Mum. Smells great.'

'Be right with you, darling. This fish is so darned fresh it is falling off my splice. You will just have to scoop it with up with a spoon.' She laughed.

Alice came into the lounge room and sat down. The table was set with precision, and of her mother's glassware, white China crockery, and cloth serviettes. The milk was in a little crystal jug and the salt was in the smallest of dishes with an even smaller salt spoon. Her mother was a stickler for settings and table manners.

After the meal, Mary cleared away the dishes then sat down with her daughter.

'Alice, are you alright? You seem a bit preoccupied. I have chatted way too much, sorry. Do you have problems at work? Was the fish so bad, or are you just tired?' Mary's attempt at humour went unnoticed.

Alice's eyes wandered aimlessly around the room. She was fixating on a small crack on the back wall near the power point, thinking that Scot would have to have a look at that. She would call him tomorrow.

Feeling suffocated, she couldn't delay any longer. There was no easy way to say it. Holding her breath for a few moments, she looked deeply into her mother's enquiring eyes, and decided there was no other way. She gripped her hand. 'Mum. Mum, I spoke to my father last night. To my dad, to Charlie, on the phone from England. We talked for a long time.'

Mary didn't answer, she didn't move. She withdrew her hand.

Her face, blank and transparent, her eyes magnified in their blackness, her mouth partially opened, but no sound came out. She started to lose her grip on her teacup. Alice quickly grabbed the cup.

'It's all right, Mum, really it is. We talked for almost an hour. He has been looking for us for the past four years. He said he has never forgotten us. Mum? Mum, look at me. It's Charlie. It's your Charlie, and he wants to see us again. He wants to talk to you.'

Mary pushed back a few strands of hair from her forehead. She looked at Alice, her voice barely audible. 'You spoke to your father? You spoke to Charlie. How is he? I mean, I mean, where is he? Oh! I don't know what I mean. You really spoke to my Charlie?'

'Yes, Mum. Yes, I did. He was very nervous and very unsure of how I would react. I was very nervous too. I didn't know what to say, as I can't remember him at all. He told me how he would bathe me and change me when I was a baby. Take me for walks in the go-chair round the streets. He said I liked to press the mother-of-pearl buttons on his saxophone and laugh when he would play a tune. He said he has a picture of the three of us taken when I was about 18 months old. He said I would stroke Jonathon's forehead in the hospital. He gave me his number he wants you to call, he said—'

Mary held her ears with both hands. 'Please, Alice, stop! Stop, no more. I can't take it all in. I just can't.'

Reaching for her inhaler she leaned back, pressing it to her lips taking two deep breaths. Her eyes closed, allowing the tears that had escaped to slide slowly down her pale cheeks.

Both women sat quietly, aware of the enormity of what had unfolded before them. They knew that from now on things would never be as they had been.

The long night edged into early morning as Alice and her mother talked. The past was so well remembered ... the future so elusive.

Mary waited almost two weeks before making the call. She had taken Charlie's number from Alice, saying she would get around to it. She never discussed it with the boys, and they never raised it with her. Only Alice was aware of the depth of Mary's torment. He was her father, but only in a mythical sense. Archie, problematic as he was, was the only father she had ever known.

With Mary it was different. She had carried Charlie in her heart from the day they first met. He fathered two of her children. He adored her, put her on a pedestal, and could not wait to be with her. Here was a man who loved every inch of her, and she him. Here was a man who fell apart when she betrayed him, a man who lived to regret the actions of his pride. A man who had ached for her for decades.

She wanted to call him the minute Alice had told her. She had wanted to call him every day since, but she was scared. Scared to hear his voice, scared that he would be disappointed in her. She waited for the right time.

That time came. It was April 25th, ANZAC Day in Australia, commemorating the landing of Australian and New Zealand troops at Gallipoli, Turkey, on April 25, 1915. Fallen heroes and returned soldiers from both world wars are honoured and remembered for their courage, mateship, and sacrifice on this day.

Mary was resting on the couch, watching the television news. A lone piper was playing *The Last Post*. The melancholy sound haunted and enveloped the crowd gathered on the steps of the Shrine of

Remembrance in Australia. She watched as bowed heads and sad eyes remembered the fallen, the brave young sons and brothers who never returned from war. Her eyes welled, watching the emotional crowd ... but *her* soldier did return from war. He did come back to find her in a dance hall in London one Christmas, and now here, decades later, in Australia. Mary dried her eyes and lifted the phone. No more waiting. It was time.

'Calling your London number now, Melbourne. Please hold!'

It rang once.

'Hello?'

She could hardly speak.

'Hello?' It was stronger this time. The line had a faint hum, but apart from that the voice was clear, soft, and confident.

'Hello, Charlie. It's Mary!'

A pause, then a breathless response.

'Mary?'

'Yes, Charlie. It's me.'

The last 38 years dissolved to minutes. Conversation was not difficult, not for a moment. They talked to each other as they always had. They rejoiced at the daughter they had created and the wonderful woman she had become, they laughed at the same things that made them laugh all those years ago, and they cried for the decades that they had lost together. They cried for a son who would never grow up.

They talked about his family and the loss of his wife. Mary briefly shared about Archie and his death. She did not want to elaborate on that part of her life at this magical moment. It could wait. They talked about his health; that was not good. He had an aggressive cancer, with some good days and some bad. Mary guessed that his time was short.

She had to see him. He needed to see her.

He was not fit enough to travel, but she knew with her medication and doctor's permission that she could travel.

Mary was going home.

Chapter 37

Two weeks after that call, Mary was revitalised. She had spoken to Charlie every day since then. Charlie's doctor had told him that his time left was to be measured in months rather than years. Mary was heartbroken. She was about to be reunited with Charlie after all this time only to lose him again. She listened with a heavy heart when he told her the prognosis. She listened, but she chose not to hear.

The family told her they had great concerns about her travelling to the other side of the world on her own. The doctor also was worried about the 26-hour flight, that she may find it exhausting. Mary was determined, assuring him that she had taken all precautions and would be fine.

One morning, while searching through travel documents, the phone rang. It was Alice.

'Hello, darling, I'm glad you called. I was going to ask you to check the expiry date on my passport. I can't remember exactly what year we went to New Zealand. Can you?'

'It's fine, Mum. Your passport is valid for another two years like mine.' Alice spoke quickly, getting to the point. 'Mum?'

'Yes, darling, what is it? What's the matter?'

'I know what this means to you, and I don't want to dampen your excitement, but honestly, I am not happy about you travelling all that way on your own. Plus, the fact—'

Mary interrupted. 'Alice, I *have* travelled you know. I and am quite capable of navigating my way around an aircraft and airports. I can talk to people and ask directions. I am not dead yet!' she laughed, albeit indignantly.

'I know that, Mum, but what happens if you have an attack? It could happen anytime, you know. I am so worried.'

'Alice, darling, the travel agent said that the airline would need approval from the doctor before I could travel, and he gave that approval … rather grudgingly, I might add. The flight crew are all aware of my condition. They have oxygen on board if I need it. The doctor said my new medication is working well and the portable nebuliser I will be taking with me should bring additional relief. He said he would give me some sleeping tablets for the flight. Oh! Alice, please don't worry. I'll be alright. You see, darling, I have never wanted anything as badly as this. I really need to see him, Alice. Please be happy for me.'

Alice heard her mother wheezing over the phone. It was only slight, but she knew it got worse when she got excited. Knowing she couldn't talk her out of this trip, she braced herself, playing her last card.

'All right, Mum. I am happy for you. In fact, I am more than happy because I'm coming with you.'

'You're what?'

'I'm coming with you. I have spoken to the boys, and they can manage the restaurant while I am away. The agency has assured me that they can provide additional experienced staff if needed, so I am not worried about it at all. I just think that whatever time Charlie has left I want to share with him. Oh Mum, I have thought about him such a lot. I really do want to see him. I want to meet my father. Is it alright, then? Can I come with you?'

Mary's voice softened. 'You want to come with me? Yes, Alice, yes! I so desperately want you to meet your father. You will just love him;

I know you will. I never ever thought I would feel this way again, and to have you with me, well, it is just so … so…' Mary began to cry softly. 'Goodbye, darling. See you tomorrow.'

The following morning, they booked two seats to London. The flight was to leave in two weeks' time, with accommodation organised at the airport in London for a rest and freshen up. Appointments were made at the hairdressers, the papers and special deliveries were cancelled, and they rang around to tell friends that they would be away indefinitely.

They decided to leave the return tickets open dated. Not knowing how long they would have with Charlie; it was the best option. Marlene had decided to take a long break and stay with her daughter in Sydney for a while. Mary's jubilant mood saddened only slightly when she spoke to Vince. He sounded tired. His family had called the night before from Queensland to wish them bon voyage. Max told her that his brother had been going downhill since catching an infection a fortnight earlier, but nothing could stop him from getting out of bed to speak to her. He said they would keep in touch and Mary promised to send them a postcard from London.

The day arrived for Mary and her daughter to start their journey to the other side of the world. It was a journey of joy, framed by sorrow. Their flight departed late in the afternoon. Scot and Billy had insisted on a big send-off at the airport. Mary protested, but only a little. She was feeling rested, energetic, and excited, and had dressed carefully for the long journey in a full skirt, loose jumper, and flat shoes. Her cabin bag was packed neatly with medication, inhalers, nebuliser, toiletries, and a good book. Alice had all the travel documents safely zipped into an inside pocket of her bag.

The international cocktail lounge at the airport was busy with passengers, families, and friends. Scot had managed to secure a table by the window. They all managed to sit around the large table. Billy ordered champagne. The glasses clinked, the champagne flowed, and chips and nuts devoured by the bowls. The happy travellers received bon voyage cards and small mementoes. The laughter was loud and the banter loving.

The party of friends and family that had gathered around the table drained the last of the champagne into Mary's glass.

'Please, no more! I am lightheaded enough already.' Mary held on to the top of the table.

Alice stood up. 'I just need to pay a quick visit to the ladies. Mum, are you sure you can wait until we get to Sydney?'

Mary looked at her daughter and laughed out loud. 'Of course, I can, darling. I am still in control, you know.'

Billy quietly got up from the table and followed his sister down the passageway. They were just out of sight of the group when Billy called after her. 'Alice. Alice!'

She turned quickly. 'Billy, I didn't realise you were behind me. What is it? What's the matter?'

Her brother's face was blank, but his voice broke. He was having difficulty getting the words out. 'Alice, I'm sorry to have to ask you this, but I didn't want to mention it in front of Mum. I need to ask you a big favour.'

'What favour? What is it? You're shaking. Come over here.' She held the crook of his arm and steered him gently to an empty lounge area on the other side of the passageway. Taking off his backpack, he laid it gingerly on his knee, undid the buckle and brought out a small metal box. It was perfectly plain except for a brass fastener on the side. He held it carefully with both hands.

Alice looked at in confusion. 'What is it, Billy? What's that?'

'It's Dad!' he said quickly. 'It's Dad's ashes.'

Alice looked at him in disbelief. 'What? What ashes? What do you mean? I thought he was cremated in Darwin.'

'Yes, he was, but in a moment of lucidity he had asked a nurse to make sure that his ashes would be scattered in Glasgow, at Ibrox Stadium. The nurse had no idea where that was when she confidently agreed. She agreed to put his mind at rest.'

Alice looked at him incredulously.

'Ali, I know it's nowhere near London, and I know it's a lot to ask, but if there is any way you can get there and do this for us it would give me and Scotty great peace. We didn't tell Mum about this, but if you want to, and the time is right, then it's okay by us.'

Alice looked at her brother's face—the hope, the plea, and the love—then she looked at the box. She thought of all the issues she had with Archie when he was alive. She remembered the hard life he had given her mother, the laziness, the gambling, the infidelity. She tried very hard to justify one good reason why she should do this for him, and she did ... she would do it for her brothers.

'Of course, I will, Billy. Let's hope he doesn't kick up a fuss going through customs.' They laughed and the tension eased.

'Oh! And, Ali, one more thing'. He pressed an envelope into her hand. 'It's his death certificate and certificate of cremation. You'll need them too, and this is from me and Scot.' He put both arms round her, squeezing her tightly. She held him closely and blinked.

Alice went to the ladies and when she returned to the lounge, she gathered her belongings and her mother. Time flew amid a flurry of goodbyes. The final boarding call for Sydney came. Mary hugged both boys for a long time.

Scot wiped her tears and smiled broadly. 'Don't worry about a thing, Mum. Treasure every moment with Charlie. Oh! And if you stop in Honolulu on the way back, can you bring us both a Hawaiian shirt?' Mary nodded vigorously through her tears.

Mother and daughter walked slowly to the departure gate, presented their tickets, then turned back for the final time to wave goodbye.

Mary sat by the window. She pushed their hand luggage under the seat, then gave the hostess their full attention for the safety drill.

The aircraft took off smoothly. Mary watched the landscape of Melbourne, her hometown, disappear beneath her. She lay back and closed her eyes. Much later, the tall blonde hostess smiled affectionately and bent over, retrieving Mary's untouched supper tray. She whispered to Alice, 'She looks so peaceful.'

The captain had started his preamble on approach to Mascot Airport, his soothing voice thanking the passengers for flying with them. He added a special farewell to all passengers connecting with overseas flights. Mary and Alice smiled at each other. No words were necessary.

When they finally cleared customs and boarded their flight to London, it was getting dark. Soon, they were airborne. The cabin lights dimmed as the captain did a banking turn, allowing passengers a better view of the spectacle beneath them.

Sydney was on display, a carpet of light from the sky above. The black waters of Darling Harbour unlocked the majesty of the Sydney Opera House and the Harbour Bridge, both magnificent structures to behold whilst on the ground, breathtaking from the air.

The night sky surrounding them was darker than dark navy blue. A margin of white held the thin orange line of the sun that was slowly disappearing from the horizon.

Alice leaned over to her mother. 'Mum, Mum! It's amazing, look at that.'

Her mother's head had turned to the window. She was already asleep. Alice placed a thin woollen blanket gently over her, knowing that she would need as much sleep as she could get. It was going to be an emotional fairground when they landed.

Heathrow airport in London at 5.00 am was alive, bright, and vibrant. Aircraft from around the world lined up on the tarmac like soldiers at muster. They taxied toward their allocated gate, waiting further instruction from the tower. Weary passengers disembarked, spilling out into the arrival's hall, looking for signs, asking for directions, collecting luggage and braving the customs queues.

Mary had slept well with the help of a tablet from her doctor, but Alice could not get comfortable enough. She had read for most of the long journey. Now, Alice found a trolley, loaded the luggage, and cleared customs. Mary quickly found a phone booth and called Charlie.

'Hello? Mary?'

'Yes, Charlie, it's me. We're here. We're just leaving the airport now to freshen up and have a rest. We may be a little late getting to Notting Hill. I—'

Charlie interrupted, his voice a whisper. 'My dear Mary, after more than three decades, does a little late matter?'

She drew in a short breath 'Oh, Charlie!' She hung up the phone.

They had decided to check in at a hotel on the outskirts of London for a few hours to rest before meeting Charlie. Notting Hill was just four miles from Central London. The airport had a shuttle bus, dropping guests at various hotels near the airport and within thirty minutes, they had arrived at the hotel, checked in and were shown to a quiet, comfortable room on the fifth floor.

Mary sat on the edge of the bed and kicked off her shoes. She turned to her daughter, who was hanging up coats and opening cases.

'I can't believe I'm in London, Alice. The last time I was here, it was like it was yesterday. Archie carrying on about the price of a Coca-Cola at the airport shops, and Scot and Billy chatting constantly and fighting over window seats every step of the way.' She smiled at her daughter. 'You know, I was so confused at that time. I knew in my heart that I was doing the right thing, but I was still wondering if I was. I had uprooted everyone, left everything that was familiar to us all, to go to God knows where, to start life all over again.' I still remember Archie carrying on. "Awstraliya?",' she mimicked him. '"Some effin backward country at the ends of the effin earth".'

They both laughed at her attempt at Glasgow slang.

'Alice, it was you that I missed so badly. I was not sure if I had done the right thing in leaving you. I wished you were with us, and all the time secretly hoped that you would appear out of the blue, on the aeroplane.'

Mary's voice was shaking as tears welled in her eyes. 'Ridiculous really. Of course, I knew you wouldn't.'

'Mum, not many women with an obnoxious husband in tow would have done that.' Alice paused. With a frown and half-smile, she turned her mother to face her. 'Well, Mum, he was obnoxious, wasn't he?'

Mary chuckled and nodded. 'He certainly was. Yes, Alice, he

certainly was. Now come on, darling, let us have room service and order a good pot of leaf tea and fresh milk. We can't settle for these tea bag dust offerings and long-life milk anymore. Not after coming halfway round the world, now can we?'

In 1982, the Falklands War dominated the United Kingdom news. The first twenty pence coin went into circulation, and Princess Diana gave birth to a future King.

As England's capital city evolved around them, and the clock ticked ever towards the future, Mary and Alice Bray indulged in a hot shower and slept for six hours.

Chapter 38

Mary took great care in getting dressed, deciding on a pale blue cotton dress, a matching short jacket, and navy-blue low-heeled shoes. Her weight and measurements had barely changed from that of the twenty-year-old girl she had once been. She worried about her hair, though. The last time she saw Charlie, it was a rich dark blonde coiled behind her ears and curled slightly upwards. He used to ruffle it and wrap it around his fingers, making ringlets. Now it was short and elfin-like. The shining dark blonde had been replaced by shades of rich brown earth and pristine clouds. In the mirror she saw a mature, confident woman whose fine features had bypassed much of the ageing process. Many years in the Australian sun had not blemished her fine lined skin. She hoped that Charlie would see glimpses of the girl he fell in love with all those years ago.

Alice went down to the front desk to settle the bill and order a cab, leaving Mary sitting by the window. Outside, the fading afternoon sun gave new life to the dull grey buildings on the street below. People were everywhere, hurrying about their business. A red double- decker London bus stopped to pick up passengers from an orderly queue of commuters. The undercarriage of a giant aircraft hovered above, waiting to land at the busiest airport in the United Kingdom.

Mary Bray ... returning to a familiar yet alien country ... was living an impossible dream.

It happened as she stood up from her chair.

It came on suddenly. Her chest tightened, her throat constricted, she felt dizzy, like she was about to fall. In desperation, she grabbed the end of the bed, all the time gurgling and wheezing. One hand was clawing at her throat, while the other blindly reached out for the nebuliser, plugged it into the wall.

Falling to the floor face-down on the carpet, she inadvertently inhaled dust and fibres, escalating her efforts to breathe. Mary Bray was fighting for her life, asking out loud in prayer, 'Please, please don't take me now … not now.'

The nebuliser was within reach. Crawling on all fours, she grasped the mask with her weak fingers, fighting to put it over her mouth. Propped against the wall, with the mask strapped around her head, she began inhaling the lifesaving vapour. Within minutes, her breathing regulated. She fell onto her side, exhausted, but she managed to pull herself up against the wall. It was over. She stood up, wiping tear tracks, from her face, she reapplied her makeup. A look in the mirror, a pat of her hair, a weak smile … she was ready again.

Minutes later Alice returned to the room, oblivious of what had just happened. She called to her mother from the bathroom.

'Alright, Mum? Cases are in the foyer, only your hand luggage is left to be packed with the nebuliser and your medication, then we're off. The bill has been paid and the taxi is almost here. The front desk told me that Notting Hill was not too far away, just on the outskirts of Central London, but traffic is heavy.' Alice frowned as she moved into the room, looking at her mother. 'Are you all right, Mum? You look a bit shaky. You sure you're up for this?'

Mary smiled at her daughter 'Am I ever!'

The taxi pulled into the motel driveway, and the driver writhed out from behind the steering wheel. He was short and robust, wearing tight black pants with a tapestry waistcoat that was holding together his drooping belly over a collarless white shirt with grubby sleeves. A shiny cap slipped over his brow, almost covering his left eye.

Quickly picking up the cases and hand luggage, he turned to Alice. 'All right, darlin, where to then, eh? Gawd, luv, what's in this bag then, yer makeup? It's bloody well evy.'

Mary put her hands to her mouth and coughed, hiding a smile, as he helped them both into the cool back seat of his London cab. They slowly pulled away from the kerb, easing into the never-ending throng of bumper-to-bumper transport city-bound.

The driver, convinced that his passengers were native Australians, started a good-natured banter. 'Them bleeding lorry drivers finks they've got a bleedin ownership on the frog-n-toads. I'm askin ya, wot gives them the right to bleedin well shove in when they bleedin well feel like, eh? Tell me that? Betcha wouldn't get this bleedin arrogance in Awstraylya, luv, would ya?'

Alice smiled at Mary.

'I think this happens the world over.' Mary laughed.

They watched his face through the rear vision mirror. It was enflamed, his mutterings became louder with every agitated driver that tried to cut him off. He kept them so amused that they had not taken much notice of where they were. He was slowing down, searching for street names. Alice caught sight of a sign saying 'Portobello Road'. She knew they were almost there.

In Notting Hill, the trees of a large garden square had shed their bare winter grey, and buds of green had started to appear on many branches. The chill that had arrived with the first light had disappeared, the morning sun was had gone, and now the afternoon sun was slowly creeping along towards night. The cast iron railings enclosing the park had no gates. Walking paths like tentacles stretched out from an imposing stone statue of a bygone era; well-manicured garden beds were in abundance. The surrounding homes were mini–Georgian mansions and elegant Victorian residences, a mixture of styles and colours. The taxi pulled over to the kerb and stopped.

They were outside Charlie's house. It was exactly 3.30 pm.

A line of young schoolchildren, wearing dark blue gabardine coats and berets, walked in pairs alongside their teacher. Black patent shoes and white socks moved with precision. They were crossing the square, their young fresh faces animated and laughing.

Mary could see their classroom in one of the buildings. It had a large bay window with colourful paper cut-outs that hung down from the curtain rails. Dull chimes announcing the end of the school day drifted through the open cab window. The children herded onto the pavement, waiting to be collected by anxious parents.

Closing her eyes for a second, she went back to another place, another time, eons ago. Mary ached with memory. She was that little girl again, a little girl who had to grow up too fast, who never had a childhood, who was never able to spend time with her siblings like her own children had. The wave of sadness was all-consuming. She blinked hard, coming back to the present.

The cab reversed expertly and parked between two cars. Mary sat upright and straightened her dress. She fastened the middle button on her jacket, unfastened it, then fastened it again. She checked her lipstick and hair, opened the cab door, and stepped carefully onto the narrow pavement. The driver unstrapped their luggage.

'C'mon, darlin. You take your andbags, and I'll get yur makeup.'

He grabbed the large suitcase and let out another uproarious laugh at his own expense. It made Mary chuckle. After carrying it up four steps, he dropped it squarely on the top one.

'See ya later then, eh, gals? And fanks for the tip.' He winked at Alice.

Mary stood still on the broad pavement, feeling exposed and vulnerable. Was he watching her from somewhere? What was he thinking? Would he recognise her? Would he be disappointed? Her hands shook, her stomach ached. Alice came up behind, gripping her shoulders.

'Go on now, Mum. You don't need me for this. It's your time now. Go!'

Mary's anxious eyes looked to her daughter as she grabbed her arm. 'Oh, Alice, I feel sick. What if he's disappointed? You know, I mean ... that I'm not what he expected. I mean, it's been such a long time. What if we ... what if we don't get on?'

Alice wrapped her arms completely around her mother for a moment, then she stepped back and cupped her face with both hands. 'Mum, these feelings are natural, but you have been waiting for this moment for 38 years. He will love you, and you will love him, and so will I. Don't you think he will be feeling nervous too?' Alice pushed her mother gently. 'He's waiting, Mum! Get up those steps now!'

Mary hesitated before tentatively climbing the few steps to the front door. She looked at the windows; all the blinds were drawn. Flicking her hand through her hair for the umpteenth time she licked her lips, swallowed, and then pressed down hard on the large brass doorbell. Its dull sound made the anticipation almost unbearable. There was no noise nor movement from behind the door ... nothing.

She looked back at her daughter nervously. Alice smiled and nodded, urging her on. Pressing the bell again, she waited. The door opened slowly, then there was a shuffle, Mary leaned forward to speak, then stopped.

At the half-opened door, he appeared, as tall and proud as she remembered, only thinner. The Adam's apple in his neck stood out as he swallowed. His hair was still a mass of unruly golden curls, only now peppered with silver. His eyes, hooded slightly, were still the same magnetic blue.

Charlie smiled and the planet stood still.

'Mary?'

His voice was thick as he let go of the door handle and held out his arms. She was there in an instant, holding him.

Alice caught her breath when she saw him. He was just as her mother had said. He was as he might have been all those years ago, only older. Here, at last, was her father. She was standing at the side of the steps behind an ornamental tree. He couldn't see her biting her lip and wiping away her tears. She waited and watched as her parents stood as one, wrapped around and supporting each other. She could hear her mother's soft cries and her father's tender voice as he consoled her, telling her that everything was going to be all right.

Alice didn't move, afraid to taint the moment. Suddenly, his head rose, searching for her, she moved from the safety of the tree. As their eyes met, she drew a deep breath, dropped her bag, stumbled, and then ran to his outstretched arms, letting out a deep moan.

'Oh, Dad!' At last, they were a family.

It was all that mattered.

For all of that week Mary and Charlie talked constantly, sometimes well into the early hours. They talked about the path their lives had taken, the highlights and the lowlights. They talked about their families, the happy times, and the sad times. They laughed at the memories of their youth and cried at the loss of their son. They talked of regret and visualised what might have been. They slept soundly together. In the crook of his arm, Mary lay on his chest in contentment, feeling the throbbing of his heart.

What they didn't talk about was what they wanted most of all ... a future together. It was left unsaid, both understanding that it would never be.

Charlie's cancer had spread. The doctor said he had only weeks, but those weeks had now stretched into months together. Mary was stoic when she was with him, talking positively and avoiding all discussion of the future. Alone with Alice, she was heartbroken.

They spent every meaningful moment together. Hours sitting by the bay window in the front room watching life move around them ... people, birds, plants, and trees. They took short walks around the square, wrapped in warm jackets and scarves. Charlie would sit in the kitchen and watch as Mary cooked. She would chat whilst spoon-feeding him samples of her efforts.

Alice could not recall a time she had ever seen her mother so happy.

But Charlie's conditioned eventually worsened. He was admitted to hospital for treatment. The cancer had travelled to his bones, he was having pain in his lower back and was very weak. He had become delirious, merging in and out of consciousness. His stay in hospital was short before moving to an adjoining hospice.

Mary never left him.

She read to him, massaged his cold hands and feet, and wiped his brow. She talked quietly to him about their marriage all those years ago, the birth of their children and his beloved saxophone. He never responded, but she knew that he could hear her.

It was late one afternoon when Charlie slipped away. His room was dark and the air was chilled. A lone candle in the corner flickered, casting a silhouette over the wooden crucifix on the wall. Outside, the sun had now slipped down behind the trees and the birds were silent. Mary lay her head on his still warm chest, her arms stretched over his body. She was inconsolable. Alice left the room.

The nursing staff gently persuaded her to leave, to go home with her daughter and try to sleep. They promised to leave him just as he was for a while. All arrangements would be made; they would call her later. Mary held firmly on to Alice as she walked slowly through the silent hallways of the hospice. Nuns leaving the small chapel approached her; they reached out for her hands, holding them as they prayed.

The taxi pulled up outside Charlie's house. Mary had been coughing and wheezing quietly into her handkerchief. Alice paid the driver and helped her mother climb the stairs.

'I think I'll go straight up to bed, Alice, and have a lie down. I'm worn out.'

Mary moved slowly, holding onto the wooden banister. Alice was behind her.

'That's a good idea, Mum. I'll put these bags down and bring you up a cup of tea.'

'No, darling,' she answered wearily. 'No tea, just a lie down. I'll be fine if I can just rest for a bit.'

Alice helped her mother onto the bed then carefully took off her shoes and pulled the satin eiderdown over her. 'I'll leave your inhaler here, on the table next to Dad's picture. Is that alright?'

'That's fine, pet.'

Alice bent down, kissing her mother gently on the cheek. Mary's eyes were closed, her mouth relaxed in a smile.

'I love you, Mum.'

'I love you too, darling.'

Alice closed the door silently and crept downstairs. In the front room she turned on the side lamp. It was dark outside. The gas heater was on low as she slumped wearily onto the sofa. It was so hard coming back to Charlie's house without him. The four months they had been here had seen it transformed from a sterile practical house into a warm, family home.

Photographs of the three of them on the mantelpiece made her smile, especially one of Mary and Charlie as they held hands. They were laughing at the pigeons in Trafalgar Square flying down like spitfires. There was another of the three of them huddled together on the banks of the River Thames with Big Ben, a monolith, behind them. A passerby took a picture of them. The young man turned out to be a tourist from Melbourne, Australia, and he was a musician. Charlie loved the Aussie accent. He engaged in a long discussion with the young backpacker about music, politics, education, and the weather. From then on, he would refer to both of his girls as *his mates!*

Her mother made their short time together cosy and comfortable, ensuring that cut flowers were always in the hallway and dining room. The table lamps that she had bought glowed invitingly in each corner of the sitting room, replacing the stark overhead lighting. Three pillar candles grouped together on the coffee table were lit nightly and classical jazz records played constantly in the background.

Alice had experienced a happiness that had eluded her all her life. She had found her father at last. It was the missing link. Whenever Mary was resting, Alice and Charlie had many long talks together. He told her of the heartbreak all those years ago when he found his lovely wife had been unfaithful, how his pride had taken a beating and that he had cried and stayed home alone for weeks. He told her how he had never stopped missing his daughter. His eyes clouded over when they talked about Jonathon, his only son, and the short time they had as a family of four.

Alice confided in her father. She told him of her heartaches with

Archie, her devastation at the tragic loss of Rena, and her sadness at not finding a life partner. She told him that this was the happiest time of her life, knowing the hardships her mother had overcome, and seeing her so relaxed and happy made all her own past trials but a memory.

The sadness of the day and the emotions had caught up with Alice. She came into the front room, lay down on the sofa, closed her eyes, and let the tears flow freely down her cheeks. Pushing her face into the soft cushions of the sofa she sobbed, then slept soundly.

Alice couldn't recall exactly what it was that woke her. There was no sound. The moon was the first thing she saw through the window; it was almost full and so clear. There was very little traffic noise from outside and although the heating was on, she felt chilled and stiff. The clock on the mantelpiece said it was a 1.45 am. She had slept for almost five hours.

Rising slowly, she began to climb the stairs to her room, pausing at her mother's door. Worried that she might not be warm enough.

The hallway light was enough for Alice to see into the room. She reached over, taking a blanket from the chair. Her mother was as she had left her last night, only now one arm was outside the covers clutching a handkerchief. Her Ventolin puffer was still on the bedside table, her nebuliser unplugged and idle on the floor. The handkerchief in her hand was sodden with phlegm, laced with red.

Leaning over, Alice called her name softly ... then louder ... finally, screaming. She knew that before even touching her mother's face that it was too late.

Mary had gone.

In shock, and unable to move, she sat for a few minutes gazing at her mother's bowed head, then taking off her shoes, she slipped slowly beneath the blanket and covered them both. With her head resting on Mary's chest, Alice cried silently, then aloud, then sobbed in silence. She pleaded with her mother to please come back. She called out for her father to take care of her mother.

Alice drifted into a disturbing slumber until morning, when daylight invaded the room.

Having lost both her mother and father in one day, Alice had to face her fears. She was alone in a country where she didn't belong and had no family support. She called her brothers in Australia. They were overwhelmed with grief, distraught at not being able to say goodbye to their mother and unable to be with their sister. They both insisted on coming to England. Alice managed to convince them that she knew what to do and had the help of the hospital and the local church. Besides, there would be no point. By the time they arrived, the funerals would be over. Scot was inconsolable and Alice learned later that Billy went into a shell and didn't speak for days.

Alice buried her mother and father together in a small, historic 12th century churchyard in Dartford, some thirty miles from London, where they had been married all those years ago. It was where their infant son rested in peace. The minister and a few of the dedicated congregation held a small service at the graveside to farewell two strangers. When they had all left, Alice stood alone, silently saying her own goodbyes to her parents.

The freshly dug graves were side by side, the ground around them was dense and brown with the remnants of dead snowdrop flowers that just weeks before had blanketed the ground in a majestic white mass, heralding that spring was on its way. An elderly gravedigger was slowly clearing parts of the ground around the plots, his gnarled hands raking and removing spindly twigs and long branches. He caught sight of Alice, and waved and doffed his old, worn cap. As she smiled and waved back, a slither of white between the graves caught her eye then disappeared.

Walking very carefully behind the majestic oak tree protecting the two plots, she looked down at the dark brown leaves and rich soil.

There it stood, behind a mound of earth, all alone. Pushing up through the dark mass, its long, thin vivid green leaves reaching up toward the only patch of sky, its white bell-shaped flower bowing and swaying in the gentle breeze.

A solitary snowdrop.

Alice was overcome, captivated by the natural splendour contrasting with the dark fresh soil. As she bent down to gently touch the leaves, the old gravedigger, leaning heavily on his rake, called out, 'Cor, blimey, missus, that's a sight for sore eyes that is! In all me years ere I ain't never saw the likes of that. Late spring and a bloody snowdrop. Well, I'll be buggered. That's a survivor for ya.'

Alice stroked the thin leaves with glassy eyes, then stood up and nodded to the old man.

'Yes, a survivor all right ... and in great company!'

Chapter 39

The overnight train from London carrying weary passengers to the heart of Glasgow terminated at Central Station. The rain had stopped, and although winter was behind them and summer was approaching, the last days of spring were wet and dismal. Commuters with raincoats and folded umbrellas got off and on trains. The manned ticket gates on leaving or arriving at platforms were guaranteed to cause chaos with impatient passengers.

Cafes displaying chalkboards offering morning fare were dotted around the exit gates. Hot bacon rolls and tea, or black pudding on toast with fried potatoes. Filling and tempting day starters for the hungry throng.

The woman in a stylish red wool coat walked quickly out of the station to a nearby bus stop. After a few enquiries at the information bureau, she boarded a waiting Glasgow Corporation double decker bus. The high collar of her coat covered her ears from the morning chill. She carried a bulky, black overnight bag. A black mohair knitted scarf that wound around her neck rested in a knot under her chin. Fashionable low-heeled black leather boots and black leather gloves ensured she stood out amidst the morning daily commuters.

On boarding the bus, she sat by a window near the door, taking in a Glasgow she hardly knew. How slowly the sad memories of long ago had vanished ... how quickly they were returning now.

The green and yellow double decker bus lumbered through the

narrow streets, as rundown and tumbling old grey tenement buildings flashed by. They were skirted by cracked pavements. Many had been vacated years ago, their doors and windows boarded up. They were a blank canvas for the graffiti artist: 'Fuck the Pope', 'Fuck King Billy', 'Up the Gers', 'Come on the Celts'.

Alice laughed aloud. Some things never change. The bus stopped abruptly at a depot. The driver called out to the few passengers inside.

'Eh, just having a wee stop here to change drivers, shouldnie be too long. Just gab amungst yersels, okay!'

Two teenage boys called out from upstairs, 'Aye, yer arse in parsley. Yer just having a fag. Think we're daft or somethin?'

The boys laughed good-naturedly with the driver.

Alice looked out the window and smiled at the banter. How good-humoured the Scots were. They were never stuck for one-liners, and were a populace with a great ability to laugh at themselves and their situations. She had forgotten just how funny they could be.

Leaning her head against the window and closing her eyes, she reflected on the sadness of the previous weeks, and of the sorrow to be when she arrives back in Australia.

Suddenly, and with no warning, a booming voice penetrated her thoughts.

'Righto then, let's get this bus movin. Did embdy else creep on in the last ten minutes? Come on noo, own up. The inspector will be on at the next stop, and you'll be thrown aff for no payin yer fare!'

The new driver was a tall, thin Indian man. He wore a well-pressed green wool uniform, spotless white shirt, a red tie, and a purple turban. His Scottish accent was a direct contrast to his appearance. The teenage boys hung down from the top deck, taunting the driver and laughing.

'Keep yer curtain on yer head, ye daft ejit. There's two wee weans under the back seat having a fag. I dare ye tay turf *them* aff.'

The driver shook his head. Alice turned away. It was pure entertainment.

'Excuse me, Mrs. You wanted aff at Ibrox Stadium, is that right?'

Alice looked up and smiled. The slim conductress with bleached white hair and black lined owl-like eyes stood at her seat, holding onto her moneybag and an overhead rail. 'Well, it's this next stop then, okay?'

'Thank you so much. I haven't been here for almost twenty years. The place has changed, but it's still the same, if you know what I mean. I'm surprised that I still recognise so much.'

The conductress let out a raucous laugh. 'Well, darlin, ye never forget yer first. First hoose, first school ... and yer first wee shag!'

Alice nodded and laughed. 'Yes, you are right, so right!'

Stepping down from the bus, she waived as the taillights disappeared around the corner.

It looked like a nice area, with many well-loved council houses and tended gardens. She could see the massive lights that illuminated one of Scotland's stand-out soccer parks: Ibrox Stadium, home of the Glasgow Rangers Football Club.

The reception area was busy with staff, supporters, and club officials all talking at once about the same thing. Football.

The girl sitting at the reception desk was young, bright, and helpful. She interrupted two argumentative football supporters.

'Hello there, Mrs. Can I help ye?'

'I'm from Australia on a short visit. I was wondering if I could just have a look around the stadium for a few minutes. I'm told it's quite famous,' Alice said.

Looking at Alice she frowned, paused for a minute, then laughed. 'Australiya? Ye don't sound Australiyan, do ye know whit ah mean? Like ye don't sound like Paul Hogan. I thought ye might have been a toff frae Kelvin Grove in Glasgow.'

Alice laughed at the girl's direct, but non-offensive attitude. 'I used to live here many years ago. I suppose it's still evident. I can hear myself talking more like a local every day.'

They both laughed.

The girl came out from behind the desk, 'Just come wi me, hen, I'll show ye the way.'

Alice thanked her, then walked alone through a long dark tunnel, into bright daylight and the massive, deserted stadium. A solitary man in the distance was marking the pitch for the next game.

Alice walked slowly onto the ground, heading for the centre, where the ever-resented referee would have stood to toss the coin. Putting her bag down, she squatted beside it and reached for the box tucked securely into a corner.

It was just as Billy had given it to her when leaving Australia four months ago. Sealed on all sides; Alice found a nail file and slipped it under the tape. Inside was a sealed plastic bag. She undid the seal.

The wind was lightly dancing around the vastness of Ibrox Stadium. It arrived with a chill. Alice stood up and tightened her scarf. She opened the bag and shook the fine grey ash high above her head. The wind carried it away, rising, falling, then scattering onto the hallowed ground. She called out but no one heard.

'Goodbye, Archie. Thank you for my brothers.'

On the night train back to London, a tired and disinterested porter showed her to her cabin. She was leaving for Australia the following night; some kind people from the church had already sent her luggage to the airport. Scot and Billy were meeting her in Melbourne. They had spoken on the phone, and neither had mentioned Archie's ashes. No one had expected her to make the effort under the circumstances. She never doubted it.

As the train slowly crawled out of the dismal, cold station, Alice opened her overnight bag, changed into pyjamas, and dimmed the lights before settling into the warmth of her sleeper. She closed her eyes. It had been an emotional yet exhilarating four months, and although physically exhausted she felt a surge of contentment and peace.

She thought of life back in Australia without her mother. They had become very close over the years. Alice's maturity had embraced her mother's twilight years. She questioned how she was ever going to survive without her, but then, she would never really be without her. Mary, in death, would be as she was in life ... always there for her. She would continue expanding the business, ensuring all of Mary's dreams would be fulfilled.

She would invest in other properties. She would take on more staff, she would diversify the company. There was an excellent prospect coming up that Mary had mentioned months previously, it was bayside on the waterfront. She would see if it was still available. It would be silver service and called 'Mary's Place'. It would have a well-stocked cellar, and a bar named 'Charlie's Bar'.

She would have music ... she would have a saxophone player ... she would ...

The rows of metal wheels beneath the sleeping passengers on the night train from Glasgow to London were grinding out a rhythmic repetitive strain, interrupted only by the train's horn and warning bells as it approached deserted stations. The night wore on. Alice slept.

The miles ebbed away as Scotland became England, then on to Melbourne, Australia ... and home.

Acknowledgements

I have been writing this story for 17 years off and on. I liked to think if I stuck with it long enough, it would reveal itself, and it has.

I am very grateful to Dr Euan Mitchell – Author, Mentor, Teacher. Who first encouraged me to write at Box Hill TAFE Victoria. Always generous in sharing his wisdom with a smile. I will be forever thankful for his guidance, knowledge, patience, and his encouragement on my road to publication.

Fiona McIntosh – Internationally best-selling author. Her Masterclass courses gave me so much fuel for my writing journey. My heartfelt thanks to Fiona, for her support, patience and precious time. Not to mention all the laughs and chocolate along the way. An outstanding author, an awe-inspiring woman ... and a friend.

Kelly Rigby, Sarah Neilson, and Tania Blanchard – A big thank you to these ladies from the 2015 Masterclass course. In the early days they all gave their time to give very constructive written feedback on my story. I refered to these notes often for encouragement over the years, right up to my final drafts!

Anne Paul – my dear Scottish bestie, who is always there for me. For her friendship over the decades, for her never-ending support, her insight, and constructive critiques, particularly with the readability of the Glasgow accent. A true friend.

Terri Parrôt — My gratitude and thanks to, my first, and only reader of the full manuscript. I drip fed her the first six chapters, before succumbing to her pleas and enthusiasm for more. She was the catalyst that gave me the push to stop editing ... and publish. Bless you Terri!

Luke Harris — Designer from Working Type Studio. For his professionalism and tolerance with this fledgeling 'mature' author, and for his insight with my cover. I gave him my idea and he produced more than I could ever have imagined. Luke genuinely cares for his clients and communicates promptly. I am so glad I found him.

Rebecca Wylie — Editor of Sage Written Word. What can I say? Rebecca went above and beyond my expectations. Her knowledge and support were invaluable to me. She easily grasped the 'Glasgow slang' dialect of my characters, and its consistency throughout the book. (Not a given for many editors) Rebecca never encroached on any of my story, for which I am very grateful, she enhanced it with improved(very) grammar and rearranging words. I highly recommend Rebecca for her professionalism, detail, understanding ... and for caring.

To my loving husband Ron Clifft. Over the years I was an 'off and on' scribing wife missing in action. He never complained,(maybe a wee bit) when I shreiked and bawled in colourful language at the computer, or lay prostrate in grief, when words or chapters went missing. A more patient man there never was... Thank You 'Oh wonderful husband!"

About the Author

This is DIANE DEEMING's fiction debut novel. She was born in England, growing up in Glasgow Scotland, before immigrating to Melbourne Australia in 1966.

Her novel is inspired by her mother, plus stories and places from her memories. It has taken some 17 years and determination, to finish.

She has had a lengthy career in Sales and Marketing with Ansett Airlines lasting 28 years.

A second career in fundraising at The Alfred hospital stretched to 16 years.

She met her husband Ron Clifft in 2006 at a music venue where he played guitar and she sang.

In 2017 they eloped, getting married on a clifftop in Queenscliff Victoria.

Diane and Ron continue with their music, playing golf, and loving life on the beautiful Mornington Peninsular.